Summer at the Lake

Summer at the Lake

ERICA JAMES

First published in Great Britain in 2013 by Orion Books
an imprint of The Orion Publishing Group Ltd
Orion House, 5 Upper Saint Martin's Lane
London WC2H 9EA

An Hachette UK Company

1 3 5 7 9 10 8 6 4 2

A CIP catalogue record for this book
is available from the British Library.

ISBN (Hardback) 978 1 4091 4599 8
ISBN (Export Trade Paperback) 978 1 4091 4600 1
ISBN (Ebook) 978 1 4091 4598 1
ISBN (Export Ebook) 978 1 4091 5162 3

Typeset by Deltatype Ltd, Birkenhead, Merseyside

Printed in Great Britain by Clays Ltd, St Ives plc.

The Orion Publishing Group's policy is to use papers
that are natural, renewable and recyclable products and
made from wood grown in sustainable forests. The logging
and manufacturing processes are expected to conform to
the environmental regulations of the country of origin.

www.orionbooks.co.uk

*This book is for Edward and Ally, Samuel and Rebecca,
and a very special little boy, my gorgeous grandson.*

Thanks and Acknowledgements

I couldn't have written this book without the help of some fantastic people who were so generous with their time and knowledge.

In Oxford I had help from the superbly efficient Digna Martinez at the Oxford Visitor Information Centre.

I was also fortunate enough to be shown round Queen's College Library by Lynette Dobson.

Closer to home, I have Grace Hulley to thank for leading me down a particular path.

In Italy, help came from some wonderful sources, in particular Rita Annunziata who, together with her *nonna,* supplied me with no end of invaluable information and patiently answered all my questions.

Help also came from Danilo who invited me for dinner and introduced me to his charming mother.

And not forgetting Mikael Mammen who inadvertently gave me a light bulb moment – I'm just sorry I couldn't find a way to use the salami submarine!

Lastly, special thanks to Sara Cilia for knowing what a nosy parker I am and taking me to see the villa, which later became Hotel Margherita.

While most of the places featured in this novel are real, I have taken a few liberties here and there. For instance Hotel Margherita doesn't actually exist, but take a trip to Lake Como and you'll find plenty of villas just like it.

When you write the story of two happy lovers,
let the story be set on the banks of Lake Como.

Franz Liszt

Chapter One

It had been a mistake to open the envelope.

She should never have done that. If only she had left it to deal with when she returned home from work, or if only the postman had been late, her day wouldn't have been ruined. As it was, her thoughts had been constantly drawn to the Christmas card from Seb with its ruddy-cheeked Santa up-ended in a snowdrift.

But it was the high-quality card tucked inside that was the real shock. Embossed with fancy gold calligraphy it requested her to save the date of 10th July next summer for the wedding of Imogen Alicia Morgan and Sebastian Hughes.

On the back was a scrawly handwritten message from Seb – *Floriana, I do hope you'll come, it would mean a lot to me.* An email address she didn't recognise had been tagged on at the bottom.

Would it mean a lot to Seb for her to be there? Would it really? Floriana found it hard to believe. For two years there had been nothing from him. Not a single text, email or phone call. Now, out of the blue, this announcement. An announcement that made her feel as though she had been slapped. Then slapped again, hard. And just when her mind managed to blank it out – *wham!* – there was another slap.

Turning off the High into Radcliffe Square, where earlier she had been explaining to an enthusiastic group of American tourists that it was England's finest example of a circular library, she hurried along in the bitter cold to Catte Street, passing the Bodleian on her left and the Bridge of Sighs on her right. It was always at this spot in the road that she warned people to look out for approaching cyclists – she had lost count of how many tourists had very nearly come a cropper here as they stopped to admire and take photographs of the bridge.

No two days were the same for Floriana; it was one of the

things she loved most about her job as an Oxford blue badge tour guide. Yesterday she had taken a group of fiercely clued-up fans on an *Inspector Morse* and *Lewis* tour – some of whom had been determined to catch her out on some minute detail or other. But blessed with an excellent retentive memory – Seb used to refer to it as her dark arts super-power – they'd have to be up early to get one over her.

Today she had been conducting what Dreaming Spires Tours called their Classic University and City Tour, culminating in afternoon tea at the Randolph Hotel. From there the group of Americans had been picked up by coach and taken to spend the night in Woodstock. Tomorrow they were scheduled to visit Blenheim Palace for mulled wine and carol singing. When Floriana had been saying goodbye to them – while accepting their discreetly palmed tips – she had inexplicably wanted to clamber on board the bus with the jolly, carefree group and run away, if only to Woodstock. Anything than go home and deal with Seb's card – a card that had scratched at the dormant and humiliating ache of her love for someone beyond reach.

But home in North Oxford was exactly where she was now heading. Avoiding Broad Street and the tangle of bus queues on St Giles, she took the quieter route of Parks Road. Usually she cycled to work, but this morning, on top of the shock of opening Seb's card, she had found her bicycle had a puncture.

Fixing the puncture was another job to add to the growing list of things she had to do. Mostly they were things she kept putting off because she couldn't be bothered to deal with them. Such as changing two of the halogen light bulbs in the kitchen that hadn't worked for the last month, or getting a handyman in to replace the cracked window pane in her bathroom. The guttering also needed clearing and that tap in the bathroom was dripping too. At the back of her mind was the thought that if she waited until everything that was going to go wrong went wrong, she'd get someone in to sort it all out in one go.

'For heaven's sake, Floriana,' her sister would say, 'stop procrastinating!' Doubtless Ann would add that they were all simple jobs anyone with half a brain could do for themselves and why on earth didn't she roll her sleeves up and get on with it?

Four years older than Floriana, Ann never put anything off; she was the last word in getting things done. She was what the world would class as a proper grown-up – wife, mother, domestic technician, and workplace Hitler. She was eminently sensible and led a thoroughly organised and blameless life and never missed an opportunity to make Floriana feel that she had somehow messed up, even when she hadn't. Her every comment, so it seemed, was weighted with the sole intention to make Floriana feel inadequate and recklessly irresponsible. And though it was true there had been times when her impulsive nature had got her into a close shave or two, she had, it had to be said, always escaped actual outright disaster.

Most notably was the occasion in her first year at college here in Oxford when she spent a night in a police cell. She had thought she'd been successful in keeping it from Mum and Dad, but then a letter for her had arrived at home with the words *Thames Valley Police* stamped on the envelope. Ann had gone to town on making a ludicrously big fuss as to why Floriana was receiving letters from the police.

'Just the one letter,' Floriana had retaliated, 'which I might add is none of your business.'

Poor Mum and Dad had been mortified when Floriana had confessed to a 'lark' that had got a bit out of hand. 'It won't be in the newspapers, will it?' Mum had asked with a trembly catch in her voice.

'Of course not, Mum,' Floriana had assured her while crossing her fingers. 'As misdemeanours go, this is very small potatoes and will be of no interest to anyone.'

'And you won't be busticated?'

'It's rusticated, Mum. And no, the college won't do that to me.' Again her fingers had been tightly crossed.

As luck would have it, both she and Seb – her partner in crime – had been let off with nothing more than a warning. The principal of Floriana's college had said, 'I'm sure you don't need me to point out the error of your ways,' and had gone on to do exactly that, detailing the folly of their drunken caper: that of scaling a wall to peer inside the building the other side of it – a building where, and unknown to them, animal research took place, which made it perhaps one of the most highly sensitive and well-guarded buildings in Oxford. The second they were atop the wall, security lights had flashed on and they'd been deafened by a siren blaring. Before they'd had a chance to scramble down, a police car had appeared and they were taken to the police station. The following morning, and after their college rooms had been searched, and their laptops and mobiles thoroughly scrutinised for any animal rights activity – they were told they wouldn't be charged and were sent on their shamefaced and chastened way.

Floriana was thirty-one years old now but Ann wouldn't hesitate to raise the incident as an example of her wilful nature always to do the wrong thing. But compared to Ann anyone would look reckless and irresponsible.

And that was Ann without an E. Giselle Anne Day had never forgiven their mother for giving them the names she had – names that would make them stand out as being different. Just as soon as she was old enough, having had enough of being teased and bullied at school, she had insisted she be called Ann and had stripped back her middle name to the simplicity of just three letters, as if that superfluous E would somehow invite further trouble.

In contrast, Floriana had loved her name as a young child and had never once been tempted to abbreviate it to Flora or, heaven forbid, Flo. Anyone who tried received short shrift. The exception to the rule had been Seb who had called her Florrie.

It was dark now and at the top of Parks Road she joined the Banbury Road and pictured Seb's handwritten message. He'd written *Floriana*, not *Florrie*, and it served to emphasise how horribly distant they'd become. Even the fact that he'd sent the card to her old address and it had been forwarded to her new home underscored the gap between them.

Yet as big a shock as it was to know that Seb was actually marrying The-Oh-So-Beautiful-The-Oh-So-Perfect Imogen, the save-the-date card was an olive branch. Unless ... unless Imogen was behind it. What if she had suggested they invite Floriana just so Imogen could show that she had won and Floriana had lost?

She turned left into the peace and quiet of North Parade Avenue, waved to Joe behind the counter in Buddy Joe's and wondered if she was being stupidly paranoid. With the passing of two years, surely the invitation was genuine and had been sent with the right motive?

At the bottom of the road she turned right and, nearing home, she reached into her bag for her keys.

But what if Seb had done this behind Imogen's back? What if

he wanted to let bygones be bygones and be friends again with Floriana? How would Imogen feel about that?

More to the point, did Floriana want to rekindle their friendship and risk being hurt all over again?

No, she thought decisively, she couldn't do that, and with equal decision, she stepped into the road to cross over for Church Close where she lived.

Strange, she thought sometime later – though with no real conscious understanding of the passing of time – why was she lying on this hard gritty surface, her face pressed to it painfully? And why did she feel so leaden, yet as if she were floating? How odd it felt.

Chapter Two

Adam Strong drummed his fingers on the steering wheel. It had been a hell of a week. But at least it was ending on something of a positive note. The sale on the house in Latimer Street he had exchanged contracts on three weeks ago had gone through this afternoon and he'd just picked up the keys from the agent. He was on his way there now.

Or rather he would be if he weren't stuck in traffic. He should have waited until tomorrow to see the house, when it wasn't dark and when it wasn't rush hour. It would have been better all round. But he needed to be busy, to keep himself from brooding.

The traffic lights up ahead changed and he slowly moved forward, at the same time acknowledging that the addition of a new project to his property portfolio would serve the purpose of taking his mind off Jesse.

Seven days ago – last Saturday – Jesse had informed him that she couldn't see a future for them as a couple, that she now only viewed him as she would a brother. And how, he thought with a flash of irritation, would she know how that felt when she was one of three sisters? *Bloody hell, a brother!* Was that what she'd felt when they'd been in bed, that she was having sex with a brother?

They'd been together for nearly two years and he honestly hadn't seen this bombshell coming. OK, he'd been working crazy long hours, so perhaps he'd been preoccupied and perhaps not quite so on the ball, but that worked both ways: she was the one who had been constantly away these last eleven months, driving round the country as a medical rep, and let's not forget those drug company jamborees and conferences she was forever attending.

She had denied there being anyone else – that had been his first question – but he wasn't so sure. Lying to him might be her way

6

of believing she was sparing his feelings. But he'd have money on someone else being in the picture, some guy she'd met while away. 'I promise you,' she'd said, 'there's no one else.'

'So why end it between us?' he'd asked, dazed with disbelief and fighting hard to keep in check the swell of painful emotion that was threatening to spill over. 'Whatever it is that isn't working between us, let's fix it.'

With tears in her eyes she'd shaken her head at that. 'Adam, this isn't something you can fix up like the houses you buy and sell on.'

He'd been stung by the accusation, as if he saw things so simplistically. 'You make me sound like some kind of emotionally challenged halfwit,' he'd said. Which he was sure he wasn't. He knew there were complexities in every relationship and that compromises had to be made. It wasn't as if he was a total rookie when it came to these things.

But he'd gone wrong somewhere along the line and missed the signs that Jesse wasn't happy. He thought back to her birthday a few weeks ago when he'd taken her for an overnight stay at Cliveden House. She'd appeared to love everything about it, particularly the spa and the Mulberry handbag, which he'd surprised her with before dinner.

Had she known then that she was on the verge of dumping him? The question, which had spun around inside his head too often this week, caused him to take the corner too fast onto the Banbury Road and suddenly he was rammed up close and personal to the car in front. Another inch and he'd have made contact.

Keeping his distance and his speed low, he reckoned the answer to his question was yes, Jesse had known for a while she was planning to leave him. Because when he looked back to her birthday, he could remember thinking that when they'd made love that night in the hotel, she had seemed less than involved, as if she was merely going through the motions. He had thought at the time that maybe she was tired, having been on the road for most of that week.

She had been staying with a friend since the weekend but was coming back tomorrow – Saturday – to move her things out. He had told her he wouldn't be at the house, but a part of him wanted to be there, to try and convince her that they shouldn't throw away the last two years.

And what about all the plans they'd made? Only a fortnight ago they'd been discussing how to carve up Christmas without offending either set of parents. Not only that, they'd booked a holiday to St Lucia for next March.

How could he have got it so spectacularly wrong? Because, he supposed, self-rationalisation and the lies we tell ourselves was human nature, it guaranteed we saw only what we wanted to see.

With a weakness for over-analysing things, he stopped the direction of his thoughts. He'd gone round in enough futile circles this week trying to figure out Jesse and what precisely had gone wrong between them.

He turned into North Parade Avenue where the shop windows were attractively lit with Christmas lights. It was an area of Oxford he particularly liked and he knew that buying here was a smart move. The university owned much of the property in the neighbourhood, but Latimer Street was one of the few roads that was predominantly residential. The house he'd bought – number six – was a compact four-bedroom Victorian villa built of yellow and red brick, and it needed gutting, rewiring, replumbing – re-everything in fact – but it would be a gem when he'd finished with it. He hadn't made up his mind yet whether he'd add it to his lettings portfolio of flats and houses, or sell it on straight away. Time would tell.

It was stupid going to see it in the dark, but ever since he'd bought his first property, it was a ritual of his to head off immediately after he'd taken possession of the keys and claim the property as his own. He would use the torch from the boot of his car and wander from room to room, confirming in his mind the plans he had in store for the house.

He'd bought his first property when he was twenty years old, borrowing an absurd amount of money from the bank to do so – those were the days when banks couldn't dish out loans fast enough. The house had been a wreck, a tiny two-up two-down, which he'd spent six months putting right – learning on the job – and effectively camping in it before selling it on for a reasonable profit, much to his parents' surprise. They'd been appalled when he'd dropped out of university in his second year and announced – rather grandly – that he was going to be a property developer.

He might just as well have announced his desire to be a drugs dealer. He'd been glad to leave university; being mildly dyslexic, he'd found it a bit of a slog at times.

He was now thirty-seven and despite the impressive buy-to-let portfolio he now had, he very much doubted if his father had given up on the idea of him one day getting a proper job like his brother, Giles, who worked for a prestigious bank in the City. But then these days, when banks were considered as great a threat to mankind's survival as nuclear weapons, prestigious was perhaps not the *mot juste*.

'There are enough over-achievers in the family as it is,' Adam had told his parents when they'd expressed their disappointment at his career choice. 'In my special and unique way I'm bringing a level of normality to the family,' he'd joked. To which his mother had told him he wasn't too old, or too tall, for her to box his ears, and what, she wanted to know, did he mean by *normality*?

At the junction with Winchester Road he turned right and had just accelerated away when a dazzling glare of lights on full beam appeared in his rear-view mirror. He knew he was doing nothing wrong, but even so he slowed down – he'd been caught by an unmarked police car on the M4 for speeding two months ago and was still in the early stages of flashing-light paranoia, worrying that any vehicle on his tail was a police car sneaking up on him. To his relief the car shot out from behind him and overtook with unnecessary speed. With a shake of his head, Adam tutted self-righteously and wondered where the police were when there was somebody seriously breaking the law.

But his relief was quickly replaced with an innate and reactive bolt of alarm. It was what his driving instructor had taught him and which he'd never forgotten – good intuitive drivers have an unconscious sense of danger being only seconds away and are perpetually on full alert for acts of arbitrary madness, because it's the unexpected that gets you killed. And something unexpected was happening up ahead: the driver who had overtaken him had simultaneously hit the brakes and swerved erratically before speeding off.

It was then, in the light cast from the street lamp, that Adam saw an elderly woman hastening towards the unmistakable shape of a body lying in the road.

Chapter Three

Esme Silcox had lived in North Oxford for over sixty years and during that time she had seen plenty of changes, along with a veritable kaleidoscope of human life.

So when she snapped her handbag shut and pulled on her kid leather gloves and Joe showed her to the door, as he invariably did when the shop wasn't busy, it was a gesture she not only appreciated but which made her think of days gone by.

To look at Joe one wouldn't expect such old-fashioned courtesy. With his shaven head and multiple piercings and curious tattoos, he looked every inch the type of man one might choose to cross the road to avoid. But Esme knew better: one simply didn't live in a place like Oxford without learning that a book should never be judged by its cover.

'You take it carefully,' Joe said in his velvety-smooth voice while towering over her. 'It's dark out there now. And don't forget, anytime you want, we'd be happy to take an order over the phone and deliver your shopping to you. Just give us a tinkle, that's all you have to do.'

Had he not spoken with such a genuinely considerate tone, she might have felt patronised, but she didn't. 'Thank you,' she said, 'that's very kind of you. I shall bear the offer in mind.'

Out on the street, with her shopping bag in one hand and her handbag hooked over her forearm, she set off in the cold evening air with a brisk determined step. At least in her head it was a brisk determined step, but given that she was eighty-two years of age, it was likely that she was being somewhat optimistic about the speed with which she was able to move.

Away from the shops and restaurants and at the junction with Winchester Road, she turned right, waited for a succession of cars to pass, then crossed over, taking care in the dark not to miss her footing when she reached the pavement on the other side. This time last year her only remaining close friend had popped out for some crumpets for tea and had slipped on an icy pavement. Poor Margaret, she had suffered the ignominy of being taken to hospital by ambulance with a broken hip and a fractured elbow and by the time she was deemed fit enough to be discharged she had lost all confidence and had gone downhill rapidly. By Easter she was dead. It happened all the time: a trivial accident and then that was that.

Perhaps if the weather did turn particularly inclement in the coming weeks, she would take Joe up on his offer and have him deliver her shopping. The previous owner of the shop had never been so thoughtful. Quite the contrary. He'd been a ghastly man, rude and bad-tempered, he'd thought nothing of arguing with his customers and snapping at anyone, particularly students, who had the temerity to touch anything. Earlier in the summer he had tried to dupe Esme. He'd called her a liar, that she had given him a ten-pound note and not the twenty as she knew perfectly well she had. The wicked man had accused her of being gaga and not knowing what she was doing. When she threatened to call the police, he backed down and handed over the correct amount of change to her. It was a month later, at the beginning of September when, without warning, the shop was stripped bare and a To Let sign went up.

Joe and Buddy arrived in October along with their attractive wicker baskets of fresh produce – bread, eggs, fresh fruit and vegetables and a delicious line in pies, pasties and cakes. They stocked all manner of organic and Fair Trade items as well as cheese, ham, salami, and olives and recently freshly made sandwiches and baguettes had been introduced, with the day's specials written on a blackboard behind the counter. Home-made soup was now being considered, so Joe had just informed Esme. She hoped their enthusiasm and enterprise would be richly rewarded with a steady flow of loyal custom. Certainly they provided everything she needed.

She was very much aware that as she grew older, her own world grew smaller, to the point that it had now shrunk to this little part of North Oxford, wedged as it was between the Banbury and Woodstock roads. Eventually, she supposed, it would shrink to just Trinity House and then quite possibly to just the one room. Life in miniature, she thought with a wry smile.

Rarely did she go too far afield these days. Occasionally she had a sudden longing to catch the bus into the centre of town, or take a taxi to see a play at the Playhouse or enjoy a concert at St Mary's, but in general she was quite content to sit alone at home and read while listening to the radio. Her favourite spot was in the window of the drawing room. From there, looking onto the road, she would watch the comings and goings of those who lived near her. They mostly seemed to be in a tearing hurry and had little or no time to get to know the people around them. They were all – just as she was – little islands of self-containment.

A long time ago she had known her immediate neighbours, but following a rapid turnaround in newcomers, the ever-changing faces had brought with them a barrier of anonymity. There had been a half-hearted attempt at a street party for the Queen's Diamond Jubilee, but Esme had not joined in. Hidden from view behind the net curtain she had watched from the window and observed people standing awkwardly in the road making small talk with glasses of wine and beer in their hands. She had feared some well-meaning soul might knock on her door and force her to participate out of a sense of pity – poor old dear, she had imagined them saying amongst themselves, we'd better invite her. But no one had come. Which had left her both relieved and perversely disappointed.

She couldn't remember who it was, but someone once said that the past is a place, not a time. It was true. For her the past was a place more richly vibrant than the present; it was crowded with memories – of climbing Magdalen Tower to watch the sun rise on May Day, of picnics down by the river drinking Pimm's and feasting on strawberries, of walks through the deer park and the Botanical Gardens, of parties talking late into the night with earnest young men and women who thought they were going to change the world. She could see them now, their eyes burning with the zealous conviction they had all the answers.

There were no answers, she had long since learnt, only questions.

As she walked in the dark along the road, she thought about the house next door to her: it had stood empty for eleven months. The owner, who had lived in London and rented it out to a succession of tenants, had died and it was only now that probate had been settled the house could be sold. Esme knew all this because she had been in the garden one afternoon and overheard the conversation taking place the other side of the wall between the estate agent and whoever it was he was showing round. Very probably, whoever bought it would do it up and turn it into flats.

She paused to shift her heavy shopping bag from her left arm to her right and heard a car behind her. Glancing over her shoulder and momentarily dazzled by a blaze of headlamps, she took an involuntary pace away from the road as the car zoomed past at a terrific speed and with a loud roar of engine. A split second later and there was a sound that made her gasp out loud.

Her heart pounding, she quickened her step.

Chapter Four

Floriana had the weirdest feeling that something wasn't quite right.

Stranger still, a man she didn't know was asking what her name was. Never mind what *her* name was, what was *his*? Who was he and why was he asking her if she knew where she was? Of course she knew where she was, she was ... she was ... Hang on a moment, where exactly was she?

She was working, that was it! She was at the Randolph having afternoon tea with her cheerful group of Americans. But where were they? Oh hell, she hadn't lost one of them, had she? That was always the nightmare, somebody wandering off. Honestly, the number of times she'd lost a person because they'd slipped away to the toilet without telling her. She turned her head to look around for her group and found that she couldn't. All she could see was a man.

He must be the man who'd asked what her name was. He had an interesting face. Sort of courtly looking with a noble nose, long and straight, and a wide forehead and a smooth jaw and chin. When she thought about it, he was awfully close to her, but maybe that was because it was dark and he couldn't see her unless he was a few inches away. He also seemed to be at a peculiar angle. Or was it she who was at a funny angle? She tried to change her position but stopped when something hurt. She tried to work out which bit of her hurt, but couldn't.

Whoever he was, she'd say this for him, he was persistent because he was asking again what her name was. To shut him up, she said, 'Floriana. What's yours?'

'It's Adam,' he said. 'An ambulance is on its way, it'll soon be here.'

'An ambulance,' she repeated, her curiosity piqued; she tried and failed to look around her again. 'Why?'

'It's probably best if you don't move,' he said. 'Just try and stay still. What's your surname, Floriana?'

Wow, was he trying to chat her up? 'It's Day,' she said. 'Floriana Day.'

She heard another voice. A woman's voice that was low and refined and had a distinct edge of authority to it. 'Ask her where she lives. Ask her if there's anyone we should telephone to be with her.'

Wondering who the woman was talking about, Floriana closed her eyes and tried to think which one of her group it was who was missing at the Randolph.

Except there wasn't anyone missing, was there? More to the point, she wasn't at the Randolph. She was ... she was walking home, that was it! And she was upset. But why?

She battled her way through the fog of confusion. It was something to do with Seb. He ... he had sent her a Christmas card. Now she remembered. He and Imogen were getting married.

As if the mere act of remembering unleashed it, a wave of pain swept through her and she suddenly felt sick. And dizzy. She began to shiver and her teeth chattered.

She started at the feel of something touching her. Opening her eyes, she realised that the man who had been asking her name was now covering her with a blanket. No, not a blanket, but a coat. A soft woollen coat that smelled nice. That was kind of him. 'What happened?' she tried to say through the chattering of her teeth. 'What's wrong with me? What have I done and where am I?'

'You're in Latimer Street and you were hit by a car,' he replied.

'Oh,' she said. 'That doesn't sound good. Am I badly hurt?'

'We don't know.'

'At a guess?'

'The paramedics will have a better idea.'

Floriana thought about this, and at the same time she tried to work it out for herself. But it was beyond her. All she knew was that she felt more tired than she had ever felt in her entire life and sort of spacey, as though she was on the edge of dreaming. The other definite was that somewhere in her body there was an epic amount of pain. Maybe if she could just sleep, the pain would be gone when she woke up. She closed her eyes and immediately felt herself drifting away. She was back at the Randolph, pointing out the Morse Bar to her group and shepherding them into the Drawing Room for afternoon tea. They were laughing and chatting amongst themselves, but one of the women was saying, 'Keep her talking, don't let her go to sleep. It's important to keep her awake.'

But it wasn't one of the American women in the group who had spoken, it was the woman who had spoken before, the one with the distinctive voice.

'Floriana,' the man said, 'can you hear me? Come on, tell me about your day. What did you do today?'

'I just want to sleep,' she mumbled, keeping her eyes closed.

'I know you do, but humour me. Tell me where you work. Or are you a student?'

With a massive effort, she opened her eyes and found herself staring straight into his. 'I'm a tour guide.'

'That must be an interesting job. I expect you meet all sorts of people, don't you?'

'Are you making me talk because you're worried I'm going to die? It's what they do in films, isn't it?'

'You're not going to die.'

'That's good to know. Are you a doctor?'

'I'm afraid not.'

'So you don't really know, do you? What did you say your name was?'

'It's Adam.'

'Well, Adam, I think I must be OK if I'm talking to you, mustn't I? Or … or am I imagining this conversation?'

'No, you're definitely talking to me.'

'But what if I just imagined you said that?'

He adjusted the coat around her. 'An interesting line of argument and unfortunately it's not one I can easily disprove for you. You'll just have to take my word for it.'

She liked the tone of his voice; it was very calming. 'My head hurts,' she said abruptly, realising that most of the pain she was feeling was located there.

'Even more reason to keep absolutely still,' he said.

'Ask if there's anyone we can get hold of for her.'

It was the well-spoken woman again. This time she sounded even more insistent.

'Who's your bossy friend?' Floriana asked. 'I don't think I'd like to get on the wrong side of her.'

'I've no idea who she is; we've only just met. But I think perhaps it's alarm and concern rather than bossiness she's projecting. Ah, that's the ambulance coming.'

Hearing the sound of a siren rapidly approaching, and the relief in the man's voice, she said, 'I've never been in an ambulance before.'

It was actually a police car that arrived first, followed quickly by an ambulance. It was when the two paramedics, having made a quick assessment of her, were lifting her carefully onto a stretcher that Floriana got a glimpse of the woman who had been giving out orders. She couldn't be sure in her dazed state, but she had the feeling she had seen her before.

The ambulance had driven off, and the handful of onlookers who had been lured out onto the street by the excitement of the sirens and flashing blue lights had now returned to their homes, their names and contact details taken by the police officer. Since they had seen nothing of any help, it was Adam and the elderly woman who were of most interest to the police officer. Their witness statements taken, the officer then set about checking the road for anything that might count as evidence.

It was now, after he'd put his coat back on and brushed the dirt from his trousers from kneeling on the ground, that Adam looked properly at the elderly woman at his side for the first time. She was small – not even level with his shoulder – and was smartly dressed in a black coat trimmed with fur at the cuffs. Her white hair was partially covered by a surprisingly stylish black beret with a brooch in the shape of a panther pinned to one side. At her throat was a red and black silk scarf and clutched tightly in her leather-gloved hands was a shopping bag, along with a handbag that looked very like it had once been part of a crocodile. Elderly and frail she might appear, but Adam strongly suspected there was steel in those old-lady bones of hers.

'It doesn't seem right the poor girl being on her own,' she said, looking up at him.

'I expect the paramedics or someone at the hospital will contact her family or a friend.'

The woman frowned doubtfully. 'I've seen her about. And never with anyone. Do you think one of us should have gone in the ambulance with her?'

'I should imagine the last thing she needed was a stranger getting in the way.'

'What if they don't?'

'Don't what?'

'What if no one rings her family or friends? What if she doesn't have anyone?'

Buttoning his coat up, Adam said, 'In the circumstances, I think we've done all we can.'

He knew it sounded feeble, but really they had, hadn't they? They had witnessed an accident, they had called an ambulance, they had waited for it to arrive and then they had left it to the experts. What more could they do?

'She seemed so young and so vulnerable,' the old lady said. 'I do hope she's going to be all right. I don't think I shall be able to rest until I know she's not too badly hurt. Aren't you in the least bit worried about her? It's outrageous that the driver didn't stop. I wish I'd been quick enough to make a note of his number plate.'

OK, this was fast turning into one of those surreal nights you never think is going to happen to you. He was now in the A&E department of the John Radcliffe and, as instructed, he was keeping schtum and was leaving the talking to his elderly companion: Miss Silcox.

Within minutes of their arrival, she had effortlessly convinced the woman behind the reception desk that she was *Mrs* Silcox, Floriana Day's grandmother, thereby getting round any potential problems regarding family members only being given information about a patient. He was pretty sure there was no need for such subterfuge in a case like this, but who was he to question her thinking? He had to hand it to her, though, she was a canny old thing. Canny enough to play on his conscience and persuade him to drive her here.

It wasn't that he didn't care about the girl who'd been knocked over, he did; he just didn't want anyone to accuse him of interfering. Odds on, the girl herself would think it weird what they were doing. In all likelihood, a friend or a member of her family – or even a boyfriend – was already on their way here and frankly it was going to look pretty strange when it came to explaining themselves. On top of that, he hated hospitals. He hated the smell. He hated the sounds. And most of all, he hated the threat of death that hung over them. The sooner he could get out of here the better.

'Shall I see if I can find us something to drink?' he asked, in need of something useful to do.

'A cup of tea would be most welcome,' Miss Silcox said. 'A splash of milk and no sugar. Thank you.'

He was about to go in search of a vending machine when a nurse appeared. 'If you'd like to come with me, I'll take you to your granddaughter,' the nurse said to Miss Silcox. 'I'm afraid she's still a little woozy, but she seems anxious to see you.'

Uh-oh, thought Adam.

Chapter Five

Floriana had been told that she was lucky.

She didn't feel lucky. What she felt was pathetically sorry for herself, lying here all alone in her curtained cubicle with her clothes stained in blood and her body feeling as though it had been put through one of those car crushing machines. No, she didn't feel as though good fortune had come her way at all.

She also felt anxious about this grandmother business. She hadn't said anything when the nurse had mentioned her grandmother was waiting to see her in case it set off the medical alarm bells and she was deemed too unwell to be discharged. The thought of being packed off to a ward for the night filled her with dread. All she wanted was to go home and get into bed with a hot water bottle and a cup of tea and a plate of peanut butter and Marmite toast and then sleep until next week.

But the thing was, she was pretty sure she didn't have a grandmother. Not a living one at any rate. If her memory wasn't altogether shot, Nanna Tricia died when Floriana was too young to remember her properly and Nanna Betsy had died a lot more recently. She was fairly sure of it because she could distinctly recall going to the funeral and feeling that it had been the saddest day of her life.

Which begged the question, who was the 'grandmother' waiting to see her?

Or did she have some sort of amnesia? Was her memory all muddled up? Was she misremembering things? God, what if she'd gone back in time somehow and had turned into a time traveller?

But that was stupid, she was letting her imagination run away with itself; better to focus on the very clear memory she had of walking home after work, her mind meshed in a tangle of thoughts about Sebastian's card and the news that he was getting married next summer. That was absolutely 100 per cent real, wasn't it?

It was just all a bit fuzzy from then on, as she'd explained in her statement to the policeman who'd showed up after she'd returned from having her head X-rayed. She still couldn't remember the actual impact of the car hitting her but the paramedics seemed to think that it must have only clipped her otherwise her injuries would be a lot worse. She squeezed her eyes shut and concentrated hard on picturing herself walking home. She could remember walking down North Parade and waving to Joe, and then crossing the road and … But no, there was nothing else. No matter how much she willed her brain to remember, it just wouldn't, and the effort of trying to make sense of those last crucial moments – and the fact that she had a grandmother who was alive and kicking – made her head feel like it was about to burst open like a watermelon dropped from a great height.

She cringed. Where had that awful image come from? Her eyes open, she put a hand tentatively to the side of her head and touched the dressing, beneath which a very nervous trainee doctor called Suzy had spent ages fumbling to put in six stitches. That was when the nurse, standing next to the trainee doctor and observing her closely, had said that Floriana was lucky because the gash was close to her hairline and the scar would eventually be hidden. She'd also had a dressing applied to her chin and her cheek, which had been badly grazed and goodness only knew how horrible that looked.

From the other side of the curtain she heard voices and footsteps, then with a sudden movement the curtain was swished back as if it was part of a magician's act and the big reveal made – *Ta-daar!* The same nurse who had been keeping an eye on the trainee doctor appeared at the end of the bed. Smiling warmly, she said, 'Here's your grandmother and a friend. I'll leave you to it for a while.'

Floriana stared first at the diminutive elderly woman, then at the tall, rather good-looking man next to her. Her gaze returned to the woman. Trim and neat, she stood ramrod straight with old-school elegance. But she was unquestionably not Nanna Betsy who had been a taller and much more rounded sort of woman.

'You're not my grandmother,' Floriana said at last.

She noticed her words made the man suck in his breath and his face colour, but the woman stepped forward. 'That's perfectly true, and I'm sorry for misleading you, but I hope you'll forgive a little subterfuge on our part. You see, we ... or rather I, told a minor fib at the desk so we could be sure of learning how you were. I was worried they wouldn't tell us if we told the truth. By the way, by name is Esme Silcox and I live in Latimer Street, not far from the junction with Church Close where you were knocked over.'

Very slowly, a piece of the jigsaw slotted into place for Floriana. 'Your voice,' she said, 'I remember your voice. You were ...'

'That's right, we were at the scene of the accident. Mr Strong here –' she indicated her good-looking sidekick – 'called for the ambulance.'

Floriana turned her attention back to Mr Strong and thought of the Mr Men books she had loved as a child; Mr Tickle had been her favourite. This Mr Strong looked extremely awkward, as if he wished he could be anywhere but here in this stifling heat and small curtained cubicle. You and me too, she thought. 'Yes,' she said faintly, 'I remember you as well now. You talked to me, didn't you? You said your name was ...'

'Adam,' he said.

'Mr Strong was wonderful,' the old lady said. 'He was most chivalrous and used his coat to keep you warm.'

Floriana smiled gratefully at him, remembering not just his name now, but how calm and reassuring he had been. 'Thank you. But why are you both here?'

'We were worried,' the old lady said, moving closer to the side of the bed. 'We didn't want you to be on your own. Is anyone on their way to be with you?'

'Um ... actually no.'

'But you have someone who will come?' she said.

'I don't need anyone, I'm fine,' Floriana said with more spirit than she really felt. 'Just as soon as whatever needs to be done, I'll be out of here.'

'Do you think that's wise?' the old lady said, surveying her patched-up head and face with a long and scrutinising stare.

'They've done X-rays and stuff and nothing's broken, so there's no need for me to stay.'

'What about concussion? Won't they want you to stay in overnight so they can keep an eye on you?'

Floriana's heart sank at hearing her fears confirmed.

'And I dare say they won't be happy unless they know there's somebody at home to take care of you. Is there somebody at home?'

What was this? Why was this old lady giving her the third degree? And why did the truthful answer reduce her to a pitifully teary state and make her wish that the one person in the world she wanted to be here with her couldn't be? Why should she even think of Seb that way when for the last two years he had been so resolutely absent from her life? One bloody card from him and she was a mess!

Anger. That was better. Better to be angry with Seb than turn into a snivelling fool. After all, it was his fault she was here. His fault entirely that she stepped into the road and ...

She stopped herself short, realising that another glimmer of memory had surfaced. She chased after the glimmer, but like quicksilver it slipped away and was gone.

'Do you have somebody at home?'

Oh, for heaven's sake, Miss Marple was at it again with her questioning! 'I think that's my business, isn't it?' Floriana replied with a show of what she hoped was assertion, but which she suspected made her sound more like a stroppy teenager.

'You're right,' Mr Strong – aka Adam – said, stepping forward and putting a hand on the old lady's arm. 'Come on, Mrs Silcox,' he added, 'I think we've achieved what we came to do, now it's time to go.'

'It's *Miss* Silcox,' the woman corrected him, 'and please don't patronise me and make out that I'm some old dear with nothing better to do than poke my nose in where it's not wanted.'

'Then let's leave before that accusation is made, shall we?'

Ooh, thought Floriana, Mr Strong lives up to his name!

But then the crestfallen look on the old lady's face had Floriana feeling sorry for her and ashamed of her own rudeness, she said, 'Please, I appreciate your concern, really I do, it was extremely kind of you both to care so much.'

'Thank you,' Miss Silcox said with a slight lifting of her chin. 'And to reassure you, I'm the last person on earth to interfere in anyone else's business, but in this instance I felt it was not only my duty as a good citizen to come here, but because ... because I should like to think somebody might do the same for me.'

Floriana now felt utterly shamed and a quick glance at Mr Strong told her he felt the same.

'How are we all getting on in here, then?'

It was the nurse from earlier.

'Fine,' Floriana said. 'Can I go home now, please?'

The nurse smiled. 'That's what I came to tell you.'

Forty-five minutes later Floriana was discharged and she gratefully accepted the offer of a lift home with her Good Samaritans.

When they drew up outside 10a Church Close, she thanked them, took their contact details, which Miss Silcox insisted she have, and waved them off with cast-iron assurances that she was absolutely fine.

She wasn't fine, and they probably knew that, but they'd been considerate enough not to push it. In the kitchen she put the kettle on and was about to load the toaster when her mobile rang. When she looked at the screen she saw that it was her sister. Floriana was in no mood to speak to her, but she could see that Ann had rung several times already.

'At last!' Ann said. 'Where've you been? I've been trying to get hold of you all evening.'

'Why, what's wrong?'

'Nothing's wrong, I'm just trying to sort out Christmas. You said you'd tell me definitely by today whether you were coming or not.' The reproach in Ann's voice pummelled away in Floriana's ear and made her head thump more painfully than ever.

'I'm sorry,' she said feebly, 'I was going to call you, I really was, only I—'

'Well, that's you all over, isn't it? You're always going to do something but you never get around to it, do you? Honestly, I give up! So, what's the excuse this time?'

'I was knocked over by a car on my way home and—'

'You shouldn't make jokes like that,' her sister said, exasperated. 'The next thing you know it will really happen – it's called tempting fate.'

'I'm not joking. A car really did hit me. I've just got back from A&E.'

There was a pause the other end of the line while her sister

24

presumably regrouped her thoughts. 'Why didn't you ring me?'

Typical Ann, no enquiring how Floriana was, just straight to indignation. 'What would be the point?' Floriana responded. 'It's not as if you could help, you're too far away. And thanks for asking how I am.'

Another pause from Ann as she realised her mistake. 'Sorry,' she said, almost sounding like she meant it. 'So how are you? You sound OK, for what it's worth.'

'I'm not, as it happens. I feel bloody awful. I've got half a dozen stitches in my head and a battered face and a body that feels like hell.'

'But nothing broken? No internal damage?'

'No, thank goodness.'

'Well, that's good,' Ann said. 'What about the car that hit you, what are the police doing about the driver?'

'The driver didn't stop.'

'*What?* Were you able to get the number plate?'

As she always did, Ann managed to make Floriana feel inept, as though she had been deliberately negligent in this oversight. She explained that she had no actual memory of being hit, that it was a blank.

'Any witnesses?'

She told her sister about her Good Samaritans, then to her horror Ann said, 'I'd come and be with you if I could, but I can't get away from work right now. Why don't you come to us?'

'There's no need,' Floriana said quickly, knowing she had to downplay the accident or who knew what her sister would unleash on her. 'I'm just a little bruised and shocked, nothing serious. Really.'

'You're sure?'

'Yes, totally sure. All I need is a good night's sleep and I'll be as right as rain in the morning.' Nothing like a bit of misplaced optimism!

The kettle began to boil and switching it off she heard her sister say, 'I think it would be better if we didn't tell Mum and Dad about this, it would only worry them and it would be awful if you spoilt their holiday. You know what Mum's like, she'd come rushing back if she knew you'd been in an accident.'

Their parents were part-way through a round-the-world cruise. The trip, many years in the planning, had been a present to themselves after Dad had finally sold the family business and retired, so Floriana knew that what Ann had said made sense, it would be wrong to ruin the holiday for them. But as was so often the way, it was the manner in which her sister made the comment that rankled.

'Of course I won't tell them,' she said defensively, 'I'm not that stupid. Now I'm sorry to hurry you, but I need to have something to eat and go to bed, I'm shattered.'

'Of course. I'll ring you in the morning to make sure you're all right. Oh, and please, have a think about Christmas, I need to know final numbers.'

And I need to come up with a twenty-four-carat-gold excuse why I can't come to you for Christmas, Floriana thought when she rang off. She feared that only her death would provide a plausible excuse for not fitting in with her sister's exacting plans.

Not funny, she told herself with a shiver. Had the timing been fractionally different this evening, that car could very well have finished her off. A tingle ran down her spine and it suddenly came home to her that the nurse at the hospital had been right; she had been lucky.

Lucky also that two such helpful people had been there on the scene. She would have to thank them properly tomorrow for their help. It was the least she could do.

Chapter Six

Saturday morning in Summertown and Adam had woken with the stark reminder that Jesse really had gone. Work commitments had meant that Monday to Friday it wasn't unusual for Jesse to be absent from their bed, but Saturday and Sunday morning she had always been there; it had been one of the constants in their relationship.

To distract himself from dwelling on her absence, and despite the perishing cold, he had gone for an early morning run and then after he'd showered and dressed, he'd walked down to the shops and returned home from the new bakers with a bag of freshly baked croissants for his breakfast.

Now, as he poured himself a second cup of coffee from the cafetière, he contemplated the day ahead.

At twelve o'clock Jesse was coming to collect her things. As originally planned, he was getting the hell out. He'd decided he wasn't going to put himself through the painful experience of witnessing her stripping the house of her presence, or of trying to persuade her that she should reconsider. Frankly he didn't trust himself not to say or do something less than dignified. With only a week since being officially dumped, it was too soon for him to behave normally around her – whatever normally was supposed to be in the circumstances.

From his chair in the Victorian-style conservatory he'd had added on to the house, he looked back towards the kitchen and where there was now a blank space on the wall above the whitewashed sideboard. A week ago the space had been filled with a large framed photograph of him and Jesse. It had been taken on holiday in the Maldives last January, the pair of them looking tanned and happy – Jesse, perfectly toned in a barely there bikini, he, less toned, in swimming shorts. During the week he had removed the picture from the wall, unable to cope with what now seemed to be mocking smiles on self-satisfied faces. He had gathered up the rest of the displayed photographs that charted their relationship and put them on the bed in the spare room. If Jesse wanted the photos, she was welcome to take them. Somehow he doubted she would.

Staring at that empty space on the wall, he was suddenly filled with an angry urge to empty the kitchen cupboards of all Jesse's herbal and green teas and health foods and supplements – the ginseng, the evening primrose oil, the ginkgo biloba, the milled organic flaxseed, the goji. He wanted to sweep it all into a bin liner along with her superfoods cookery bible and then do the same in the bathroom, clearing the shelves of all trace of her expensive beauty products. But he steeled himself to resist the urge. He didn't want to give Jesse any reason to accuse him of petty vindictiveness.

So better all round if he made himself scarce today and allowed her to go about her business as she saw fit. He would rather be deemed a coward for avoiding her than run the risk of reducing himself to any unedifying behaviour he would later regret. A man has his pride, after all.

His breakfast finished, he tidied the place up, taking care to empty the rubbish bin in the kitchen, thereby removing all take-away evidence from last night – a dumped boyfriend cosying up with a takeaway was just too much of a cliché.

He'd called in at the Bangladeshi restaurant on his way home last night after firstly stopping off in Church Close and then Latimer Street, where, to their mutual surprise, it turned out that the property he'd just bought was next door to Miss Silcox's house. What were the odds?

'I imagine you'll be turning the house into flats,' Miss Silcox had said to him, when he'd got out of the car and had gone round to the passenger side to assist her. She had already ex-tracted from him what he did for a living.

Not prepared to disclose his plans, not when she would probably have the news spread to the entire neighbourhood by breakfast, he had merely said, 'I've yet to decide what to do with the property.'

In the dark he had escorted her up the steps to her house and stayed with her until she had removed her gloves in order to locate her keys from her crocodile handbag. With the door open, she turned to look up at him. 'Goodnight, Mr Strong,' she said. 'Despite the rather unfortunate nature of our meeting, I've enjoyed making your acquaintance. Thank you again for giving up your Friday evening, especially as I'm sure you had other plans for it. I wish you well with whatever you have in mind for next door. Goodnight.'

For all the finality of her words, he had known they would not be the last she exchanged with him. Back behind the wheel of his car, deciding to put off stumbling around in the dark to inspect his purchase, he'd driven the short distance to North Parade. Plans, he'd thought. No, he'd had nothing planned for the evening. Just an evening of sitting at home brooding in front of the telly.

Determined not to succumb to any brooding this morning, he came to a swift decision: seeing as he'd missed his chance to view his new house last night, he would go and take a look now.

He was in his car, the heater on, when he made a further decision and one that took him by surprise.

With the cake box placed for safekeeping on the front passenger seat, he headed for Church Close.

His rational self told him he had nothing to apologise for, but he couldn't shake off the feeling he might have given a poor impression of himself last night. If there was one thing he abhorred in others it was a belligerent manner, or worse, a lack of manners, and the more he thought about it, the more he was convinced he had displayed both of these characteristics last night. Put it down to his pride, but he felt duty bound to put the record straight to both Miss Silcox and Floriana Day.

Whenever he thought of the latter, he pictured her lying helplessly on the ground, the blood trickling down her face from under her beanie hat, which was skewed and partially covering one of her eyes. As gently as he could, he had carefully removed it so she could see better, and more importantly so he could see what kind of damage was going on underneath. His behaviour had been fine then, it was later when he had not exactly excelled. He'd probably come across as stand-offish in comparison to Miss Silcox who had been thoroughly effusive with her willingness to help. At the time he had thought her a meddlesome old dear getting her kicks by being caught up in somebody else's drama. And dragging him along in her wake.

It was her comment about hoping somebody would do the same for her if she were in an accident that had given him cause to rethink. Her kind help, for that was what it was, had put his behaviour under the microscope and found it severely wanting. Yes, he'd done what was expected of him at the scene of what the police officer had called 'a failed to stop accident', but he had perhaps viewed it as no more than his duty, and his duty done, he had wanted to be on his way. But how would he feel if, for instance, his father was involved in an incident like that? Wouldn't he appreciate, on his father's behalf, the kind of help Miss Silcox had been so quick to offer?

So he was on a mission to make good his reputation and, if he were scrupulously honest, to ease his conscience. He just hoped the recipient of his gift would welcome it and that she wasn't like Jesse, permanently on a diet.

Jesse had hotly disputed that she was ever on a diet – 'I just like to watch what I eat,' she would say. Which meant no cakes, except for special occasions. Bacon butties were a no-go as well. Along with chocolate, crisps, pizzas, sausages and potatoes. Basically anything with a calorific content greater than a rice cracker was considered toxic. Of course, there was no getting away from how spectacular Jesse looked as a consequence of all the working out she did and the 'watching' of what she ate.

He knocked on the door of 10a Church Close. It was a quarter to twelve, which he hoped was late enough not to disrupt a lie-in but early enough not to coincide with lunchtime. Although it was highly likely that following last night's accident, the occupant's normal Saturday morning routine, if indeed she had one, would have been cast aside.

Still in her vintage rose pyjamas with a slouchy cardie in place of a dressing gown, Floriana put down the book she'd been trying to read, and went to answer the door, being careful not to slip on the tiled hall floor in her chunky-knit socks. She wondered if it was the police community support officer back with a question he'd forgotten to ask her earlier. It had been a follow-up visit, he'd explained, a: to check her statement and b: to see if she had remembered anything else that might be useful. She hadn't. And that bothered her. She hated knowing that there was period of time, if only a few seconds or maybe minutes, that had been taken from her.

'Oh,' she said, when she saw who it was. He looked different to how she remembered him. Maybe that was because yesterday he had been wearing a suit and a smart black overcoat. See, she told herself, there's nothing seriously wrong with your memory, you just need the right stimulus. Today Mr Strong was Mr Casual, wearing jeans with a navy-blue jacket under which was a grey sweater and a navy-blue scarf wrapped loosely around his neck.

'I hope it's not a bad time to call,' he said, 'I just wanted to check that you were all right. And I've brought you' – he held out a white box decorated with a Christmassy red and green ribbon – 'some cakes which I thought might help to make you feel better. How are you?'

Surprised and touched, she said, 'You know the phrase "hit by a truck"? Well, that pretty much covers it. But at the mention of cake, I suddenly feel a whole lot better.' Despite knowing she looked ghastly, she added, 'Would you like to come in?'

His hands still holding out the box, he hesitated. 'I don't want to intrude.' His gaze dropped from her face to her cardigan and pyjamas, just as the policeman's had.

'If it would help, I could get dressed,' she replied. She had no intention of doing so, but she didn't want him to rush off, she wanted to thank him properly for what he and Miss Silcox had done for her. 'I don't know the precise contents of that box,' she went on, 'but if left alone I might eat the lot in one sitting, something I'm more than capable of doing. So, please, Mr Strong, you have to save me from myself. And apart from that, given my fragile state, if you keep me arguing on the doorstep a moment longer, I'm likely to die of cold, which would be a shame after coming so close to meeting my demise last night.'

He gave her a quick sidelong smile. 'Put like that it would be churlish and irresponsible of me to abandon you to your worst excesses. And please, call me Adam.'

'In return you must call me Floriana,' she said, while closing the door. 'There, we've now been properly introduced.'

'We did that last night, actually.'

'True, but I prefer my introductions to be done when I'm not spreadeagled on the tarmac.'

Taking possession of the cake box, she offered to make them a drink.

'A better idea would be for me to make it for you,' he said, 'given your *fragile state*.'

'Under normal circumstances, I would wrestle you to the floor rather than agree to such an outrageous suggestion, but frankly I don't have the strength today. Nor do I have the energy to go upstairs and get dressed. Do you think you could just avert your eyes to save our mutual blushes?'

He gave a small nod of his head. 'Have no fear, my eyes will be averted at all times.'

The matter settled, his coat and scarf hung up, Floriana perched on a stool at the small breakfast bar and watched her Good Samaritan go about the business of making coffee in her minuscule kitchen. Everything about 10a Church Close was minuscule; it was the smallest house in the street and looked as if it had been forced to hold its breath so it could be squeezed into place between its larger neighbours. A cottage with a sash window to the left of the front door and a window above, it was very much a two-up two-down affair – sitting room and kitchen downstairs and a bedroom with a bathroom upstairs. The original brickwork had been rendered many years ago and was painted white. She called it The Toy House.

Pouring boiling water into two mugs, and as if picking up on her thoughts, her helpful guest said, 'How long have you lived here?'

'Since August. I'd been renting before on the Iffley Road.'

He raised the carton of milk with an enquiring glance.

'Please.'

'It's a nice property,' he said, now looking out at the small paved back garden where there was a bird table, a couple of old wooden chairs and a dilapidated shed and not much else. Her plan, when she got around to it, was to buy a pretty table and chair set and put up fairy lights to illuminate the garden. 'And in a good area,' he continued. 'A very good area. Are you renting?'

'No, it's mine,' she said. 'And have I remembered correctly, did you mention in the car last night to Miss Silcox that you're some kind of property developer?'

'Perfectly remembered. So go on, get it out of your system.'

'Get what out of my system?'

'That you think people like me in Oxford are the lowest of the low, that I'm the scourge of a fine and beautiful city destroying its architectural heritage. And don't forget that I'm just another scamming buy-to-let landlord swindling the poor to fill my gold-lined pockets.'

'And are you?'

'No. As a landlord I take my responsibilities very seriously.'

'Phew, that's a relief. I'd hate to think I was keeping such poor company.'

He smiled. 'It turns out I've just bought a house next door to Miss Silcox – a scary coincidence, wouldn't you say? Do you want to drink your coffee here?'

'No, it's more comfortable in the other room.'

He followed behind her carrying the tray of mugs, plates and cakes. After she'd cleared away a basket of knitting, he placed the tray on the coffee table and waited for her to sit on the sofa before opting for the armchair to her right. In keeping with the size of the house, all the furniture was smaller than average and the armchair, which she had bought from a second-hand shop on the Cowley Road and only recently finished reupholstering, was far too small for him and she could see he immediately regretted his choice. 'The sofa might be better for you if you'd prefer,' she said.

'No, no, this is fine.'

Her aching sore face twitched with a smile at his polite stoicism and she remembered how calm and reassuring he had been last night and how he had kept her talking and covered her with his coat. Ironically he was exactly the kind of person you'd want in an emergency. Miss Silcox had described him as 'chivalrous' and he was certainly living up to that description by coming here.

'I'm glad you called round,' she said, after she'd reached for her mug of coffee, 'and not just because you came bearing gifts, but because I wanted to thank you for all that you did last night. I think I may not have expressed my gratitude as well as I should have. I'm sorry if I came across as bolshie and ungrateful.'

'Not at all. In fact, I wanted to apologise to *you*.'

'Really? What on earth for?'

'For my behaviour at the hospital; they bring out the worst in me. When I was seven years old I had a prolonged stay in one and ever since I've preferred to keep my distance.'

'I know what you mean. I couldn't wait to leave, I was terrified I'd be forced to stay the night.'

'Is that why you went along with Miss Silcox's ruse that she was your grandmother?'

'Yes. I thought they'd force me to stay if they didn't think there was someone here to fuss over me.'

She sipped her coffee cautiously, taking care how she placed the mug against her mouth. Last night the pain to her cheek had been relatively localised, today it had spread to her entire face despite regular doses of paracetamol, which also seemed not to touch the thumping headache she still had. The swelling and bruising had also spread and after a fitful night's sleep she had been shocked to look in the mirror this morning and find she had a black eye. The nurse had warned her it might happen, that the bruise from the blow to her head would extend to her eye and beyond.

As if picking up on her thoughts again, he said, 'Did you manage to sleep?'

'Not much.'

'Is there anything you need doing?' he asked. 'Any shopping I could fetch for you? Any errands you need running?'

For reasons she couldn't explain, she suddenly felt close to tears. 'Please,' she said, flapping a hand, 'don't be so helpful or I might not let you leave!'

As though guessing she was about to embarrass them both, he eased himself out of the chair and reached for a plate and passed it to her. 'Cake,' he said. 'Marie Antoinette's answer to all of life's ills. What would you like?'

Shaken by her near loss of control, Floriana swallowed back the lump in her throat and murmured, 'The mince pie, please.'

The awkward moment defused, he helped himself to a chocolate éclair and sat down again. She saw his gaze come to rest on the mantelpiece where one solitary Christmas card stood – the one from Seb, the cause of her present predicament. 'What are you doing for Christmas?' he asked. 'Are you staying in Oxford?'

'Oh,' she said as carelessly as she could muster, 'normally I'd go to my parents, but they're away on a world cruise right now which leaves me trying to get out of going to stay with my sister.'

'You don't get on?'

'We get on fine, so long as I never forget that I'm the clumsy, irresponsible younger sister.'

'Are you clumsy and irresponsible?'

Unable to open her mouth too wide, not without causing a great deal of pain to her jaw, she nibbled carefully on the edge of the mince pie. 'I have my moments,' she said. 'Look at me now, covered in more bruises than a rotting banana and quite possibly of my own making.'

He frowned. 'I hardly think you can blame yourself for being hit by a reckless driver.'

'Hmm ... well, the trouble is, and my memory still isn't clear on this point, but as I told the policeman who was here earlier, it's highly likely I stepped into the road without looking. My mind was definitely elsewhere. I know that for a fact.'

'Even so, the driver should have stopped. So what will you do if you don't go to your sister's?'

'I shall lie low.'

'No friends you can go to?'

'I'd hate to impose on them. It's family time, isn't it? What about you?' she asked, tired of his constant questioning. Or rather, tired of the direction of his questions, which all too pointedly underscored just how few close friends she had. As if that hadn't been made abundantly clear last night when she didn't ring anyone to be with her.

The thing was, she had plenty of what she called casual friends – work colleagues and ex-college buddies who she hadn't seen in a long time because they were scattered far and wide – but only one good close friend here in Oxford, the sort she could ring in an emergency, and that was Sara. But Sara had gone home to Argentina last week to spend December with her family. Of course, before Sara, Seb had been the one to whom she could always turn. But that had stopped when Imogen had appeared in Seb's life and ruined everything.

'I'll be with my family,' her guest said, curtailing her thoughts about Seb. 'What will you do about work? You said last night that you're a tour guide. Is that here in Oxford?'

'Yes, and I've already called in to say I can't do my two tours tomorrow. It's left them in the lurch, but I'm hoping I'll be OK by Monday.'

'You don't think you should give yourself more time to re-cover, at least until the bruising has faded?'

'You mean, until I no longer run the risk of frightening people with my hideous face?'

He smiled with a sudden flash of engaging frankness. 'Might be all right if you're doing a ghost tour.'

'I'll be fine,' she said firmly. 'I'll slap on some industrial strength make-up, wear a hat pulled down low and a muffler pushed up high so only my eyes show. By the way, this mince pie is delicious. Thank you so much for coming and for bringing such a thoughtful gift.'

His thoughtfulness went to further lengths before he left. He insisted on washing up the mugs and plates, replacing the halo-gen bulbs in the kitchen, and bleeding the radiator in the sitting room, so, as he pointed out, it would stop gurgling and heat the room more effectively. When he was putting his jacket and scarf back on at the front door, he said, 'You're absolutely sure there's nothing else I can do?'

'Well, there is that cracked window pane in the bathroom that needs fixing and a tap that's leaking.' Seeing him hesitate with his jacket, she said, 'I'm joking! You've done more than enough. Go on, you must have better things to do than be here. Go and have some Saturday afternoon fun.'

'I'm going to go and inspect my new house, as a matter of fact.'

'In that case, would you do one more thing for me? Would you call on Miss Silcox and thank her for her help last night?'

'Consider it done.'

He held out his hand to her. 'Goodbye and take care. And as I said before, anything I can do to help, don't hesitate to give me a ring. You have my card, don't you?'

Mr Strong, she thought, waving him off, how very apt his name was. Strong and eminently dependable, and altogether a very interesting man. She had never knowingly met a property developer before, but he didn't fit the profile of what she im-agined one to be.

Listening to the sound of his car driving off, she stood for a moment wondering what to do next. Then her gaze fell on Seb's Christmas card on the mantelpiece. No. Not that. She wasn't in any fit state to think about replying. It could wait.

Chapter Seven

From her customary seat in the drawing room window of Trinity House and with her cat – Euridice – settled on her lap and purring happily, Esme observed the ebb and flow of activity on Latimer Street. A car had just gone by with a large Christmas tree ineptly tied to the roof; it had looked like it would slide off at any minute.

That was what age had done to her; it had turned her into an observer rather than a participator. Yet she was quite happy to live vicariously; after all, she had more than enough memories to keep her company. She also had a natural disdain for getting involved in other people's lives.

However, there had been no avoiding that young girl's accident last night, or from getting involved. Nothing on earth would have made her walk away. As she'd told the community police officer who'd visited earlier, when a person was in need, it was basic humanity to help.

On the table in front of her lay that morning's copy of *The Times*, the crossword only partially completed. Normally by now, before she sorted out something to eat for lunch, she would have it finished. But her mind wasn't on it. She kept thinking about Floriana Day. Such a pretty and unusual name, she mused, absently scratching the top of the cat's head and wondering if the girl's roots were Italian.

'So what shall I do, Euridice? Shall I forget about Miss Floriana Day in the hope that she's all right, or shall I add further weight to her conviction that I'm a bothersome old lady?'

Purring with increased rapture, the cat squeezed its eyes shut and pushed its head against Esme's hand.

'Yes, I rather thought that's what you would say, which, I might add, isn't all that helpful.'

Out on the tree-lined road, a car appeared in front of Trinity

House. Leaning forward, Esme watched it come to a stop in front of the neighbouring property to the left. The driver was none other than Mr Strong. She watched him step out of the car and survey next door. Her own house had been built around the same time and was similarly constructed of red and yellow brick, but whereas number six was a modest Victorian villa, Trinity House was of a larger and more elaborate construction. With pointed arched windows and an elevated front door set deep within an arched and slated porch, it was a modestly scaled-down version of the more lavish Gothic-style residences to be found on the eastern side of the Banbury Road in Norham Gardens.

He was a fine-looking man, she thought, as Mr Strong continued to scrutinise the exterior of his house from the pavement. Self-assured, but in no way arrogant. A little taciturn, perhaps, but that was preferable to a loquacious nitwit. She had noted the absence of a wedding ring last night and while she was all too aware that people today didn't necessarily marry their life partners, or indeed wear a ring to display their marital status, it had not slipped her notice that at no stage did Mr Strong telephone anyone to say he'd be late home, which left her with the conclusion that he very likely lived alone.

Just as Floriana Day did. Which was why Esme was so concerned about her. She couldn't get it out of her head that the poor girl didn't have someone on hand to turn to, and while she herself was not one to succumb to self-pity, she knew how it felt to be unwell and alone and how vulnerable it made one feel.

Out on the street, Mr Strong's attention had been diverted: he was now staring at Trinity House and even though she was hidden behind the net curtain, Esme hastily moved away from the window, not wanting his opinion of her to plummet yet further, to be dismissed as a common curtain-twitcher.

At the disturbance, Euridice sprang from her lap and landed on the floor with a startled meow. She gave herself a little shake, followed by a stretch, then stood and looked at Esme as if to say, 'Now what?'

For answer, there was a vigorous knock at the front door.

'It seems we have a visitor,' Esme said, glancing quickly at her reflection in the mirror above the fireplace and smoothing back her hair. 'And taking into consideration who it is, I think we should both be on our best behaviour, don't you?'

The cat meowed again and scampered off to hide behind an armchair; she was always wary of company.

Once again, Adam was being offered something to drink. This time it was tea, which he politely declined. He hadn't planned to cross the threshold, his intention solely to relay a message, and to apologise for being offhand last night. But in the same way that Floriana had pointed out it was too cold to talk on the doorstep, he had agreed to come in for a few minutes.

Before stepping into the hallway with its ornate coving and dado rail and faded runner on the tiled floor, he had half expected to enter a gloomy netherworld of Miss Havisham meets Miss Doily-Kitsch, fragranced with eau de mothballs and musty old age. He couldn't have been more wrong. The gracefully proportioned, high-ceilinged room Miss Silcox had led him to – cobweb-free as far as he could see – was comfortably furnished with polished antique furniture, pieces of china, shelves of books, and a conspicuous quantity of paintings. Delicate watercolours rubbed shoulders with large oils, along with what looked like experimental acrylics. There were landscapes, still lifes and portraits, some of them good, some of them extremely good. One large painting in particular caught his eye; it was of a strikingly attractive young blonde girl sitting in the dappled shade of a tree. She had a book in her hands, but she wasn't looking at it, her gaze was engaged directly with whoever had painted the picture.

'You're an art lover, I see,' he commented, when he had been invited to sit in a comfortable leather armchair and she had taken a more upright wing chair. 'Or are you the artist?'

'Are the two mutually exclusive?' she asked with a raised eyebrow.

He immediately apologised. 'Sorry, that was clumsy of me.'

'My father was the artist,' she said, 'I'm merely the custodian. Now tell me about Floriana. How is she *really*? And do you think there's anything more we can do to help?'

He shared with her what little he'd picked up on during his visit and finished by saying, 'I'm sure she'd like it if you were to call round.' He had no way of knowing if this was true but felt it could do no harm. Floriana didn't appear to have a surfeit of ready help available and Miss Silcox seemed genuinely keen to help, so why not encourage her?

Meeting the old lady again, and in less dramatic circumstances, Adam was fast reviewing his opinion of her. She was not, as he'd thought previously, a do-gooding sticky-beak, she was an intelligent woman who, along with her house, intrigued him. With the weak afternoon sun pouring an aqueous light across the charmingly serene room, he felt oddly at ease chatting with her and he rather hoped there would be other moments such as this in the course of doing up his house next door.

'Really?' Miss Silcox asked. 'You don't think Miss Day might see it as interference?'

He was about to answer when a small and pretty ginger cat peered out cautiously from behind Miss Silcox's chair. It looked steadfastly at Adam then slowly, with dainty little steps, padded across the rug towards him. After pausing by his foot, it sprang gracefully up onto his knee and stared unblinkingly at him. Keeping perfectly still, he stared back, and as if happy with the arrangement, the cat made itself at home on his lap and began to purr.

'Gracious,' Miss Silcox said, 'I've never seen her do that with anyone else before. You're greatly honoured. Generally she's as timid as they come.'

Adam relaxed further into the squashy softness of the chair and stroked the cat. 'What's her name?'

'Euridice.'

'And is there an Orfeo?'

He saw a flicker of surprise pass across the old lady's face, followed by an imperceptible nod of satisfaction, as though he'd passed a test. 'No,' she said, 'it's just the two of us. How about you, Mr Strong, do you have a significant other?'

He decided to be honest. 'I did until last Saturday.'

'Oh, dear. May I ask what happened last Saturday?'

'My girlfriend reached the decision I was too much like a brother to her.'

'Ah, I see,' she said after a meaningful pause. 'The spark had gone out for her; it happens. You probably won't think so right now, but I'd advise you to take heart, for there are worst ways for a relationship to come adrift. Had you been together for long?'

'Long enough for me to think we might end up making a life together.' The words out, he thought of Orfeo's love for Euridice and the famous aria – 'What is Life?' – from Gluck's opera, which his mother, a keen singer and opera buff who died twelve years ago, had often claimed was quite possibly one of the most hauntingly beautiful arias ever written. It wasn't often he heard the piece of music, but when he did he was always reminded of her.

Whether it was the unexpected reminder of his mother, or talking about Jesse leaving him, or maybe the combination of the two, a great sadness came over him. Fighting it, he concentrated on stroking the purring cat.

'I'm sorry,' Miss Silcox said quietly. 'You must be devastated. But is it really hopeless? Is there no way you can win her back?'

He swallowed and looked at his watch. 'She's at the house now, clearing it' – his voice cracked – 'clearing it of her things. And I have absolutely no idea why I'm telling you this.'

'Well, I'm glad you did,' Miss Silcox said briskly. 'Bottling things up serves no purpose at all. Better to get them out.'

She rose slowly from her chair and, standing before him, put her hands together. 'Would you care to join me for some lunch, Mr Strong, and when duly fortified you can go next door and get on with whatever it is you came to do?'

Carefully removing Euridice from his lap, he placed her on the floor and stood up as well. 'I will if you'll call me Adam,' he said.

She smiled. 'And you must call me Esme.'

Chapter Eight

Sunday dawned grey-skied and frosty.

From her bedroom window Esme looked out at the whitened garden. Perched on a bare tree branch, the bossy blackbird – the self-appointed autocrat of the walled garden – gave a flap of its wings and swooped down to the ground beneath the holly bush and pecked for fallen berries amongst the petrified leaves. From the stone bird bath, a robin watched the blackbird and, as if weighing up its chances, flew over to the holly bush to see what pickings he could find. But the blackbird was having none of it and shooed him off at once with a volley of vicious pecks.

Esme tutted. 'Such wickedness. This cold weather really does bring out the dictator in that wretched bird.'

At her side and sitting on the dressing table, Euridice licked her paw, dabbed it delicately behind her ear, then yawned as though any uncivilised behaviour going on in the hurly-burly of the garden was quite beneath her.

Breakfast was always the same for Esme – tea and a slice of toast with marmalade followed by some fresh fruit, depending on what was in season. If she didn't have any fresh fruit, she would have tinned; she was particularly fond of tinned pineapple. Today she took two clementines from the bowl on the dresser and sat at the table in one of the Windsor armchairs with Bach's Sonata in G minor playing on Radio Three.

During lunch yesterday with Adam she had told him that having lived alone for so many years she was a fastidious creature of habit. In return he'd said that he never knew from one day to the next what he was going to do, that he thrived on the unpredictable nature of his work. How very alien her world here at Trinity House would be to him. Of course, it hadn't always been like this, but as she had explained to him, gradually, with the passing of years, one adapts and learns to subsist on a sort of cheeseparing way of life, is even grateful for the solace it brings.

Breakfast eaten and tidied away, she went back upstairs to dress, thinking that as much as she relished the pleasantly ordered tranquillity of her routine, she did not find the disturbance to it since Friday evening's twist of fate in any way disagreeable. It would naturally run its course and all would soon be just as it was before.

She opened the larger of the two mahogany wardrobes in her bedroom and pondered what to wear for her outing.

Just as Adam had suggested, she was going to pay a call on Floriana, but now that the time was upon her, she was suddenly tremendously occupied with the anxious hope that her visit would be well received. Adam, a most sincere and genuine young man, had been in no doubt that it would be, so she must try to allay her anxiety and put her trust in him. And in the gifts she would take with her: a pot of indoor cyclamen and a very small box of Champagne chocolate truffles, bought yesterday afternoon from Buddy Joe's after Adam had left to go next door. Surely such offerings would prove her intentions were well meant?

But by the time she was dressed and had applied her make-up, her anxiety had multiplied – what if Floriana wasn't at home? The thought of her short journey being a wasted one, of having to return to Trinity House with her gifts, pained her so abruptly, she lost her nerve and wondered if she shouldn't forget the whole enterprise. Why not stay here and be content with her usual Sunday of listening to the radio while reading and maybe tidying the larder, a job which was long overdue? Why risk going out in the cold, especially as the pavements would probably still be covered in a treacherous layer of slippery frost just waiting to catch out a foolish old woman who should know better and stay inside?

Floriana had given herself a good talking to when she'd woken that morning. There would be no more lazing about the house in her jammies feeling sorry for herself. There would also be no more putting off a very important phone call.

Accordingly, she was now dragging herself out of bed and fully determined to tell her sister that she had her own plans for Christmas. She would tell Ann she was going to friends, not just for Christmas, but for New Year. No way was she going to let her sister bully her into spending any of the festivities with her.

It wouldn't be so bad if it was only Ann and her husband, Paul, and their two children, but the whole Brown clan would be there – Paul's parents, plus a stray uncle and Paul's ultra sensible brother, Robert. Ann had some crazy notion that Robert was perfect for Floriana and that she was a fool not to appreciate how fond Robert was of her and that at her age she shouldn't look a gift horse in the mouth.

Mum and Dad never went on about her still being single, but Ann had an unhealthy fixation about it and could always be relied upon to know why her younger sister was incapable of finding a decent man. It came down to many things, but chiefly it was her 'ridiculous dress sense' as Ann saw it. 'You're not a student any more,' she would say in exaggerated bafflement at the latest quirky outfit Floriana had put together. 'It's time to grow up and settle down,' was another refrain.

Settling down implied settling in Floriana's mind and she didn't want that. The sad truth was, for the last two years she'd lived with the realisation that if she couldn't have Seb, she didn't want anyone.

She certainly didn't want her sister's brother-in-law. In his late thirties – going on fifty – Robert was a personal injury lawyer and in the light of her accident, which Ann had admitted yesterday on the phone she had mentioned to Robert, she could just imagine what the hot topic of conversation would be if she joined the Brown clan for Christmas.

Now dressed, she took the stairs slowly – her head still ached and if she moved too quickly she felt dizzy. The swellings on her face had gone down a bit, but the technicolor bruising was increasing. Just call me freak-face, she thought as she reached the bottom step and winced as a sharp pain shot through her hip and back. She was beginning to worry that she wouldn't be well enough for work tomorrow. She hoped she would be; she hated letting people down. She also needed the money. But the thought of wandering round the streets of Oxford in the cold in her present state didn't feel like the most sensible thing to do.

Making herself some breakfast, she recalled Adam's words of caution yesterday, and his kindness. The kindness of strangers, she thought, was so much more palatable. Often benevolence from closer to home was harder to accept, mostly because it frequently came with too many strings.

Yesterday her sister had kept her promise and duly phoned to see how she was, but her main concern, apart from badgering Floriana about Christmas, was that under no circumstances was she to let on to their parents about the accident. Feeling that she was being warned – no, *lectured* – like a naughty child to do the right thing, Floriana had regretted she'd ever mentioned it to Ann.

Usually there was no problem with Christmas, because normally it was under Mum's control and they all went home to her and Dad and Ann's need to boss everyone about was held in check. This year Mum and Dad would be somewhere between Borneo and Vietnam on Christmas Day, on their way to Ho Chi Minh City. Mum had been unsure about being away during December – she had been all for choosing a different itinerary for a different time of the year – but in a rare moment of unyielding strong will, Dad had held firm and gone ahead and booked the cruise, saying Ann and Floriana were old enough to organise themselves in their absence. Which, of course, they were. Floriana had at once got it all perfectly planned, she and Sara would spend Christmas together, but then Sara's family in Argentina had insisted she go back to them for the whole of December.

Plans, thought Floriana as she cautiously chewed on a piece of soft buttery toast – her jaw was still very tender – was there any point in making them? Before Seb's card had arrived, she had planned to spend some of the weekend sorting through the storage boxes on top of her wardrobe, put there temporarily when she moved in and which had stayed there untouched ever since. But the thought of climbing onto a chair to get them down had been beyond her yesterday. Maybe later, after she'd rung her sister, she would summon the energy to face the job.

Her breakfast finished, she heard a knock at the door.

Floriana ushered her unexpected visitor in from the cold.

'Normally I wouldn't dream of calling unannounced,' said Miss Silcox, 'especially not on a Sunday.' Her cheeks were flushed from the cold, her eyes a little watery and her words tumbled from her lips in a breathless flurry. She sounded quite different to how Floriana had remembered her, not at all the authoritative figure giving orders.

'I would hate to be guilty of a breach of manners,' her visitor went on, 'but I wanted to put my mind at rest and see for myself that you really were on the mend.'

'Seeing is believing,' Floriana said with as much of a smile as her sore face would allow, 'so I hope your mind is at rest now. What's more, I've put away my self-pity and have officially rejoined the human race today. Yesterday I was a lazy couch potato; I didn't do a thing. Let me take your coat.'

The coat hung up on the hook in the hall, she led her guest through to the sitting room. 'I take it Adam passed on my message to you yesterday?'

'Oh, yes, it was most kind of you to ask him to thank me,' Miss Silcox said, removing the fabric cover from the basket she was carrying. 'Very thoughtful indeed. I brought these for you, a small offering to cheer you up. But I'm delighted to see that you're already remarkably chipper, considering what happened to you.'

'Oh,' cried Floriana, 'how sweet of you. But really, I feel such a fraud. First Adam bringing me cakes and now you with chocolates and flowers; I should get run over more often.'

'Perhaps that's a little drastic, my dear. Where would you like the cyclamen?'

Floriana took the pot from her guest and surveyed the small room. 'I think here on the window sill would be perfect, don't you?'

'You'll have to find something for it to sit on, or it will make a terrible mess.'

'No problem, I'll fetch a saucer while I make us a drink. What would you like, tea or coffee? Or, seeing as it's so cold, shall we be very indulgent and have hot chocolate to go with one of those delicious truffles you've brought?'

Settled with their drinks, Floriana was thinking how pleased she was that this elderly, doll-sized woman had come to see her. The more snippets of information she winkled out of the old lady – she had lived in Oxford all her adult life, had worked as a librarian at Queen's, then an archivist at the Bodleian, and had never been married – the more Floriana itched to know. She also realised that she recognised Miss Silcox, had seen her about since moving to Church Close, very likely at the shops in North Parade.

Composed and perfectly at ease in the chair where her guest yesterday had looked anything but comfortable, Miss Silcox was dressed in a smart navy blue two-piece suit with a cream silk blouse, her stockinged legs placed neatly together at the knees and ankles and tucked to one side in a very ladylike fashion. Her patent court shoes with a two-inch heel were blue to match her outfit, along with her handbag and gloves. Her silver hair, elegantly pinned up, was surprisingly thick and luxurious for a woman of her age, which Floriana guessed was late seventies. Her eyes were blue and alert, and probably missed nothing, and were surrounded by a tracery of fine lines.

She must have been a very attractive woman when she was young, Floriana found herself thinking, mesmerised by the old lady. She watched her wipe the corners of her pearly-pink lip-sticked mouth with the paper napkin from the packet Floriana had dug out from the bottom of the drawer in the kitchen – Adam had been awarded no such treatment, not even a bit of kitchen roll. But then having Miss Silcox here was a bit like having a visit from the Queen. Though what had she been thinking, giving her royal guest such a clunky old mug? It looked like a bucket in Miss Silcox's small elegant hands – hands that were doubt-less more accustomed to delicate teacups made of expensive fine bone china.

'Please don't think we were gossiping about you,' Miss Silcox said, meeting Floriana's gaze over the top of the huge mug, 'but Adam mentioned that you seemed to think you were at fault for the accident. Surely you can't really believe that? The car, after all, was going much too fast.'

'I'm afraid I was at fault to a degree,' Floriana responded. 'I still can't actually recall the impact of the car hitting me, but I do remember stepping into the road without looking. I feel rather silly about the whole business. To be honest, I feel a bit sorry for the driver.'

The old lady's silver eyebrows rose at that. 'But he didn't stop,' she said, clearly taken aback. 'He could have left you for dead.'

'I know, but the thing is, there was nothing premeditated about it and I can easily understand that he, or she for that mat-ter, probably panicked and just took off.'

47

'That's a very generous attitude on your part, but don't you think the driver ought to be taught a lesson, if only to stop him, or *her*, from doing it again?'

Floriana thought about this and with a truffle held between her thumb and forefinger, she dipped it into her mug of hot chocolate. 'I agree, in principle,' she said, 'but how do we know the driver hasn't spent the weekend in a frenzy of regret and self-recrimination? Would being sent to jail and punished for an accident they didn't cause be truly just? I'm not sure I'd want that on my conscience when I know that I'm partly to blame, that were it not for the fact my mind was elsewhere, I would have reached home quite safely. And you know, if the timing had been different, it could have been Adam's car I stepped out in front of.'

Miss Silcox pursed her lips. 'An admirable approach and I applaud you for that. We live in an age when too many people refuse to accept responsibility for their actions and rush pell-mell to blame others for their mistakes. Yet I still hold the view that I'd think better of the driver if he'd had the courage to stop and help. As for Adam knocking you over, had he done so, he would most assuredly have stopped to help you. I barely know him, but he's a man of integrity, that I'm sure of.'

Floriana popped the warmed softened truffle into her mouth and let it melt on her tongue. At length, she said, 'We can never really know how a person will react when faced with a moral dilemma, can we? Likewise, we all make mistakes. Haven't you done something which you've regretted the instant you did it?'

As she heard herself ask the question, Floriana wondered with a spark of irritation if she wasn't thinking about something altogether different.

About Seb.

About *her* and Seb.

She flushed with annoyance, for betraying the depth of her feelings, that Seb was never far from her thoughts. Unwilling to pursue the conversation further, she offered Miss Silcox another truffle.

'No thank you,' the old lady said, 'they're for you. And yes, I've done many things I've regretted, but just as many I don't, though perhaps some I ought.'

In the silence that followed, while Floriana tried to think of something else to talk about, Miss Silcox looked about her. When furnishing the room Floriana had had shabby chic in mind, but even she had to admit she had only achieved the shabby element of the design.

She watched her guest's sharp eyes roaming over the packed bookshelves either side of the fireplace, the cast-off television from her parents, the basket of knitting on the floor – she was making a pair of fingerless gloves for her niece – the solitary Christmas card on the mantelpiece, the wonky lamp, the candles, and the tatty beige carpet with its blackened edges which the previous owner had left behind and which Floriana longed to be rid of. Taking up the carpet was another job on her To Do list, a list that seemed to grow on a daily basis. If only the number of available hours in the day grew exponentially. She didn't know what sort of house Miss Silcox lived in, but she guessed it was a lot grander than her much-loved Toy House.

'May I ask you something?' Miss Silcox asked when her scrutiny had been exhausted and she had placed with deliberate care her finished mug of hot chocolate on the table. 'It's rather personal, so please tell me to mind my own business if I've gone too far.'

Floriana nodded, and tucked her feet under her on the sofa, curious to hear what this woman considered to be personal. Maybe she was going to offer some interior design tips.

'It was at the time of the accident,' Miss Silcox said, 'when Adam was ringing for an ambulance and when you were not quite compos mentis; you kept repeating something.'

'Really? What was it?'

'I can't be one hundred per cent sure, but I think it was a name. Does the name Seb mean anything to you?'

Chapter Nine

Floriana first laid eyes on Sebastian Hughes when she was fourteen years old and was helping out in her father's shop during the long summer holiday.

Day & Son had been a family-run business since 1872 when Floriana's great-grandfather had opened a small hardware store selling ironmongery and decorating equipment. By the time her father took it over, not only had the Kent village of Stanhurst expanded to being a small town, but the shop had spread to the two premises either side and its stock was comprised of a vast selection of DIY equipment and general household items, including an extensive range of kitchenware and garden furniture. Then last year, after several approaches from a large supermarket chain, her father reluctantly accepted an offer to sell the shop so the site could be converted into a sizeable convenience store. It wasn't a decision he made lightly, and not surprisingly it wasn't met with universal approval.

But back when Floriana was a child, and just as soon as she and her sister were old enough, they had both worked Saturdays and holidays in the shop and on this particular busy afternoon when Floriana was filling the shelves with pest control products, she noticed a boy about the same age as herself searching for something on a nearby shelf. She'd never seen him before, so took a moment to give him the full once-over. Like most teenagers, his jeans were baggy and where they dragged on the ground they were torn and frayed at the heels of his trainers. He was wearing a black T-shirt, the front of which showed a skull with a crown of barbed wire. His hair was thick and messy, as if he hadn't brushed it in days. He was, she thought, not bad-looking in a quirky sort of way.

She watched him take a mousetrap from the shelf and to her amusement he pulled back the metal spring and stuck his finger experimentally in the bit where the mouse would meet its snappy end. She waited for the inevitable yelp, but it didn't happen. Removing his finger, he released the spring, then casually slipped the trap into his pocket.

Petty thieving went on all the time in the shop, but never had Floriana actually witnessed somebody do it right under her nose. Shocked she looked around for one of the full-time assistants, but there was nobody else about. Determined he wasn't going to get away with it, she stopped what she was doing and followed him as he coolly ambled towards the main door.

Out on the street, she tapped him on the shoulder. 'I think you've forgotten something, haven't you?' she said, mimicking the snooty tone of voice her sister used whenever she was telling her off about something.

He swung round so quickly she thought he might hit her and make a run for it. But he hit her with an awkward smile instead and said, 'Oh hell, I don't suppose you could let me off, could you? I mean, it's just a mousetrap. Seventy-five pence worth of wood with a bit of metal is hardly going to make a difference, is it?'

'Of course it makes a difference!' she said indignantly.

He shrugged. 'What do you care, you only work here, don't you?'

'This is my dad's shop,' she said, 'which means I care lots.' She held out her hand. 'So stop kidding yourself you're Robin Hood or Dick Turpin and give me back the mousetrap.'

He lowered his gaze and looked quizzically at the open palm of her hand, in a way that suddenly made her feel very foolish. 'See here,' he said, pointing with a finger, 'that line there shows you have a strong spirit and that you're not easily manipulated by others.'

Furious, she snatched her hand away. 'Don't change the subject. Just give me back the mousetrap or ...' Her words trailed off and she floundered. Just what would she do?

'Or what?' he asked. He didn't sound like he was challenging her, merely as if he was trying to be helpful. Which made her feel a hundred times more foolish.

'Or I'll call the police!' she blurted out, knowing that her face was now the same colour as the red polo shirt Day & Son employees wore. Worse still, she wasn't just mimicking her over-bearing sister, she was turning into Ann!

He took a step back and stared at her. 'Bloody hell, you're serious, aren't you? You really would call the police, and over something as stupid as a shitty bit of wood and a spring.'

'It's you who's put yourself in this situation,' she said, her indignation fizzling out. 'All I'm doing is giving you the choice to do the right thing.'

'And do you always do the right thing?' he asked. There was mockery in his eyes.

Her indignation spluttered back into life again. But only because he'd hit home so closely, because more often than not if there was a simple choice between doing the right thing and doing the wrong thing, Floriana could make the choice that would get her into hot water. She saw it as being individual, not wanting to be a sheep, one of the boring crowd, but her teachers saw it differently and called her stubborn and rebellious. She had once been sent to the head for being rude to a teacher, something she hotly denied; all she'd done was correct his spelling. I mean, come on, an English teacher who couldn't spell?

'Right,' she said decisively, grabbing hold of the boy's arm, 'you're coming with me.'

Except he didn't budge, being much taller than her there was no chance of her dragging him back inside the shop. To her further annoyance, he laughed. 'What's this, a citizen's arrest?'

Cross that he was laughing at her, she let go of him. 'Oh, sod you!' she said, wishing she'd never got involved. Why couldn't she have been working in another part of the shop when he'd come in to help himself?

A moment passed, during which neither of them seemed to know what to say next. Finally he broke the silence. 'I'm sorry,' he said. 'Look, have it back if it means so much to you.' He pushed the mousetrap into her hands.

'You could just pay for it,' she said, 'as you pointed out your-self, seventy-five pence isn't that big a deal.'

'Yeah, well, it is if you don't have any money.'

His reply surprised her; from the second he'd opened his mouth, he had looked and sounded exactly the sort to have plenty of money, if not in his own pocket then certainly in that of his parents'.

'What do you want a mousetrap for?' she asked, as he started to walk away from her.

Twisting his head round, he looked at her as if she was a complete idiot. 'Why does anyone want a mousetrap? To catch mice, of course.'

She watched him go off down the street. He had a long loping stride and an air of vague distraction about him.

Two days later when she had shown a customer where to find the descaling products, she felt someone tapping her on the shoulder.

It was him.

'Hello,' he said, 'I'd like a mousetrap, please. And before you get uppity with me, today I'm in the fortunate position to offer you seventy-five pence of the sovereign realm. God save the Queen!'

In spite of the excruciating memory she had of his previous visit, and how small and mean she had felt for the rest of the day, she smiled.

The transaction completed, he said, 'What time do you get off work? Or does your father keep you here overnight stocking shelves?'

By the end of the school holiday not only had they become friends but Floriana's father had agreed that he could work Saturdays in the shop.

Seb and his mother had moved to Stanhurst following her divorce and he described their situation in terms of living in genteel penury. It was an expression which Floriana had come to know as being a typical Seb remark, in that it was loaded with sufficient exaggeration and irony to appear comical, but in actual fact belied just how difficult things were. It was a defence mechanism, she came to realise.

He'd apologised for trying to steal the mousetrap, explaining that he and his mother had been in their new house less than twenty-four hours when they'd discovered they had company. With his mother screaming hysterically every time a mouse poked its head out of a drawer or a cupboard and her bank account seriously in the red, Seb had taken matters into his own hands. And failed. 'Clearly I'm not cut out for a life of crime,' he'd joked, adding more seriously, 'any more than my mother is cut out for marriage and motherhood.'

This was his mother's second marriage to end in divorce.

Seb's father – Husband Number One – had long ago remarried and contributed haphazardly to his son's well-being, the money mostly going towards paying the fees for the private school he attended. Husband Number Two felt no inclination to support a child that wasn't his. 'I can't say I blame him,' Seb said of the man, 'why should he just because he married my mother?'

Although Seb was the same age as Floriana, he seemed older and altogether more worldly and astute. He claimed he was steeped in cynicism and that tricked people into thinking he was smarter than he really was. 'Put it this way, I've been on a steep learning curve,' he said one day when she asked him how he always managed to sound so positive and pragmatic.

'Since when?' she'd asked.

'Since I was born.'

Of his mother he said, matter-of-factly, 'It's a shame, but she's not very good at being married. The trouble is, she's not very good at being on her own either.'

It didn't take long for Floriana to realise that Seb had his hands full taking care of his mother, who in Floriana's opinion was a lazy, selfish woman who needed to stop moaning about how unfair life was. Some days she stayed in bed, awash in her own misery, not giving a thought to Seb who was left to fend for himself. Not once did he ever criticise or complain; he just accepted the situation and got on with it.

It didn't even bother him when, six months after moving to Stanhurst, his father wrote to say he could no longer afford to pay Seb's school fees. At the start of the next term he transferred to the comprehensive which Floriana attended, and where her sister had also been a student – a model student as was pointed out to her all too often. It was then that Floriana more or less dropped her immediate circle of friends and she and Seb became inseparable and were dubbed the Gang of Two.

Floriana's mother adored Seb and made him an honorary member of the family, saying he was welcome any time he wanted. Unbeknown to Floriana, she was regularly sneaking food parcels into his bag to take home with him. Floriana only found out when she caught her mother red-handed fiddling with Seb's bag when he was spending Sunday afternoon with her to do some last-minute revision for their GCSEs. Telling Floriana to *ssh!* her mother confessed that she had been doing it for months. 'He has his pride, Floriana,' her mother said, 'so don't say anything to him.'

Mum wasn't the only one to fall for Seb, a high percentage of girls at school did as well, but he somehow kept them at arm's distance without actually upsetting or insulting anyone. In private to Floriana he said he had enough on his plate as it was without taking on the demands of a needy girlfriend. 'Not all of womankind is as needy as your mother,' Floriana had rebuked him.

His attitude towards girls changed when they went to university.

They hadn't planned to go to the same university, let alone go to Oxford. Forever one for the path of ease and least resistance, Floriana hadn't considered it, but her History teacher urged her to give it a go. 'I know you hate hard work,' he'd said, 'and coast along by relying on that near-photographic memory of yours, but Oxford would give you the stimulus you need. What's to lose?'

Precious time preparing herself for the stress of it all, had been Floriana's private opinion. But once Seb had said he was apply-ing – just for the sheer hell of it – a competitive streak she didn't know she possessed kicked in and the next thing she and Seb, along with four other sixth-formers, were heading to Oxford for an overnight stay and a round of interviews.

During the train journey back home afterwards, and nurs-ing spectacular hangovers following a night of what Seb called 'acquainting ourselves with college life', Floriana had known that if she wasn't offered a place, she would be devastated. She had fallen in love with Oxford. She loved everything about it; its velvet green lawns and ivy-clad walls, its architecture, its ethos, its tradition, and its sense of place in time and history. Never had she wanted something so much. Sitting next to Seb on the train, she had pulled off her gloves and asked him to read her palm. 'Tell me what it says,' she'd said. 'Am I going to Oxford?'

He'd held her hand in his and in an act of solemn divination stared at it thoughtfully. 'Yeah, Florrie, you're going, no ques-tion.'

She'd giggled. 'And you?'

He'd raised his own and studied it for a long moment. 'It says wherever my best friend goes, I go too. What's more, it says we're going to go travelling together one day.'

They'd slept the rest of the train journey home, Floriana's

head against his shoulder, his arm around her. Anyone looking at them would have assumed they were boyfriend and girlfriend. People, including her sister, could never get it into their heads that they really were just good friends. How could there be anything else, Seb would say, when Floriana and her parents had effectively become a surrogate family to him? To be anything other than friends would just be plain weird. He truly was like a brother to her. So no, there was never anything remotely sexual between them.

Just as there was no truth in Seb's ability to read palms. Other than knowing a few rudimentary things about palmistry, it was, of his own admission, another of his charlatan tricks to fool people into thinking he was something he wasn't. For all that, it had become a light-hearted joke they often resorted to when in need of reassurance about something. Or to reaffirm the dreams they had for themselves.

In this instance, the palm reading got it right and the following October Floriana took up her place at St Anne's College to read History and in his typically laid-back fashion, Seb said he was embarking on three years of dossing about at Keble to idle his way through the odd work of literature.

Away from home, and as though now free of the responsibility of caring for his mother, Seb threw himself into college life – mostly the social aspects. He was making up for lost time, he said, and while he began working his way through a series of girlfriends Floriana started seeing a rugby-playing chemist called John from Merton. He lasted almost to the end of that first Michaelmas term but parted with Floriana when he realised she was discussing their relationship in intimate detail with Seb. 'But why wouldn't we?' Floriana retaliated. 'We tell each other everything.'

'But some things are private,' John had argued back.

Her next boyfriend had been a fellow History student, but he stopped seeing her after her escapade with Seb which had resulted in them spending a night in a police cell. He didn't want to be tainted by association, she supposed.

Though she and Seb were the closest of friends, there was nothing possessive or exclusive about their friendship, both of them were quite happy with the other to have a life of their own. More than once Floriana found herself thinking that she could not contemplate a long-term relationship unless it could be carried out along the same lines.

Meanwhile, Seb was getting through girlfriends at an alarming rate; he had a different one every time Floriana saw him. It seemed to her that it was nothing but sex for him, the more casual and meaningless the better. As the weeks, months and terms passed, she saw a recklessness to his behaviour that worried her.

Chapter Ten

Sunday evening, and although he had been expecting it, the ringing of his mobile still took Adam unawares.

He cautioned himself not to rush to answer it. He mustn't appear too eager. Better to play it cool. Cool but not cold. Definitely not cold. Cool but not desperate.

Was he desperate?

Yeah, he was desperate all right. All last night he'd sat here thinking how much he missed Jesse and how he hated the sight of the empty spaces she'd left in the house while he'd been out yesterday – the empty cupboards, the bare shelves. Then today, all morning and all afternoon, he'd been on tenterhooks waiting for this call, deliberately staying no more than a few yards from his mobile in case he missed it ringing. But just as a watched pot never boiled, nor did a watched phone ring, so it was inevitable that the minute he'd turned his back and got on with some work, the call would come through.

It might not be Jesse, of course.

Or if it was, she might not be going to say what he hoped she would; that she'd had second thoughts, that packing up her things had made her think again.

For pity's sake, just answer it!

He reached across the breakfast bar for the phone that was behind his laptop; a picture of Jesse stared back at him from the small illuminated screen.

'Hi, Jesse,' he said, hoping he would come across as happy to hear from her, but not so happy that she thought he wasn't missing her.

'Adam,' she said.

Not exactly breezily upbeat, he decided, but then not too downbeat either. So far so good. A sum total of three words exchanged between them and all still to play for.

He waited for her to speak again – after all she was the one who wanted to talk to him. When he'd returned from Latimer Street yesterday, he'd found a note on the worktop from her. It had been friendly enough, just a few lines saying she hoped he didn't mind but she'd made herself a drink and she would ring the following day as there was something she wanted to discuss with him. Eaten up with curiosity – and hope – he'd been tempted to ring her straight away, but he hadn't.

When she didn't say anything further, he said, 'Did you manage OK yesterday? Find everything you needed?'

'Yes, thanks.'

There was another pause. He was about to fill it with some inanity when she said, 'This isn't easy, is it? It's not how I thought it would be.'

Bloody hell, he thought, you should try it from where I'm standing! But sensing a chink in her defences, perhaps even a hint of the regret he'd hoped for, he said, 'Would it be easier to have this conversation face to face?'

'No,' she said quickly. Too quickly. 'No, I don't think so,' she added.

'You're sure?' he said. 'There'd be no pressure. Just the two of us talking. You saying whatever it is you want to say, me listening. Maybe some coffee involved. Or maybe dinner?' He gripped the mobile and cringed. Too pushy! Way too pushy. He waited for the knock-back.

'That's ... that's really sweet of you that you could suggest something like that, because that's how I'd like things to be between us. You know, being friends and being able to speak to each other without any bad feelings.'

His hope took a nosedive. 'Friends,' he repeated. 'Is that why you wanted to speak to me? To establish we could be *friends*?'

'Yes,' she said. 'If you think it's possible.'

Hurt and anger welled up in him. And disappointment. 'You mean, if I can be with you and not wish it was how it used to be between us? But hang on, that was when I was like a brother to you. I'm getting confused, is it a friend or a brother you want?'

'Adam, please don't make this any more difficult than it already is.'

The phone clamped to his ear, he whirled round on the spot and willed himself to stay calm. Sarcasm was not going to help his cause. He closed his eyes and from nowhere came the image of being in Esme Silcox's house, the sun pouring in through the window of the large elegant drawing room and Euridice purring on his lap. The old lady's words echoed in his head: *Is there no way you can win her back?*

He cleared his throat. 'I promised myself I wouldn't get upset,' he said, 'but I miss you, Jesse, and I wish you were here now. I keep thinking of all the good times we had. And the good times we could have in the future.'

'I miss you too,' she said. 'I miss how you could always be so reassuring and make me feel better about—'

'Then come home,' he cut in, unable to stop himself. 'Let's forget this awful week ever happened. Just tell me how to make things better between us and I'll do it. I ... I love you.'

There was a long silence. It was so long he wondered if the signal had died.

'Are you still there, Jesse?'

'Yes, I'm still here.' He heard her take a deep breath and fearing the worst – adamant rejection – he leapt in with both feet again.

'Look,' he said, deciding to act on the advice Miss Silcox had given him, 'why don't we put off making any definitive decisions right now, when maybe neither of us is thinking straight? Why don't we put things on hold and take time out to think things over?'

'Are you saying you want us to be on a break?'

He tried to lighten the tone. 'I know it sounds like something from an American sitcom, but yes, I am. If it would help. If it would give us both space to think things over, to know what it is we really want.'

He was met with another silence. 'What do you think?' he asked. 'Would it help?'

Chapter Eleven

It wasn't until Tuesday that Floriana went back to work.

The office for Dreaming Spires Tours was on the High, just down from St Mary's. The bulls-eye bay-fronted windows looked festively charming and to Floriana's mind – because she had done them herself last week – were tastefully decorated with just the right amount of ye olde worlde Christmas schmaltz.

Since it was only just after nine o'clock and they didn't open until nine-thirty, it was too early for any customers yet, but Tony, her boss, was there before her. When she walked in, he looked up from where he was tidying the booking counter. He made no attempt to disguise his alarm at the sight of her. 'Floriana, darling, you look awful!'

'Thanks, that's just what I need to hear.'

Taking off his glasses and letting them dangle from the chain around his neck, he came out from behind the counter. 'I had no idea you were in such a bad way. I thought it was more shock that you were nursing rather than actual physical damage. You poor thing. Why didn't you tell me it was this bad?'

Disappointed that her attempts at concealment – a beanie hat pulled low, strategically applied make-up and her hair worn down so it formed a partial curtain over one side of her face – had been far from successful, she said brightly, 'I'm fine. Really. It's just bruising.'

He tutted and shook his head. 'But your cheek, it looks like someone took a cheese grater to it.'

She winced at the description. Yesterday she'd had enough of the dressing on her cheek and had carefully removed it, deciding that it would heal faster uncovered, just as her mother used to say whenever she'd grazed her knees as a child – let the air get at it.

'I need to work, Tony,' she said. 'I can't sit moping around at home any longer; I've done enough of that already.'

'Are you sure? I could give Damian a call and see if he's free to step in. You're down for the Potter tour, aren't you? He could manage that without too much trouble. And then you could help me here in the office today, that would be much easier for you.'

Everyone at Dreaming Spires Tours knew that Tony had the screaming hots for Damian Webb and chose to overlook the fact that he wasn't a qualified guide. Damian was an actor whose claim to fame was as an extra in an episode of *Inspector Morse* – 'Death is Now My Neighbour' – in which he'd played a don walking through the front quad of Brasenose College. That was way back in 1997 but boy, he never let anyone forget it. He'd also appeared fleetingly in a couple of *Midsomer Murders* episodes. When he was between acting jobs, which happened a lot, he offered his services to Tony, and while his knowledge as a tour guide was woefully inadequate and thankfully precluded him from leading the more in-depth tours, the tourists who didn't know the first thing about Oxford, and could therefore be easily fooled, lapped him up, especially if he regaled them with his luvvie tales of being on set with John Thaw and Kevin Whately.

Privately, Floriana thought he was nothing but a show-off and made a mockery of the hard work she and all the other blue-and green-badge guides put in – the many hours of study for the exams they had to sit as well as the regular workshops attended in order to keep up to date.

However, what bothered her more was the thought of Damian getting the payment she was due for leading her group this morning. 'But, Tony,' she said, trying to appeal to his desire for Dreaming Spires Tours never to be accused of second-rate service, 'you know Damian gets carried away with the sound of his own voice and just makes it up as he goes along. That's hardly good for our reputation, is it?'

'Oh, he's not that bad,' Tony said, 'and his patter goes down well enough. Most of the punters don't know that he's ad-libbing and a lot of them want nothing more than a good yarn to share with the folks back home.'

While that was true on one level, Floriana still wasn't going to let an amateur steal her show. 'I'll be fine to take my group,' she said, 'and by the time I've got my Professor McGonagall hat on and wrapped a Hogwarts' scarf around my neck, they'll hardly notice the bruises.'

Tony raised his glasses to inspect her more closely. His expression was sceptical. 'All right, but' – he wagged his finger at her – 'no overdoing it.'

Relieved that she'd convinced Tony she was fit for work, she went through to the back office. Now all she had to do was convince herself she could get through the day without keeling over or experiencing a panic attack.

She was disconcerted that she felt so utterly exhausted before the day had even properly begun. She felt jittery as well, sort of hollow and wobbly inside. Perhaps she should have caught the bus in and not walked, but she'd thought the walk would do her good and help to get her back into the swing of things. But she'd misjudged it badly, for every time a car had come too close to her she had let out an embarrassing cry of panicky alarm and jumped away from it, her heart racing and her hands literally shaking. At one point she was scared she was going to have a full-on panic attack. It had been a huge relief when she'd reached Radcliffe Square and escaped the traffic.

As much as it grieved her, it looked like Esme Silcox had been proved right when she'd said that Floriana should take another day off, if not the whole week, before returning to work. 'No one in their right mind would expect you to rush back before you were fully recovered,' the old lady had said.

The trouble was, as Floriana had explained to her, being freelance meant she was paid by the tour, so the more she did, the more money she had in the bank. As well as tours she also did shifts in the office when Tony needed extra help, which she quite enjoyed but really being out and about as a guide was what she loved to do. She enjoyed the interaction with a group, seeing herself as part teacher and part entertainer. Just not the kind of entertainment Damian Webb advocated.

She was the only one of the guides to add a flourish of costume to her tours. Initially Tony hadn't been keen for her to do it. Ironically, given his penchant for hammy old Damian luvving it up, he'd been worried it would give the wrong impression, that they wouldn't be taken seriously. But Floriana had gone ahead with it and the feedback Tony received was that her tours were always thoroughly enjoyed, both for their content and style, which she kept light and engaging, but grounded in solid fact. She had also become something of a familiar sight in Oxford as she led her groups through the streets and colleges, which was quite something in a city that was full of eccentric sights, both in human and architectural form.

She opened the cupboard where she kept her 'theatrical props' and found an envelope with her name on it – it was a Christmas card from Sandra, one of the other guides who specialised in garden tours and stained glass. It was a reminder that Floriana had to get on with buying some cards herself and start writing them. There was also the small matter of Seb's unanswered card to deal with.

All that free time at home and she hadn't managed to bring herself to reply to him.

She had thought of Seb, though. She had thought of him too often, to be honest. Esme Silcox was partly responsible for that.

It had come as a shock to Floriana when Esme had told her that she'd been mumbling Seb's name at the time of the accident. Perhaps she had been blaming him, Floriana had suggested.

'Oh no, I wouldn't say that at all,' the old lady had said. 'You uttered his name wistfully, as if you wanted him there with you.'

That had been too much for Floriana to hear and after disappearing to the kitchen to bury her tender face in a handful of tissues, she had returned to the sofa and told Esme exactly who Seb was.

'Oh, you poor dear girl,' the old lady had said when she'd finished. 'How cruel life can be to us.'

'It's my own fault,' Floriana had said. 'I'm always putting things off. It'll be written on my gravestone – *Here lies Floriana Day, the greatest procrastinator of them all.* I just didn't realise I loved Seb until it was too late.'

'Did you never tell him how you felt?'

'Only when it finally dawned on me he'd fallen in love with someone else.'

'Do you still love him?'

'I don't know, is the honest answer. I thought I'd got him out of my system, but then this arrived.' She had gone over to the mantelpiece for the Christmas card and the save-the-day card inside it. Giving them to Esme, she'd said, 'That's what I was thinking of when I stepped out into the road on Friday night.'

'Will you go to the wedding?' Esme said after reading the two cards and passing them back to her.

'Again, I honestly don't know. I don't know if I could put myself through the pain of it.'

'Why do you think he has written very specifically that he'd like you to be there at his wedding?'

'It's an olive branch, of course, I can see that. I'm not so stupid as to think he wants me there out of spite.'

The old lady had smiled. 'Well, you certainly don't need to decide categorically one way or another right now. This card is only asking you to save the day, isn't it? Do you have any idea where the wedding will take place?'

'None whatsoever,' she had said. 'My guess is that it won't be in this country; everybody seems to be getting married abroad these days. A save-the-day card is a warning to invited guests to set aside time and money. And if that's the case, if Imogen has set her stony heart on somewhere extravagantly exotic, this whole dilemma is hypothetical as I won't be able to afford to go.'

'But meanwhile, you can simply accept the olive branch, can't you? What's the worst that can happen as a result of doing so?'

Recalling that conversation now, Floriana thought how wonderfully simple the clear-thinking Esme had made it sound. But then from the outside looking in, it probably did look simple. All she had to do was send a card to Seb saying she would save the day, because in no way did it commit her. And really, just how difficult would it be to do that?

The difficulty lay not so much in writing the words but in what might follow. What if Seb made contact again? What if he wanted to resurrect their friendship? Could they ever do that with Imogen in the picture?

Clearly Seb, in offering her this olive branch, had forgiven her. But the real question was, could Floriana forgive Seb for falling in love with Imogen?

His ticket bought and displayed in the windscreen, Adam locked his car and crossed the road. He had three-quarters of an hour until his meeting with his accountant, which gave him time to nip into Blackwell's for the Haruki Murakami book he wanted to buy for his brother for Christmas. God help him, he might even take a look at the self-help shelves where doubtless he'd find any number of books along the lines of *How to Survive While on a Break*, and *How to Win Back Your Girlfriend*.

Having negotiated a way to get Jesse to reconsider their relationship while on a month-long break, he'd initially been full of optimism that he could turn things around, but now hope had been eclipsed by doubt and anxiety.

How the hell did he think he could win her back when he couldn't see her? What was he supposed to do in the next four weeks? And what did being 'on a break' actually mean? Was Jesse free to see other men? Were they supposed to see other people as some sort of test, to see if there was anyone better out there?

It was that thought that was driving him mad. Forty-eight hours into this half-baked agreement – an agreement that he had engineered – and he wasn't sure he'd done the right thing at all. He was used to being proactive, making things happen, getting things fixed, now, quite possibly for the first time in his adult life, he was powerless. He could do absolutely nothing but wait for Jesse to decide what she wanted.

In the interim, he was in limbo. He couldn't help but wonder whether he'd been better off before when he'd believed it was definitely over. Hope was one thing. But false hope was quite another matter.

His purchase made, he held the door open for a mother with a child in a pushchair and stepped onto the pavement.

It was a cold, damp and dreary day and after the warmth of the shop it felt even colder and damper outside. Buttoning his coat, he noticed a group of tourists on the other side of the road in front of the steps of the Sheldonian. In all the years he'd lived in Oxford, he'd seen any number of tourists in Oxford trailing round after their guide, but never had he given them, or their guide, much thought before, other than annoyance if they got in his way. Having met Floriana Day, he now gave the group opposite him more than a passing glance. And then, in spite of how awful the last forty-eight hours had been, he found himself smiling at the sheer daft coincidence of it.

He crossed the road for a better look, taking care to keep his distance, not wanting to distract her, not when he could see how keenly her group was listening to her, hanging on her every word by the looks of things. He didn't blame them; with her hands waving about her, she looked extraordinarily animated. The black cape, scarf and witch's hat she was wearing added another dimension of vibrancy to her. How amusingly unconventional she looked.

She was ushering the group up the steps of the Sheldonian when she noticed him. Just as he had done, she did a double take. Then smiled and gave a little wave.

Feeling it would be rude not to, he crossed the road and approached her. 'Nice hat,' he said.

'Professor McGonagall,' she said by way of explanation. 'I'm doing a Potter tour.'

'Sounds fun. How are you?' Now that he was close up, he thought she didn't look much better than when he'd last seen her, though perhaps that was because she had removed the dressing from her face. It looked a terrible mess.

She glanced over her shoulder at the group that was drifting further away, some of whom were taking photographs, others were consulting their maps, and the rest were looking back at her as if anxious she was about to abandon them. 'I'm OK,' she said, 'busy right now, as you can see.'

'Sorry, I didn't mean to interrupt you. I'd better let you go.'

'It was nice seeing you again,' she said.

'You too.' He turned to walk away and then something took hold of him. 'I don't suppose you're ...' He stopped himself short. It was a crazy impulse and one that would put her on the spot. So no. Better not to ask.

'What?' she asked

He shook his head. 'No, forget it. It's nothing.'

'Oh, don't do that to me. I'll now spend the rest of the day wondering what it was you wanted to ask.'

He hesitated. Oh, why not! 'I was going to ask if you could give me your advice on something. Over lunch maybe. That's if you're free today. That's if you even have a lunch break.'

'I'll be free at half past one if that's any good.'

'That would be perfect.'

'Now I really must go.' She started to move off.

'Where shall I meet you?' he called after her.

'In St Mary's in the Vaults. They do great soup. And cakes nearly as good as the ones you gave me on Saturday. See you!'

*

'I really should have warned you before, giving advice isn't exactly my strongest suit,' Floriana said after they'd queued for their lunch and were now seated – they'd both opted for hearty plates of lasagne in preference to the soup. She was glad of the chance to sit down. She was exhausted and looking forward to getting home so she could crash out.

'But I'd be interested to hear what you think,' Adam said, passing her one of the paper napkins.

'Go on then, tell me what it is you imagine I can help you with.'

He ate a mouthful of the lasagne, chewed, took a sip of his fizzy water and said: 'Have you ever been on a break from a boyfriend?'

She shook her head. 'Nope.'

'Do you know what the ground rules are?'

'Nope. Sorry.'

'Right,' he said with a frown. 'That was short and sweet.'

Seeing his obvious disappointment, and wishing she could be of more help, Floriana said, 'Why don't you give me the context of why you want to know?' She knew from her chat with Esme that Adam had very recently broken up with his girlfriend, but without admitting they'd discussed him behind his back, she couldn't acknowledge that she knew about Jesse.

'My first reaction is to tell you to let Jesse go,' she said, when he'd explained, 'and to impress upon you that there's nothing worse than clinging onto something you can't have.'

His face dropped.

'But,' she said, hurrying on, 'what I'm actually going to say is, if you love Jesse, do all you can to win her back. If that means giving her a month to reconsider, or perhaps even longer, then so be it. If you have the patience and you truly believe she's worth it, hang in there. What have you got to lose?'

'You sound so sure,' he said.

'Trust me, I wrote the book when it came to missing my chance. I know exactly what you can lose.' And because he'd been so candid with her, and because it seemed so vitally important that he didn't make the same mistake as she had, she told him why she knew what she was talking about.

When she'd finished raking through the embers of her history with Seb, and suddenly feeling self-conscious, she said, 'I know that receiving his wedding invitation has stirred things up for me, but amazingly I haven't spoken to anyone about him in ages, now here I am telling you all about him when I hardly know you, just as I did with Esme on Sunday.'

'That makes two of us,' Adam said. 'I told her about Jesse on Saturday when I called round, so perhaps she's some kind of divining conduit.'

'Either that or she's a witch,' Floriana said with a laugh.

A slow smile spread over his serious face, a face she'd noted that tended towards solemnity all too frequently. 'Talking of witches,' he said, 'I'm disappointed you're not wearing your Professor McGonagall hat for lunch. I was looking forward to that.'

'Now that's just plain creepy,' she said. 'Any more of that talk and I'll start to revise my opinion of you.'

Chapter Twelve

The house looked like somebody had lifted it up and shaken it hard, and then, just for good measure, turned it upside down and given it another shake.

It was less than a week until Christmas and with Adam's help Floriana had moved all the furniture from the sitting room and squeezed it into the kitchen and hall. She was now sweeping the dusty bare floorboards in readiness for the arrival of the new carpet while Adam put the old one out by the front door to be taken away.

With an impressive army of people at his disposal who could provide or fix almost anything at a few hours' notice, Floriana had voted Adam to be the most useful man on the planet. Last week he had not only mended the puncture on her bike but had arranged for one of his helpful men to replace the broken window in her bathroom. She didn't really know what the going rate was for a job like that, but the bill was for such a small amount she was suspicious Adam had intervened and negotiated a reduced figure.

The same was true of the carpet today. 'It's the end of a roll,' he'd explained airily when she'd been surprised how cheap it was. 'No more than an offcut that I'd put to one side to use at a later date.' He spoke like a man who had any amount of carpet offcuts just lying about. He'd brought a sample round the other day to see if she liked it and it had been just what she'd had in mind – a light oatmeal shade.

This was after she'd pulled up a corner of the old carpet and, seeing the state of the wooden floorboards beneath, had decided replacing the badly stained carpet with a new one was easiest and cheapest. She had asked Adam's advice, seeing as he seemed to be an expert on anything to do with houses, and he'd said that he knew a man who could probably do a good job of sanding and polishing the floorboards, but the estimated cost had brought Floriana out in a cold sweat. Even factoring in paying a bit extra to get this bargain-priced carpet laid on a Sunday afternoon, it was still cheaper, and by a huge margin.

In the weeks since she had met him, it had become very obvious to Floriana that Adam's cash flow was vastly different to hers, but in no way did he flaunt it. 'Admirably modest' was how Esme described him in one of her typically discerning remarks. They both agreed he played his cards pretty close to his chest, thereby making it difficult to know at times what he was thinking. But given the choice, Floriana would rather be around someone who was taciturn and genuine than a showy big-mouth. What he lacked in blether he certainly made up for in thoughtfulness and dependability.

Outside on the street, a white van pulled up behind Adam's car. Seconds later a squat man the shape and size of an Olympic weightlifter was opening the back of the van and chatting to Adam. Together they carried the rolls of underlay and carpet into the house.

In what seemed no time at all the furniture was back in place and the manky old carpet was on its way to the tip in the back of the van. Job done.

'Thank you so much, Adam,' Floriana said, looking round delightedly at her transformed sitting room. 'You're a miracle worker. Do you walk on water as well?'

'You're pleased with it, then?'

'I'm over the moon! And if we weren't due at Esme's, I'd throw myself on the carpet and roll about like a demented dog for the next hour!'

He raised an eyebrow. 'Go ahead, don't let me stop you enjoying yourself.'

'Second thoughts,' she said with a smile. 'Maybe I'll save that pleasure for when I'm alone tonight.'

By the time they'd cleaned up and Floriana had changed into some kind of weird extensively layered ensemble that looked like she hadn't known what to put on so had decided to put on everything, along with a pair of clompy boots, the first snow of winter began to fall from the darkening sky. All day the sky had been ominously leaden and the temperature had steadily dropped.

They were on their way to Trinity House to have tea with Esme; it was to be the first time since the night of Floriana's accident that all three of them would be together again. They had each independently called on the old lady – Adam because he was frequently at his new house next door, and Floriana because she was fascinated by the old lady and wanted to get to know her better.

'There's just something about her,' Floriana had said to Adam. 'She's so inscrutable and just when I think I've got her sussed, she'll say something to make me rethink. I wouldn't be at all surprised if she turned out to be a cold-war spy and being a librarian was just a cover!'

Wildly random statements from Floriana were fairly standard issue, Adam had come to realise; they were as richly flamboyant as her quirky dress sense, which very much reflected her haphazard and impulsive personality.

There again, for all he knew there might be nothing haphazard or impulsive about her appearance, she might actually spend hours carefully crafting her look. After all, what did he know about fashion? Although under Jesse's guidance he had learned to appreciate the sleek and stylish look she had mastered. Updating his wardrobe had been one of the first jobs she'd carried out when they'd got together. She'd rifled through his less than impressive selection of clothes and after much tutting and head-shaking had taken him shopping.

'It's weird,' Floriana said now as they stood at the junction between Church Close and Latimer Street and waited for a car to pass, its wipers working at keeping the falling snow from settling on the windscreen, 'but whenever I'm with Esme at Trinity House, I feel like I'm in a parallel world, a more interesting world. I think it's one of the reasons I like being with her.'

'I know what you mean,' Adam said. 'I've decided it's all those interesting paintings she has; they create an atmosphere all of their own.'

'Yes!' she cried excitedly, turning to look at him so fast the pom-pom hanging at the end of the long tassel on her hat – a multicoloured hat with earflaps that looked hand-knitted – whipped round and bounced off her nose. Flicking it away with a mittened hand, she said, 'You're absolutely right. I know it might sound fanciful but I keep thinking that each one of those paintings tells a story of her life, you know, like a photograph album.'

'I hadn't thought of it exactly like that, but it's a nice idea. Have you asked her about them yet?'

Her eyes sparkled with mischief. 'I'm working on it.'

Adam didn't doubt it for a minute. It was another of Floriana's traits: an instinct for gathering information. Of her own admission, she was a hoarder of useful and not so useful trivia, and as he'd already witnessed, she could summon any of it from her mind at a metaphorical click of her fingers. 'I just have that sort of a brain,' she'd told him, when at his prompting to give an example of what she meant, she'd rattled off a list of proverbs from around the world, including a Russian one that he particularly liked, something about when being engaged in a fight, it's not the time to part your hair. 'My brain just collects data at will,' she'd said, with a shrug, 'whether I want it or not.'

He supposed that's what made her enjoy her job as a tour guide so much; she could easily absorb facts and recall them effortlessly. He, for one, would never be able to retain the necessary information.

Esme had been preparing for this afternoon for the last three days. Having decided the dining room would be the best place to host her tea party, she had asked her cleaner to give it more than a cursory flick with the feather duster. Krysta came to her once a week and spoke as much English as Esme spoke Polish. Clean Sweep – the agency Esme had contacted when her previous and long-standing cleaner had moved away – had sent Krysta to her three months ago and in all that time the only words the woman had uttered with any great fluency were *Hello* and *I finish now, goodbye*.

Once the dining room had been thoroughly dusted and polished, Esme had dug out the best tablecloth only to find it had been stuffed in the drawer so long it needed to be washed and ironed to make it presentable. That done, she had sorted through the box of table decorations she hadn't used in a very long time and decided they were too shabby so had gone to the art gallery in North Parade where they were selling a small stock of Christmas bits and pieces. She had settled on an arrangement of pine cones and some apple and cinnamon scented candles, along with a poinsettia from Buddy Joe's and some red and green garlanded paper napkins.

Buddy Joe's had also provided her with the means to create a menu of turkey and mushroom vol-au-vents, smoked salmon blinis, and cocktail sausages wrapped in bacon with a cranberry relish. For afters there were mince pies, and a chocolate Yuletide log. For drinks, she had mulled wine simmering gently on the hob and a limited selection of spirits if something stronger was requested.

Now, with the candles lit and the lamps switched on and the gas fire hissing faintly as it warmed the room, she checked the table to make sure she hadn't forgotten anything.

Her real concern was not that she had overlooked something but whether such a formal tea table might seem embarrassingly quaint and unfashionable to her young guests. She was hopelessly out of practice when it came to entertaining. It was rather mortifying to know that she couldn't remember when she last invited anyone to tea.

Years and years ago she and her father used to enjoy tea at the Randolph, then more latterly she and her friends – Margaret, Dorothy and Nina – had frequented the Old Parsonage which had been far cosier. But her father and those friends were all gone now. Just the memories remained, some of which were little more than vague recollections and some so sharply in focus the events could have happened yesterday.

She looked at the painting above the fireplace and studied the young girl gazing back at her. There was a pensive intensity to the girl's expression that never went unnoticed by anyone who took the time to study the portrait. However, it was the subtle blend of innocence and boldness that Esme had always thought made it the arresting picture it was. She had never thought of the face as being beautiful or even pretty – the chin was too pronounced, the cheekbones too defined and the hairline too low – but it was an interesting face and that counted for so much more in her opinion.

She was eighty-two years of age and had lived with this painting of herself since the day her father had finished work on it and presented it to her on her eighteenth birthday. The funny thing was, there were times when she could view it entirely objectively and feel she hardly knew the girl at all.

The painting on the wall opposite, a head and shoulders self-portrait of her father, was a very different matter. When she looked at his face, partially in shade from the hat he was wearing, the years rolled away and she could hear his softly spoken voice as clearly as though he were standing in the room with her.

Next to his self-portrait was a smaller painting; it was another portrait of Esme when she'd been ten years old. Dressed in a plain blue pinafore dress and a white blouse and socks that were sagging and wrinkled, she was sitting on a low wooden stool, her shoulders hunched, her face flushed and turned towards her father in a way that suggested he had just disturbed her. It was one of her favourite paintings and showed how clearly she resembled her father and not her mother; something for which she had always been grateful.

Reminding herself that her guests would soon be here, Esme returned her attention to the table, surveying it for a missing plate or a piece of cutlery out of line.

'What do you think?' she asked Euridice who was sitting at the French window watching the snow fall outside. 'Will it do?'

The cat slowly swivelled her head and blinked.

'I shall take that as a yes and hope for the best,' Esme said. 'Now then, come with me, I'm not leaving you alone in here, not when there's so much tempting food on the table.'

The cat obediently followed her out of the dining room.

When she opened the door to her guests Esme was most amused to be greeted with a brief chorus sung by Floriana of 'We *Two* Kings of Orient Are', and with Adam looking on awkwardly.

'Granted we haven't travelled that far,' Floriana said breathlessly, her face pink from the cold as they stood in the hall in a mêlée of hats, coats, gloves and scarves being removed, 'but we do come bearing gifts. You have to keep them until Christmas though, no opening them before. Do you want us to take our shoes off?'

'Heavens no! Not unless you have a burning desire to do so. Come on through to the kitchen and warm yourself up and tell me how you both are.'

'I expect Adam needs to sit down and rest,' Floriana said with a merry laugh. 'I've worked him hard. I'm now the proud owner of a beautiful new sitting room carpet, which is something of a milestone; I've never owned a new carpet before. I can't tell you how properly grown up I now feel.'

Esme smiled fondly at her, then at Adam who was probably wondering if he would ever be allowed to get a word in. 'That being the case,' she said, 'I think we need to raise a glass in celebration of such an important milestone in your life.'

Not for the first time Esme thought how different this bright-eyed, chatty Floriana was to the one she had met at the time of the accident. Her face still bore signs of faint bruising and the scar where she'd had stitches was a long way from fading, but her true personality had since been revealed. She was charmingly irrepressible, a delightful bundle of energy and enthusiasm and Esme never failed to enjoy time spent with her.

It wasn't only her spirited nature that had come to the fore since recovering from the accident, there was now no mistaking how pretty she was. Esme's father would have had fun painting her; he'd have caught the sparkling vitality in those large hazel eyes of hers with their long lashes and her delicately pointed chin and her straight dainty nose. She had a rare face, in Esme's opinion – one that seemed incapable of a mean or disagreeable expression.

Any reservations Esme had previously experienced about her guests not enjoying her tea party were quickly dispelled when she took them through to the dining room with their glasses of mulled wine.

'How wonderful!' Floriana cried when she saw the table. 'But you shouldn't have gone to so much trouble.'

'Well, since I have, let's make the most of it. I know it's not politically correct these days to suggest such a thing, but I'm feeling subversive so, Adam, would you like to sit at the head of the table? And Floriana, you sit opposite me. There now, that's perfect. And if Euridice bothers you, take no nonsense, just push her firmly out of the way. Ah, Adam, I see she's made a beeline straight for you.'

'It's all right,' he said, as Euridice planted herself next to his chair and stared devotedly up at him. 'I don't mind.'

'I want to know why she never comes to me,' Floriana said.

Esme gave her a playful look. 'I think she likes Adam because he has such a quiet and calming aura about him.'

Floriana laughed. 'Are you saying I'm too noisy for her?'

'Lively is the word I would use, my dear; energy bounces off you at every turn. Wouldn't you agree, Adam?'

Adam raised his hands. 'I'm saying nothing.'

'Forever the solicitous diplomat,' Esme said, passing round plates of food. 'So tell me what your plans are for Christmas.'

Floriana groaned. 'Adam, you go first, I need to eat something before I can stomach the idea of describing the hell that will be my Christmas *chez* Brown.'

Esme gave Adam a wink. 'I believe you've been given permission to speak. If I were you I'd grab the chance while you can.'

Helping himself to a smoked salmon blini, he said, 'It's the standard family Christmas for me, at home in Thame. My brother will be there as well.'

'And do the two of you get on?'

'Yes, we do.'

'Is he married?'

'No, he has a worse track record with women than me.'

Esme tutted. 'This is a Christmas tea party, not a pity party, so we'll have none of that talk, Adam. Come the new year I predict things will change for you, and for the better.'

Floriana laughed heartily. 'See, Adam, we were right, she is a witch!'

'I think you'll find it was you who reached that conclusion,' he said with a frown.

'Ooh, how ungallant of you!'

Amused, Esme said, 'My dear girl, what on earth put the idea into your heads that I have supernatural powers?'

'Because you have this sneaky knack for getting information out of us while revealing hardly anything of yourself.'

'Glory be, I had no idea I was the subject of such marvellous speculation! I feel flattered. But I assure you; I'm nothing more than a harmless old lady who asks too many questions. Sausage roll, anyone?'

'See!' cried Floriana. 'That's how you do it, you distract us with questions of your own!'

'Then I shall cease doing so at once and answer any question you put to me. Who wants to go first?'

Adam looked at Floriana and made an eloquent gesture of 'over to you' with his hand.

'Well,' Floriana said, her gaze settling on the painting above the fireplace, 'is that you?'

'Indeed it is.'

'And?'

'And what?'

'Tell us more. When was it painted? How old were you and who did it? Was it your father?'

Chapter Thirteen

The painting marked a turning point in Esme's life. For her father as well.

Five months before Esme's eighteenth birthday, her mother died quite unexpectedly of a heart attack. Most people had thought she would live for ever, if only to vex those around her.

Violet Silcox – née Bradbury – had not been a happy woman. The only daughter of a Nottinghamshire engineer who'd made his money in mining machinery, she had been brought up to believe that she was a great beauty with the world at her feet. The truth was, she was no such thing and despite her parents' ambitious intentions for her to marry into a family of greater wealth and position than their own, she failed to attract the slightest interest. But then along came William Silcox, a gentle, quiet-mannered man who worked for her father as a patent lawyer, a man who was trusted and liked by both her parents. Younger than Violet by four years, he didn't stand a chance when she decided at the age of thirty-two he was the man she wanted to marry – it was him or the shame of spinsterhood stretching out before her. He came with none of the wealth and position her parents had dreamt of for their daughter, but instead they saw a presentable and well-educated man who would cause them no trouble as a malleable son-in-law and who could at least make Violet happy and provide them with grandchildren.

But William couldn't make Violet happy. No one could. Especially not Esme when she was born two years after her parents had wed and moved into Hillside, a stern Victorian house some three miles from where Violet had grown up at Abbey Vale.

Knowing how much it would please her father, Violet had badly wanted a boy, and she was so convinced she was going to produce a son that when she was told she was the mother of a fine baby girl, she had refused to believe it. 'But it can't be!' she

79

had screamed hysterically at the midwife and doctor in the high-handed manner she had been brought up to treat anyone she considered unequal to her in social standing. She had no sense of how ridiculously she was behaving and cared little that the cook and maid downstairs could hear her every word and would soon be relaying it round the village, its apocryphal echoes reaching Esme's ears when she was old enough to understand what people said of the goings-on at Hillside and the derision in which her mother was held.

When war broke out in 1939, Esme was eight years old and of an age to know the implications: that her father might have to go and fight and never come back. But her father was deemed unfit – a legacy of his childhood, part of which had been spent in a sanatorium being treated for TB.

Most wives would be relieved that their husbands wouldn't be at risk, that they could instead throw themselves into the war effort at home, but not so Violet. She wanted to be married to a hero, better still a dead one, as she had actually said on one occasion to William in a fit of petulant temper when yet again he came home late from work – Bradbury Mining Tools was now producing machinery for the war effort and the workshops were running twenty-four hours a day; it was all hands on deck. 'What are you doing there that's so important?' she'd demanded. 'You're only a lawyer!'

Just as motherhood had proved to be a bitter disappointment to Violet, marriage was not what she had thought it would be. She had perhaps imagined something more akin to her parents' marriage. Her father, who she adored above all else, was a tall powerful man who asserted himself as charismatic master of the house and was forever indulging his wife and daughter with whatever they desired. But the qualities Violet had once admired in her fiancé – kindness and gentleness and an artistic temperament – she now took to be signs of embarrassing weakness in a husband.

More embarrassment came when towards the end of the war Violet's adored father was accused of profiteering from it. The accusations were not made outright, not at the start, but after William resigned from the firm and initially refused to say why, rumour and gossip quickly gained momentum, and before long the family was shunned in public. Violet held her husband solely responsible for people turning against them. William defended his actions saying that he simply couldn't continue working for her father when he knew what was going on. 'So a person makes one little mistake and you can't forgive them?' she railed.

'I have to live with my conscience,' he said.

From a young age Esme had become adept at listening in to the conversations between her parents, though in truth it didn't take any stealth to eavesdrop as more often than not her mother's condescending tone was raised and clarion-clear for all to hear.

By the time the war was over, so too, to all intents and purposes, was the marriage. Esme's father wanted a divorce but for his daughter's sake he couldn't bring himself to go through with it. Moreover, Violet had warned him that she would never agree to anything that would bring further shame on the family. She also threatened that she would never allow William to see Esme if he tried to leave her. It seemed that a marriage in name only for Violet was better than no marriage at all.

An impasse reached, Esme's father spent longer and longer hours at the firm he now worked for and it was only at the weekend when Esme saw him. But that time together was precious to her, and to him as well. They were as close as they were each distant to Violet, who never showed more than a passing interest in Esme's well-being; what interest she did show was merely to criticise and correct. The only person Violet cared about was herself and she started to feed her self-absorption, quite literally, gaining weight at an alarming rate by gorging herself on mountains of food, particularly anything sweet.

When Violet's mother died of a stroke and then six months later her father was killed in a shooting accident – some said it was suicide with the cloud of rumours still hanging over him – she took up with a new circle of friends and became obsessed with the spirit world. She would hold regular seances at Hillside, desperate to make contact with her dead father and mother. All the while her mental state was visibly unravelling and her mood swings intensified.

One evening Esme's father came home from work to find that every single one of his paintings he kept in his studio in the garden had been slashed. But not a word did he say. Which Esme knew had infuriated her mother and she taunted him cruelly, saying he wasn't man enough to react or stand up to her.

She had frequently dismissed him as a third-rate amateur, talentless and lacking in originality, and this spiteful destruction was a culmination of that growing disdain, and jealousy. Unrepentant at what she'd done, she told him his style was so disgustingly sentimental it made her skin crawl and that she had done him a favour in ridding the world of such nauseating tosh. His only comment had been to ask her what kind of mother could slash paintings of her own daughter?

An unhinged mother was the answer, but who in their household was brave enough to say it?

Esme's father didn't paint again until several months after Violet's sudden death. The first painting he did was the portrait he gave Esme on her eighteenth birthday. It was after he'd shown it to her that he said he wanted to talk to her.

He invited her to go out to the garden with him and with her arm linked through his, he said, 'We've never discussed money before, but, as you know, and despite all the advice she was given, your mother didn't ever get around to making a will. That being the case, everything comes to me. And by that, I mean it comes to *us*. But I'm sure you had already worked that out for yourself.'

Esme had nodded, unsure where this was going.

'So what I propose, now that the legal side of things has been sorted out, is that we leave this ghastly house and everything associated with it and move somewhere of our own choosing, somewhere we can start afresh and be happy.'

She had smiled at that. 'That sounds perfect. But why do I feel that isn't all you have in mind to tell me?'

He had returned her smile and she had thought how good it was to see him smile more often, now that they were free of the tyranny of her mother. 'That's very astute of you,' he said, 'but then I should have expected nothing less. How would you feel about postponing going up to Oxford and coming on an adventure with me?'

For so long gaining her place at Oxford to read English had been Esme's dream, but putting her trust in her father, she said, 'What sort of adventure?'

Chapter Fourteen

'No! You can't stop there; you have to tell us what happened next. What was the adventure?'

A little surprised with herself that she had gone into such detail, Esme reached for her long-forgotten glass of mulled wine, which was now cold. 'My dear, surely you don't want to listen to me prattling on any more?'

'We do! We do!' Floriana enthused exuberantly. 'Don't we, Adam?'

Adam nodded his agreement. 'But only if you want to tell us more,' he said. 'Perhaps we should give you a chance to have something to eat first, you've barely touched a thing, unlike us.'

'Good idea,' Floriana said, quickly picking up a plate of smoked salmon blinis and offering it to Esme. 'A good raconteur marches on its stomach, after all.'

Esme laughed. 'Very well,' she acquiesced, 'but while I eat, you must tell me why you're now going to your sister's for Christmas when I'm sure you previously mentioned you were hoping to avoid such an arrangement.'

Floriana let out her breath in one long weary sigh. 'As usual, it was my own fault and I should have acted sooner, but, tipped off by my sister that I'd turned her down, Mum and Dad phoned me to ask who I was spending Christmas with. I never have been able to lie to them, not convincingly anyway, and I ended up throwing in the towel and agreeing to go to my sister's after all.'

'So why will it be so awful?' Esme asked.

'Because without Mum and Dad on hand to rein Ann in, I shall be endlessly bossed about and reminded that it's time I grew up and found myself a proper job. Not only that, Ann will try to fix me up with her husband's brother, a nice enough man if you go for the ultra-mature type, but he couldn't be more wrong for me.'

Not without sympathy for Floriana, Esme said, 'Why does

your sister think being an Oxford tour guide isn't a proper job?'

'In her opinion I've wasted my education and squandered it on something that doesn't stretch me enough or have any real prospects.'

'And what does she do that makes her so superior to you?' asked Adam.

'She works in the HR department of a large insurance firm and, of course, runs her home and two children like clockwork. Everything runs perfectly in Ann's world. I'm talking about a woman who irons her dishcloths!'

'What? You don't iron your dishcloths?' Adam said with a deadpan expression, passing Esme the plate of vol-au-vents. 'But I thought everyone did.'

Floriana laughed and helped herself to a vol-au-vent after Esme had taken one. 'In Summertown maybe.'

'Do you think your sister is jealous of you?' Esme suggested. 'From where she's standing your life must seem wonderfully unencumbered and spontaneous compared to hers.'

Floriana let out another laugh. 'Jealous of me? Ann would no more want my life than she would want typhoid fever. No, the long and the short of it is she loves to disapprove of me; it comes with being the older sister, I guess.'

'What a shame, but since it's the job of the young to exaggerate, I'm inclined to take some of what you say with a pinch of salt, because I refuse to believe your family isn't proud of you.'

'Oh, Mum and Dad are OK with what I do,' Floriana said, 'but I'm sure they, in common with Ann, thought I'd come to something more. It's the Oxford thing; it raises expectations to absurd heights. In Ann's eyes I should, at the very least, have what she has: a husband, two children, a large four-bedroom detached house with two cars on the drive, blah, blah.'

'And do you see that as something you'd like one day?'

'Come on, Esme, look at me. Do I look like I aspire to that kind of lifestyle? I'm happy with my life as it is, thank you very much. OK, a bit more cash in my pocket would be good, but I can't complain, not when I have a job I love and my very own home. For which I have to thank my grandmother; the money she left me when she died went towards the deposit, no way could I have bought it without that gift from her. Ann got exactly the same amount and has it invested to pay her children's school and university fees. See, different priorities again,' she added with a shrug.

Esme was about to ask something else when she heard the sound of ringing coming from Adam.

'Sorry,' he said, a hand darting to his trouser pocket. Esme had never used a mobile herself, but she was sufficiently acquainted with them to know that when one rang or buzzed, it demanded immediate attention, no matter the situation.

'Please answer it,' she said, noticing that Adam's expression had dramatically altered on looking at the screen of the mobile.

'I'll take it out in the hall if I may,' he said as the ringing continued.

When he'd closed the door after him, Floriana leant across the table. 'I bet that's Jesse,' she whispered.

'Was he expecting her to get in touch?' Esme's voice was equally hushed.

'He's been expecting her to call ever since he sent her a Christmas card. He's bought her a present as well.'

Knowing how taciturn Adam tended to be, Esme said, 'How do you know that?'

'He told me. He wanted my opinion on whether he'd done the right thing or not.'

'I do hope she's not stringing him along, I'd hate to see him go through any unnecessary pain.'

'Me too. But as my mother, that ardent fan of a happy ending, would be the first to say, time apart worked for Prince William and Kate. Which,' she said with a smile, 'backs up my theory that procrastination isn't always a bad thing.'

Wiping the flakes of vol-au-vent pastry from her fingers and then dabbing her mouth with the napkin, Esme said, 'Does that mean you still haven't replied to Seb's card?'

'Let's just say it's a work in progress. So what are *you* doing for Christmas? Will you spend it with anyone?'

'I shall have a very quiet day here on my own with Euridice, as I always do,' Esme said, noting how deftly Floriana had diverted her from the matter of Seb and his card. 'Goodness,' she then exclaimed, 'I've just realised that wily cat must have followed Adam out of the room, she seems to have become utterly devoted to him.'

At which point the door opened and Adam, with Euridice

hot on his heels, reappeared. 'Sorry about that,' he said, his face bright with what Esme took to be good news.

'Was that Jesse?' Floriana asked, when he resumed his seat at the table.

'Yes,' he said with a look of surprise. 'How did you know?'

'Ooh, just a guess. What does she want?'

'She wants to meet to exchange Christmas presents tomorrow evening. I don't know what's surprised me more – the fact she's bought me something or that she's prepared to meet.'

Esme wanted to urge him not to read too much into it, largely because people often behaved hypocritically at Christmas and did what they thought was expected of them, rather than what they really wanted to do. Keeping her thoughts to herself, she said, 'I'll make us some tea now, shall I?'

It was dark and snowing heavily when they left Trinity House and set off for Church Close. Passing cars had churned up the snow that lay on the road, but no one had so far walked along the pavement and the pristine covering of snow sparkled in the glowing light cast from the street lamps.

'Here,' Adam said, giving Floriana his arm to hold on to when she'd come close to falling over for the second time. 'Let's not risk you hitting your head again just as you've healed so well.'

'Thanks,' she said, gratefully hooking her arm through his and giggling.

'What's so funny?'

'You living up to your name, Mr Strong.'

'I could easily become Mr Mean and push you over and stuff handfuls of snow down your neck.'

'Ah, but you wouldn't, you're much too nice.'

'Don't bet on it. Remember, I'm a property developer, which means I'm ruthless to the core and act only out of self-interest.'

'No you're not, you're one of the most considerate people I know.'

He groaned. 'Party food and a couple of glasses of mulled wine and you go all cheesy on me.'

'Am I embarrassing you?'

'Excruciatingly so.'

'Thank goodness for that, I thought I was losing my touch.' It always amused Floriana that Adam was such an easy target to tease or wrong-foot. He was too serious for his own good; he needed to lighten up.

They walked on in silence, the dry powdery snow crunching underfoot. A car passed by at a snail's pace and when it had gone, its red tail lights disappearing into the distance, Floriana said, 'If I wasn't going to my sister's for Christmas, I'd invite Esme to come to me. It seems all wrong that she should be alone.'

'How do you know she's going to be alone?'

'I asked her when you were on the phone. She said it would be just her and Euridice.'

'Hmm ... I agree with you, that doesn't seem right.'

'It's obvious she doesn't have the busiest of social lives, but I'd imagined there would be at least one relative or old friend with whom she'd spend the day.' Floriana paused. 'When are you back from Thame?'

'Probably Boxing Day evening. Why?'

An idea had occurred to her. 'Why don't we arrange something for Esme when we're both back in Oxford? We could invite her to lunch, or perhaps dinner? I'm not the best of cooks, but I'll give it a go. I could even have a crack at doing a turkey. I've never cooked one before, but how difficult can it be? It's just a chicken on a bigger scale, isn't it?' Gripped with sudden enthusiasm for the idea, she said, 'I wasn't going to bother, but this would give me a reason to buy a Christmas tree and put up a few decorations. What do you think?'

'I think your mind's now made up and I'm happy to go along with you. I'd also hazard a guess that you're after the next instalment of the story – What Esme Did Next.'

Floriana laughed. 'And if your mobile hadn't gone off when it did, I would have kept Esme on track and we'd know exactly what she did next.'

They turned into Church Close and with it being a cul-de-sac and not having attracted any through traffic, not even a resident's car had been in or out, they were presented with a scene of magical winter wonderland. Whether Adam was right and she was mellow with mulled wine and party food, but the sight filled Floriana with a comforting surge of childlike awe and joy.

'You're welcome to come in for a warm and a drink before going,' she said, when they got to work clearing the snow from Adam's car.

'Thanks, but at the rate this snow is falling if I come in for any length of time, the car will be covered again.'

He was right; the snow was coming down so fast they themselves were beginning to resemble a pair of snowmen. But observing Adam across the bonnet of his car, she was struck how incredibly earnest he looked as he worked methodically at clearing the windscreen. A mischievous thought came to her.

Don't do it, the sensible adult in her warned.

But the naughty child in her wasn't listening – the naughty child was too busy scooping up a handful of snow and taking aim.

He ducked but not quickly enough and the snowball caught him on the shoulder. 'What was that for?' he asked.

'No real reason, other than it felt like fun. You do know what fun is, don't you, Adam?'

He stared at her, and for an awful moment she thought she had gone too far. But then he began to scoop up a pile of snow from the roof of the car and patted it into shape. 'You wouldn't be accusing me of being boring, would you?'

'I certainly am!' She dropped to her knees behind the car as the missile flew overhead, causing just a small shower of snow to fall on her. 'And you're a useless shot into the bargain!' she laughed back at him.

'Oh yeah? We'll see about that!'

As raucous snowball fights went, it was up there with the best. Floriana scored the first direct to the face, followed almost immediately by Adam doing the same to her. Their cries and laughter rang out in the quiet still air and when a nearby dog joined in and began barking, they decided they'd disturbed the peace of the neighbourhood enough and called a truce.

Shaking the snow from her hair and leaning against the car and panting with exhileration, her face and hands stinging with cold, Adam stood next to her brushing the worst of the snow from his coat and trousers. 'Thank you,' he said, his breath ragged and his eyes shining in the street lamp.

'What for?'

'For making me behave like a kid. It's a while since I've done anything so stupidly good fun.'

She smiled. 'It's a while since I've had anyone to enjoy a snowball fight with. I'm definitely out of practice.' In her mind's eye she could see the many fight-to-the-death battles she and Seb used to have.

'Bloody hell,' Adam muttered, 'I'd hate to see you when you're match fit in that case. Go on,' he added, 'you'd better go inside and get dry, I'll be off now.'

She pushed herself away from the car. 'Drive carefully, won't you?' she said, when he had the door open.

'Will do.'

'Hey,' she said, suddenly thinking of his call from Jesse. 'Good luck for tomorrow evening. I hope it goes well. But don't expect too much. Just go with the flow.'

He nodded. 'Message received loud and clear. No putting any pressure on her.'

'Or yourself.'

He closed the door and she watched him set the windscreen wipers going, along with the heater. He then lowered the window. 'I'll give you a ring about your idea for Esme,' he said, 'and we can decide which day to do it. OK?'

'Excellent.'

She watched him drive slowly down the street and after she'd let herself in and shrugged off her wet things in the hall, she went through to the sitting room in her stockinged feet. At the sight of her lovely new carpet and the transformation it had made to the room, she wished she'd remembered to thank Adam again for his help.

No doubt about it, he was one of the good guys. Whatever Jesse's problem with him was, she had better get her act together because men like Adam didn't grow on trees.

Chapter Fifteen

The country was in the grip of an Arctic Big Freeze, which was newspaper hyperbole for twenty-four hours of snow.

Adam's concern about the weather was that it might prevent Jesse from meeting him as arranged. Putting aside his selfish need to see her, he'd texted her earlier to give her the option to postpone meeting until the weather had improved, but she'd replied that this evening was the only free slot she had, as her diary was full right up until Christmas Eve when she finished work.

While he waited for her to arrive, Adam didn't know whether to feel encouraged that she was so determined to see him tonight and was prepared to brave the roads, or disheartened that she had referred to this evening as her only free slot, as though he was just another appointment fitted into her hectic schedule.

He was reading too much into the evening, of course, but it was hard not to. He felt that everything was riding on how well it went; more precisely, how well he performed. It was like he was a prisoner up for probation!

Floriana had texted him in the afternoon to wish him luck again and to thank him for the carpet which, she'd joked, she had yet to roll around on.

He'd half expected her to be the kind of girl who would pepper her messages with *lol* and *lmao* and the ubiquitous smiley or unhappy face, but he was pleased to be proved wrong. He was firmly of the opinion that that sort of thing was strictly for teenagers, that anyone older than twenty had no right to use urban slang or send messages containing text abbreviations – his dyslexia meant he found the latter particularly tiresome. It was a pet hate of his, but there was nothing worse than someone his age trying to behave like a school kid.

At the back of his mind there was a small but growing worry that he was in the early stages of turning into a grumpy old man.

What was it Floriana had said yesterday? 'You do know what fun is, don't you, Adam?' And then had come his admission that he'd forgotten how much fun a snowball fight was. He and his brother used to have some marathon fights in the snow. Being as competitive as they were with each other, they'd keep going until they'd either used up all the available snow or one of them was hurt.

He wondered when Giles has last thrown a snowball. He suddenly felt compelled to call his brother and ask him. But that would be stupid. Besides, there was no time. Jesse would be here any second. She was ten minutes late, but that was understandable, the roads were lethal after yesterday's snow and the fresh fall today, but the real danger was that the temperature hadn't risen so what lay on the ground was now icy and treacherous. It had dropped to minus ten in the night; the coldest it had been so far this winter.

Before going to work this morning, Adam had cleared the pavement in front of his house in Summertown and he'd noticed when he'd returned an hour ago that his neighbours had done the same, which meant the pavement now resembled something fans of mogul skiing would have fun tackling.

He thought of Latimer Street and hoped Esme hadn't ventured out. If he'd had time he would have driven over to see if she was all right. He could have phoned but he reckoned her response would be an automatic everything's-fine-don't-worry-about-me. And maybe it was wrong of him to assume that Esme would welcome help from him. It was always possible that she would view it as interference – after all, she'd managed perfectly well before they'd met. He remembered how fiercely independent his grandparents had been right up until the end when, one by one, they'd died – but they'd died in their own homes and with the conviction that they would do things their way. So he could understand how Esme might bristle at being considered incapable of caring for herself. Nobody wants to feel they're on the slippery slope.

Adam took one look at Jesse and knew that this was going to be one of the most difficult nights of his life.

Having invested so much time and effort into trying to keep a lid on his emotions and not raise his hopes, it shocked him how easily the mere sight of her made a mockery of that determination and distilled into one painful blow the desolation her absence had caused him.

'You look great,' he managed to say, hanging her coat up and taking in the emerald-green top and skinny jeans with black patent ankle boots he didn't recognise, with heels so high they made her nearly as tall as him. Everything about her looked fresh and shiny new. And disturbingly altered. She even smelled differently.

'You've had your hair cut,' he said, trying to keep the disappointment out of his voice.

'Yes,' she replied, giving her now collar-length hair a self-conscious flick. 'I decided it was time to shake things up, go for a dramatic change.'

You're not kidding, he thought. He had always loved her long straight hair; it had been one of the first things he had noticed about her when they'd met at a wedding – he'd been at university with the groom and she was a cousin of the bride. They'd been nicely set up, conveniently seated next to each other for the reception after the ceremony. They had chatted effortlessly from the get-go, an easy and spontaneous attraction on both their parts.

Now as he looked at her, he mourned not just the loss of all that silky waist-length hair the colour of ebony, but the absence of effortless dialogue between them. How could it have come to this? This appalling awkwardness?

'Please,' he said, gesturing the way through the house as though she was visiting for the first time, 'I've just opened a bottle of wine.'

'I'd rather have a soft drink, please. Since I'm driving.'

'Right, of course.' *Damn!* He hadn't been shopping for a few days and was pretty sure there was nothing suitable in the cupboards. 'Um ... I'll check to see what there is.'

A quick look in the kitchen confirmed that, other than tap water, he had nothing that didn't have an alcoholic content. 'How about some coffee?' he offered.

'Decaf?'

Shit, this was going from bad to worse. 'Tea?' he offered in desperation.

She smiled and pulled out what looked like a chunky square-shaped wallet from her handbag – the handbag that wasn't the

Mulberry one he'd bought her for her birthday. Had it been consigned to the past already? When she unzipped the wallet, he saw that it fell open like a concertina and each compartment contained an individual sachet of tea. This was something else that was new about her. She passed him a sachet, which declared itself to be rosehip tea.

In an agony of discomfiture, he boiled the kettle, poured the water over the teabag in a mug with a teaspoon and passed it to her to deal with. Meanwhile, he poured himself a glass of wine – large and purely medicinal; something to help relax him so he could talk to her as a normal human being.

The teabag dispatched to the bin under the sink, Jesse walked round to the other side of the breakfast bar and pulled out a stool. Adam took it as a clear message that she wasn't going to cross the boundary to the sitting area and make herself comfortable on the leather sofa. Opting for the bar stool made it plain she was all business.

In turn he leant back against the worktop and raised his glass. 'Happy Christmas,' he said, failing miserably to inject even a trace of festive cheer into his voice.

'Happy Christmas,' she murmured. 'Have you told your family about us?'

He shook his head. Apart from Floriana and Esme he hadn't told anyone. He'd deemed them as safe to tell; they weren't part of his immediate circle of friends. 'Not yet,' he said. 'It wasn't something I wanted to say over the phone.' The truth was, it wasn't something he wanted to discuss with anyone who had known them as a couple. It was the sympathy he dreaded. Or worse, the plenty-more-fish-in-the-sea banality that he could imagine any number of his friends saying. But odds on, the crossover between some of their friends would soon have the news spread.

'Does that mean your father and Joyce are still expecting me to join you for Christmas?' Jesse asked.

When he nodded, she said, 'Oh, Adam, that's not fair to them. It's not fair to me either.'

'I suppose not,' he said, not really sure why it wasn't fair to her. As he took a large reckless swallow of his wine and watched her sip cautiously at her drink, he thought how it hadn't occurred to him to tell his family about being on a break with Jesse. That was the good thing about his family: rarely did they ask or share things of an emotional nature. Questions of that sort were cast aside in favour of assumptions. So yes, the assumption was that Jesse would be arriving with him as had been arranged when it was discussed at the start of December.

'When you've explained the situation to them,' Jesse said, 'will you pass on my best wishes, please?'

'I will,' he said. 'And likewise to your parents.'

In the protracted silence that followed, he snatched at the first thing he could think to say. 'I'll get your present.'

It was almost a relief to leave the claustrophobic atmosphere of the kitchen and escape upstairs to fetch the present he'd wrapped and left on their bed.

His bed.

No, *their* bed, he corrected himself. It was still their bed until the very last drop of optimism had been completely drained from him.

He hoped Jesse didn't think he'd spent too much and would interpret his gift as an extravagant attempt to buy her back. After spending hours online, he'd narrowed the choice down to a Hermès enamel bangle or a Gucci pair of leather gloves. In the end he'd opted for the bangle and a bottle of her favourite Prada perfume, which he'd wrapped as one present so as not to appear too showy or overgenerous. He'd always teased her that she had an unhealthy interest in anything that had a designer label attached to it, and she'd countered that as vices went, it was her only one and was harmless enough. Her credit card statements had told a different story and he'd been shocked at the start of their relationship to discover how much debt she had racked up. What had surprised him more was how freely she discussed the amount she spent and what she owed. 'I expect you're in debt far more to your bank than I am to Visa and American Express,' she'd said with a shrug.

'But that's different,' he'd said. 'That's a business loan and I'm fully on top of it.'

Smiling, she'd said, 'Who says I'm not on top of my loan?'

She hadn't been on top of it though and six months later he'd helped to pay off the majority of it and put together a spreadsheet on how to manage her money better.

Back downstairs, he breathed in deeply and stepped into the

kitchen and put the wrapped present on the breakfast bar. 'No opening it until Christmas Day,' he said lightly.

In front of her was a much smaller wrapped parcel. 'Ditto for you,' she said, sliding it towards him. At least it wasn't socks, he thought, guessing from its shape that it was a CD.

It was then that he noticed her mug was empty. Surely she couldn't have drunk it all while he was upstairs? He hadn't been that long. A spark of bitterness ignited deep within him. She had probably tipped the tea down the sink so that she didn't have to drink it and prolong her visit any longer than was necessary. Was it so bad being here with him?

Perhaps it was, because right now he didn't much like being around himself. This wasn't the real him. He was on edge and constantly struggling to think of things to say, and everything he did say felt false and forced.

'You must have been thirsty,' he said, looking pointedly at the empty mug.

Not meeting his eye, she said, 'I was.'

'Would you like another one?' Now he was just being cruel. For which he got what he deserved.

She slipped off the stool and took the mug over to the sink. 'No thanks,' she said. She glanced at her watch. 'I really ought to be going.'

His heart sank. 'No, don't rush off,' he said, 'let's have something to eat. I thought maybe we could have a takeaway. Or go out.'

'I'm sorry,' she said, actually looking like she meant it, 'I can't stay, I'm meeting some friends in town.'

'*Friends?*' he repeated, immediately regretting it.

'Jackie and Amanda from work,' she said with a flare of defiance. 'We're having dinner together. I'm not going on a date, if that's what you're thinking.'

If he carried on this way, she soon would be, he thought miserably. 'Sorry,' he said. 'Sorry for ...' He threw his hands in the air and turned away. 'Sorry for everything. I seem totally incapable of getting this situation straight in my head. I get the feeling I'm doing and saying everything wrong.'

She came towards him. 'It was you who wanted us to be on a break,' she said softly.

Suddenly scared she might pull the plug on him there and then, he forced himself to smile. 'I'll eventually get the hang of it,' he said. 'And I'm glad you came. It's been good to see you, if only for a short while.'

She mirrored his smile but with a sadness he found unbearable, then picked up her bag and present and moved around him towards the hall.

He followed behind, helped her into her coat and stood back, unsure whether a goodbye kiss on the cheek would be contravening any of the rules by which she was playing this. 'Well then,' he said with excruciating brightness and sounding like an anxious parent talking to a teenage daughter going out for the night, 'have fun in town. Say hello to Jackie and Amanda from me.'

As if she couldn't take the forced cheeriness from him, she leant in and kissed him lightly on the cheek. 'Goodbye, Adam,' she said. 'Take care.'

The close proximity of her, the gentleness of her voice, the spicy new fragrance she was wearing, the familiar blue of her eyes, it was all too much and he closed the gap between them and kissed her on the mouth.

For a split second he thought he was doing the right thing. The soft warmth of her lips against his convinced him that this was all he'd needed to do right from the moment she'd arrived – just one kiss and she would come back to him and life would be as it once was.

But it was over before it had begun because no sooner had her lips responded to his – and he was sure they had – than she was pushing him away. 'No,' she said, 'please don't, Adam, that's not the answer, it will only complicate matters.'

'No it wouldn't,' he said, reaching for her again. 'It would simplify matters.'

She looked at him with what he could only call horrified disdain.

His face burning with shame, he stood back and watched her pull open the door. 'I shouldn't have come,' she said. 'It was a mistake.'

Later, when he'd finished off the bottle of wine and had made inroads on another and was doing the man-thing of lying on the sofa and controlling the universe with the remote control, he knew he'd blown it with Jesse. Every time he thought of what he'd said – that kissing her would simplify matters – he wanted to rip his tongue out and stamp on it, because frankly, it was sod all use to him if it was going to go round spewing crap like that.

Never in the history of dumb things to say had he sunk so mortifyingly low. And never would he be able to rid himself of the memory of that shameful utterance.

Oh, he'd really covered himself in glory, hadn't he?

Chapter Sixteen

Christmas Eve and never had the journey back to Kent seemed so tortuously endless or so full of opportunities to bail out. Every time the crowded train stopped at a station, Floriana had been tempted to gather up her things and make a run for it. But the thought of having to explain herself to Mum and Dad, not to mention Ann, had kept the temptation at bay.

Before catching the train from Oxford she had called in to see Esme to wish her a happy Christmas and in return she had been given a pep talk from the old lady, urging her to be more positive about the days ahead and to consider the possibility that her sister might want her presence to offset the weight of her husband's family. 'For all you know,' Esme had said, 'Ann might feel outnumbered by them and want you there as support.' It was a nice idea, but Floriana had yet to see any evidence of that since arriving.

She had had another reason for calling in at Trinity House; it was to deliver the invitation for Esme to join her and Adam for lunch when they were back in Oxford. She had also asked if Esme had heard anything from Adam about Jesse, but she knew less than Floriana did.

Floriana had texted Adam the day after he was seeing Jesse and all she'd had back from him, other than agreeing to the date she'd suggested for their get-together with Esme, was that it hadn't gone well. He hadn't expanded and she'd been too busy to call him, what with work and making a frantic and statutory last-minute start on her Christmas shopping.

So here she was, Christmas Eve *chez* Brown, a scant two miles from Stanhurst where she and her sister had grown up and where they'd always celebrated Christmas. For the first time since they'd gone on their trip, Floriana really missed Mum and Dad: it didn't feel like Christmas without them.

Standing at the kitchen sink peeling potatoes for tomorrow's lunch, behind her Ann's mother-in-law was banging on about the terrible state of the roads. Where were the gritters? Gillian Brown wanted to know. And why hadn't the neighbours got together to clear the roads on their development of houses? It was as slippery as an ice rink out there. A death trap.

'Paul and I have done our best to clear our part of the road,' Ann said, opening the fridge that was nearly as big as Floriana's kitchen, 'but not all the neighbours appear to be as like-minded.'

'Community spirit just isn't what it once was,' declared Gillian with an exaggerated huff. 'You young people don't know how to pull together like our generation.' Not much older than Mum and Dad, the woman had an annoying way of speaking that gave the impression she was a war veteran who with her bare hands had dug out survivors of the Blitz during WWII. In reality the only war she'd ever encountered was a face-off within her local choir when a new woman had tried to oust her as main soprano – it was Gillian who ousted her and the choirmaster when it was revealed the two had been cheating on their partners and sleeping together. Gillian never tired of telling the story of the successfully defeated coup.

Only halfway through peeling the mountain of potatoes, Floriana observed her sister wrestling with the main guest for tomorrow's lunch – a comedy-sized turkey, which she had now manhandled out of the fridge in its roasting tray and dumped on the work surface with a thud. It looked big enough to feed the whole bone-idle neighbourhood, never mind the Brown clan. And why was it only the women in the kitchen? Why weren't any of the men helping to peel all these bloody potatoes? Why did they get to hang out together in the sitting room with the kids playing on the Xbox? What kind of example did that give her niece and nephew, that cooking was strictly women's work?

At seven years old Thomas was already remarkably efficient at telling his five-year-old sister, Clare, what to do. Only earlier, when Floriana had been reading to them on the sofa, Thomas had interrupted her and asked his sister to fetch his slippers from his bedroom upstairs. Popping her thumb out from its customary place in her mouth, Clare had dutifully slithered off Floriana's lap, but Floriana was having none of it. 'Fetch them yourself, lazybones,' she'd said, nudging Thomas with an elbow.

'But she likes doing things for me,' he'd said, astonished at her intervention.

'Yeah, and I like squishing lazy nephews who boss their little sisters around.'

It was an uncanny reminder of when she and Ann had been children and Ann had constantly bossed Floriana around.

Another potato peeled, and behind her Gillian was off again, asking Ann if it wasn't time the children were in bed.

'Perhaps you'd like to do it for me?' Ann said, her right arm disappearing inside the turkey.

'I thought I'd do the children's stockings.'

'I've done them already,' Ann said, now removing her arm from the turkey with a gruesome squelching noise and, in the manner of a midwife, presenting the huge naked beast with a large bag of giblets.

Seeing a chance to escape peeling any more potatoes, Floriana said, 'I'll get the children ready for bed if you like.'

'No,' Ann said firmly, 'the potatoes are more important. You haven't done very many, have you?'

'Hey, I'm going as fast as I can,' she retaliated. 'Now I understand why you were so keen for me to come,' she muttered under her breath. 'You needed a slave.'

'What's that?' her sister said.

'Nothing.'

Half an hour later, and still bristling from Ann's assertion that the children's stockings were sorted, Gillian – determined she wasn't going to lose out in the ongoing power struggle – went upstairs to fetch the small presents she was adamant had to be included.

The children were no nearer going to bed – there was a great deal of high-pitched squealing coming from the sitting room – but the potatoes were now done and Floriana was about to ask for a vodka and tonic as her just reward when her sister dumped a sack of Brussels sprouts on the draining board.

'You're joking,' Floriana said as Ann returned to the fridge for an equally large sack of carrots and a slightly smaller one of parsnips.

'Do I look like I'm wearing my joker's face?' she said.

'I didn't know you had one,' Floriana fired back, not caring that she was sounding so insubordinate.

'Go ahead, moan all you like if it helps to get the job done any faster.'

'It's never like this at Mum and Dad's,' Floriana grumbled, thinking she might have to review her proposed turkey lunch for Esme if it was going to involve this amount of work. There again, there would only be the three of them.

'That's because Mum has the luxury of time to do it all before we arrive,' Ann said. 'Whereas I work,' she added self-righteously.

'Mum's always worked.'

'Her current charity work of two afternoons a week doesn't compare to the hours I put in.'

Floriana was about to say that Mum did a lot more than her two shifts at the Cancer Research shop when a voice at the kitchen door said, 'Anything I can do to help?'

Ah, it was the man himself, Robert Brown – Ann's idea of the dream catch for Floriana – and he was incongruously dressed in a pair of blue and green tartan trousers – or would that be trews, strictly speaking? Strictly speaking they were a tribute to thunderously bad taste. No grown man in his right mind should be seen dead in a pair, but for some reason Robert thought they were absolutely the thing to wear to celebrate the birth of Jesus Christ. That and a yellow-and-blue-striped rugby shirt. He swore he wasn't colour-blind, but Floriana, who wasn't averse to wearing some pretty odd clothes and colour combinations, had her doubts.

'No, no, nothing you can do here, all under control,' Ann said brightly, reverting to perfect 1950s housewife mode and straightening her Cath Kidston apron.

What? Floriana wanted to scream at her sister, gripping the vegetable knife in her hand. *Nothing to do, are you mad? It's like below stairs at Downton-bloody-Abbey here!*

'How about I give you a hand with those sprouts,' Robert said, smiling genially.

'Good idea,' Floriana said quickly, before her sister had a chance to veto his offer of help.

He turned out to be as deftly skilled with a knife in one hand and a sprout in the other as he was as a terrier seeking out the details of Floriana's accident. He'd touched on it earlier during the short drive from the station – he'd been the one to offer to pick her up – but now she felt as if he was really getting down to business and cross-examining her properly, grilling her on what actual forensics had been done at the crime scene. It all sounded overly melodramatic for such an insignificant accident, especially one of her own making. Though she hadn't brought up that bit – no way was she going to admit to being distracted, that would lead to telling her sister about Seb and his getting married. Better all round that his name wasn't mentioned.

'I don't have a clue about any forensics,' she said in answer to Robert's question. 'I wasn't at my most alert lying there in the road.'

'What about the two witnesses you referred to?'

'What about them?'

'Presumably they gave reliable accounts of what they saw and heard? Have they been asked if they've remembered anything else since those original statements?'

'They gave all the information they had at the time,' she said tiredly, 'but the subject hasn't risen again between us.'

On and on the interrogation went. Question after question.

'Did you take any photographs of your injuries?' he asked after he'd concluded the police had probably overlooked vital pieces of evidence that would have led to tracking down the driver, such as flakes of car paint on her clothing or on the ground.

'I can honestly say that whipping out my iPhone and taking a few snaps of my bruises and stitches was the last thing on my mind to do,' she said. 'But next time I'll be sure to remember that helpful tip.' She winced at how snarky she sounded. Robert didn't deserve that; it was his way of being helpful. It was just so difficult to take advice from a man dressed as Rupert Bear. The sooner he found the woman of his dreams, the better, she thought. Because then, with any luck, she would sort out his dress sense.

They both reached for a sprout at the same time and as their hands touched inside the bag, their eyes met. Poor Robert as good as jumped at the contact and his face coloured. He wouldn't have started more had she jabbed him with a taser.

'Tell me, Floriana,' she imagined someone saying to her, 'when did the two of you realise you loved each other?'

Cue the ha-ha-ha laughter track. 'Oh, it was love at first sprout.'

Chapter Seventeen

Christmas Day and Adam woke early to a bright and clear morning and, in an act of determined self-mastery, he resolved to bring about a fresh clarity to his mood and thinking.

By rights he should have a monumental hangover after staying up late drinking with his brother, but amazingly he didn't. Now out of the shower and wrapped in a towel, he stood at the window of his childhood bedroom and looked down at the snow-covered garden. This had been the family home since he was six years old. He could remember the day they moved in, how he and Giles had raced around the garden and orchard in awe of its grandeur and size, so many places to hide, so many places to build dens, so many trees to climb. And fall out of, which they did with careless and happy regularity. Fortunately, they both seemed to bounce well rather than end up with anything broken.

That was until Adam was seven years old and he climbed a tree higher than he'd ever climbed before and in a moment of boastful triumph that he'd gone further than his brother, he'd slipped and hurtled towards the ground with alarming speed. A broken femur condemned him to a month-long stay in hospital on traction. It was assuredly the most miserable period of his childhood, and had instilled in him a near pathological dislike of hospitals.

These days it was almost *de rigueur* to complain about a blighted childhood, but he couldn't find a single fault with his – apart from his own clumsiness falling from that tree, it had been pretty much perfect. His parents had never given any indication that they were anything but happily married and he and Giles never wanted for love or encouragement.

Their mother's death twelve years ago hit them with a shattering broadside blow that was as incomprehensible as it was unexpected. Mum had been perfectly healthy one minute and then after suffering a series of debilitating headaches, she was diagnosed with an inoperable brain tumour. She was dead within six weeks of the diagnosis and literally faded away before their eyes, the life seeping from her as she lay in the hospital bed drifting in and out of drug-induced sleep.

Two years later their father married again. An old friend of the family whose husband had died some five years previously, and who had been at school with Mum, Joyce was an ideal match and no one was unduly surprised by their announcement to tie the knot. Unable to have children, Joyce had thrown her maternal instinct into being a fun and loving honorary aunt to Adam and his brother when they'd been little, and now she was their stepmother, and a very good one into the bargain.

It was Joyce who had been the first to ask Adam where Jesse was when he arrived yesterday.

It was unquestionably wrong of him not to have told them beforehand that he'd be coming alone, but he really hadn't been able to face doing it over the phone. He couldn't even face thinking about Jesse, not after the humiliating mess he'd made of Monday evening. The expression on her face after he'd kissed her was still painfully etched on his memory.

So as cowardly as it was, it had seemed so much easier, and not to say self-explanatory, to arrive on his own. Both Joyce and his father had taken the pragmatic view that a thing wasn't over until it was over and he should just hang in there until Jesse had sorted herself out.

His brother's response was to pour him a large tumbler of whisky and say, 'Come on, Adam, man up!'

The subject was neatly side-stepped during dinner, probably on the grounds Dad and Joyce thought they'd said all they could say on the matter, but it was afterwards, much later, when it was just Adam and his brother still up, that Giles pressed for further details and the levels on Dad's decanters began to drop.

'I know you don't want my advice,' Giles said, 'you never have, any more than I've wanted yours, but in my opinion there's only one option open to you.'

'I'm listening.'

'Forget about Jesse and move on.'

Adam raised his glass to his brother. 'That's the best advice you can offer? You, the brilliant Cambridge man with a double first in PPE. Priceless.'

'OK, I could give you any amount of philosophical reasoning to assuage your disappointment, but you know deep down as well as I do that there isn't a more realistic option.'

And that, thought Adam as he finished dressing and could hear the rest of the household moving about, was what he had to accept. There was no other option. Yes, he could stick to the agreement he'd made with Jesse that they were on a break, but was there any point?

He didn't think so. Because whenever he remembered that look of utter disdain on her face after he'd kissed her, he could not imagine her ever looking at him the way she used to. That crushing moment would always be between them. So wouldn't it be better to pre-empt matters himself and end it with Jesse?

'*Man up!*' Giles had said. Well maybe they were the wisest words his brother had ever spoken.

It was a long time since Esme had had any presents to open. The last one she had been given had been from Margaret; it had been a CD of Monteverdi Vespers. They were funny things, presents, you could manage quite well without them, but when an unexpected one came along, it was all the more precious and enjoyable to open.

With great restraint, Esme had waited to open the presents Floriana and Adam had given her until she had eaten her lunch of roast chicken with sage and onion stuffing, roast potatoes and petit pois with some ready-made gravy and a dollop of cranberry sauce from a jar. Too full to eat the miniature Christmas pudding she had bought from Buddy Joe's, she had decided to save that for later.

But now, sitting in the drawing room with a glass of port and the gas fire gently hissing an accompaniment to carols from Christ Church College playing on the CD player, and with Euridice at her feet, it was finally time.

She took a sip of her port, then reached for the first of the two nicely wrapped gifts: the one from Adam, which was book-shaped. The red and gold wrapping paper dispensed with, she nodded with approval. 'What a perfectly thoughtful present from your new best friend,' she said, showing Euridice what it was – *The Times* Cryptic Crossword Puzzle Book.

Having removed the wrapping paper with great care and folded it with equal care, Esme placed it on the table beside her ready to be put away in her may-come-in-handy-one-day drawer. Then taking another sip of her port, she reached for Floriana's present.

'Now what do you suppose this is?' she asked the cat, at the same time giving the soft bulky package an experimental squeeze. 'No clues there,' she said. 'Yes, I know what you're thinking, Euridice: for heaven's sake, you foolish old woman, get on and open it!'

As silly as it was, Esme wanted to savour the moment, for once she had opened this present, the fun would be over. She had been the same as a child, eking out the pleasure and anticipation of present-opening, particularly if it was something from her father. And it didn't matter how much she loved what she had been given, there would always be a feeling of anticlimax when there was nothing else left to open. It was a natural form of greed, of course, and one that her mother had been only too quick to stamp on, prohibiting any extravagant gifts, or the quantity given. There were times when Esme had feared her mother would put a stop to Christmas and birthdays altogether, and as a consequence the fear had only endorsed her desire to draw out the process even longer.

She didn't doubt that there would be those who would say her father had been a weak and ineffectual man, he certainly didn't have the bullish temperament that her mother had inherited from her own father. Yet his strength lay not in his ability to stand up to his wife, but more – for Esme's sake – in his resilience to withstand marriage to a woman who openly despised and ridiculed him, never letting him forget that she was the one with all the money, wielding the power it gave her over him with a vindictive zeal that was unreasonably cruel and would have had a lesser man walking away from the situation, no matter how much he loved his only child.

Esme returned her attention to the package on her lap. She pulled on the bow of the silky red ribbon Floriana had used to tie the present and with the same care she'd used for Adam's wrapping paper, she removed it along with a layer of bubble wrap. She smiled delightedly at what Floriana had given her – a bone china chinoiserie teacup and saucer, prettily decorated with flowers, butterflies and a kingfisher. A card with its edges cut with pinking shears was attached to the handle of the cup and the writing on it was so small in order to fit, she had to put on her reading glasses.

Happy Christmas, Esme – it has been decreed that this cup and saucer must be brought with you when you next visit me.

Nestled inside the cup was a small grey knitted mouse with a length of string for its tail. There was another note, its edges also cut with pinking shears: *Happy Christmas, Euridice!* On the reverse side of the label was written: *Hand-made by Floriana.*

Esme was deeply touched that two people whom she had known for so little time had gone to such trouble for her. Her throat tight with emotion, she acknowledged that their kindness served to emphasise how insidiously the loneliness of old age had crept up on her, and what a barren state it was.

She held the mouse aloft for Euridice to see, realising then that there was a small bell inside the toy.

'Look,' she said, 'this is for you from Floriana. From now on, I want you to stop ignoring her; do you hear me?' She waved the knitted mouse at Euridice and the sound of the tinkling bell made the cat stretch up on her hind legs to investigate. Holding the knitted mouse by its tail, Esme dangled it in front of her and the cat batted it with one of her paws. Dropping it to the floor, Euridice instantly pounced on it. She then picked it up and carried it in her mouth over to the hearthrug where she patted the mouse about, turning it round as if inspecting it.

'Well,' said Esme, holding the teacup up to the light and admiring it, 'what lovely generous new friends we've acquired.'

There was just one more thing to open. It was the card Floriana had called round with yesterday. Esme could have opened it right away, but she had wanted to save it for today – something else to savour. Assuming it was a Christmas card, she was surprised to see that it was an invitation and written in what she now recognised as Floriana's hand, the style forthright and fluid and very expressive, just as the girl herself.

Miss Esme Silcox
you are cordially invited to join
Adam and Floriana for lunch
at 10a Church Close
on 28th December, 12.30 for 1.00.
RSVP asap.

Written on the back of the card was Floriana's telephone number. After removing her spectacles and taking another sip of her port, Esme wondered when she had last enjoyed a Christmas Day as much as this one.

Some time later, and succumbing to a pleasing torpor, she placed her now empty port glass on the table beside her and closed her eyes.

Chapter Eighteen

It was the last week of May when they took the train from Venice to Milan and where they stayed for just the one night.

Post-war Italy was rife with shocking stories of what the country had endured during the war, and though it was irrational, neither Esme nor her father felt inclined to linger in a city where, only five years before, in the Piazza Loreto, the bodies of Mussolini and his mistress had been gruesomely strung up with piano wire and their corpses spat upon and shot at. So after a tour of the *duomo* and with the help of a porter on the crowded station, they boarded the train to Como and with their tickets purchased on the waterfront they then took their seats on the steamer boat. Signora Bassani had offered for someone to meet them in Como, but Esme's father had sent a telegram saying they would be happy to make their own arrangements.

They had been travelling now for more than seven weeks, varying the length of time they spent in each place depending on their level of interest and the weather. They had commenced their tour in Pisa, followed by Siena, the Amalfi coast, Rome, Florence and Venice, and while every day had brought them plenty of new experiences to explore and enjoy, Esme was looking forward to the months ahead when they would be stopping at the lake for the rest of the summer. It would be a time to unwind after all the weeks of sightseeing.

The ghost of her childhood left far behind in Nottingham, this was the adventure her father had wanted to take her on, their very own version of the Grand Tour. Some might say they were heartless to be so happy, when her mother had been dead only a year, but the way Esme saw it, they were finally free and she for one was going to make the most of this wonderful opportunity. Occasionally she would catch herself wondering what her mother would think of them travelling round Italy like a couple of carefree gypsies, but the thought was fleeting, soon lost in the heady pell-mell of sights to see, trains to catch and people to meet.

Everywhere they went they met somebody new and interesting. In Siena a delightful Belgian couple had befriended them with their extraordinarily well-behaved children and in Rome there had been a widowed English woman – Elizabeth St John – who had seemed quite the jolly eccentric aristocrat, until she had let on that she was no such thing.

'Not even a minor-ranking member of the aristocracy,' she had whispered to them over a game of cards one afternoon when a heavy downpour of rain had put paid to their excursion to Tivoli and the gardens at Villa d'Este. It was all an act, she had explained, a way to impress and appeal to the proprietor of the small hotel where they were staying. 'It goes down frightfully well,' she confided, 'by hinting that I'm a "*somebody*" travelling incognito but I don't want any fuss, it ensures that I always get the best service. The American tourists love it, too. In exchange for a gin fizz, I'll tell them my fascinating tales of when I met Edward and Wallis Simpson, oh, they just love it!'

'And did you meet them?' Esme had asked eagerly and with instant and regrettable naivety.

'I should say not!'

Esme had felt quite sad to say goodbye to her when she and her father moved on to Florence. But not, Esme suspected, as sad as Elizabeth St John was to see William depart. 'A lucky escape there, I think,' her father had said later when he'd recovered from Elizabeth's farewell embrace; an embrace that had necessitated his being clutched tightly to her mighty bosom. Moments before they had left, and while her father was preoccupied with their luggage and checking their train tickets, Elizabeth had given Esme two pieces of advice: 'Firstly,' she had whispered to her, 'you must be brave and throw yourself into as many new experiences as possible while you're here in Italy. And secondly, and this is the best advice I can give you, you must fall in love! You are not to go home until you have had at least one grand passion!'

In Florence they had stayed in a charming hotel just off the Piazza Santa Maria Novella. La Residenza Santa Maria was ideally placed to visit the main sites – the Uffizi Gallery, Giotto's bell tower, the Ponte Vecchio and, of course, the cathedral of Santa Maria del Fiore and the Church of Santa Maria.

They soon slipped into an agreeable routine of spending the morning sightseeing together, then after lunch her father would devote the afternoon to sketching or painting the city from its many vantage points, leaving Esme to further her Italian language studies, and then when she'd had enough of grammar and verbs, she would go for a walk.

Enthralled with everything she saw, and not surprisingly, since she was reading E.M. Forster's *A Room With a View*, she readily surrendered herself to Elizabeth's advice that she must fall in love and fancied herself in the role of Lucy Honeychurch.

Or if not love itself, she conceded, then to be romanced.

How perfect it would be to experience her first kiss here, she thought with a happy thrill one afternoon as she paused in front of the *duomo* where a handsome young couple strolled by arm in arm and looking impossibly glamorous – the girl in a navy-blue dress cinched in at the waist with a white belt and the man in grey trousers with a white shirt, the sleeves rolled up to his elbows and a jacket slung over a shoulder.

But there was no romance for her that day, only an interesting conversation with Professor Banes – a retired American professor of history who she recognised as a fellow guest from La Residenza Santa Maria. She had spotted him during dinner on their first night at the hotel, a plump, pink-faced man who had occupied a table the other side of the dining room.

Seeing her admiring the doors to the Baptistery, he tipped his hat and came over to say hello and to enquire after her father. 'Then since you are alone, permit me to be your guide for the rest of the day,' he said, dabbing his glistening pink face with a neatly folded handkerchief. 'Now what do you know about these splendid fellows?' he demanded, pointing at the doors with his silver-topped walking cane.

She told him what she'd learnt from her guidebook, that they were by Ghiberti and Pisano and had been removed for safekeeping part-way through the war and were later returned in 1946.

'Yes indeed, you are perfectly correct,' the professor replied. 'But these particular doors, facing east, are by Ghiberti. Michelangelo said they were worthy to be the gates to paradise.' The professor then went on to explain how when it was deemed safe to bring the doors back to Florence, it was decided to give them a polish; only then was it realised that the doors were not made of bronze, but of gold. 'Imagine their surprise,' he declared. He held out his arm. 'Shall we venture inside *paradise* and investigate further?'

Professor Banes introduced Esme and her father to a wide circle of his associates in Florence. He jokingly referred to them as relics of the British colony, who, like Ghiberti's gates, had returned to this great city once the war was over and were now replicating their glory days of life before the war. They spoke about Florence with a critical and proprietorial fondness, as though the city were a wayward child in need of their steadying hand.

'You see,' said an opinionated man with a lamentable habit of dominating any conversation and waving his pipe at Esme in a way she didn't much care for, 'this is the trouble with Italy, and with Florence in particular. Beauty and history have been commandeered by these damned communists – they know a honey pot when they see one and have no qualms in abusing wealthy foreigners like us.'

While certainly not siding with the communists, Esme could however understand the basis of their ideology. But more importantly, she didn't like this self-satisfied man pontificating at her and, unable to let his lecture go unchallenged, she said, 'But isn't it more a case of the tourist trade dropping off in cities like Florence that has caused greater numbers to be unemployed and thereby given communism its appeal?'

The man had thrown back his head and let out an unpleasantly patronising laugh that filled the salon in which they had congregated for pre-dinner drinks. 'Silcox, old man, I see you have a Marxist for a daughter! You'd better watch her.'

'I'm entirely in agreement with Esme,' her father said mildly, breaking off from chatting to an antiquarian bookseller from Kensington. 'After all, how can we truly understand the mind of an Italian when one moment he has been ordered to fight the Americans and the British, and the next he is fighting with them?'

'Quite right,' Professor Banes joined in. 'Is it any wonder things are as chaotic as they are when, within ten years of turmoil they have been expected to respect a dictator, then a king, followed by a republic?'

A woman wearing an expression of intense boredom added

her laconic voice to the debate. 'Oh, let's face it,' she said with an aloof flick of a well-manicured hand, 'Italians are natural anarchists. Now, please, will someone make me another Americano, I'm gasping?'

Leaving behind them La Residenza Santa Maria, the beautiful sunsets over the Arno and the Ponte Vecchio, the Giotto frescos, the fountains, the hills of Fiesole and Professor Banes' eclectic circle of friends, they set off for Venice where they encountered an equally cosmopolitan crowd.

Esme's first sighting of the beautiful city was as she and her father stepped outside of the railway station – the Venezia Santa Lucia – and there directly in front of her was the Grand Canal. During the train journey from Florence she had read from her Baedeker what to expect, but the preparation had been in vain. In a daze of mute astonishment she stood looking at the Grand Canal while her father located the boat stop. Then in rapt wonder they travelled by motor launch to their hotel, weaving their way through the traffic of *vaporetti* and gondolas.

As a treat, her father had booked them into the Hotel Danieli for the first four days of their stay. Next door to the Doge's Palace and the Ponte dei Sospiri, her room overlooked the lagoon and the island of San Giorgio; to the right was the Grand Canal and the Santa Maria della Salute in all its magnificence. It was a truly spellbinding view.

Surely here she would fall in love, she thought wistfully.

The next morning she awoke early to the sound of bells ringing across the city, and rushing to the window, eager to greet the day, she had flung it open and absorbed the intoxicating atmosphere. Wanting to soak up every sight, sound and smell, to be a part of it, she had hurriedly dressed and without bothering to disturb her father in the room next door, she had quietly crept out to explore on her own. She had only walked as far as the Piazza San Marco when she came to a stop. Seeing the great square deserted, save for the pigeons, she stood with the basilica behind her in a trance of lost enchantment.

Just a few months off her nineteenth birthday, she considered herself quite grown up, but the child within her – the child that her mother had kept squashed under her thumb – wanted to be let loose and run impulsively through the pigeons. And deciding that since it was not yet six o'clock and there was no one about, she could do exactly as she wanted with perfect impunity. So, with her arms stretched out either side of her, she ran at the birds and to her inordinately silly satisfaction they rose as one with a noisy flap of their wings and wheeled up into the pearly dawn sky in a burst of panic.

Laughing aloud, and with her eyes shut, she spun round and round like a whirling dervish. Then opening her eyes, she turned and started to run the way she'd just come, only to crash head-long into the handsomest man she had ever set eyes on.

'*Buongiorno*,' he said, smiling at her.

Her cheeks flaming with a deep flush of embarrassment, at the same time denied the power of coherent speech, all she could do was stare back at him in a horribly gauche manner. So much for the sophisticated young woman she had believed herself to be since coming to Italy!

'You are English?' he said, more of a statement than a question.

She nodded and finally found her tongue and the confidence to speak in Italian. '*Sì, signore*,' she said, '*sono Inglese.*'

The smile increased and showed off two rows of white teeth against a tanned face – a face that was beautifully aesthetic, like that of a Renaissance statue. '*Brava, parla Italiano?*' he said.

'*Un po*',' she managed to say, thinking that his eyes were quite literally as blue as the Adriatic and that he wasn't much older than her.

Perhaps guessing he had exhausted her Italian vocabulary, he said, 'You like to frighten the pigeons? It is a game for you?'

She shook her head. 'I've never done anything like that before, I just suddenly felt like being extremely silly.'

'Good! I think it is very good to be silly at times. Too many people are too serious. And anyway, the pigeons are much too big for their bots, they need to be chased now and then.'

'*Boots*,' she corrected him. Then immediately regretted it. 'I'm sorry,' she said, 'that was rude of me.'

'No, no. It is the best way to learn, to be taught the correct words and pronunciation. I very much want to speak *l'inglese corretto*. You are here alone in Venice?'

'I'm here with my father.'

'For how long?'

'A couple of weeks, then we're going on to Lake Como.'

'*Bello*. Do you know where at the lake you will stay?'

She shook her head again, noticing that the pigeons had re-turned to the piazza and had completely surrounded her and this charming young man with his oh-so-blue eyes and his jet-black hair. 'We haven't booked anything yet,' she said. 'We're taking each day as it comes.'

She went on to tell him that this trip to Italy was a chance for her father to explore his love of painting, 'Although he would never describe himself as anything other than an amateur art-ist,' she said, 'but, and perhaps I am a little biased, I think he's genuinely talented.'

'Then may I make a suggestion?'

'Please.'

'I have an aunt who runs a modest hotel on the shores of the lake. It is not one of the very grand establishments, but it is com-fortable and very tranquil. The views would not disappoint and would be perfect for your father. And for you also,' he added with a smile that made her heartbeat quicken and her legs feel as wobbly as cooked spaghetti.

It was then that he held out his hand to her and introduced himself as Marco Bassani and explained that he was in his first year of seminary studying to be a priest.

Her heart almost crashed to a stop.

All along the lake, the steamer dropped people off and picked others up. Standing at the prow of the boat, and with growing ex-citement, Esme stood next to her father and watched the passing scenery. Pretty villages nestled in the lower slopes of the hillsides, tiny cottages and palatial villas lined the foreshore, and gardens lush and bright with azaleas and oleanders in full bloom dazzled the eye with flowers of vermilion and creamy yellow, pink and white, all contrasting vividly with the dark green cypress trees that stood tall and proud like sentinels on guard duty.

It was every bit as beautiful as Marco had said it would be. And it was here he had grown up, adopted by his aunt – Signora Giulia Bassani – after the death of his parents when he'd been a boy. It was difficult to imagine how he could bear to leave this beautiful place to go off and become, of all things, a priest.

Esme tried not to give in to the thought too much, but a less than worthy part of her considered it a waste for Marco to give his life to the Church, but as she and her father had become better acquainted with Marco during their stay in Venice, which they had prolonged by an extra week, she had begun to appreciate the sincerity of his faith and belief that the path he had chosen was the right one. 'In life,' he had told her, 'we are each called to do something special and when we know in our hearts what it is, we must do it, for then it will not be a duty, but a pleasure.'

Esme had found his company considerably more interesting and engaging than the crowd of diplomats, industrialists and so-called intellectuals they had met in Venice – a self-serving bunch she had soon grown weary of. Marco had been very much a breath of fresh air.

Her father nudged her and pointed towards a pale yellow villa with dark green shutters. 'According to the directions, that's Hotel Margherita,' he said. 'The next stop is ours.'

As the boat slowed and sailed closer to the shoreline, Esme shielded her eyes from the sun and took in the substantial villa and its grounds that sloped gently down to the water's edge. Positioned as it was on a promontory, and with nothing else around it, it was as if Villa Margherita stood atop its very own private island.

So this was home for the rest of the summer, Esme thought happily.

It was the ringing of the telephone that woke Esme. So deeply had she been dreaming, it took her a moment to orientate herself, to realign her mind with the present and to relinquish the powerful hold of the past, to which, in sleep, she had surrendered herself entirely.

But by the time she made it to the hall in the semi-darkness, switching on the lights as she went, the ringing stopped.

'Who could it be?' she said to Euridice who had followed behind her. 'Nobody rings us on Christmas Day.'

She was on her way to the kitchen to put the kettle on and make a pot of tea, when the telephone started up again.

'Hello,' she said guardedly, expecting it to be a stranger who had misdialled.

'Esme, is that you?'

'It is,' she said, still guardedly, not recognising the voice at the other end of the line and blaming her befuddled state on her mind which was still lagging behind in Italy.

'It's me, Floriana. I just wanted to wish you a happy Christmas.'

At the girl's words, her throat bunched tight with emotion, just as it had earlier when she'd opened her presents and had been so moved by the thoughtfulness of her two young friends.

'Esme? Are you still there?'

'Yes,' she said croakily.

'Are you all right?'

'I'm fine,' she said, battling to pull herself together. 'Just a little groggy, I was fast asleep.'

'Oh, I'm sorry I disturbed you.'

'My darling girl, don't apologise, it's lovely to hear from you. I'm very touched that you should think of me, and thank you for my beautiful present, and for Euridice's mouse. You've quite spoilt us. Are you having a good Christmas?'

There was a long and exaggerated groan in Esme's ear. 'I'll tell you when I'm back. By the way, are you free that day for lunch?'

'Wild horses wouldn't keep me away.'

'Brilliant.'

Later, when she was settled with a cup of tea and a mince pie and she had shaken the last vestiges of the past from her mind, Esme focused her thoughts on the present and in particular her new friends, Floriana and Adam.

She knew she was getting ahead of herself, and as different as they were in temperament, she detected the signs of a very pleasing chemistry between the pair of them; it was there in the easy way they interacted and in her opinion it quite belied the length of time they had known each other.

Esme had never played at matchmaking before, but she was quite tempted to do so with these two. However, she would have to tread carefully for very likely Adam had a long way to go yet before he would be over Jesse, and goodness only knew how Floriana felt about this Sebastian character.

Chapter Nineteen

A grey cold sky had wrapped itself around Oxford since the New Year and today the city lay submerged beneath a shroud of freezing fog making it feel as though it was cut off from the rest of the world.

January was the quietest month of the year for Floriana – not surprisingly people weren't keen to sign up for tours when it was so perishing cold – instead, and because this was the time of year when they were inundated with bookings for when the season took off around Easter, she helped in the office. But this morning a hardy Russian couple from Moscow – Mr and Mrs Zhukova – had requested a personal three-hour city tour. Dressed in thick woollen overcoats and fur hats, they hadn't once objected to the biting cold wind that numbed Floriana's hands and feet and whipped at her face bringing tears to her eyes – maybe for them this was a mild spring day.

Dreaming Spires Tours had only the one Russian-speaking guide – Martina, who was unfortunately off sick – but thankfully the Zhukovas had a more than adequate grasp of English and Floriana had encountered no difficulties in talking to them. The only hitch she'd had was trying to explain to Mr Zhukova – a thickset man with a permanently nodding head as he listened to her every word – that none of the colleges were for sale. He'd given her a steely look when she'd had to repeat this in the front quad of Christ Church after he'd interrupted her part-way through explaining about Christopher Wren's Tom Tower and its seven-ton bell known at Great Tom. 'Not true,' he'd said, shaking his head vigorously. 'Everything for sale for right price.'

The other problem she'd encountered was that Mr Zhukova's mobile kept ringing. He was taking a call now, speaking loudly in Russian, his head nodding non-stop, his expression unreadable. And while he continued his conversation, and Floriana shivered and breathed in the icy lung-numbing air and tried to chat politely with his wife, she started to lead them back towards the High where they'd begun the tour outside the office, and where the couple's driver would be waiting to whisk them back to London. It had crossed Floriana's mind more than once that this visit to Oxford for the couple had in actual fact been a buying expedition and they were now leaving disappointed. Her imagination running away with itself, she imagined Mr Zhukova consoling himself with a bunch of oligarch pals in a swanky Mayfair bar tonight, hitting the vodka shots and planning his next move: Cambridge.

Esme was always laughing at Floriana for having what she called a fertile mind. 'Is that what you call it?' Adam had remarked in his habitually droll manner. 'Not just plain bonkers, then?' He'd made the comment at the weekend when he'd invited Floriana and Esme to have a look round his new house. Since buying it, he'd had builders in to rip out what a series of previous owners had done by way of supposed improvement. He wanted to return the property to its original Victorian roots, he'd explained. 'Complete with parlourmaids and bootboys, no doubt?' Floriana had joked. 'Could I be the po-faced housekeeper? I can be really stern when I want to be.'

'I'd figured you for the mad woman in the attic,' he'd said with a sardonic lifting of an eyebrow.

'Watch it, mister,' she'd laughed. 'Come the next lot of snow, I'll have my revenge.'

With no heating in the property, they hadn't lingered for long and had quickly retreated to the warmth of Trinity House where Esme had treated them to tea and crumpets. After some surreptitious questioning from Esme, Adam had admitted that he'd cut short the month-long break with Jesse and ended things himself. 'And, please, no more on the subject,' he'd said, raising a warning hand. 'Certainly no platitudes.'

'As you wish,' Esme had said quietly, exchanging a look with Floriana.

It had been the first time they had managed to get together again since the lunch Floriana had cooked for them. To her surprise, there had been no disasters and her first attempt at cooking a turkey had been declared a triumph, and in the way that Adam always managed to come up trumps, he'd not only supplied the wine for the meal but the table and chairs – something she had completely overlooked in her haste to host the lunch. He'd offered the furniture for her to keep but as she'd pointed out, there just wasn't room for it on a permanent basis.

Outside the office on the High now, Floriana was all set to launch into what she always said at this point – a thank you to the customer for choosing Dreaming Spires Tours – when Mr Zhukova moved in alarmingly close and thrust something small and hard into her gloved hand. For a crazy moment she thought it was a gun.

'For you, Miss Day,' he said gruffly. 'You need better coat to keep you warm and proper fur hat, that silly knitted thing you wear is best only for English teapot.'

It wasn't until the Zhukovas were installed in the back of the black Mercedes and she'd waved them off that Floriana checked what was in her hand. She was shocked to see it was a roll of cash, and by all appearances a considerable amount. Amazed at the generosity of the tip, she stuffed it quickly into her coat pocket, turned away from the kerb and pushed open the door to the office.

It was there that she received her second surprise of the day.

'When I didn't hear back from you, I knew there was only one thing to do – I had to come to Oxford and do this face to face.'

'And what exactly is it you want to do face to face?' Floriana asked, playing for time. She was miserably on edge, struggling to think straight, struggling even to sit still after being press-ganged into agreeing to have lunch in Quods. How could he do this to her? How could he just turn up out of the blue like this?

Opposite, the cause of her anguish was looking her unnervingly square in the eye. It was more than two years since she'd last seen Seb and he looked transformed. Gone was the trademark shaggy hair of old that had made him seem just a bit out of kilter, now his hair was closely cropped, giving him an oddly vulnerable appearance. But then there had always been something vulnerable about Seb beneath the outward show of confidence and swagger.

'I want to know that you'll be at my wedding,' he said.

She gave a tense little laugh. 'You came all the way from London to do that?'

'Oxford isn't exactly at the far ends of the earth.'

'But you took the day off work to come and all on a wing and a prayer that I'd be here. I could have been anywhere.'

He shrugged. 'Not exactly. I phoned your office yesterday to check you'd be working today and simply lay in wait.'

'No one in the office would give out personal information like that,' she said. But then she remembered Damian Webb had been working yesterday. Spin the right line to him and he'd probably give out her bank details if he had them to hand!

'I pretended to be a potential customer, gave some story about you being personally recommended to me,' Seb said. He suddenly smiled. 'I'm sure you can remember how persuasive I can be.' But then the smile dropped and his expression was serious and she knew the awkward exchange of polite query and response was over and it was to the heart of the matter. 'Don't you think this silliness has gone on for long enough?' he said, matter-of-factly.

Stirred by a flash of irritation Floriana sat up straight – twice now in less than thirty minutes the word silly had been applied to her: first Mr Zhukova and now Seb. 'Is that what you'd call it?' she said as a jumble of emotions and memories raced chaotically through her head ... angry words exchanged ... accusations made ... love declared ... love rejected ... humiliation complete ... a friendship lost.

Without answering her question, Seb said: 'Why didn't you reply to my card? And please don't say "what card?", that would not just insult my intelligence, but yours.'

She swallowed and looked around for their waitress. How long did it take to make a cup of coffee and pour out a beer? Seb had suggested tequilas for old times' sake, but she'd refused – no way was she going to consume any alcohol when she needed all her faculties in full working order to survive this ordeal. 'I just didn't get around to replying,' she said blandly. 'I was busy in the run-up to Christmas.'

He shook his head sadly. 'You're such a bad liar, Florrie.'

'Don't call me Florrie!' she snapped.

The pained expression on his face was so acute she might well have slapped him. Silence weighed heavily between them.

'I'm sorry,' he said finally. 'Sorry for many things. But chiefly for what happened to us. I always believed we were invincible, that nothing could ever come between us. I still believe it.' He glanced over her shoulder, distracted by something. 'Ah, at last, our drinks, which I know you were anxiously awaiting in the hope they would provide you with a convenient distraction.'

She gritted her teeth.

'Don't grit your teeth,' he said, when the waitress had left them, 'the wind will change and they'll all drop out. Or something equally hideous will happen to you.'

'Something hideous will happen to you if you don't be quiet,' she said, picking up her cup and taking a sip. Annoyingly it wasn't as hot as she'd like.

The corners of his mouth tilted up into a cautious smile. 'That's more like it, that's the Florrie – I mean, that's the Floriana I know and love. Come on, let's put all that ... all that stuff behind us. Let's be friends again.'

Classic Seb, she thought, trust him to dismiss the single biggest heartbreaking event in her life merely as 'stuff'.

'I'll beg if I have to,' he said when she didn't reply.

There was a tenderness to his voice that made her heart turn over and she felt the carefully constructed defences she had worked so hard to put in place begin to weaken. 'Are you sure you need an old friend like me in your life?' she asked.

'What you're really asking is will Imogen mind me having you as a friend again, isn't it?'

'And will she?'

'She knows that you're my oldest friend and that I've missed you these last two years. She's made it very clear that what went on before is all in the past and she's ...'

'She's what?' Floriana asked, leaping on his hesitation. She knew Seb well enough to know that he didn't hesitate without good reason.

'She's forgiven you.'

It took all of Floriana's will power to refrain from saying, *That's bloody big of her!* but tipping her cup up so she was virtually hiding behind it, she drank the rest of her lukewarm coffee in one long swallow.

When she put the cup down, she found Seb's dark contemplative eyes fixed on her. Oh, how well she remembered those eyes, the deep intensity of them, the little flecks of amber that had always fascinated her and which could make his eyes literally glitter. He had once convinced a gullible girl at school that staring at the sun when he'd been a baby had caused the flecks.

As a teenager, and in the way that close friends can be wholly objective, she had always considered Seb to be good-looking, but if she had been asked to describe him back then she would have failed to do so, because his features, so very familiar to her, had been as good as invisible to her, in the same way the faces of her sister or parents were. But sitting here across the table from him, seeing him anew and taking in the clean, sharply defined features of his face, the smoothness of his skin that gave him a forever-young appearance, and experiencing the way he could fix his unblinking gaze on her and make her feel he could read her mind, it was a stark and painful reminder of when she had realised that her feelings for him had changed from friendship to love. The realisation had hit her so suddenly and with such force it had turned her world upside down and then the day had come when she could bear it no more and she had been compelled to tell him that she loved him. But it had been a disaster, the very worst mistake of her life.

Now, against all the odds, she was sitting close enough to reach across the table and kiss him, just as she had wanted to do the last time they'd spoken. But there had been no kiss, just a terrible argument and the shattering suggestion from Seb that perhaps it would be better if they never saw one another again.

Remembering that day, she felt her throat constrict with a sadness that made her want to run far away from him. She didn't think she would ever forget the pain of being banished from the world they had once shared, and all because she had spoken the truth. But it was a truth he hadn't wanted to hear, let alone believe.

'What about you?' he said now, his gaze fixed on her with unblinking intensity. 'Have you forgiven me for falling in love with Imogen?'

She was saved from answering by the arrival of their lunch – pumpkin ravioli for her and steak and fries for Seb. The disruption in the conversation gave her the chance to change the subject when the waitress had left them.

'So where are you getting married?' she asked brightly.

There wasn't a doubt in her mind that he knew she had refused to answer his question and what that meant. But either deciding to come back to it later or forget it altogether, he said, 'Lake Como.'

Her first thought was, Oh, what a coincidence! On Sunday, while they'd been enjoying tea and crumpets at Trinity House, Esme had told Floriana and Adam about her trip to Italy with her father when she'd been a young girl and how they'd gone to Lake Como to spend the summer there. But as Esme always did whenever she shared anything with them, she had brought the story to an abrupt stop just at a tantalising point in the tale.

However, Floriana's second thought was one of relief. Because right there was her cast-iron excuse for not putting herself through the agony of watching Seb marry Imogen. No way would she be able to afford to go. She was off the hook. *Three cheers for being a lowly, cash-strapped tour guide!* In an instant her mood lightened and she said, 'A fancy-schmancy wedding, I should have expected nothing less.' What she really meant was that she would expect nothing less of Imogen. The girl's class and moneyed background made Floriana look like trailer trash.

'Not that fancy,' Seb said. 'It'll be fairly low-key. Just three hundred close friends and family.'

'*Three hundred!*'

He smiled. 'I'm joking. It'll be about seventy or eighty guests.'

'Still, that's quite a big do.'

'You will come, won't you?'

'Seb, you don't want riff-raff like me there. I'll only get horribly drunk and let the side down.'

He frowned. 'Since when did you become riff-raff?'

Since you got involved with Imogen and her super-rich family, she thought. 'Well, we do move in slightly different circles these days, don't we?' she said. 'There's you, the top-flight ad exec living in high-achieving splendour in Belsize Park, and there's me slumming it in Oxford.'

'Hardly that,' he said tersely.

'You know what I mean.'

She watched him chew thoughtfully on a piece of steak, then reach for his beer. 'Money isn't the issue here, though, is it?' he said when he set the glass down.

'That, my friend, just goes to show that you know nothing; it's *all* about the ker-ching. It always is when you don't have much of it. Those chips looks good.'

He moved the salt and pepper pots out of the way so she could reach. 'Help yourself,' he said.

She did, offering him some of her ravioli in return.

He scooped up a piece with his fork. 'Mm ... not bad.'

And magically, as if they had somehow negotiated the rocky terrain and dangerous precipice of the last two years and were now on safer ground, they embarked on the process of catching up properly. She told him that her parents had sold the shop and were away on a world cruise. 'They've been gone since the end of November and are due home next week.'

'And Christmas, what did you do in their absence?'

Remembering how he and his mother had once spent Christmas with them, and how his mother had got embarrassingly drunk and they'd had to put her to bed in the spare room while they opened their presents downstairs, she told him about going to Ann's. It was when she was fully engrossed in hamming up her story of the Christmas from hell and was pushing a hand through her hair, that he noticed the scar, which was still quite livid in colour. 'How'd you get that?' he asked with a frown. 'Looks like it must have been painful.'

So out came the story of her accident. 'I blame you unreservedly,' she said. 'If you hadn't sent me that blasted invitation I wouldn't have got knocked over.'

'On the upside, if I hadn't sent that *blasted* invitation we wouldn't be having lunch. God, it's bloody good to see you. I've missed you.'

When she didn't say anything, he said, 'That's your cue to say you've missed me. You have, haven't you?'

She nodded, not trusting herself to answer.

There was an awkward silence while they concentrated on eating. 'Will you promise me something?' he said at length.

'Depends what it is.'

'Please don't say you won't come to my wedding because you can't afford it.'

She put down her knife and fork. 'Seb, the truth is, I don't have the money. Just about everything I earn goes on my mortgage. Trips abroad are a luxury I can't afford.'

As if missing the point of what she'd just told him, he said, 'You got around to buying something, then?'

She told him about her grandmother dying and leaving her

enough money to get a deposit together. 'I decided to be sensible with the money and invest it by getting a foot on the property ladder. I'm living in North Oxford now.'

'Well done.'

'Hey, I'm not looking for a pat on the head.'

He rolled his eyes. 'Then shut up and listen to what I'm going to suggest.'

She listened and when he'd finished, she shook her head. 'No. Absolutely not.'

'I knew you'd be bloody awkward and say that.'

'Then you shouldn't have wasted your breath on asking.'

He leant across the table, his brows drawn, the flecks of amber glittering in his eyes. 'Look, Imogen doesn't need to know if that's what's worrying you.'

She jerked back from him, stunned. 'Oh, that's very good, Seb, starting off your marriage with a secret! And a secret about me, well, that's just a genius idea!'

'OK, OK, I'll tell Imogen if it makes you feel better. But I owe you, Florrie. You and your parents were always so good to me. And don't forget what I was like here in Oxford, I was a mess for most of it. You saved me from myself.'

Chapter Twenty

Adam liked nothing more than to get in the car and drive around. It was a good way to keep an eye on what was going on property-wise. Keeping his ear to the ground, he liked to call it.

After lunch and bored rigid with paperwork – the bane of his life – he'd told Denise he'd be back in a few hours. Denise had been his PA at Strong Property Solutions for nearly a decade now and was quite used to the way he worked – basically he hated to be confined. He'd much rather be on the move and taking calls on his mobile than be stuck behind a desk. His being away from the office suited them both as not only did he trust Denise to run things smoothly in his absence, he reckoned she preferred it when he left her to it. Many a time people had assumed she was the boss and he'd never had a problem with that.

His first destination had been Headington, where a tenant had reported a problem with the central heating. All his maintenance men were busy, so it was no big deal for him to go instead. Turned out it was a minor fault with a valve in the airing cupboard, which Adam had fixed himself.

He was now driving round the narrow streets of Osney. It was doing exactly this that had led him to find his very first house. It had been a wet and dreary day and he'd noticed a particularly shabby end of terrace with its guttering hanging off in places, an upstairs window boarded up and the paintwork seemingly all that was holding the window frames together. With nothing to lose, he'd knocked on the door and explained to the elderly owner that he was interested in buying a house just like this one. As luck would have it, the man had been considering selling and over the following days they came to an agreement on the price and made a deal. Because there were no agent fees involved, Adam was able to offer a good and fair price and so both parties were happy. Six months later – re-wired, re-plumbed and thoroughly modernised – the house was sold for twice what he had originally paid for it.

That property still meant a lot to Adam; it was where it all started for him. He'd acquired dozens of properties since then and learnt a ton of stuff along the way, including down-to-earth practical skills and fundamental dos and don'ts when it came to investing in property, which he could boil down to just two simple golden rules: You make the money when you buy, not when you sell. And: Buy in haste and you'll repent at leisure.

While he still got a thrill out of finding a place and turning it around, nothing had given him as much pleasure as that very first purchase.

Until now.

The house on Latimer Street had come to mean more to him than merely another acquisition to do up and sell on, or to offer for rent. Without intending to, he'd become attached to it. As a consequence, and having decided he was going to start the year afresh, he was contemplating renting out his house in Summertown and moving to Latimer Street. Usually any property-based decision he made was reached through object-ive evaluation, but in this instance it was purely an emotional choice he was making. More than likely he'd grown attached to it because it was synonymous with two new friends whose very diverse company he valued. There had been many times since meeting Esme and Floriana when they had distracted him from dwelling on Jesse, and for that he was grateful.

He turned into East Street and stopped the car in front of his very first purchase, which overlooked the Thames. Staring at the well-cared-for house – smart pale yellow-painted rendering, white front door and white window frames – he remembered how he'd slept on a mattress on the bare floorboards in the back bedroom while he did it up.

Recalling the satisfaction he'd got from the experience, he had a sudden vision of doing the same thing in Latimer Street. The idea had instant appeal to it and he knew then that his mind was made up; moving would give him the new start he needed.

On New Year's Day, he'd heeded his brother's advice and ended things with Jesse. The relief in her voice when he'd phoned to say he didn't see any point in dragging things on any longer had told him all he needed to know: she'd had no intention of coming back to him. It was far from the outcome he had hoped for before Christmas, but now he saw that shock and disappointment, as well as a massive blow to his pride, had blinded him to the obvious, that the relationship was dead in the water.

So, enough was enough. It was time for him to move on. In more ways than one. His house in Summertown was too full of Jesse-related memories and Latimer Street wouldn't only give him a new start, more importantly, it would be something tangible in which to pour his energy, both physical and creative. He would take his time restoring the property; it would be a labour of love.

A car horn hooted and acknowledging the driver behind him, he drove back to the office in Summertown. But unable to resist the symbolic gesture, he made a quick detour to Latimer Street where he stopped outside his new home.

Yes, he thought, looking up at the attractive bay-fronted Victorian house, it would be good living here. His glance slid along towards Trinity House where he saw Euridice looking out at him through the window. Another impulse had him switching off the engine. Seeing as they were going to be neighbours, it seemed right that Esme should be the first to know of his decision.

An hour later, the afternoon light all but gone, he walked into the office and asked Denise if there was anything urgent for him to deal with.

'This may surprise you, but the world kept spinning quite happily without you,' she said, pulling open the top drawer of the filing cabinet next to her desk. She gave him a hard stare when she'd put the file away. 'You're looking pretty pleased with yourself, what've you been up to?'

'Oh, you know how it is,' he said carelessly, 'this and that.'

'Now you're scaring me, you're positively jaunty.'

He waved vaguely in the direction of her cluttered desk. 'Haven't you got any work to do?'

'Plenty,' she said. 'But you're worrying me. You haven't looked this cheerful in ages.'

'You mean, not since before Jesse dumped me?'

He saw the surprise in her face and it was little wonder. Despite knowing each other for as long as they had, he had specifically asked Denise not to discuss Jesse with him. He'd always suspected that she had never taken to Jesse and so any advice from her would have been skewed. Rarely did he put forward his personal life for discussion in the office, but Denise had got it out of him in the run-up to Christmas, that he and Jesse were on a break, when she'd asked him what they would be doing for the festive holiday.

'Yes,' she said, 'that's exactly what I was thinking. Are the two of you back together now?'

'No. And nor will we be. Have you got the Roper file? I need to speak to the planning department.'

She gave him a look that he knew of old. It said, *I'm holding off for now, but this isn't finished.* And because he was feeling generous as a result of his good mood, he said, 'I've decided to move house.' Then he told her why.

Chapter Twenty-One

It was dark when Floriana cycled home and just to make her misery complete it had started to rain. Annoyingly, if she hadn't stayed on to help in the office and discuss the idea with Tony of adding *Endeavour* to sit alongside the *Morse* and *Lewis* tours, she would have made it home in the dry.

With traffic rumbling past and icy pinpricks of rain stinging her face as she pedalled furiously along St Giles, passing the Eagle and Child on her left where, as she informed her groups, C.S. Lewis and Tolkien used to hang out together, she was conscious she had to keep her wits about her – the last time she had had any contact with Seb she had got herself run over.

To say his appearing so unexpectedly had caught her on the back foot was a massive understatement; it had stirred up no end of feelings. She was desperately trying to convince herself that she was happy Seb had sought her out in the sneaky way he had, happy that he had come to Oxford with the sole intention to reunite them.

But happiness was not what she felt. How could she when Seb's words played on constant loop inside her head?

Imogen's forgiven you. Imogen's forgiven you. Imogen's forgiven you.

Omit those words from their lunch together and maybe then Floriana could allow herself to be happy – after all, she should be happy for Seb that he was marrying the woman he loved. Happy also that he wanted Floriana back in her life. That's how friendship worked; you cared about somebody, you wanted them to be happy. Hadn't she always said Seb's happiness was as important to her as her own? So even when she forced herself to be utterly objective and accept that Seb would never view her as anything other than a friend, why couldn't she feel happy for him? Why, when she tried to give that emotion space to bloom, did she feel only sadness and the awful certainty that he was making a terrible mistake marrying Imogen?

It would be easy to dismiss her reaction as nothing more than jealousy, but until Imogen, the girls that came and went through the revolving doors of Seb's love life in Oxford, and then later after graduation when he moved to London, had never bothered Floriana. It had been a long-standing joke between them, in the same way that Seb would tease her about the duds she had got through.

A few of her boyfriends had been wise enough to cotton on to the fact that when compared against Seb, they didn't measure up. The last one, a tutor from the language school on the Banbury Road, had realised before she did that she was in love with Seb. There had been no rancour in him when he'd confronted her. 'It's not fair to you or your boyfriends to go on pretending you don't love him,' Jules had advised. At first she'd protested her innocence, declaring Jules to be mistaken, or perhaps jealous of her close friendship with Seb. 'There's only one mistaken person in this relationship,' he'd said, 'and it's not me, Floriana.' He'd wished her well and the next she'd heard he was seeing one of his ex-students, a pretty Spanish girl.

Looking back on it now, Jules probably had been jealous of Seb; it stood to reason. After all, a number of the girls who had lasted as long as a month with Seb hadn't exactly approved of Floriana's presence in his life.

However, she had known straight away that there was something different about Imogen, and not just because she was stunningly attractive and came from a very different world to theirs. No, it was actually Seb's behaviour that had alerted Floriana to the suspicion that this girl might be a keeper. He had brought Imogen with him to spend the day in Oxford with Floriana and from the moment he introduced this latest girlfriend, she had sensed a curious mixture of pride and nervousness in him. It later dawned on Floriana that he was anxiously seeking her approval; something he had never previously needed.

It was shortly afterwards that she broke up with Jules and the true depth of her feelings for Seb crystallised and Floriana finally admitted to herself that she loved him. This new-found knowledge didn't make her happy, though. All she could see ahead for herself was misery. Just endless misery. Misery that she would have to pretend nothing had changed between them and misery that she would forever be just good old Floriana; Seb's oldest and closest friend, the one he could always rely on to have a good laugh with.

Over the weeks and months that followed, she waited for her feelings to revert to how they'd once been, but it didn't happen. She also waited for Seb to tire of Imogen, but the hope was in vain. He couldn't stop talking about her whenever they spoke on the phone or got together, which happened less frequently as time went on. It was all about Seb and Imogen; they had become quite the domesticated couple and there was no room for an old pal now.

And all the while as she succumbed to the most awful feelings of jealousy towards Imogen, Floriana grew more convinced that Imogen wasn't right for Seb. She was too high maintenance. Too frivolous. Too self-absorbed. Just too plainly wrong. What was more, it was clear she hated Floriana.

On one occasion, when the three of them met up for Sunday lunch in Richmond, and while Seb was ordering their food at the bar, Imogen, in a light-hearted jokey voice and with a rise of her perfectly arched eyebrows, had said how lucky Seb was to have a friend like Floriana. 'You're like a lovely little lapdog the way you're always there for him, aren't you?'

She had been so taken aback by the sheer bitchiness of the re-mark Floriana hadn't been able to think of a suitable reply. Nor did she know what to say minutes later, when Seb had returned from the bar, Imogen had linked her arm through his and said, 'Goodness, I don't know how poor Floriana puts up with us, we're like a boring old married couple, aren't we?'

But then fate, or so it seemed, had intervened and provided Floriana with the perfect means to convince Seb that Imogen was not all he believed her to be. But it backfired horribly and Floriana ended up accused of being a liar, and a lot more besides.

Earlier, when they'd finished their lunch at Quods, Seb had asked Floriana to take the rest of the afternoon off so they could continue catching up, but she had said that Tony needed her in the office. His disappointment had been all too evident. 'If you had warned me you were coming, I might have been able to switch my shift with somebody else,' she had said when their waitress brought them their bill.

'If I had warned you, you might not have agreed to see me and that was a risk I wasn't prepared to take. And since you've been bleating on about being a pauper, put your money away, I'm picking up the tab on this.'

She had tried to make a grab for the bill so they could split it, but he'd been too quick for her. 'My reactions always were faster than yours,' he'd said with a laugh. 'Remember all those crazy games of snap we played? I recall you slapping my hand with rather too much relish on one occasion. If I think very hard I can still feel the pain of it.'

'I expect you deserved it,' she said lightly. 'If not specifically for beating me at snap, then for some other crime.'

The bill dealt with, he'd put his wallet away and helped her into her coat. It was no more than a friendly and considerate gesture, but it felt far too intimate, made her want to spring away from him. He must have sensed her anxiety and decided to confront it head on by suddenly wrapping her in a massive hug when they were outside in the cold damp air. 'Please don't be awkward around me, Florrie,' he'd said.

Helplessly, she had stood frozen in mute shock, wanting to sink further into his embrace but also wanting to break free and dash across the road to the safety of the office. Chin raised, she'd blinked hard, marshalling what was left of her dwindling strength to prove she wasn't at all awkward in his presence.

In return, tipping his head back to look at her, his gaze fixed so fast on hers she felt there was nowhere for her to hide, he took a deep breath. 'Whatever misunderstandings we had before,' he said, 'let's forget they ever happened. Let's promise never to let anything come between us again. You're the nearest I have to family. You're all I have.'

His parting words had been to extract a promise from her, to accept his offer and come to his wedding.

Mentally crossing her fingers behind her back she had mumbled the assurance he wanted, but had no idea how she would stick to the agreement. To do that she would have to find a way to over-come the damage inflicted by his blindness to her feelings and her own blinding resentment towards the woman who meant the world to him. It was, she concluded, another thing to put off, another bridge to cross when the time came.

Leaving the noise of the traffic behind her, she turned into

North Parade and, stopping off at Buddy Joe's for some pasta and pesto sauce for her supper, she then cycled on to Latimer Street where she stopped again, this time to call in to see Esme.

To Floriana's disappointment she had received news yesterday in an email from her friend Sara that she wouldn't be returning to Oxford after all; she had been offered a job as a graphic designer in Buenos Aires. A previous email had left Floriana with the distinct impression that her friend sounded happily settled where she was, so hearing that she was going to stay shouldn't have come as a shock, but it had. What was more, it had left Floriana feeling unusually alone and isolated.

So with no one else in whom she could confide, Floriana had known the moment she set off from work that she would call in to see her elderly new friend and pour out the events of the afternoon. She saw Esme as a safe pair of ears, someone who didn't know Seb and would therefore be scrupulously objective in her opinion.

But really, once again she was being disingenuous and kidding herself. It wasn't an objective opinion she wanted; she wanted somebody to agree with her and make her feel better. To go straight home now would only lead to a miserable evening spent brooding, which would end in her wrapping herself in a consoling layer of sanctimonious martyrdom and that, she knew from past experience, would never do. In contrast, Esme would cheer her up enormously.

Esme greeted her with her habitual warmth, which always seemed to be tinged with a degree of delighted anticipation, as if she had been waiting for Floriana to show up any minute on her doorstep.

'Adam was here earlier,' she said, before Floriana had even removed her coat. 'He popped in to give me the splendid news he's not going to rent out next door, but live in it himself.'

'Did he say what's brought this change of heart on?' Floriana asked, noting the animated manner in which Esme delivered the news, and which only highlighted how dismally wretched she felt. Clearly Esme was going to enjoy having Adam as her neighbour. As Floriana knew all too well, he was a handy man to have around.

'No, but I should think it's obvious, isn't it?' Esme said. 'He's making a fresh start.'

'Is there such a thing?'

Esme's expression altered at once and tilting her head to one side – putting Floriana in mind of an inquisitive bird – the old lady looked at her sharply, her greyish-blue eyes keenly alert. 'Hmm ... I think you should come and sit down by the fire and tell me what's made you say something as uncharacteristically gloomy as that.'

'Well now,' Esme said. 'You either go to Seb's wedding or you don't, a choice that hasn't changed since December when you received that save-the-day card. However, what has changed is that you now know that Seb did not send the card as a random act of politeness. But then I suspect you knew that already deep down.'

Swallowed up in the large armchair, her stockinged feet tucked under her, Euridice on the hearthrug playing with the little mouse Floriana had made for her, her young friend nodded. 'But don't forget, the location of the wedding is an important factor in the decision-making process,' she said. 'I can't afford to go swanning off to Lake Como and I absolutely refuse to accept Seb's offer to pay for me.'

'I agree, that would put you in an awkward spot. But aren't you just a little bit curious to go? It's quite beautiful, you know.'

A small frown appeared on the girl's face, but then it cleared and she said, 'I'd sooner hear about the time you were there. Go on, tell me all about it. Did you fall in love there? Did you have a grand passion?'

Esme smiled at Floriana's clever change of tack and her blatant fascination for delving into Esme's past. It had become rather an amusing game on her part to tantalise the girl with snatches of her life, often punctuated by pointing out a relevant painting and explaining how and where her father came to paint it – that was me in Siena ... and that was on the Ponte Vecchio in Florence ... and oh, that was in Venice the day we saw Maria Callas enjoying an aperitif in the Gritti Palace. There were many paintings yet to be explained, but the one which Floriana knew nothing about and which would intrigue her most was upstairs in Esme's bedroom.

'Very well,' she said, thinking that Floriana could do with something to distract her from this wretched Seb character who'd appeared out of the blue to further torment her – a young man who was plainly used to having his cake and eating it. 'I'll make us a couple of large gin and tonics and then I'll tell you about my summer at the lake. How does that sound?'

Chapter Twenty-Two

Esme had fallen completely in love with the quiet seclusion of Hotel Margherita.

After the hurly-burly of all those busy cities, it was heavenly to be here in this enchanting oasis of tranquillity enjoying the chorus of birdsong coming from the magnolia trees. It was late morning and she was alone in the dappled shade of the vine-covered terrace, save for the occasional appearance of a finch darting in and out of the branches behind her.

Immediately below the rose-covered balustrade of the terrace, there were bushy mounds of lavender that gave off a fresh tangy fragrance in the heat. Beyond this was a fountain and a wide well-tended lawn that sloped gently down to a blaze of vermilion oleanders and two stately cypress trees reaching up into the china blue of the summer sky. Between the cypress trees was an ornamental gate and stone steps that led to the water and a boathouse and jetty. A short distance from the shore, and only for hotel guests to use, there was a sunbathing raft to swim out to.

To her right, the other side of the pleached beech hedge, Alberto, the gardener, wearing the traditional *zoccoli* – wooden clogs – was clipping the low box hedge, which formed a parterre and enclosed a herb garden. Beyond the parterre was a vegetable garden ringed with fruit trees that Alberto, along with his young grandson, also took care of. Every morning Elena the cook would come out with two baskets – one for herbs and one for vegetables – and pick what she needed for lunch, then later in the afternoon she would reappear to gather what she needed to prepare dinner for those guests who chose to dine here rather than eat at any of the nearby tavernas.

It was now the middle of June and Hotel Margherita had been Esme and her father's home for nearly three weeks and one by one the days had dissolved into this dreamy paradise. They had not, as before, rushed to go sightseeing, rather they had dispensed with their guidebooks and followed Lucy Honeychurch's example in *A Room With a View*; instead of acquiring information, Esme had begun to be happy.

Just as Marco Bassani had said it would, the scenery and quality of light had truly inspired Esme's father; he was in heaven! Never before had Esme seen him so relaxed, or so free. He was a changed man, a man who no longer had to hide his talent for painting from a wife who had inhibited his gift by constantly undermining and humiliating him.

A few days ago, during lunch, the Kelly-Webbs – an American couple from Baltimore on their honeymoon – had begged her father to let them buy one of his paintings of the lake to take home as a memento of their blissful time here. Predictably William had shied away from any sort of financial transaction, but Esme had encouraged him to take the money, not because they needed it, but to convince himself that he was a bona fide artist who could sell his work for no other reason other than it was admired and appreciated.

The Kelly-Webbs' delight soon spread round the small hotel and other guests had since approached William for a painting to take home with them.

After breakfast this morning, and taking with him his canvas bag of paints, brushes and block of watercolour paper, along with a picnic lunch specially made by Elena, William had set off to explore the lake in a wooden sailing dinghy. Alberto's grandson, Cesare, a boy of only twelve years of age, had given him a lesson yesterday in how to sail the boat and as the heat of the day intensified Esme hoped her father had remembered to take his hat. She also hoped her father had been able to understand what Cesare had told him as the young boy, like Alberto and Elena, spoke in a thick impenetrable local dialect.

Thinking she really ought to summon the energy to go for a walk, Esme heard footsteps approaching.

It was Signora Giulia Bassani.

A handsome woman with heavy-lidded dark eyes, Signora Bassani was always immaculately dressed and held herself tall and proud. Often there was a brusqueness to her manner that initially had made Esme awkward around her, but she soon came to realise that the woman's coolness masked a sadness that she kept locked deep within her.

Marco had explained to Esme and her father that his aunt had been widowed during the war, just months before Italy joined the Allies against Germany. The strain of trying to keep the family business afloat in such dire times was too much for Alessio Bassani and he suffered a heart attack. He was just recovering from this when a fire ravaged the factory down at Como and all was lost. He died a month later.

For several centuries the Bassani family had been at the forefront of silk manufacturing in Como. Alessio Bassani and his brother, Romano – Marco's father – had taken over the business from their own father, but then when he was eight years old Marco's parents had died in a car crash, leaving him to be brought up by his aunt and uncle, who had a son a couple of years older than him. Alessio Bassani continued alone with the business but without his brother at his side, who, it was rumoured, was the more astute of the two, things began to slip away from him. Then war broke out.

It wasn't from Marco that Esme had learnt the more intimate details about the Bassani family, but from an English couple staying at the hotel. Gerald and Josephine Montford had been coming to the lake since well before the war – and to Hotel Margherita four years ago when it first opened – and were, as they liked to say, very much a part of the furniture, practically family if they were to be credited. *You wouldn't believe the changes we've seen here at the lake!* was a constant refrain from them. As first-timers to the hotel, Esme and her father had been singled out on arrival, not just as a captive audience, but also to be put under the Montford microscope to discover whether they were worth cultivating.

Now as she looked at Signora Giulia Bassani, Esme felt she knew rather too much about the unfortunate woman whose circumstances had been so dramatically altered as a result of the war and her husband's death. Turning the family home into a hotel to make ends meet must have come at great cost to her honour and pride. From being the lady of the house, she was now reduced to being at the beck and call of strangers who slept in rooms once occupied by several generations of the Bassani family.

'*Buongiorno*, Signorina Esme, you did not want to go out with your father today?' The woman spoke excellent English, but her words were always spoken with grave civility.

Esme smiled politely. 'No, I thought I'd have a quiet day here on my own and read.' She indicated the book on the table in front of her – *The Enchanted April*.

'You read a lot,' Signora Bassani said. 'Every time I see you, you have a book in your hands. I fear you must be very bored here at Hotel Margherita.'

'Goodness no!' Esme exclaimed. 'How could I possibly be bored here?'

'You are so much younger than the other guests, there is no one of your own age to talk to.'

People were always leaping to this conclusion but so accustomed to her own company, and that of her father, Esme really had no need of people her own age. 'Please don't worry about me,' she said, 'I really couldn't be happier.'

But later, when Esme was taking her seat for lunch on the terrace after her walk, Signora Bassani approached her once more, but this time the woman wasn't alone.

'*Signorina*, may I present my son, Angelo, to you? He is home from Milan for the weekend and if it is agreeable to you, I wondered if he could keep you company while you have lunch. Maybe you could help to improve his English – like many young men of his age, he is lazy and refuses to study as he should.'

Inclining her head in acknowledgement, Esme regarded the extraordinarily handsome man beside Signora Bassani, a man who held himself in the same tall proud manner as his mother. His thick black hair was pomaded into place with a polished sheen, and with dark intelligent eyes, a broad forehead and aristocratic Roman nose, he gave off an air of easy entitlement.

It did not go unnoticed by Esme that in the split second it took for her to observe him, he had done the same with her.

Holding out his hand, and offering a smile of surprising warmth, he said, 'Please to not listen to my *mamma*, I am the perfect student, the problem is I have not yet the perfect teacher.'

Shaking hands with him, Esme couldn't help but think that while there were a few physical similarities between him and his cousin, Marco, he was an altogether different kind of man.

This was confirmed during lunch.

Self-assured and bristling with a restless energy, he entertained her with stories about his job in Milan as a newly qualified *avvocato* – a lawyer – breaking off now and then to enquire if her *pesce persico* – the local fish from the lake – was cooked to her liking, or to top up her water glass. He was an exuberant dining companion, keeping not just her amused but the guests around them, including the Kelly-Webbs who were back from an outing to Tremezzo, and a Canadian couple who had arrived from Turin last night. Gesticulating wildly with his hands, his dark eyes flashed with humour as he gave a highly amusing impersonation of Elena scolding Alberto for dirtying the floor of the holy temple of her kitchen.

He was a natural mimic, as well as a charismatic raconteur – even in a language that wasn't his own – which for someone only four years older than Esme struck her as exceptional. But then she supposed that following the death of his father he'd had to grow up fast and adopt an older and more worldly manner.

'I believe it is Marco who we must thank for persuading you and your father to stay here with us,' he said, lighting a cigarette and pushing aside the bowl of perfectly ripe cherries Maria their young waitress had brought for them to share. The other guests had drifted away and it was just the two of them on the terrace now. 'My cousin is the good and devout member of our family. Sadly, I am –' he shrugged his shoulders expansively – 'I am, how you say, the black ship.'

'Black *sheep*,' she said gently, not wanting to appear pedantic.

He slapped his hand down on the table and laughed. 'Ah, yes, there is big difference, ship and sheep, such a difficult language you have.'

Hardly daring to imagine why he was casting himself as the bad lot of the family, Esme watched him blow a long, curling ribbon of smoke into the air. 'I think you're much too modest,' she said, 'you speak English extremely well and to the detriment of me learning Italian.'

He frowned and arched one of his well-defined eyebrows. '*Detree ... detreement*? What is this?'

'Sorry, it means disadvantage.'

His expression still one of puzzlement, she said, 'What I mean is, I shan't be able to learn your language if you continue to speak such fluent English with me.'

His expression now broke into what she could only describe as a wolfish grin. A hungry wolf at that! 'You want to learn?' he asked.

'*Sì*,' she replied, suddenly shy.

'*Perfetto! Allora*, if you are not busy, your first lesson will be this afternoon. We shall go for a nice long walk and I shall be your *professore*. But in doing this we shall pretend to my *mamma* that you are teaching me the English. Yes?'

'*Va bene*,' she replied with a complicit nod, thinking that she might learn a lot more than just a language from this charming and charismatic man.

Chapter Twenty-Three

The following day, and shortly after Angelo had returned from Mass with his mother, he invited Esme to take the steamer across the lake with him to Bellagio where he had some business to attend to. When he'd finished he would take her to the Hotel Grand Bretagne, he explained, which he was confident she would like.

Esme and her father had been looking forward to visiting Bellagio together and she saw the disappointment in his face at Angelo's suggestion. There was wariness in his expression also. But with assurances from Signora Bassani that Angelo would take good care of Esme, he agreed for her to go.

'I don't think your father approves of you spending the day with me,' Angelo said now as the steamer pulled away from the boat stop with a loud grind and clank of machinery followed by a sudden bump that had him putting a hand out to stop her toppling forwards.

'He was merely being protective,' she replied, conscious that Angelo made no attempt to withdraw his hand despite the danger of her falling having passed. 'He is my father, after all, it's his job to look out for me.'

At that Angelo turned and flashed her one of his absurdly wolfish grins. 'My *mamma* is also doing her job and says that I must behave as a perfect English gentleman. What do you think? Would not another English gentleman be boring for you? Would you not like something different? Perhaps I could play the part of an *innamorato* for you? It would be more fun, don't you think?'

Esme willed herself not to blush. 'More fun for me or for you?' she asked.

He threw back his head and laughed. He laughed a lot. But from what she had seen so far of him in the twenty-four hours since they had met, he seemed to do everything in excess. He talked, laughed and smoked incessantly – she had never known anyone smoke so much as he did. He could also, as if a switch flicked inside him, suddenly appear almost morose. But essentially he devoted himself to flirting with her; an amusement that came as naturally to him as it did to breathe, she suspected.

'I think it would be fun for us both,' he said, sliding his hand to her waist and resting it there with a firmness that felt both improper and deliciously thrilling.

As a rite of passage it was very tempting for Esme to allow herself to believe she could fall in love with this confident and charismatic man. Would the experience not make her time in Italy complete, just as Elizabeth St John had urged? Certainly standing here with him on the prow of the boat, the wind blowing at her hair and the sun caressing her cheeks, she couldn't think of a single reason why she shouldn't make the most of his attention.

As if responding to her thoughts, he increased the pressure of his hand and gently pulled her closer to him. With his other hand he pointed to a spectacular-looking palazzo in the distance with two striking *campanili*. 'For now I must concentrate and be your personal tour guide,' he said. 'That is the Villa del Balbianello. Originally a Franciscan monastery, it was built for the Cardinal Angelo Maria Durini.'

As the boat drew nearer and they cruised around the wooded promontory on which the villa was perched, Esme marvelled at the beautiful terraced gardens and the handsome loggia. 'It's beautiful,' she said.

'There is much here that is beautiful,' he said, switching his gaze from the scenery to her.

Now her face did flush and feeling the full force of his potent masculinity, butterflies took wing in her stomach. As unfamiliar as the feeling was, it was far from unpleasant.

Her father often described her as beautiful, but she had never thought of herself in that way. She was more inclined to believe what her mother had said of her, that she was too small and too thin, that she lacked the appropriate womanly curves men would find attractive, and that her waist-length blond hair was too fine and unmanageable. As for her face, in her opinion, it didn't conform to any notion of what was considered classically beautiful. 'Beauty is in the eye of the beholder,' her father constantly reminded her when she sat for a painting for him, 'and what others see in you is quite different to how you see yourself.'

After the boat had stopped at the village of Lenno, it went on to Tremezzo and Cadenabbia and once again Angelo adopted his role of tour guide, pointing out the Grand Hotel Tremezzo where Greta Garbo had stayed and the Villa Carlotta known for its colourful garden of azaleas and rhododendrons and where Esme and her father had visited; it was one of the few excursions they had made. 'And there,' Angelo said, 'is the church specially for you English protestants. Maybe next Sunday you will go with your father.' He gave her a sly smile. 'Maybe by then you will have done something bad and will be in need of forgiveness.'

Biting her lip, she let the remark go and continued to admire the view in what she hoped was a sophisticated and enigmatic manner.

From Cadenabbia, the boat swung out towards the middle of the lake where on the far shore and shimmering in a bluish haze was their destination: Bellagio.

Left to explore on her own while Angelo went for his meeting, Esme quickly orientated herself, noting Hotel du Lac on the waterfront where she was to find Angelo later, and set off.

Compared to the serenity of Hotel Margherita, Bellagio came as something of a shock; it felt crowded and claustrophobic. In part this was because it was so pretty and attracted tourists from all around the lake. It was smaller than she had imagined, and with its warren of dark and narrow cobbled alleyways it reminded her of Venice, except here the streets were all steeply inclined.

At the top of one of these narrow streets, Esme found herself in a small piazza where on her left, according to her guidebook, stood the Romanesque church of San Giacomo. A cursory glance inside the cool interior presented nothing of any great interest for her and she decided to go back down to the waterfront and find somewhere for a cold drink.

She had only gone a short distance when she caught sight of a familiar figure some yards ahead of her. Too far away for her to call out to Angelo, she hurried to catch him up, but stuck behind an elderly couple struggling to negotiate the steepness of the steps, she lost sight of him. But then turning to her left, she saw him again in a narrow alleyway.

He wasn't alone though; he was with four other men. Admittedly she hardly knew Angelo, but knowing his background they didn't seem to be the type of men with whom Esme would expect him to associate, they looked much too rough and ready, decidedly disreputable. One of them opened a canvas duffel bag and handed a bundle of paper to the man on his right who began leafing through it. It was a few seconds before Esme realised that it was a thick wad of lire notes he was not so much leafing through but counting.

An instinct she didn't question told Esme to take a step back into the doorway of a shop and, peering cautiously out from her hiding place, she watched Angelo take the money and tuck it inside the soft leather briefcase he'd brought with him on the boat, a case she had assumed contained important papers and documents for his meeting here. Never had she imagined the meeting would be with such shady-looking ruffians who, for all she knew, could be gangsters. Then a more alarming thought occurred to her; maybe they were members of *Cosa Nostra* – the Mafia?

Back in Florence and Rome there had been much talk of what went on in Sicily, of the thriving black market and the protection racketeering, and the killings. But surely that didn't go on here, not in this charmingly picturesque little town. Yet if it did, what on earth was Angelo doing mixed up in it?

No, she had to have got it wrong; she was letting her imagination get the better of her and leaping entirely to the wrong conclusion.

Later, in the garden at the Hotel Grand Bretagne, where Angelo was met with smiles and handshakes by a number of people who knew him by name, they were shown to a table overlooking the lake.

A party was in full flow, and in the heat of the afternoon sun, the air fragrant with the smell of crushed grass, couples of all ages were dancing on the lawn – the men in suit trousers and shirts with ties loosened at the neck and sleeves rolled up to their elbows, the women elegantly attired in colourful sundresses either fashionably cinched in at the waist, or cut to suit the fuller figure of the older women. They were dancing to music provided by two singers accompanied by a small band with an accordion player.

The song being performed was one that Esme was sure she recognised, and watching the rhythmic way in which the couples were dancing, it came to her where she'd heard the song before; it had been in Rome in a trattoria with her father and a radio had been playing and when this song came on everybody had joined in and sung along. Glasses of grappa had then appeared and their waiter had explained that it was a popular Neapolitan song sung by the renowned Trio Lescano.

Their seats turned towards the band, and nodding his head in time to the music, Angelo lit a cigarette and smiled at Esme. Trying to rid herself of the unease that had dogged her since witnessing him in the alleyway with those shifty-looking men, she returned the smile aware that Angelo was not the cheerful loquacious man with whom she had come to Bellagio just a few hours ago; he was in a much darker and reflective mood.

Watching the dancing couples, she wondered if he would ask her to dance. She half hoped he would, especially if he held her as close as these couples were holding each other, but the other half of her – the Esme who, at the hands of her mother, had lived a life as sheltered as that of a nun – trembled at the thought. The only dancing she had ever done had been at school, when her partners had been other girls.

'You know the song?' Angelo asked, blowing a long stream of smoke into the air.

She nodded.

'You like it?'

'Very much.' And deciding to cut herself loose once and for all from the immature Esme of her childhood, she said boldly, 'Shall we join in and have a dance?'

To her surprise and embarrassment, he regarded her with a deeply saturnine air as if she could not have disappointed him more. Crossing one leg over the other while absently flicking ash from his cigarette onto the grass to his right, at the same time attracting the attention of a waiter, he said, 'I would rather not.' Then to the waiter now standing to attention by their table, he said, '*Due martini. Grazie.*'

When the waiter left them, and feeling deflated and almost in tears with humiliation, Esme said petulantly, 'I might have liked to choose my own drink; I'm not a child.'

Angelo's jaw tightened and he stubbed his cigarette out with considerable force, even though it was only half smoked. '*Scusa*, I was forgetting my manners, of course I should have asked you what you wanted, after all, you are the independent and sophisticated young woman.' His tone could not have been more sarcastic or cutting.

Too stung to respond, Esme watched him fiddle with his packet of cigarettes, lining it up against the small silver lighter that was engraved with his initials. An eternity seemed to pass before he raised his gaze and, seeming to have regained a more insouciant manner, he said, 'I'm sorry, but I think it is not the cocktail that has made you cross, is it? Is it because I refused to dance with you?' He put a hand on her wrist and stroked it with one of his fingers. 'Is that it, *tesoro?*'

So much for shaking off her childish self! Now Esme felt infinitely more immature and about as sophisticated as a wet sock.

When she didn't reply, he stared at her with patent intent and leaning in close, he pressed his lips very lightly against hers, then slowly increased the pressure, in the same way he had increased the pressure of his hand around her waist on the boat earlier.

Her first kiss, she thought as she melted against the warmth of his mouth and tasted the bitter tang of tobacco on his breath. Remember this moment, she told herself, remember the smell of his cologne, the feel of his rough chin grazing her mouth, the firmness of his lips. Remember it all!

With her eyes closed in rapture and wonder, and her mind racing to capture the experience, she almost missed the moment when Angelo pulled away. It was the band striking up with their next song and adopting a change of tempo, causing a delighted cheer to go round the garden, that brought her to her senses with a sharp and embarrassing jolt.

What a strange day this was turning into, she thought when she tried to think how she felt about Angelo kissing her. But there was no time to measure her reaction, for their drinks arrived and after the waiter had left them, Angelo was raising his glass to her.

'*A te*, Esme,' he said, 'may you always be as *carina* and may you never forget your summer here at the lake.'

'I won't,' she said, chinking her glass against his, her composure very nearly restored. She took a fortifying sip of the drink, enjoying its cool dry flavour and the warmth that then spread to her throat. 'As good as the ones I had in Venice,' she declared, deliberately trying to show Angelo she wasn't as naive or inexperienced as he thought. 'How did your meeting go?' she asked.

'*Bene*,' he said lightly, his hand reaching for his cigarette packet and fiddling with it again.

'No problems, then?'

He shook his head and took another sip of his martini. '*Tutto a posto*. All is in order.'

As the music played on and people danced with ever more carefree enjoyment, Esme remembered Angelo's briefcase and, seeing it close to his chair, she suddenly understood why he wouldn't dance with her: he couldn't leave the case unattended when it was full of money, could he?

The realisation instantly lifted her spirits, and scolding herself for thinking the worst, that he had deliberately and cruelly snubbed her, she said, 'Perhaps we could go dancing together another time?'

He smiled broadly. '*Sì*, I would like that. It is just that today I am not in the mood to dance.'

'That's all right,' she said airily. 'I quite understand.' And without meaning to, her glance dropped to the ground where his briefcase lay. His reaction was to tuck it further under the table completely out of sight.

Chapter Twenty-Four

Out of sight was what Angelo became in the following week, but he was far from being out of Esme's thoughts.

Her father clearly suspected this and as they relaxed on the terrace, he looked up from the book he was reading and repeated the question he had asked her last night, a question she had hoped she'd answered sufficiently well to satisfy him. It appeared she had failed in that.

'You're absolutely sure you're not bored, aren't you?' he said. 'Only you've been very quiet since Monday when Angelo went back to Milan. I suppose it was much livelier here for you having him around. He's a ... a very compelling young man.'

Watching Alberto dead-heading the roses at the far end of the terrace, and all too aware that her father had chosen his words with considerable care, she said, 'I'm perfectly happy, you really don't need to worry about me.'

'But I do, Esme, your happiness is of paramount importance to me.'

'As yours is to me,' she said, turning away from Alberto to look at her father. 'What shall we do today?' she asked, changing the subject.

He drank the last of the strong black coffee which he had grown so fond of since coming to Italy. 'What would you like to do?'

'Do you want to paint? You still have that portrait of the Kelly-Webbs to finish.' So pleased had the honeymoon couple been with the picture of the lake William had sold them, they had implored him to paint another, this time a picture of the two of them with the Hotel Margherita in the background. 'It will be something for our grandchildren to remember us by,' they had joked.

'I asked what *you* would like to do,' her father said. 'As for the Kelly-Webbs, they've extended their stay by another week so there's no hurry. Actually, what I should like to do is paint you.'

'Again?'

He smiled, making the lines at the corners of his eyes in his tanned face – caused by squinting into the sun while painting – deepen. 'You're changing on a daily basis and I want to capture this latest change in you.'

Without asking him what change it was he could see in her, she said, 'Then seeing as we plan to go to Varenna tomorrow, let's do it today since everyone else has gone out for the day and we have the place more or less to ourselves.' Even Angelo's mother, Giulia Bassani, had disappeared first thing that morning for the day, something she hadn't done in all the time Esme and her father had been here.

After she had changed into a prettier dress than the one she had previously been wearing, Esme took up her position in the leafy shade of the chestnut tree, which her father had selected as the ideal location for the picture. While she made herself comfortable, she fondly watched him set up his easel and methodically lay out his brushes and paints on the wooden table placed to his right.

Settled now with her hands decorously placed in her lap, Esme considered how blessed she was to be here with her father in this wonderful place. Was it terribly wrong of her to be glad her mother had died? It was not a thought she would ever utter aloud, but one thing she knew with resolute certainty: if her mother were still alive, she would not be here experiencing this enchanting place. Nor would she and her father have become as close and as intuitively in step as they were now.

She closed her eyes and let her thoughts wander to Angelo. During dinner last night Giulia Bassani had said that he had telephoned to say he wouldn't be returning to the lake for the weekend as he'd hoped he would. Esme had tried not to show her disappointment and later in bed she had comforted herself with the thought that Angelo would surely return the following week. She had then indulged herself in imagining all sorts of romantic possibilities and scenarios for his next visit.

'I had rather hoped to paint you wide awake, Esme.'

She flicked her eyes open. 'Sorry,' she said, 'I was miles away.'

Her father raised an eyebrow at her. 'I can't think where.'

Minutes passed, during which Esme followed her father's instruction and tilted her head so that the light filtering through the canopy of leaves and branches of the tree fell in exactly the right place. She never minded posing for her father; she enjoyed the quiet time it gave them together. It also gave her the opportunity to daydream unashamedly of Angelo. Yet her thoughts about him were mixed, coloured by their outing to Bellagio and the scene she had witnessed between him and those sinister men in the alleyway. She hadn't mentioned it to anyone, because what was there to say, other than she had observed a mysterious transaction of money? What business was it of hers what Angelo got up to?

'You've moved your head,' her father said, when he'd been painting for a while. 'More to the right, please. That's better. You're thinking of Angelo, aren't you?'

'I was thinking of my trip to Bellagio with him,' she said with partial honesty. 'You and I must go there together,' she added. 'You'd like it.'

'I'm sure I would.' He paused, removed his gaze from the canvas in front of him, wiped his paintbrush on a bit of cloth, then looked directly at her. 'Will you promise me something?'

'I'll do my best. What is it?'

'I know that Angelo has had a great effect on you, but please don't let him change you too much.'

'If I'm changing, Father,' she said, choosing her words with care, 'it's because I'm growing up.'

'I'm aware of that, just so long as you don't do it too fast.'

'Meaning I must take care with Angelo?'

His brows drawn, his lips pursed as he selected a tube of paint from his box, he said, 'Yes, I believe you should.'

'You don't approve of him, do you?'

'Let's just say I would want to know him a lot better before I trusted him completely, especially with something as precious as my daughter.'

Esme was about to ask why her father felt the way he did, when her attention was distracted by the appearance of a figure up on the terrace. It was a figure that was vaguely familiar. But surely she was mistaken? Turning her head to get a better look and ignoring her father's protestations, she saw that she was indeed correct. 'It's Elizabeth St John!' she cried. 'Look, there on the terrace.'

'Good God, so it is.'

'My dear, this is just too thrilling! I remembered you saying you hoped to come to the lake, but I had no idea where you planned to stay. But fate has brought us together again. How simply marvellous!'

'It's good to see you again, Mrs St John,' Esme said, and meant it. There had always been something wonderfully refreshing and engaging about their jolly friend from Rome. Even so, and fearing the woman's voice could be heard on the far side of the lake, she was glad there were no other guests around to be disturbed. Besides Elena in the kitchen, Maria their waitress who had laid a table for three for lunch and Alberto and his grandson Cesare who had carried the woman's things up to her room, the hotel was still deserted.

Grabbing hold of Esme's hand, the woman said, 'I've told you before; you must call me Elizabeth. I don't want any formality between us. Now where has your father got to? Such a dear sweet man. He's looking well; the lake obviously suits him. How tanned he is!'

Smiling to herself, and picturing her father fending off Elizabeth's attention in the coming days, Esme said, 'He's putting his painting things away. He'll be back any minute for lunch. How long do you plan to stay?'

'Heavens! I've only just arrived and already you're trying to get rid of me!'

Esme laughed. 'Not at all. It's going to be lovely having you here with us.'

'That's more like it. Now tell me everything. How was Florence and what did you think of Venice? And what about the other guests here? Please tell me they're more fun than that stuffy lot in Rome. Goodness, one can do without another mob of that order! And have you fallen in love with a beautiful Adonis yet? I so hope you have.'

Seeing her father emerging through open French doors behind them, Esme said, 'There is somebody, but I'll tell you about him later.'

Grabbing hold of Esme's hand again, this time clutching it

to her cushiony bosom, she said, 'How splendidly thrilling, my dear, I can't wait to hear about him!'

Elizabeth St John wasn't the only surprise arrival at Hotel Margherita that day.

Already dressed for dinner that evening and making her way downstairs with her father, and Elizabeth who would be joining them, she heard voices, one of which belonged to Giulia Bassani. She was speaking in Italian and so fast Esme had difficulty in understanding her. But when she descended the final flight of stairs that led directly to the tiled hallway, her heart gave a little leap.

But how different he looked compared to the last time she had seen him. The transformation was shocking. Shoulders hunched, his face pale and gaunt, dark shadowy arcs beneath his eyes, he looked alarmingly unwell. A handkerchief pressed to his mouth, he coughed and as though the effort was too much, his body sagged and he dropped into the nearest chair; Giulia Bassani was immediately at his side. Caught between wanting to know what was wrong with him, but feeling she was intruding, Esme didn't know what to do. But then he raised his head and spotted her.

And again, her heart gave another leap as her gaze connected with that of Marco Bassani.

Chapter Twenty-Five

It was early in the afternoon and the doctor from Menaggio – a personal friend of the Bassani family – had been and gone.

It was his third visit to check on Marco since he arrived four days ago from Venice with his aunt. The diagnosis was chronic bronchitis and instructions had been given that his patient was to be confined to bed in a well-ventilated room with regular steam inhalations given, poultices applied to his chest and medicine taken three times a day to ease his cough. A light diet was advised and only when Dottor Romano permitted it would Marco be allowed to venture outdoors.

The light diet was anathema to Elena the cook who was of the opinion that doctors knew nothing and what Marco needed was building up with hearty dishes of beans, polenta and pasta. With tears in her eyes and much crossing of herself and repeated exclamations of *Grazie al cielo!* she had told Esme in the herb garden yesterday that she had known Marco since he was a small boy and had seen him nearly die from whooping cough. Ever since then he had suffered with a weak chest and every day she had doubted the wisdom of his leaving the lake where the air was so much better than in Rome where he was in his first year in seminary. And as for doing pastoral work in the orphanage in Venice, where everybody knew the air was riddled with foulness, that was surely the last place on earth he should be! To further the cause of his recovery Elena was now attending church twice a day to pray and light candles for him.

An hour after Dottor Romano's visit, clouds of smoky-grey amethyst lay thick and heavy in the sultry sky and then the first fat drops of rain began to fall. Alberto had warned them at breakfast that the lake would not be so *allegro* today. His prediction was that a cooling wind from Colico, in the north of the lake, would bring with it a change in the weather. For some reason Alberto blamed a lot of things on Colico.

Within no time of those first drops of rain falling, there was a distant roll of thunder and the heavens opened, sending guests scurrying inside for cover. In the drawing room and looking out of the rain-lashed window, the lake was the choppiest Esme had ever seen it; it was covered with racing white horses. The mountains were entirely hidden in the driving torrent.

Not heeding Alberto's advice at breakfast, Esme's father and Elizabeth, along with the Kelly-Webbs, had taken the steamer across to Bellagio for the day; Esme hoped they wouldn't have too bad a journey back. She had planned to go with them but had woken this morning with a headache, another presage of the storm, she thought now.

Alone in the elegant drawing room with its ornate cornices, Venetian glass chandelier, faded rugs and large oil paintings of preceding generations of the Bassani family, Esme wondered what to do next. For the first time during their stay at Hotel Margherita she was at a loss how to occupy herself.

Hearing the hurried tap-tap of heels on the marble floor, she turned to see Giulia Bassani enter the room. It must have been a worrying few days for her. The first she had known of her nephew being ill was when she received a telephone call from the orphanage. She had then arranged with somebody there to accompany Marco on the train to Milan where she had met him and brought him home.

'How is Marco?' asked Esme.

His aunt shook her head. 'No better, I'm afraid. Dottor Romano says it will be a long time before he is well enough to return to his duties. He also thinks the climate here at the lake is better for Marco. In summer, Venice can be so very hot and the air stagnant and particularly unhealthy for someone who has a chest as weak as his.'

Here at least was something Elena and the doctor agreed upon, thought Esme. 'I don't have any nursing experience,' she said, 'but is there anything I can do to help?'

Giulia smiled tiredly. 'You're very kind, but really there isn't anything you—' she broke off. Then, as if reconsidering, she said, 'Perhaps you could be of help. But maybe you will think it inappropriate, especially with your father not here.'

'Whatever it is, I'm sure my father won't mind. He would rather I was useful, if I can be. What would you like me to do?'

'Would you keep Marco company this afternoon? He's complaining that he is bored and sadly I am too busy to sit with him, and there is no one else. Perhaps you could read to him.'

'Of course I'll do that,' Esme said, pleased to have something constructive to do.

Sitting in the chair beside his bed, and just as his aunt had suggested, Esme was reading to Marco. She was doing so self-consciously and a little nervously.

When she and her father had spent time with Marco in Venice, she had managed to quell the initial reaction she had experienced when she'd first met him, and had gone on to regard him purely as a friend. But the reaction she'd had the evening of his arrival here – that split second when their eyes had met – had been a denial of what she'd convinced herself to be true. To her very great consternation she was forced to admit that there lay within her heart feelings for Marco that were wholly at odds with how she should feel towards him, given the life he'd chosen for himself.

'You have a beautiful clear voice,' he murmured.

She looked up from the book she was reading to him – *A Room With a View*.

'I think you're feeling so ill you would enjoy a parrot squawking to you just as much.'

A faint smile passed across his harrowed face. 'I don't think so.'

She continued reading and when she paused to turn the page, he said, 'Do you think we could leave Lucy Honeychurch and Miss Bartlett for now?'

'Of course.' She closed the book, disappointed that she had bored him so thoroughly and so quickly. 'I'm sorry, was that too dull for you?'

'No, no, it is I who am sorry, I see I have offended you.'

'Not at all. I could try reading something Italian, if you want.'

'I would prefer to talk with you if—' Whatever he was about to say got stuck in his throat as his chest heaved and he coughed. His chest rattling audibly, he coughed again, then didn't seem able to stop. His hand covering his mouth, and beads of sweat forming on his flushed face, his whole body shook and shuddered as he tried to catch his breath.

Alarmed, Esme jumped to her feet as though that in itself would somehow help him. She had never seen anyone so ill before and panic-stricken he might actually die right before her eyes, she blurted out, 'I'll go and find your aunt!'

With a grimace he shook his head and pointed to a pile of freshly laundered handkerchiefs on the bedside table. She hurriedly passed one to him, nearly knocking over his water glass as she did. Oh, what a terrible nurse she made!

Pressing the handkerchief to his mouth, he coughed violently several more times and then, as if finally spent, he lay back against the pillows exhausted, his face flushed and glistening. When his hand unfurled and released the handkerchief, Esme saw with shock that it was spotted with blood.

His body now completely inert, she stood watching the only part of him that moved – his eyes flickering restlessly beneath closed lids. Realising she was holding her breath, she breathed out slowly and sat down.

Hardly daring to move in case she disturbed him, she sat perfectly still for some minutes just listening to the rain hammering in time with her heartbeat at the window and the crashing of thunder overhead. All the while she watched him intently, taking in his face that at first glance bore a passing similarity to Angelo's, but which was in fact quite different. It was like comparing a Caravaggio painting with a Raphael masterpiece.

In comparing the two cousins, Esme could see that Angelo's attractiveness lay in the raw and petulant arrogance of his unpredictable manner. She had confided in Elizabeth, telling her all about Angelo and how he had kissed her. Elizabeth had at once declared him the sort of man she had met many times in her life. 'I guarantee he knows all too well the effect he has on a pretty young girl such as yourself. My advice is to enjoy his flattery and if you must fall in love with him, do so in the knowledge that it will be temporary and entirely one-sided; it always is when the man is in love with his own reflection. And take it from me,' she'd added with a voluble laugh, 'most Italian men are!'

Esme could readily believe that of Angelo, but surely Marco was different?

Watching the laboured rise and fall of his chest as he slept, she wished she had her father's talent for sketching and painting. She should have liked to capture how peaceful Marco looked. But to sketch a man when he was so desperately sick, what sort of an idea was that?

Easing herself forward, taking care not to make any sound that would waken him, Esme carefully removed the bloodstained handkerchief from his now open hand and, holding it between her thumb and forefinger, dropped it in a wicker basket under the bed where she could see other used handkerchiefs had been deposited.

To be on the safe side, she crept quietly from the room and went to the nearest bathroom to wash her hands. When she returned he was still fast asleep and resuming her seat she leant forward, close enough that she could practically count his long black eyelashes, thinking that he had such a gentle face. By rights he should be called Angelo, she thought with a smile.

She thought back to that first encounter with him in St Mark's Square, remembering how embarrassed she had been to be caught acting so childishly. She remembered, too, her first reaction to him, how handsome she'd thought he was, and how blue his eyes were, and how instantly disappointed she had been when he'd said he was training to be a priest.

With a wistful sigh, she wondered how he could never want to fall in love and to marry and have children.

With the rain still falling, dinner was served in the dining room that evening, and as had now become the pattern for their evening meal, Elizabeth joined Esme and her father, along with the Kelly-Webbs.

'And what does Alberto, our resident forecaster, predict for us tomorrow?' Elizabeth asked Maria as the young girl placed bowls of ham and cannellini bean soup on the table.

At Maria's confused expression, Esme said, '*Il tempo per domani, bello o brutto?*'

For answer the girl pulled a face and pointed at the dripping window. 'Rain. More rain.'

'Oh dear, that's not at all what I wanted to hear,' Elizabeth said when Maria hurried back to the kitchen – with all the guests opting to eat in tonight she and Elena were rushed off their feet. 'I was rather hoping you'd accompany me to the Villa Carlotta tomorrow, William. I'm very anxious to see the *Amore e Psiche* sculpture, I hear it's perfectly beautiful. Not to say exceedingly sensual.'

'It is,' Helene Kelly-Webb said, 'although of course it's not Canova's original, that's in the Louvre.'

'I think, darling, you'll find it's the Hermitage in St Petersburg,' her husband corrected her gently and with a look of great tenderness in his expression. He was such a gentle and adoring husband.

'Yes, of course, it is,' Helene said with a flutter of her hand. 'What a goose I am. Just goes to show my brain can only absorb so much.'

'That goes for us all,' Esme's father said diplomatically.

'Lord, I'm the biggest goose of all!' Elizabeth exclaimed with a volley of laughter that made her bosoms wobble and the other diners look towards their table. Unaware of their stares, or maybe undeterred by them, she said, 'So what do you propose we do tomorrow to amuse ourselves, William?'

Stifling a giggle, Esme kept her head down and concentrated on her soup.

'Something amusing you there in amongst the cannellini beans?' her father asked.

'No,' she said, fixing her eyes on her spoon. She knew that if she met his gaze she would laugh out loud, which would be very rude and not for the world did she want to hurt Elizabeth's feelings. But really it was so funny how tenaciously the woman had latched onto her father.

'What about you, Esme?' asked Elizabeth. 'Will you be attending to the *signora*'s poorly nephew again tomorrow?'

Now Esme did look at her father. When he and the others had returned from Bellagio, soaked to the skin and in need of a hot bath, he had been surprisingly perturbed by the news that she had spent most of the afternoon alone with Marco in his bedroom. 'I wonder at Giulia's sense of propriety,' he'd said.

Defending both herself and Giulia Bassani, Esme had said, 'She was concerned whether or not you would approve and I said you'd prefer I was of use rather than being idle and doing nothing.'

'It's not what Marco would do,' he'd replied. 'I trust him completely – it's what others will say that concerns me more.'

'It's 1950, not the 1900s!' she'd said hotly. Then more calmly:

'Besides, what do any of these people matter to us? When we leave here, we'll never see them again. I thought we'd left all those boring old-fashioned mores behind us in England.'

'So what do you think, Father?' she said now, 'will you let me?'

His soup finished, he picked up his wineglass and drank from it. 'What if you become ill as a result of spending time with Marco?'

'I'm fit and well, I doubt I'll catch anything from him.'

'Oh, do let her, William,' urged Elizabeth. 'Who knows, this might awaken a calling in her to train to be a nurse.'

'Or a doctor,' Esme piped up, glad to have somebody on her side.

'We'll see,' her father said.

From across the table, Elizabeth winked at Esme. Esme could guess what she was thinking: with his daughter out of the way, William would be conveniently free to spend time with her.

Chapter Twenty-Six

Almost three weeks since Marco's arrival, he was sitting in the garden for the first time and enjoying the warmth of the July sun on his pale face. Keeping him company was Esme and her father, along with Elizabeth and Angelo who had arrived home late last night from Milan.

Behind them, up on the terrace, Maria was clearing the lunch tables while being subjected to a severe scolding from Elena for breaking a plate. Esme had noticed the girl had come in for a lot of scolding from the woman recently and increasingly Maria's pretty face was soured with a sullen expression. Though whenever Angelo was around the expression always brightened, Esme had also noted.

Making her way slowly down the steps from the terrace, Elena approached the group with a tray of drinks, muttering all the way about how Maria could not be trusted to do the simplest thing. Setting the tray on the table in front of them, she launched into one of her fussing sessions with Marco – was he warm enough? Was he too warm? Had he eaten enough at lunch? Was he sure he wasn't overdoing it? When she had finished with him, she turned her attention to Esme.

Much to everyone's amusement, Elena was adamant that it wasn't just thanks to *Dio* that Marco had made such a good recovery, it was also down to Esme. She further claimed that Esme had been sent by the angels themselves to minister to him. It didn't matter how often Esme said she had done nothing but read to Marco or play board games with him when he had regained sufficient energy, Elena refused to believe she hadn't been blessed by God with the gift of healing.

'If that woman's praise of you continues you'll become a figure of devotion and there'll be a chapel built here in your honour,' Elizabeth joked when Elena had left them. 'Or if not an actual chapel, then one of those little shrines where people light candles and leave flowers.'

Angelo shook his head and blew a long stream of smoke into the air. 'That will not be enough for Elena, she will not rest until she has taken Esme to the Vatican to be made a saint by the Papa himself.'

'Oh, stop it all of you,' Esme said, her cheeks reddening. She hated to be the focus of attention.

Next to her Marco said, 'I think you must take your medicine of praise and swallow it like the good patient you said I must be.'

'Please don't you start as well,' she said.

Her father laughed. 'Marco, I'm afraid you'd do better to save your breath, she is completely determined to be thoroughly ungracious. See how she has stubbornly set her chin, that means she will listen to no one but herself now.'

'I disagree,' Angelo said, 'that is not the chin of a stubborn person, it is the chin of a saint!'

'Goodness!' Esme exclaimed. 'Won't you all just stop it and leave me alone?'

'But you give us such pleasure,' Angelo said, with a wink.

'In that case, I'm going for a swim.'

Rising from his chair, Angelo said, 'In that case I am in the mood for a swim also.'

They swam out to the raft and after Angelo had given her a hand up, they lay in the hot sun, the water softly lapping at the wood beneath them. Regularly swimming twice a day Esme could not only now swim like a fish, but her pale white skin had an unrecognisable golden hue to it, a sight that took her by surprise whenever she looked in the mirror. Hello, my new self, she would think with a happy smile.

But as she always did when alone in Angelo's company, Esme felt very much her old self – horribly gauche and out of her depth.

It was different when she was with Marco, there was nothing threatening or intimidating about his presence and the more time she had spent in his company during his period of recuperation, listening to his stories about his parents when he'd been a young child and his plans for the future, the surer she had felt in his company. With him she could relax and be entirely herself.

In contrast, with Angelo she always felt the need to prove

herself to him; to the point of trying to be someone and something she wasn't. During his visit home to the lake last weekend he had insisted on taking her for a drive in his new car, a Fiat Topolino. It had not been the romantic tour of the lake she had thought it would be – instead he took her to Dongo to show her where, dressed in a German soldier's uniform, Mussolini had been captured with his mistress, Clara Petacci. He told her about the missing vats of gold and important war documents that locals were convinced lay somewhere at the bottom of the lake. The gold he referred to had been wedding rings given by villagers – so poor it was all they had left to give – to support the war effort and collected by soldiers passing through the villages. 'Your Winston Churchill came last year to look for those documents,' Angelo had gone on to say. 'It was an unofficial trip, people were told, that he was here to paint, like your father, but everyone here knows the truth, that he and the British government wanted to find letters that had been exchanged with Il Duce.'

Esme had no idea if that was true, but saddened by the thought of all those poor men and women handing over their precious wedding rings, she had asked Angelo if he thought the gold would ever be found. 'Who knows,' he said with a careless shrug, 'maybe it has already been found and stolen.' He then drove back the way they had come, stopping off to show her the spot in Mezzegra where Mussolini and his mistress had been shot.

It was a macabre trip for him to take her on and Esme had wondered if it was another of his tests he liked to put her through. In the same way kissing her in the car before they returned to Hotel Margherita had seemed to be. She had allowed him to do it, but when his hands had begun to explore her body she had, after a moment's hesitation when curiosity and a tiny thrill of excitement had caused her to wonder what it might be like, pushed his hands away. He had made no comment, had merely smiled, lit another cigarette and driven on, leaving her with the distinct impression that his actions were nothing more than a perfunctory exercise for him. Which, and not at all to her credit, had left her feeling childishly sulky for the rest of the day.

Marco never made her feel this way. Being with him was infinitely more straightforward, she never had to worry that he might do or say anything improper with her. Yet there were definitely times, especially when his health had improved and their conversations became more animated, when she forgot that he was a priest in training and viewed him as she would any other man. She had said this to him once and he had laughed and said he would much prefer that she did exactly that. He didn't want to spend the rest of his life being treated as an oddity, he said, that wasn't what his calling was about.

She admired him for knowing with such certainty what he wanted to spend the rest of his life doing and had said she wished she had the same clear vision. 'It will come to you one day,' he assured her. 'Better to wait than to rush into something that is wrong for you. I had to wait until I had completed my studies at university before I really knew what I wanted to do.'

'You are very quiet today, *amore*,' Angelo said, interrupting Esme's thoughts.

'I'm often quiet,' she said, hoping she sounded enigmatic rather than just plain boring.

'Yes, but today you seem too serious.' He trailed a finger along her arm. 'Do I not make you laugh any more?'

'You haven't said anything to make me laugh,' she said.

He stroked her arm again, his fingers slowly moving from her shoulder down to the tips of her fingers. With her eyes squeezed shut, she gave an involuntary shiver. A shiver that she knew would not go unnoticed by Angelo. Beneath her she felt the raft rock slightly as he shifted his position and then she felt his warm lips kissing her shoulder, following the route his hand had just made. Then, as if her body had a mind of its own, she turned over and looked up into Angelo's face above her.

'I have been patient enough with you,' he said gruffly, his dark eyes glittering, 'now I am going to kiss you as I know you want me to kiss you.' With unexpected force his mouth connected with hers and he kissed her fully and deeply and for a very long time, his tongue forcing her mouth to open wider still.

She put her arms around his broad and muscular back, then moved her hands to the nape of his neck. His response was to kiss her with greater strength and passion, pinning her to the raft. He gripped one of her legs with his hand then, running a hand the length of her thigh, he pushed her legs apart.

But she felt nothing. She wanted to – why else would she have turned over? – but all she felt was an awareness of the mechanics of what Angelo was doing to her. It was as if she was having an out-of-body experience, was merely observing what they were doing. What was wrong with her? Why was she so passive, why couldn't she enjoy herself? Was she frigid; was that it? She had overheard girls at school discussing the problem some women had, their jokes and laughter suggesting it was not something to own up to.

Angelo suddenly pulled back from her. For an awful moment he was so still and stared at her with such contempt, she held her breath fearful what he might do or say.

'Am I boring you?'

'No!'

'What then? Why do you just lie there, like you are asleep?'

She couldn't speak.

'You have much to learn, Esme,' he said, turning from her and sitting up, the palms of his hands flat on the surface of the raft as if preparing to launch himself off. 'You should not tease men the way you do, one minute blowing hot, and then cold.'

'I wasn't teasing you,' she murmured, stung by his words. 'I'm sorry ... I thought I wanted to ... I mean, I tried, but ...' Her words trailed off hopelessly. 'I'm sorry,' she repeated.

'Desire is not a conscious decision,' he snapped. 'It is one of the most natural and spontaneous things a man and a woman can experience.'

Sitting up, she tried to appease him. 'You're right,' she said, 'I have a lot to learn.'

His mouth clamped shut, the muscles ticking at his jaw, he kept his gaze fixed on some faraway point across the lake. 'Just not with me,' he said finally.

'Perhaps not,' she murmured, realising with new understanding that she had just learnt something crucially important: she could never love somebody like Angelo. 'I'm sure I'm no more than a diversion for you,' she said lightly. After all, he wasn't going to claim to be broken-hearted at her rejection, was he? Surely it was nothing more than a glancing blow to his vanity he was suffering?

He turned his head and at the flicker of what looked like fire in his eyes, she wondered if she had been too flippant and under-estimated how he might feel.

'Perhaps,' he said slowly, 'you are no longer interested in me because you are now more interested in somebody else? Marco, for instance?'

So that was it! He was jealous of her friendship with his cousin. How petty of him. Well, enough of his accusations, she would take no more of them! She leapt to her feet. 'If you're going to start talking such nonsense, I'm going back.'

Quick as a flash, he was on his feet also, making the raft rock violently beneath them, and with a movement that took her by surprise, he grabbed hold of her chin between his thumb and forefinger and forced it up sharply. 'Look at me and swear it is not my saintly cousin Marco who interests you more now. And don't lie to me, I have seen the way you are around him.'

Filled with outrage, she glared at Angelo and thrust his hands away from her. 'You arrogant pig! Don't you dare ever touch or speak to me that way again.' And pushing past him, she dived into the water and swam back to the shore, her legs and arms powered by furious indignation and the awful and mortifying knowledge that Angelo was right.

To make matters worse, when she reached the jetty, Marco was standing at the top of the stone steps looking down at her. 'Is everything all right, Esme?' he asked, concern written all over his anxious face.

'No!' she said with a tearful cry, grabbing the towel she'd left on the steps and running past him and almost colliding with Alberto who was pushing a wheelbarrow across the lawn. 'Everything is not all right!'

Half an hour later there was a knock at her bedroom door. Lying on her bed, her swimsuit now exchanged for a dress, her hair still wet and wrapped in a towel, she ignored whoever it was who had come to pester her. In a state of abject shame, she couldn't talk to anyone right now.

A second knock followed.

And a third.

'Esme, it's me, Marco. Tell me what is wrong. Are you unwell?'

She stifled a cry of alarm. Not Marco. Anyone but him! 'Please go away,' she said.

'No, *cara*, not until I know what is wrong with you.'

'There's nothing wrong.'

'Then come to the door and prove it to me.'

Reluctantly she got off the bed and opened the door.

His handsome face drawn into a frown, Marco's worried gaze swept over her. 'You have been crying, *poverina*. Why?'

Her lips shut tight, she shook her head.

'May I come in so we can talk in private?'

She hesitated. To be alone with him now after what Angelo had said, no, she mustn't.

'Please,' he persisted, 'I am so worried about you.'

Against her better judgement, she gave in.

The door closed, he went over to the window that overlooked the garden and lake, and turned to face her. 'I think you have been crying because of something my cousin has said. Or maybe something he has done. Will you tell me what it is? Did he hurt you? I saw the two of you on the raft,' he added, not quite meeting her eye. 'I saw you dive into the lake. You looked very angry.'

She swallowed, filled with yet more shame – just how much had Marco witnessed? Oh, how could she have allowed Angelo to kiss her the way he had when all along she hadn't felt a fraction of what she felt for dear sweet Marco? Why had she encouraged a man who seemed to enjoy her discomfort, especially if he was the cause of it? What a childish and treacherous game she had been playing. 'I can't tell you,' she said. 'I'm too ashamed.'

Marco moved away from the window and came towards her. 'I am right, Angelo did do something to you!'

'No! It was me. It was my fault.'

'Esme, you are in many ways so very clever, but you are young and I know my cousin, he can be very persuasive and has a certain reputation in these things. If he made you do something you regret, it is not your fault.'

Aghast at what Marco might imagine had taken place, she said, 'It's not as bad as you think. It's just that he accused me of something and though I denied it to him, I know that it's true.'

'My cousin has no right to accuse you of anything.'

'Maybe he does if it's true.'

He stepped closer to her and placed his hands on her shoulders. 'As always I think you are being too generous of spirit. But I hate the idea of you being upset. Is there anything I can do to cheer you up?'

'Thank you, but no.'

He sighed and seemed visibly to sag before her. 'I am going

to rest now,' he said, putting a hand to his forehead and pushing back the hair that had flopped down onto his eyes. 'I am tired, but perhaps later you will come for a walk with me before dinner?'

In the end Marco overslept and didn't surface for dinner until quite late. By then arrangements had been made for Esme's father and Elizabeth to join a couple from Bath in a game of bridge after dinner and so Esme was free to sit with Marco on the terrace.

She was still deeply ashamed of her earlier behaviour with Angelo, but her overriding concern now was to readdress the balance of her feelings for Marco. Yes, she had fallen in love with him – she could admit that now, at least to herself – but since nothing would, or could, ever come of it, she wanted to enjoy his company as she always had, before Angelo had made everything sound so sordid.

To her profound relief there was no sign of Angelo that evening – as Marco had just explained, he was meeting a client in Como.

'He has a lot of clients here at the lake, doesn't he?' Esme said.

'Yes,' Marco said simply.

'What kind of clients are they?'

'The usual kind.'

'Are they Mafia people?'

Marco looked at her startled. 'Why do you say that?'

She shrugged. 'I saw him being given what appeared to be a lot of money when we were in Bellagio some weeks ago. The men who gave it to him didn't look very nice.'

Marco leant forward, his expression serious. 'You must not ever talk of this with anyone. You have not done so already, have you?'

'No. So is it the Mafia?'

He shook his head. 'The men would have been *spalloni*. You have heard of them maybe. They are smugglers.'

Esme had vaguely heard about the smuggling that went on and had even spotted the occasional Guardia Finanza boat patrolling the lake. 'Is Angelo involved?'

Marco nodded. 'Many are involved. It is a way of life.'

'But it's illegal. Angelo could go to prison, surely?'

He put a finger to his lips, urging her to lower her voice. 'What is illegal, Esme?' he said quietly. 'Is it not more illegal that there is so much poverty in our country that men and women are forced to find such ways to survive? The true crime is that ordinary people have to put up with the way our beloved country is ruled so badly. It is the bureaucracy that is the biggest crime, not hungry people seeking ways only to feed their families. Have you not thought before of the unfairness that Alberto's grandson, Cesare, had to leave school at age eleven to help provide money for the family? Does this happen in England? No! But here, too many children are denied their education at too young an age. It is wrong!'

She had never heard Marco speak this way before, so ardently. 'There doesn't seem to be much poverty here, none that I've noticed,' she said.

'I could take you to places only a short walk from here where you will see all the evidence you need to be convinced of its existence. Here at Hotel Margherita much is done to protect the guests from seeing it. We need guests to be happy so they will keep returning to the lake, bringing with them their prosperity.'

Mulling over what he'd said and experiencing a wave of guilt at the privileged life she led, Esme said, 'What does Angelo actually do?'

'He is what you call a go-between. He helps with the transactions, he makes sure the money ends up where it should.'

'Does his mother know?'

'Probably.'

'But nobody talks about it?'

Marco nodded. 'And now I see you are shocked. But please, do not judge those who do such things, not unless you are prepared to walk in another man's shoes and encounter his struggle.'

'I wouldn't dream of judging anyone,' she said.

'I'm sorry,' he said quickly, 'I can see from your face that I have insulted you. Forgive me, please.'

'Nothing to forgive,' she said. 'But why does Angelo do it when he has a perfectly good job as a lawyer in Milan? Why take the risk?'

'It's the adventure he seeks. The excitement. He wants to be part of something bigger than he is. He has a rebellious nature; this is his way of satisfying it. He hates to sit in his office all day, he would rather be a true *spallone* hiding out in the mountains and risking his life by carrying the heavy packs of whisky and cigarettes on his back.'

'Is it dangerous what they do?'

Marco nodded. 'Very dangerous. But remember, you must not speak of this to anyone. Do you promise?'

'I promise.'

Staring out at the inky night sky, the stars shining brightly like the purest of diamonds, Esme thought what a lot she was learning this summer. But mostly she thought how at peace she felt sitting here with Marco.

If only it could go on for ever and ever.

Chapter Twenty-Seven

It was supposed to be a surprise, but Elena had let the cat out of the bag yesterday afternoon when Marco had been in the kitchen helping himself to a glass of water. She had begged him, so he later confided in Esme, not to let on to anyone, especially not his aunt, that he knew there was to be a party for him this evening.

Now, on what had been the hottest day of the summer, and with everyone gathered on the terrace after dinner – friends, family and hotel guests had been invited – Elena had the honour of presenting Marco with his birthday cake. After she had carefully set it down on the table, Marco kissed her and thanked her for being such a good *nonna* to him. Calling her his grandmother could not have pleased her more, and dashing tears away from her eyes, she straightened her apron and looked at him adoringly while patting him on the cheek. Turning then to his aunt Giulia, Marco thanked her for arranging the party.

'*É un piacere*,' she said kissing him, her face soft with affection for him.

While Elena cut the cake into slices to be distributed to the guests, Elizabeth leant in close to Esme. 'I swear, if I were thirty years younger, I would do my damnedest to persuade that divine young man not to become a priest.' She laughed. 'Yes, I know what you're thinking, just the mere thought of that would have him running to the nearest monastery double quick!'

Esme smiled. 'I was thinking no such thing.'

'So what were you thinking, may I ask? That it's a tragic waste for a man as attractive as he is to become a man of the cloth?'

'I think it's a fine and noble thing he's doing,' Esme said firmly, hoping Elizabeth wouldn't pursue any further this particular line of conversation. Many times the woman had tried to lure her in to discussing Marco, but Esme had always found a way to deflect or distract her, usually by mentioning Angelo, who

Elizabeth considered excellent company, but a spoilt mamma's boy who should have been spanked more as a young child. In this instance, distraction was conveniently at hand in the form of Maria appearing with plates of birthday cake. Esme thanked the girl, but receiving not so much as a nod of acknowledgement, she was once again left with the growing impression that Maria didn't like her. At a guess, she would say it was something to do with Angelo.

When Maria had returned to Elena to fetch more cake for guests, Elizabeth said, 'Do you think your father will ever marry again?'

As relieved as she was by the rapid change of subject, Esme was nonetheless taken aback by the question. 'I should imagine only he could answer that,' she said. 'But he's been a widower for so short a time, I doubt he's given the matter any thought.'

'It wasn't a happy marriage, was it?' Elizabeth continued. 'Not from the little he's discussed with me.'

'No,' Esme said warily. Since coming to the lake rarely did she think of the life she and her father had left behind. They had arrived at the end of May and it was now August and the thought of leaving this idyllic paradise – even if it was only surface deep, as Marco had pointed out to her – and returning to England filled her with dismay. But they would have to leave, she knew that, just as the Kelly-Webbs had reluctantly left for Baltimore several weeks ago.

'Ah, William!' exclaimed Elizabeth. 'There you are, we were just talking about you, weren't we, Esme?'

'All complimentary, I hope?' her father said with a ready smile. He was looking exceptionally suave this evening in his cream linen suit that was neatly pressed and a new silk cravat at the open neck of his white shirt.

'Sadly not,' Elizabeth said. 'We were being disgracefully rude about you.'

He laughed. 'I expect I deserved it.'

'Where were you?' Esme asked. 'You missed Elena presenting Marco with his birthday cake.'

'I was inside having a word with Angelo.'

'Is he here? I didn't think he was coming home until tomorrow.'

'He arrived a few minutes ago.'

'What were you talking about?'

'Oh, nothing special.'

Esme could tell from the exaggerated casualness of his voice that her father was lying. But why? What could he possibly have to say to Angelo that he couldn't share with her? Unless it was to do with her?

Two weeks had passed since Esme had last seen Angelo and still that angry and humiliating scene on the raft was etched on her memory as though it was yesterday. How she wished she had never gone swimming that day, that Angelo had never had the chance to be alone with her. She wished too that she had reacted differently to his accusation. As it was, her anger would have only convinced him he was right. Now she dreaded seeing him again in case he decided it would be fun to goad her some more. Would he really be so petty? He was a grown man turned down by a silly young girl; surely he wouldn't have given it another thought?

'*Signora* and *signorina*, how is the cake? Do you like it?'

It was Marco and dressed in a pair of smart grey trousers and a shirt that matched perfectly the blue of his eyes, Esme thought he'd never looked more handsome. He now looked as well as he had when she'd first met him in Venice, if not better. There was a vitality to him now that shone out of his eyes.

'It's *buonissimo*,' Elizabeth answered for the two of them. 'Happy birthday to you, Marco. May all your birthdays be as jolly!'

Smiling, he handed Esme's father a plate of cake. 'Signor Silcox, for you, I noticed you had not been given any.'

William took the plate, wishing him a happy birthday.

'I hear there is to be music and dancing,' Elizabeth said.

Marco nodded. '*Sì*, this is true, I hope to have the pleasure of dancing with you, *signora*.'

'You may certainly dance with me, young man, and the pleasure shall be all mine. I shall dine out on the memory for the rest of my life!'

He laughed and turned to Esme. 'And you, Signorina Esme, will you dance with me on my birthday?'

'Of course she will,' Elizabeth piped up.

But it wasn't Marco who approached Esme first when the music started and the dancing began: it was Angelo.

'How pretty you look this evening,' he said, after giving her no opportunity to refuse his request. Grasping her firmly around the waist with one hand and gripping her right hand tightly in his left, he twirled her forcefully round the terrace which had now been cleared of tables and chairs. Remembering how she had wanted to dance with him across the lake at Hotel Grand Bretagne, it was ironic that now she was, she wished wholeheartedly she wasn't. *Careful what you wish for* – how true that was.

'Are you not talking to me, Esme?' he asked when she made no effort to respond to his compliment.

'I'm concentrating on the music,' she said.

'No, no, that is not the right thing to do. You must relax and let me guide you. That is how you learn. You follow the man.'

Suspecting he wasn't only talking about dancing, she said, 'You're assuming I want to learn.'

He laughed and squeezed her waist. 'How sad you will be when Marco, your *innamorato*, leaves the lake next week. It is why my mother is giving him such a good party tonight. It is a great kindness that she does, no?'

This was news to Esme and as distressing as it was, she kept her voice calm. 'Marco is not my *innamorato* and I'd prefer it if you didn't speak that way about him.'

'I give you permission to fool yourself, Esme, but please, do not try to make the fool of me. Not when I know that Marco desires you just as much as you desire him.' He winked at her. 'Forbidden love is the sweetest of fruit, is it not?'

Livid with loathing for him, she tried to wriggle free from his strong grasp. But he held her even more firmly, pressing her against his body that was hot and clammy with the sultry heat of the night. 'No,' he laughed, 'the dance has not yet finished. And why do you want to run away from me like a silly schoolgirl when I am only speaking the truth? Are you so scared of the truth?'

'You're hurting me,' she said, 'let go of me, please.'

He loosened his grip, but there was no way for her to escape. 'Come on,' he said, 'enjoy the music. Was it not you who wanted to dance with me when we went to Bellagio together? Oh, how I remember the disappointment on your face when I said no. Now you look like you would rather dance with a snake. Have I become so very disagreeable to you?'

'Right now, yes,' she said through gritted teeth.

'And this is because I tell you that Marco feels the same way you feel for him? Why is that so bad? Why does that not make you happy?'

'Because you're playing a cruel game and all because you didn't get your way with me on the raft. You're nothing but an arrogant and narcissistic bad loser.'

He threw his head back with a disdainful laugh and spun her round and round until she was dizzy and the lights on the terrace were a blur. When he brought her to a stop and caught her in his arms and the terrace had stopped spinning, she saw that Maria was watching them. Never did Esme think she had witnessed such hatred in a person's face as she did in that moment.

'I am the bad loser, am I?' Angelo said, jamming her against his chest, his breath hot on her face. 'Where as you, my little Esme, are a shameful liar because you will not admit your love for my cousin, instead you teased me with your kisses. It was not I playing the cruel game; it was you! You could not have Marco, so you flirted with me. I was just a poor substitute for what you really wanted. Is that not the unkindest thing you ever heard?'

'That's not true!' she cried. 'I didn't flirt with you. You kissed me and—'

'And what?' he interrupted her. 'What did you do? You kissed me back. You cannot deny that.'

'I was curious,' she said. 'Was that so very wrong?'

'It is if you were imagining it was my cousin you were kissing!'

'Please,' she pleaded, looking anxiously about her – she could see her father dancing with Elizabeth and glancing over to her, so too was Marco as he danced with a delighted Elena, her head tipped back with a beaming smile of happiness on her wrinkled face – 'keep your voice down, others will hear you.'

His dark eyes stormy, he flashed her a look that scared her rigid, making her realise that there was something inherently reckless and dangerous about him. It was just as Marco had said; there was a rebellious streak to his nature that made him deliberately seek out danger, in any form.

'Do you think I care if they hear?' he snarled. 'Would it not be better for everyone to know that I have been used and that Marco is not the saint they think him to be? All my life it is the wonderful Marco I have to hear about. Everyone loves him.

Everyone thinks he is perfect. But he is not perfect!'

'So that's what this is all about? You're jealous of your cousin and you want to hurt him, is that it?'

'Jealous? Me? What does he have for me to be jealous of? It is the fairness I want. For people not to think I am the bad one of the family and he is the good one. Has he not said bad things about me to you?'

'You couldn't be more wrong. And if you believe he would, then you don't know him.'

'Ah, of course, you have known him for five minutes and know him better than me!'

Appalled at the bitterness she was now witnessing from this man and shocked how wildly she had misjudged his character, she said, 'My father was right about you. He warned me to be careful around you and he was right.'

'Yes, your father does not approve of me, we both know that. He spoke to me earlier this evening when I arrived. He made it very clear that I was not to upset you, that I was to leave you alone.'

'And yet you have upset me.'

He smiled sardonically and to her very great relief the music came to a stop and he released her. She couldn't get away from him fast enough and without really thinking where she was going, she left behind the gaiety of the party on the terrace and slipped into the quiet darkness of the garden.

She ran the length of the lawn, passed through the ornate gate, took the steps down to the lake and sat on the bottom step, deliberately choosing a spot behind a large stone urn, which she hoped would keep her from being seen.

Her hands pressed to the sides of her face, she listened to the music now playing on the terrace, while staring at the inky surface of the water and the twinkling lights of Lezzeno in the distance. Above her, a silver arc of moon shone so brightly it had the look of being newly polished. There wasn't a breath of wind and insects buzzed and fluttered in the syrupy warm air. Somewhere, not so far away, a church bell was softly chiming.

She sighed. What a mess she had made of things, and the worst of it was, it was of her own making. Angelo was right; she *was* guilty of using him. Being as sharp as he was, he had known before she did what she was doing. Oh, she was nothing but a very silly child. Tears of self-pity filled her eyes and spilled over, streaming down her cheeks.

'Esme, are you there?'

She started at the sound of Marco's voice in the shadowy darkness and tried to hide herself further behind the urn.

'Esme?'

She held her breath, hoping he would go back to the party.

But he didn't. Still holding her breath, her heart thumping in her chest, she listened to his footsteps on the stone steps. And then he was there, looking down at her. 'Why are you hiding here?'

When she didn't answer him – her throat was too constricted with tears to speak – he sat on the step next to her. 'Why are you crying?' he asked. 'What is making you so sad?'

She shook her head. 'Nothing,' she managed to say.

He pulled a handkerchief from his trouser pocket, but instead of passing it to her, he pressed the folded white linen to her cheeks. 'There, that is better. Now tell me what is wrong.'

'I can't tell you,' she said.

'You said that before when Angelo upset you on the raft. And now you are saying it again after Angelo has danced with you.'

She shook her head. 'It's not him; it's me. I've been very silly.'

'Then tell me what it is you have been so silly about and I will decide if it is worth crying over.'

'Are you asking me to confess to you, as if you were a priest?'

He took her hand in his. 'No, *mia cara*, I am asking you to talk to me as a friend. We are friends, are we not?'

She swallowed. 'Yes,' she murmured, a fresh burst of tears spilling from her eyes.

He gently pressed the handkerchief to her eyes. 'I think I must be a very poor sort of friend if I make you cry like this.'

'Please don't be so sweet; I can't bear it. Not when I've behaved so badly.'

'Who has said you have behaved badly? My cousin?'

'No, me. I know I have. I thought I was being so clever and grown up, whereas the truth is, I'm hopelessly naive.'

'We are all naive and we all make mistakes. I have made plenty myself. For instance, perhaps it is a mistake for me to sit here with you.'

She looked up into his face. 'Why?'

'Because ever since I met you in Venice I have wanted very much to kiss you.'

She swallowed. 'Really?'

'Yes. I will never forget the sight of you spinning so happily in your red skirt in San Marco. I thought only a person who was truly happy could express joy so freely and so simply.'

She smiled at the memory.

'Every day since, I have thought of you. And wondered what it would be like to kiss you.'

'But you can't, can you?'

'I could.'

'But you mustn't.'

'One kiss would not be too bad. It is my birthday.'

'But I'll be responsible for making you go to hell, or ... or something far worse. Excommunicated before you're even ... communicated,' she said, scrabbling for the right words and failing miserably.

He smiled and took her hand in his again. 'One kiss does not mean I will be eternally damned. And I am a long way from taking my vows yet, so I am happy to take my chances. One kiss and then you must come and dance with me. Will you do that?'

She contemplated his face so close to hers, the smoothness of his olive skin, the darkness of his blue eyes and the intensity of expression within them that held her rapt, drawing her to him like a candle in a darkened room. Yet for all the compelling strength of his gaze, there was nothing to fear in it and she suddenly knew that he was not going to force her to do anything she didn't want to. This was entirely her decision.

Chapter Twenty-Eight

It was a sweet and tender kiss, like nothing she had experienced before. There was no anxiety to it, no fear that she was doing anything wrong or that she was being toyed with, as there had been when Angelo had kissed her.

With Marco, the world no longer existed; it was just the two of them and the silky, warm softness of his mouth against hers. She could sit here kissing him for eternity, and still want to go on kissing him. Nothing, absolutely nothing, would ever compare to this heavenly moment.

'Happy birthday,' she murmured, when at last they drew apart and she looked at him dazed and a little breathless.

'This will be a birthday I never forget,' he said solemnly. 'I shall remember this always.'

There was such finality and certainty in his voice, Esme's heart missed a beat. 'I will as well,' she said.

'I leave for Venice next week,' he said flatly, gazing out at the lake.

'Are you sure you're well enough to go back?'

He half turned to look at her. 'Yes, I am more than well enough. Despite what Elena might say,' he added with a smile.

'I shall miss you when you've gone,' she said. 'It won't be the same here without you.'

'I shall miss you as well.'

'Do you think you might be able to return for a few days before my father and I leave to go home to England?'

'It might not be possible, but if it is, I will come. I promise.'

For some minutes they sat hand in hand in companionable silence just staring at the lake and watching a small boat puttering by, its lights winking in the darkness.

'Would you do something for me?' Esme asked, when the boat had passed and they were left with the sound of small waves lapping at the shore just yards from where they were sitting. 'Would you let my father paint you, please? I should like to have something special to remember you by.'

Squeezing her hand, he said gravely, 'And what will I have to remember you by?'

'Given the circumstances perhaps it would be better that you forget me.'

'How quickly you have forgotten what I said only a few minutes ago, that I shall remember this moment for ever.'

'If that is true then you don't need anything to remind you of me,' she said lightly.

'But I should like something. A small token that I shall always keep.'

With a sudden thought, she smiled. 'I know the perfect thing.'

'What is it?'

'It will be a surprise for you, but I promise it will always make you think of me.'

'Then it will be something I will treasure.'

The mood eased between them, he said, '*Allora*, we must go back and join the others or we shall be missed. And you will dance with me, yes?'

'Are you sure you wouldn't rather dance with Elizabeth?'

He laughed. 'I have that pleasure to come.'

They had gone a short way up the stone steps when Esme caught the unmistakable and familiar sound of a lighter being flicked, then followed the equally familiar smell of cigarette smoke. Her heart in her mouth, she saw a figure noiselessly materialise from behind one of the tall cypress trees, the red tip of a cigarette glowing in the darkness. It was Angelo and his brooding face was a shadowy mixture of malevolence and grim satisfaction. Saying nothing, he merely turned on his heel and made his way back up the garden.

Either Marco was an excellent actor or he genuinely didn't care what his cousin thought, but not a word did he say. Esme, however, spent the rest of the night worrying just how much of their conversation Angelo had overheard. And more importantly, what he had seen.

Chapter Twenty-Nine

Her mind in a whirl, her body restless and clammy, Esme scarcely slept that night and when the first rays of daylight showed through the pearly bloom of dawn, she pushed back the tangle of bedclothes and went and sat on the window seat. She had left the window wide open and unshuttered in the hope of benefiting from a cooling breeze, but not a puff of air had blown in while she'd tossed and turned, both physically and mentally. Already she could feel it would be another stiflingly hot day.

Resting her elbows on the sill, she leant out of the window and stared wistfully at the lake and the mountains beyond which were shrouded in a shimmering apricot haze. It was a magical scene and it was no wonder her father frequently rose at this early hour to capture the first luminescent light of day.

She hadn't had a chance to ask him last night, but at breakfast Esme planned to ask her father to paint Marco before his departure next week. She had no doubt that he would know the reason behind her request, and that he might consider it unwise to return home to England with such a poignant keepsake, but she simply had to have it, nothing mattered to her more right now.

Throughout their time in Italy she had taken plenty of photographs with the box Brownie camera her father had given her, and had taken a number of photographs of Marco, one or two when they had been in Venice, but a painting of him would be so much better. She knew that her father had the skill to produce more than a mere two-dimensional picture, that he would capture Marco's true spirit – his kind and gentle nature – for it was that which she had fallen in love with.

Her head told her that it had been wrong to kiss Marco in the garden last night, but her heart said otherwise. It was that dilemma that had kept her awake. Reason told her it was not so much about right and wrong, but about reality and honesty, and when confronted with Marco's own honesty, she hadn't want to be anything but sincere with him.

The Kelly-Webbs had said that they wanted Esme's father to paint a picture of them to show their future grandchildren one day – 'Something to prove to them we had once been young and beautiful!' they had joked. Esme could now relate to that same sentiment. She had no understanding of what it would feel like to be old, but when that day came, she wanted to be able to look back and remember Marco Bassani just as he was. She wanted him – and this summer – to be preserved in time for ever.

Voices and the sound of gravel being crunched underfoot had her leaning further out of the window. It was Angelo saying goodbye to his mother; he was going back to Milan. Relief swept over Esme. Now there was no danger of bumping into him, she decided to go for an early morning swim.

Later, when she had showered and changed into a sundress, she went to find her father for breakfast on the terrace, where all evidence of the party the night before had been cleared away. She greeted her father apprehensively, convinced that everybody was watching her – she was paranoid word might have gone round that she had been seen kissing Marco.

'No Elizabeth?' she said, battling her guilty conscience and trying to adopt a cheerful tone.

'Not as yet. I suspect she might be having a lie-in this morning, she was pretty merry last night and might well be nursing a sore head. How are you feeling?'

Esme shook out her napkin. 'I've been awake for most of the night.'

'Yes,' he said softly, 'I imagined you might be. Tea? Or would you prefer coffee? I haven't ordered anything to eat yet, I was waiting for you.'

'Tea is perfect. Here, let me do it.' Reaching across the table, she took the teapot from her father and filled her cup.

Maria appeared at their table, and at the sight of her expression – there was an unpleasantly mocking sneer to it – Esme felt queasy with fear. Had Angelo said something to the girl? Or had she, too, been skulking in the shadows last night and seen her kissing Marco?

They ordered their breakfast, and when they were alone, Esme asked her father why he'd thought she might have been awake for most of the night.

'I could lie to you and suggest that an excess of excitement had kept you awake,' he answered her, 'but since I'd rather be frank, I'd sooner say that I'd never seen you looking more radiantly beautiful than when you danced with Marco last night. I doubt I was the only one to think that.'

'Oh dear. And I suppose everyone considers me a wicked and corrupting influence on him. Is that what *you* think?'

'Esme, what on earth could make you say such a thing?'

'Because we didn't just dance last night, we ... we kissed.' She'd had no intention of admitting this to him, but now that the confession had slipped out, she was glad; it felt good to say the words aloud rather than have them spinning reproachfully round and round in her head.

She watched her father take stock of this as he lowered his cup. 'I can't say as I'm terribly surprised,' he said quietly.

'Has my behaviour been that obvious?'

He frowned. 'Why is this all about you, Esme? Does Marco play no part in it?'

'You sound cross.'

'I'm cross that you should feel you alone are responsible for the situation in which you and Marco find yourselves. You're two young people who have been attracted to each other from the day you met.'

'You've known all along, haven't you?'

He smiled. 'I would have to be devoid of every one of my senses not to have guessed.'

'Is that why you didn't want me to be alone with him when he was so ill?'

'Yes, I was concerned about the appropriateness of the two of you being alone together and what might transpire, and how it would affect you, and the consequences.'

'The consequence is that I feel wretchedly miserable,' she said gloomily.

He put a hand out to her. 'Don't be miserable. I won't allow that. Instead, I want you to treasure what you've experienced here. It will inevitably come to an end, but the memory will last as long as you want it to last.'

'You sound as if you've put a lot of thought into this.'

'Anything to do with you I put a lot of thought into. It's why I told Angelo to leave you alone last night. I should have done that at the start, but I didn't want to appear too heavy-handed and, I'm afraid, some lessons in life have to be learnt the hard way.'

Filled with love for her father, she rose from her chair and hugged him. 'I don't deserve you,' she said, 'you're too good to me.'

He hugged her back. 'Nonsense, I just want you to be happy.'

When she sat down, and after Maria had appeared with their boiled eggs and toast, Esme explained about her wish for him to paint Marco's portrait.

'I was going to suggest that myself,' he said.

Tapping at the top of her egg, Esme said, 'You're incredible, you know that, don't you? You understand me so well.'

'Not incredible at all. I'm just trying to make up for the ruined years of your childhood.'

'You don't have to. It wasn't your fault. Besides, it wasn't all bad.'

'Even so, I should have stood up to your mother more. It's my greatest regret.'

'Another life lesson learnt the hard way,' she said. Minutes passed, then dipping the corner of a piece of buttered toast into the yolk of her egg, and wanting to lift the mood between them, Esme said, 'So what about you and Elizabeth? What are you going to do about her?'

Her father laughed. 'What indeed?'

'She's very taken with you.'

'Are you saying you'd like her as a stepmother?'

'She would bring some fun and laughter into your life when I'm away at college.'

'And drive me mad into the bargain!'

'Oh, she's not that bad. She has a good heart.'

'She's perfectly barmy in a very charming and eccentric way, but I intend to return home to England a single and relatively unscathed man. Now then,' he continued, and swiftly changing the subject, 'this picture of Marco: oil or watercolour, and where would you like me to paint him?'

'Oil,' she said decisively. 'On the stone steps leading down to the lake.'

They soon realised that since the stone steps were in the full glare of the sun for most of the day, there was no way Marco could sit in the scorching heat for so long. Instead, he was positioned in the shade of the majestic cedar tree on a white-painted wicker chair reading a book. Except he wasn't reading, he was chatting with Esme who was sitting to his right in another chair.

The painting took three days to complete but at no stage during its creation would William let anyone look at it and if Elizabeth or any of the other guests so much as hinted at wandering over to get a glimpse, he immediately covered it with a large cloth.

Elena was given the honour of being the first to see the portrait and took them all by surprise by bursting into tears at the sight of it. She fled back to the kitchen, her face buried in her apron. Within seconds Giulia came out to see what could have reduced her cook to such paroxysms of distress and her reaction, while less dramatic, was still a reaction worth observing. She was plainly moved by the portrait. 'William,' she murmured, 'this is an extraordinary likeness; you have captured him perfectly. *Bravo!* And though you couldn't possibly know, you have somehow caught the similarity with his father.'

Longing to see the painting for herself, Esme bounced on the balls of her feet. 'Let me see, let me see,' she cried excitedly. 'It's not fair that everyone else gets to see it before me!'

Laughing, her father invited Esme and Marco to take a look together.

'My aunt is right,' Marco said slowly, 'I do look like my father. Or, at least, how I remember him.'

He turned to shake hands with William. 'Thank you, *signore*. If you ever tire of the painting, I would happily give it a good home.'

Neither Esme or father said anything, both knowing that would never happen.

The following morning, and to Esme's dismay, she awoke with a blinding headache and nausea, which put paid to her joining her father and Elizabeth and a number of other guests on a trip across the lake to Lezzeno to see the grotto there. Alberto had taken great pleasure in telling them that Lezzeno had once been a stronghold of witchcraft and myriad grisly evil goings-on. Another of his tales revolved around a tragic love story.

'*Troppo sole ieri*' – too much sun yesterday – was Elena's diagnosis when Esme didn't make it down for breakfast. Elena consequently appeared in person with a tray of tea and a freshly baked roll with some jam, which she insisted Esme try.

She managed to drink the tea and then went back to sleep. When she woke the hotel was very quiet. The clock on her bedside table showed it was half past twelve. Feeling guilty that she had slept for so long, she tentatively sat up to judge how she was now feeling. To her relief she no longer felt sick and the hammering pain in her head had magically gone away.

Hearing a quiet knock at the door, she assumed it was Elena or Maria back for the tray. '*Sì*,' she responded.

But it wasn't either of them; it was Marco with another tray. 'How are you feeling?' he asked, coming into the room and letting the door close behind him, while solicitously avoiding looking directly at her in bed. 'Are you well enough for a glass of lemonade? Or perhaps you would prefer tea? I have brought you both.'

She hastily readjusted the bedclothes as he settled the tray on the ottoman at the end of the bed. 'I'm feeling a lot better, thank you. It's very quiet.'

'Everyone has gone out for the day. My aunt, too, she has gone to the bank in Como. It's just me, Maria and Elena here. It was Elena who said I should bring you something to drink. This is not the usual lemonade she makes, this is her special version made from her own mother's recipe. But knowing your fondness for it, I decided tea might be better for you. So you have the choice.'

'In that case, I'll have a cup of tea and work my way up to Elena's special lemonade.'

He poured her a cup and brought it over to her. 'Would you like me to leave now?' he asked, standing a few feet from the bed, his hands crossed behind his back.

Her head was telling her he shouldn't stay, but the chance to be alone with him was too great to pass up. 'Perhaps you could stay for a little while,' she replied, hoping to placate the voice of her head.

He pulled over a chair and sat down. He did it so quickly, she wondered if he was worried she might change her mind. 'To return your favour when I was ill,' he said, 'would you like me to read to you?'

'No, talk to me instead. Tell me ... tell me how I'm going to cope with never seeing you again.'

'You are going to be fine without me, Esme,' he said solemnly. 'You are going to return home to England and happily fall in love many times and then you will meet the man who will be perfectly right for you. And you will have children; a sweet little blonde girl and a mischievous dark-haired boy. They will both have blue eyes just like you.'

'How can you be so sure?'

'Because I will pray for this to happen for you. This is the future I want for you, Esme, to be the happy wife and mother in England. One day you will return to the lake and you will bring your husband and children to see where you once stayed and you will tell them you had a good friend here who loved you greatly. And who knows, we might meet again some time.'

The cup he'd given her rattled in the saucer and she began to tremble so much she had to put it down on the bedside table. 'I don't think I want to hear any more of that future,' she said, blinking back tears. 'I know we've only known each other for a few months, but I'll never feel for anyone else what I feel for you.'

'Don't cry,' he said, reaching out for her hand. 'I need to leave here knowing that I have not made you sad. You must promise me that.'

'I can't! Oh, why do you want to be a priest?' she cried, her voice rising tremulously. 'You could be anything you wanted!'

'I know that, but this is what I have chosen, and what has chosen me. Listen, *mia cara*, love does not come without sacrifice. When we choose to love someone, it will always cost us something. Remember that. Remember also that true love lasts for ever; my love for you will always be in your heart.'

'But never to see you again,' she mourned, 'that's too big a sacrifice. Won't God let you change your mind?' she persisted.

'Of course he would.'

'But it's what you want to do, more than anything else in the world, isn't it?'

'Since I made the choice I have never once doubted it, not ...' He hesitated, his gaze drifting from her face. 'Not until I met you.' He smiled, his blue eyes soft and filled with tenderness. 'But I am glad I have known such temptation; it will make me a better priest.'

She stared back at him disbelievingly. 'But there must have been girls you liked before me who … who *tempted* you?'

He shook his head. 'There has been no one like you, Esme. You are unique. Never forget that.'

His words were too much and she started to cry; she felt as if the world was ending for her. He took her in his arms and held her. She cried and cried, shuddering inconsolably against his shoulder. He shushed her and stroked her back, briskly at first, his hands comfortingly warm and sure, then slower until it was a soothing languorous caress.

'Please don't cry,' he murmured, his lips moving against her neck. 'To remember you this way will be more than I can bear. You have no idea how painful it is for me to know that I am hurting you so much.'

Breathing in deeply, she struggled to pull herself together and little by little, through her subsiding tears, she eventually fell quiet.

'That's better,' he said softly, his hands still moving in slow circles on her back and shoulders.

When she was sure she wasn't going to cry again, she sat up straighter and tilted her head away from him. She was about to apologise for making a scene, and for looking a fright, when he put one of her hands to his lips and kissed the fingertips. 'You have such a generous soul, *cara*, it is that which makes you compassionate towards others. Never lose that. If only because I fear you will need it in order to forgive me for hurting you so badly. *Ti amo tanto.*'

'I love you too,' she said.

He stroked her face and she closed her eyes. His touch was light and delicate and made her senses spiral. Trembling with joy and something else she couldn't name, she felt intoxicated with love for him. When she opened her eyes and gazed into his sensitive face, she saw a look of total adoration in it. But suddenly his expression altered and she saw a new emotion blaze in his face; it was an emotion that went deeper than just adoration. It was then that she felt the moment spark between them and his lips met hers and he kissed her deeply.

She kissed him back with sad and fierce longing, feeling the tension in him as his hands began moving over her, caressing and exploring. Her mind and body suffused with an unfamiliar warmth, she pulled him closer to her and leant back with him against the pillows. His breathing quickened and she felt the thud of his heartbeat through the thin fabric of his shirt. With trembling hands, he unbuttoned the front of her nightdress. Now at his touch, she quivered, overwhelmed by the mounting sensations he was making her feel. She watched him pull off his shirt, flinging it to the floor, and when she traced her hands over his smooth chest, he looked at her almost shyly. '*Ti amo*,' he repeated and lay down beside her.

Chapter Thirty

'Seb's invited me to his wedding,' Floriana blurted out.

It had been the last thing she had intended to say and just as she was imagining a large cartoon hand slapping her mouth shut, her sister threw her one of her classic looks, the one that said, *Oh, for goodness sake, why does everything have to be about you?*

For once Ann had a point, this wasn't the time or place to talk about Seb, this was all about their parents and welcoming them home after their three-month trip away and giving Dad the chance to show off the holiday DVD he had compiled of their holiday. While Mum had been dealing with the shock of readjusting to normal life after having everything done for them onboard ship and was reacquainting herself with the kitchen and washing machine, Dad had been in the spare room editing the epic number of hours of video footage he'd taken during the cruise.

But no sooner had Floriana arrived and was removing her hat and coat, Mum had pounced and pointed in horror at the scar on her head, demanding to know how it had happened. Explaining as briefly as she could, Mum had been appalled.

'But why didn't you tell us you'd been in an accident?' she had cried, at the same time dragging Floriana into the sitting room where the light was better and she could get a closer look. It had probably been on the tip of her tongue to say it wasn't too late to apply some arnica. Arnica and a nice cup of tea were Mum's two weapons against anything bad life could throw at her.

'It was hardly an accident at all,' Floriana had said, studiously avoiding any eye contact with her sister who was almost certainly giving her the *What-did-I-tell-you-about-not-worrying-Mum-and-Dad?* look.

Mum's interrogation hadn't let up until she'd extracted a full confession from Floriana and the news about Seb spilled.

'Getting married, is he?' Dad said now in the hush created by Mum's sudden and meaningful silence. Ever since their falling out, Floriana had insisted, a bit dramatically she could now see, that Seb's name was never mentioned in her hearing and, to their credit, her parents had respected her wishes. Though what they said and thought in private was another matter. She knew, however, only after Mum had let it slip last year, that they had sent Seb a birthday card. They didn't hear back from him though.

'That's a turn up for the books,' Dad went on awkwardly, giving an excellent impression of a man who'd been given a very hot potato to hold and was passing it from one hand to the other in the hope of dumping it on somebody else. 'I didn't really have him down as the marrying kind.'

'Who's getting married?' asked Clare, looking up from the game Thomas was playing on his Nintendo and which he'd allowed her to watch over his shoulder, so long as she didn't put her thumb in her mouth and make the squelchy sucking noise he particularly hated. 'Can I be a bridesmaid?'

'No you can't,' Ann snapped. 'It's just some silly old friend of Auntie Floriana's.'

Crestfallen at her mother's harsh tone and forgetting her brother's rule, Clare slid her thumb into her mouth and sucked on it so hard the action could have cleared a blocked sink.

'Eu-*uw*,' Thomas said, jabbing his elbow into her chest. 'That's *so* gross.'

'Take your thumb out of your mouth!' Ann barked. 'How many times do I have to tell you, you're not a baby?'

Thumb-sucking had been outlawed *chez* Brown since the New Year, but Clare's addiction to it was showing no sign of weakening. Her face crumpling ominously, she mumbled into her thumb that she wasn't a baby.

'Yes you are!' Thomas taunted. 'You're the grossest baby on the planet!'

The crumpled face gave way to full-blown disintegration and Clare began wailing while simultaneously walloping Thomas on the top of his head and proving, if proof were needed, that she was far stronger than any baby.

'Mu-*um*,' Thomas yelled, giving his sister another vicious poke with his elbow, 'make her stop!'

The volume of Clare's crying now at fire alarm level, her

brother gave an almighty shove that knocked her off her feet and, toppling backwards onto the coffee table, she knocked flying the bowls of nibbles that Mum had put out in readiness for when they sat down to watch Dad's blockbuster DVD.

'Bloody hell, you two, can't you behave for two seconds without kicking off, I'm trying to send an email.'

'Paul,' Ann reprimanded her husband, 'don't you dare swear at the children like that! And I thought we were having a BlackBerry-free day?'

'This is important.'

'Isn't it always!'

'It's all right, everybody,' Mum said with a calmness that was distinctly at odds with the speed with which she had thrown herself onto the floor to pick up the mix of popcorn, olives and crisps before it was ground into the carpet. A SWAT team wouldn't have reacted faster.

'See what you've done,' Ann hissed.

'How am I to blame?' Floriana asked incredulously. Stupid question. Of course it was her fault. It always was in Ann's eyes.

Her sister glared at her. 'If you hadn't started on about Seb's wedding this wouldn't have happened. Don't just stand there, go and fetch a cloth! Better still, get some kitchen roll and a dustpan and brush!'

The commotion dealt with and the carpet saved, and on the pretext of helping, Floriana was in the kitchen with her father – the two of them enjoying a sneaky and recuperative glug of Dad's home-made damson liqueur while the kettle boiled. 'I take it the news about Seb's impending nuptials was a surprise to you?' he said above the noise of the kettle rumbling like a jumbo jet about to take off.

She nodded.

'Will you go?'

'I don't know. He came to Oxford to see me a few weeks ago to twist my arm.'

'He's keen then, really wants you there?'

She shrugged, unable to answer.

Pouring them both another measure of the liqueur, her father said, 'Come on, drink up quick before your mother finds us and tells me off. I'm on a strict diet now, limited to just one glass of alcohol a day.' He patted his stomach. 'I've put on nearly a stone.'

Floriana scoffed. 'You look fine to me. Better, perhaps. You were whippet-thin before.'

He smiled. 'Would it be so very awful for you to go to Seb's wedding? I've no idea what went on between the two of you, but don't you think it would be an opportunity to accept the olive branch he's offering? You two were so close, it's a shame to lose a friendship, especially one that was so important to you both.'

She shook her head, feeling sorry for her father; he'd always liked Seb, had secretly seen himself as a bit of a father figure for him. 'The wedding's in Lake Como,' she said, 'which pretty much means I can't go.'

'Why?'

'Moolah, Dad.'

The kettle now boiling, he switched it off and made a pot of Mum's favourite Earl Grey tea. He then refilled it to make coffee for Paul and a decaffeinated tea for Ann. 'We could always help you out, you know that.'

'What, and have Ann accuse me of not being able to stand on my own two feet?'

'She wouldn't need to know.'

Floriana drained her glass of liqueur. 'Now you're sounding worryingly like Seb.' She explained about Seb's terrible idea to pay for her to go.

'Goodness, that's very *terrible* of him. What a swine to offer such a thing.'

'Don't be a tease, Dad, you know what I meant. I can't accept his charity.'

'It's hardly that. More like a kind gesture. As I said before, it must mean a lot to him to have you there. You're his oldest friend. Who knows, he might not have any friends now who mean half as much to him.'

This wasn't the first time Floriana had heard this; Esme had said much the same, then more recently, when she'd had dinner with Adam, he'd made the same remark.

'Are you sure you're not using money as an excuse?' her father said, hunting in the cupboard for Ann's box of decaffeinated teabags. 'There are some amazingly cheap deals on flights these days.'

'It is an issue, but not an insurmountable one,' she conceded. During dinner with Adam, and to prove a point, he'd gone on-line with his mobile and shown her what she could expect to pay. She'd argued that by the time she'd made her mind up the cheap deals would have all evaporated. 'Even more reason to book now,' Adam had maintained.

'So, it's not just the money,' her father said, 'and you didn't see me do that,' he added when he gave up rummaging in the cupboard and put a lethally caffeinated Tetley teabag into Ann's mug. 'What then is really holding you back?'

'Any chance of those drinks appearing this side of Easter?' Ann said, poking her head round the door of the kitchen.

'On their way, on their way,' Dad said, hastily blocking Ann's view of the mug and teabag that was, if she were to believed, likely to keep her up all night. Which would be a just punishment in Floriana's view, given the way Ann had spoken to her earlier. Honestly, her sister was as grouchy as hell these days; just what was her problem? Apart from the obvious – two squabbling kids and a husband who was fast turning into a boring middle-aged grump. Always quick to rush to anybody's defence, Mum claimed Paul worked too hard, that he was never off his mobile or dealing with some pressing problem or other from the office. Privately, Floriana reckoned Paul deliberately kept busy to escape the constant barrage of diktats from Ann.

Hugging Clare on her lap while they watched the DVD of Mum and Dad's trip of a lifetime, Floriana thought of Esme's own trip of a lifetime to Italy when she'd been a young girl.

It was a fortnight since that evening when Floriana had listened in rapt attention to her elderly friend's story. How tediously dull her own life story would sound in comparison.

'Look!' squealed Clare, uncorking a soggy wrinkled thumb from her mouth and pointing at the television screen that was showing a swimming pool, a row of sun loungers and a jacuzzi. 'There's Nanna in a bubbly bath!'

'So it is,' Floriana said. 'Hey, nice work in the jacuzzi, Mum, and would that be a glass of champagne in your hand?'

'It certainly is. And before you ask, my face is pink from the sun, not from what I'm drinking.'

Floriana laughed. 'Of course, Mum, perish the thought we'd

think anything else. And who's the gigantically huge man with you?'

'That's Jim Romano, he's a district attorney from Chicago. We often had dinner with him and his wife. She called him Big Jim.'

'I bet she did,' Floriana said with a laugh.

'Why's he having a bath with you, Nanna?' asked Clare.

'*Ssh!*' Ann hissed from the sofa, where next to her Paul was surreptitiously fiddling with his BlackBerry.

'I'll tell you later,' Floriana whispered in her niece's ear as on the screen Big Jim grinned a toothy smile for the benefit of the camera.

It was probably the association of an Italian-sounding name that had Floriana's thoughts drifting from her parents' cruise back to Esme's time in Italy. To her dismay, and just at the crucial bit in the story, Esme had abruptly broken off with an awkwardly murmured apology, saying she was too tired to talk any more. Floriana had respectfully left shortly afterwards and had telephoned the old lady the following day to check that she was all right. 'I'm fine, my dear,' Esme had said, 'just suffering from a surfeit of nostalgia.'

Much as she was intrigued to know what happened next in Esme's story, Floriana hadn't wanted to push her luck, though she was guilty of speculation and discussing it with Adam, concluding that Marco really must have been the love of Esme's life and that was why she had never been married.

Watching her mother posing for the camera – now in full evening wear and with another glass of champagne in hand – and listening to her father's affectionate and amusing commentary, Floriana reflected on their own romantic story – they'd met as teenagers at school, dated a while, split up, then a few years later, the way Dad always described it, he'd found himself drawn back into Mum's gravitational force field and that was that, there was no one else in the world for him: Mum was the true love of his life.

Floriana couldn't help but think of Seb. Was he her one true love? He had never actually been a boyfriend, but undoubtedly she had never felt for anyone else what she had felt for him. Would she ever? Was there a second chance out there for her, another Seb?

Or was she destined to grow old and alone like Esme? And

would that be so awful? Catching the threatening looks being exchanged between Ann and Paul as he continued to defy her by using his BlackBerry, Floriana thought spinsterhood really wouldn't be that bad an option.

Steve had assured him it would be a laugh. Which begged the question: what the hell passed for a laugh in Steve's world these days? Root canal work?

Not so long ago Steve would never have contemplated a place like this for a drink, but whether or not he was having an early mid-life crisis, he was now a proud member of Oxford's latest lounge bar in George Street, an establishment aimed at the city's so-called elite party crowd. It boasted, of all things, a 'fair door policy' to ensure like-minded people could safely rub shoulders with the select few. What a joke that was, Adam thought as he surveyed the assembled bunch of alpha males suited and booted and the ranks of girls who were trying too hard in their false eyelashes and towering heels.

'Right,' Steve had said when Adam had told him on the phone about Jesse, 'no more crying into your Adele CDs, let's get you party-hearty and back out there!'

Party-hearty was the last thing Adam felt as he tried to chat with the two girls who had latched on to them when they'd arrived. 'We're in with these two,' Steve had said with a wink. 'Got ourselves a couple of Kardashians and make no mistake! Grab those seats over there while I get the drinks. I'll let you choose which of the girls you want. But only this once, mind.'

Getting drinks was no mean feat; the bar was five deep in places and Steve had been there an age, leaving Adam to talk to the two girls. From the little conversation he'd got from them so far, he reckoned they were merely biding their time until something better came along. Apparently there was some soap star currently in a play at the Playhouse and who, it was rumoured, favoured the club – perhaps they were hoping to snag him?

Above the noise of music that was pounding the foundations of the building, one of the girls was saying something to Adam. He put his hand to his ear, indicating for her to repeat what she'd said. He caught the words *Take Me Out* ... had he watched it last Saturday? His expression a rictus of feigned interest and feeling like a hard-of-hearing, befuddled uncle that was being humoured, he said, 'No, sorry, I must have missed that.' At least he knew what programme she was referring to – he'd accidentally watched part of an episode one evening while waiting for Jesse to dry her hair before going out. These two girls struck him as ideal contestants.

With that line of conversation thoroughly dried up, they tried another. Shrieking at him, the one he thought was called Shelly wanted to know if he knew anything about the DJ here tonight. Was he any good? They'd heard R 'n' B was his thing. Adam silently groaned – the ageing deaf uncle had now morphed into the bewildered grandfather fumbling for a Werther's Original in the pocket of his cardigan.

His ears thrumming with noise and his boredom threshold severely breached, he did the only thing he could: he took out his mobile pretending that it had just rung. 'Sorry,' he said, waving the phone at the two girls and then at Steve who had made contact with a young lad behind the bar and was communicating by sign language.

Grabbing his coat, he climbed the stairs fast, dodging incoming punters, and ducked onto the street. Outside on the pavement, he negotiated the huddle of smokers and the beefy guy in the ill-fitting suit with an FBI-style earpiece standing guard over the ridiculous red carpet – his job to ensure the club's 'fair door policy' wasn't compromised.

Away from the noise, Adam breathed in the cool night air. What the hell was he doing here? This wasn't his scene. It never had been. Even in his twenties he'd been too old for this kind of place. A car with a something-to-prove exhaust and check-me-out music blasting from its four lowered windows drove slowly by. It was the final nail in the coffin of his evening and without a backward glance, he strode off down the street, thinking that all it had taken was one phone call from a friend he hadn't seen in ages, and *bam!* he'd agreed to a night from hell. Oh please! Had he really been so desperate to kick-start his social life?

He thought back to this time last week when he and Floriana had gone for dinner at the Trout in Wolvercote. Granted it had become something of a tourist trap, thanks to *Morse* and *Lewis*, but it was still a safe bet in a mad and crazy world full of elitist malarkey. Smiling, he remembered how he and Floriana had experienced a moment of being star-struck when they'd spotted

Thom Yorke and his family having a meal together. They were there just like any other ordinary family having a quiet night out; there was nobody hassling them. Driving home afterwards Floriana had burst into song with a surprisingly good rendition of 'I'm a Creep'. Caught up in her enthusiasm he'd joined in with her and they followed it up with 'Karma Police', though not necessarily with all the right words or right notes.

Thinking of Floriana, and acting on impulse, he sent her a text. He knew that if she were able to reply she would. What was more, she would say something that would cheer him up. She usually did. *Hope you're having a better Saturday night than me*, he texted.

Ten seconds later his mobile rang. 'I trump your shitty Saturday, Mr Strong, with a squally nephew and niece and a sister who can give the US a run for its money when it comes to policing the world.'

'Not even close, Miss Day,' he said, pleased to hear from her. 'I've been holed up in a club with two girls who wouldn't know where to place the US on a map.'

'But are they cute?'

'No.'

'Not even a little bit?'

'You're not hearing me, are you? I'm in dire need of immunisation from catching stupid sickness, so for the love of God say something intelligent to save me. Give me one of your amazingly obscure facts.'

There was a small pause and then: 'Did you know that Mozart had a pet starling that would mimic the music Mozart played on the piano?'

'Did he?'

'He surely did. Mozart kept the bird as a pet for three years and when it died, he wrote a poem for it and put on a lavish memorial dinner in its honour.'

'How extraordinary.'

'More extraordinary still, the bird did something that nobody could understand because, despite being able to mimic perfectly the notes Mozart played, there was one piece of music that contained a note that should have been G-major, but the bird always sang it as G-sharp.'

'Now that's one impressive starling. Almost as impressive as you.'

'Why thank you. Feeling better now?'

'Infinitely.'

'In that case, get back into that club, Mr Strong. You have a duty to perform.'

'What duty?'

'To dazzle and impress the two hotties. Go throw some moves on the dance floor.'

'Not a chance. I've had enough, I'm heading for home.'

'Wuss!'

'And a goodnight to you too!'

Smiling happily to himself, he picked up his pace and set off down the road, turning left onto St Giles where he'd left his car.

He was unlocking it when he remembered Steve. Hastily he sent him a text – *Sorry, emergency problem I had to deal with, speak to you tomorrow*. He then drove on to Summertown humming to himself.

He was letting himself in at home when he realised what he'd been humming – the overture from *The Marriage of Figaro*. Could the starling sing that? he wondered. And would Floriana and her whirring database of a mind ever cease to surprise him?

Chapter Thirty-One

It was a beautiful morning in March, the softly blue sky was clear and beguiling and from her bed Esme could see the daffodils down in the garden heralding the true start of spring, taking over from where the hellebores and snowdrops had hinted at what was to come.

Under strict doctor's orders – orders that bordered on the draconian – she was feeling wretched and confined to bed for the foreseeable future, yet the sight of those simple yellow flowers cheered her immensely. She loved daffodils; they were such valiant, no-nonsense flowers with their perfectly formed trumpets serenading a song of optimism after the long dark months of winter. A humble flower in so many ways, it symbolised friendship, which was something Esme had come to value again since Adam and Floriana had come into her life. It wasn't that she had been antisocial before she'd met them, it was simply that her previous friendships had dwindled as, one by one, her friends had died. She had known Adam and Floriana for a scant three months but had become extremely fond of them; she would hate to lose their companionship now.

On the bed with her, Euridice was kneading the coverlet with her paws, getting herself comfortable. In front of the cat was the toy mouse Floriana had made for her. She was so attached to it, she often carried it round with her in her mouth; it was like a kitten to her. 'You're in hiding, aren't you?' Esme said in a voice little more than a raspy whisper. 'You're scared to be alone with Krysta.'

Settled now, the cat blinked back at Esme, but flinched at the sound of the vacuum cleaner starting up on the landing and bumping against anything that got in its way – skirting boards, tables, chair legs, and a small cat if it should happen to make the mistake of getting in Krysta's formidable path.

Closing her eyes, Esme leant back tiredly, sinking gratefully into the softness of the pillows. She hated to be confined like this, but the terror of her health worsening and being hauled off to hospital, as she'd been threatened with, was enough to make her do exactly what the doctor had instructed so that she would recover from an infuriating chest infection which, to her dismay, had turned into pneumonia. Rest, warmth, plenty of liquids and regular nourishing food were the orders she had been given. Bless them, both Adam and Floriana were doing sterling work keeping an eye on her, as well as trying to amuse her and lift her spirits. How would she ever repay their kindness?

Adam was now living next door – though perhaps camping was a better way to describe the basic manner of his existence amongst the rubble and chaos of the rebuilding work that was going on – but as busy as he was, he had still found time to install a television and a mini hi-fi system with a radio and CD player in her bedroom, both items he said he had going spare. The television was the biggest revelation to her, not just because she had always considered it disgracefully decadent having one in the bedroom, but because she hadn't bothered with a set in years.

'But I don't have a licence,' she had said to Adam.

'Don't worry about that,' he'd assured her, 'I'll get one sorted for you.'

After she'd insisted on paying Adam to organise it, she hoped he had, as otherwise it might not be the hospital she was taken away to, but prison!

It was good of him to provide her with something to keep the boredom at bay and once she'd had the energy to stay awake long enough, she had begun to watch a selection of programmes during the day, which left her thinking that the world was currently obsessed with buying and selling property and antiques, and when they weren't doing that they were cooking.

From beyond the bedroom door the roar of the vacuum cleaner stopped and then came the sound of voices. Opening her eyes, Esme recognised Floriana's voice. Some sort of discussion appeared to be taking place, then light footsteps hurried up the stairs. At the sound of a knock on the bedroom door, Esme managed a feeble, 'If that's you, Floriana, come in.'

'And if it isn't me,' the girl asked, stepping in, 'what should I do?'

'I'll decide that later,' Esme said with a smile as Euridice went over to the edge of the bed to say hello – no longer did she spurn the girl in the way she used to. But Adam was still her favourite; her special one.

'How are you today?' Floriana asked, removing her coat and hanging it on the back of the chair next to the bed. 'Feeling any better?'

'A little.'

'Bit by bit, then.' She sat down and at once Euridice sprang onto her lap. 'I bought you some chicken soup from Buddy Joe's,' she said. 'I'll reheat it when you're ready for your lunch. Oh, and Buddy and Joe say hi and want to know if there's anything they can deliver.'

'Oh dear, you're all being so sweet; I feel I'm putting everyone to so much trouble. Shouldn't you be at work?'

'I'm on my way there next; Tony's got a group of children lined up for me.'

'What is it today, the Potter tour?'

'Not specifically, this is one for deprived children; it's to give them a taste of something inspiring, not to say aspirational. They have a tour round Brasenose, a quick look in the Ashmolean and then we end up at Christ Church for Evensong.'

'I haven't done that in a long while,' Esme said wistfully. 'I used to love going to Evensong at Christ Church; it was always the best in my opinion.'

'When you're well enough, we could go together, if you want. Better still, we'll rope Adam in and he can drive us there in his flashy new Mercedes.'

Unable to imagine having the strength or energy to go downstairs, never mind get across town to Christ Church, Esme said, 'He didn't tell me he'd bought a new car.'

Floriana smiled and rolled her eyes. 'You know what he's like, you have to wrench things out of him.'

And you're just the person to do that, thought Esme with a half smile.

'Is the doctor calling in today?' Floriana asked, stroking Euridice's back and making her purr.

'I fear he will be. He has the coldest hands of any person I've ever known.'

Laughing, Floriana bent down to her bag on the floor. 'I've

brought you something else,' she said. 'It's not a present, per se, but something Adam and I thought would be useful to you, maybe even fun.'

'You really shouldn't, you've spoilt me too much already.'

'Don't get too excited, it's only a mobile phone. It's an old pay-as-you-go one I had knocking around at home. I've topped it up for you. If you're feeling well enough, I'll give you a crash course in how to use it, if you like.'

Esme stared at the device doubtfully. 'But I have a phone, right here,' she said, indicating the one on the bedside table.

'True. But this mobile will give you the convenience of being able to contact Adam or me with a text when we're unable to answer a call from you.'

'But I can leave a message on your phones as it is.'

'Yes, but this way we can text you.'

'Would you want to?'

Floriana laughed. 'Why don't you give it a try? Most people think they won't benefit from a mobile initially, but they soon discover the convenience and fun of it. Here, let me show you how to send a text. We'll send one to Adam, shall we?'

'I don't want to bother him,' Esme said apprehensively.

'Trust me, he'll be delighted to hear from you. Then when we've done that, I'll heat up your soup for lunch.'

To Esme's profound surprise, not only did she manage to follow Floriana's patient instructions, but within a few seconds the mobile trilled in her hand and a message appeared on the screen. 'Look!' she said excitedly, putting her reading glasses back on. 'Is it from Adam?'

'Touch the icon for MESSAGE and see. That's it. What does it say?'

'*Hi Esme, I see Floriana's talked you into the mobile. Well done!*' Feeling absurdly thrilled, she said, 'How do I reply to him?'

'See, one text and you're hooked already!'

Following Floriana's instructions, Esme painstakingly tapped out a reply – *Awaiting Dr Death and his cold hands* – then tapped SEND.

A loud knock at the door made them both jump.

It was Krysta, looking as unsmiling as ever. 'I finished. I go now.'

'Thank you, Krysta,' Esme said, 'I'll see you next week.'

When the front door banged shut downstairs, Floriana said, 'She's a bit scary, isn't she?'

'She's a good worker, if a little brusque. Oh, what's this?' Esme held up the trilling mobile for Floriana to see.

'Looks like another message from Adam.'

Esme tapped the MESSAGE icon as before. 'It's more than a message, I think.'

Putting Euridice on the floor and leaning over to get a better look, Floriana said, 'He's sent you a photo. Tap there and you'll see it in a bigger format.'

'Oh, how clever, it's a picture of him at a desk. It must be his office.'

'What does his message say?'

'*Welcome to the technological age,*' Esme read. '*Next stop, the internet!* Now that,' she said with a weary shake of her head, 'I can promise you will most certainly not happen.'

'I wouldn't count on it,' Floriana said with a smile. 'Now while I leave you to reply to Adam on your own, I'll get your lunch ready. Does Euridice need feeding?'

'No, Adam saw to her first thing this morning before he set off for work.'

'What a minxy little thing you are,' Floriana said to the cat, 'you've got Adam completely wrapped around your little paw, haven't you?'

Down in the kitchen, she tipped the soup into a pan, found the orange juice and wholemeal bread she bought yesterday, buttered a slice and laid a tray to take back upstairs.

Esme had been ill for nearly a fortnight now, but today Floriana was convinced there was a definite improvement in her; there was a little more colour in the old lady's face.

It had been Adam who had been the first to realise just how poorly Esme was. He had called round one morning, not got a response from the door, and noting there were no lights on that evening when he'd tried again when he was back from work, he'd resorted to ringing her. Only then when she answered the phone by the side of her bed did she let on that she wasn't feeling very well. Which proved to be a massive understatement.

That was when Operation Esme had swung into gear and

Floriana and Adam took it upon themselves to ring the health centre on the Woodstock Road for a home visit. It had been touch and go whether Esme would have to be admitted to hospital, but to her very great relief the doctor had said she could stay at home on the condition she would be well taken care of.

Carrying the tray upstairs, Floriana thought of the first time she had entered Esme's bedroom two weeks ago. Once she had recovered from the shock of seeing her elderly friend looking so frail and ill, she had then noticed the paintings on the walls, one in particular, directly opposite the bed, a portrait of a young man sitting in the shade of a tree on a white wicker chair with a book in his lap – it had to be none other than Marco Bassani.

Every day she visited Esme, Floriana tried not to look at the painting too overtly. Or at least not do so when Esme was awake. A couple of times when the old lady had drifted off to sleep, Floriana had seized her opportunity and studied the painting in depth, desperately wanting to know what had happened next to Esme and Marco at the lake all those years ago. Not another word on the subject had Esme since uttered and certainly while she was so ill, Floriana had no intention of referring to it.

But each time she set eyes on the portrait she had the same reaction: *Where are you now, Signor Marco Bassani?*

She was at the top of the stairs when she heard ringing coming from her mobile which was in her bag in Esme's room; she quickened her step to answer it.

With her head tilted to one side and her eyes closed, it looked as if Esme had fallen asleep. Setting the tray down on the chest of drawers, Floriana grabbed her bag inside which her mobile continued to ring.

'Hello,' she said cautiously, not recognising the number that showed on the screen.

'Is that you, Floriana? It's me, Seb. Is it a good time to chat?'

Seb, no time is good to chat to you, she thought with a rush of pulsating nervous energy. 'Not really,' she said turning round to look at Esme, who she assumed would have woken by now. But the old lady hadn't stirred.

Suddenly concerned, and thinking she looked alarmingly still, Floriana said, 'Esme?'

'What did you say?'

'Sorry, I wasn't talking to you, Seb. Look, this isn't a good time, can I call you back later?'

'Tell me when would be better and I'll call you then.'

'Better if I ring you.'

There was a pause. 'But will you?'

'Yes,' she said quickly.

She cut him off without another word and approached the bed.

'Esme?' she repeated.

The moment was too reminiscent of that awful day when, home for a weekend, Mum had given Floriana a cup of tea to take in to Nanna Betsy who, since suffering a stroke, had been living with Mum and Dad. But when Floriana had gone into her grandmother's bedroom, she had been unable to wake her. She was dead.

Swallowing back the rising panic within her, Floriana bent over Esme's bed.

'Time for lunch,' she said, her voice unnervingly loud in the quiet room. Please don't let her be dead, she urged whatever unearthly power would listen to her.

Chapter Thirty-Two

At the sound of her name being called, Esme woke with a start. Disorientated by the fug of a profoundly deep sleep, it took her a moment to work out not just where she was, but who was looking at her with such an anxious expression on her face.

'I'm sorry,' she said woozily, sitting up straight and rubbing her eyes whilst trying to gather her wits, 'I must have dropped off.'

'That's all right,' Floriana said brightly, the concern now gone from her face. 'I've got your lunch ready here for you.'

'Lunch, is it really that time? Has Krysta been?'

'Been *and* gone,' Floriana said.

'Really?' Puzzled, Esme turned to look at the clock on the bedside table, but was distracted by the sight of an unfamiliar object on the bedcover. She picked it up, and slowly it came to her – Floriana had given the mobile phone to her. She then remembered their previous conversation, as well as Krysta's visit, and with her mind now clear and working properly, she suddenly felt very foolish. 'Oh dear, you're probably thinking I'm turning into a dotty old lady who can't remember what day of the week it is.'

'That couldn't be further from my thoughts,' Floriana replied, carefully placing the tray on her lap. 'There's nothing wrong in dozing off when you're unwell. Perhaps I should have let you sleep on.'

'Goodness no, not when you've gone to the trouble to make me something to eat. Besides, I can sleep when you've gone. Mmm ... this soup smells delicious. Thank you so much for doing this for me.'

'It's no trouble,' Floriana said, settling herself in her chair again. 'Don't forget to take your antibiotics, I think they may have rolled under the plate.'

Having located the tablets Dr Death had prescribed for her, Esme swallowed them down with some orange juice, briefly closing her eyes as she did so. At once she felt the pull of the dream in which she had been so deeply immersed – she had been with her father at Christ Church for Evensong and they had reached the part in the service that always moved her: the Magnificat. She opened her eyes and, stirring the bowl of soup in front of her, she reflected that since she had been stuck in bed, the past was constantly insinuating its way into her head, reminding her, like a reverberating echo, of all that she had lost.

Being ill had made her maudlin; it was not a trait she usually suffered from. Yet repeatedly she was being made to believe that the scales of life measured everything in terms of loss and gain. She had never thought that way before, she had always been happily of the pragmatic belief that one came into this world with nothing and when one no longer had the gift of tomorrow one exited the same way, with nothing.

Looking up from the bowl, she met Marco's gaze staring down at her from the painting on the wall opposite the bed – the painting that had been both a comfort and a torment.

'Don't let your soup go cold,' Floriana said quietly.

Esme smiled fondly at her young friend, amused how studiously the dear girl tried not to stare at the portrait. 'For one so curiously inclined,' she said, 'I'm surprised you've never asked me about that painting.'

Without being told which picture Esme was referring to, Floriana's gaze slid towards it. 'I was tactfully waiting for you to tell me about it. Is it the portrait your father painted of Marco?'

'It is.'

'He was a bit gorgeous, wasn't he?'

With a small laugh that made her chest rattle, Esme said, 'Yes, he was rather.'

'Do you have any photos of him?'

'I'm afraid not. Some years ago the roof leaked and all the boxes of things I'd stored up there were ruined.'

'Oh, what a shame! So this painting is all you have?'

'And all the memories,' Esme said. 'Now then, and to prove I'm quite with it, and that you don't need to worry that I'm going senile, I clearly recall you saying that you have a group of youngsters to educate and inspire this afternoon.'

Floriana looked at her watch. 'I've got another ten minutes before I need to leave. Just time to make you a cup of tea and get some more water for you. I'll call in on my way home later this afternoon.'

'Do you have your key?'

'Yes, so no worrying about opening the door to me.'

'You're an angel, you really are. When I'm better, I'm going to have to find a way to repay your kindness. You and Adam.'

Pedalling hard, knowing that she was cutting it fine, Floriana passed Keble College and because of its association with Seb, she remembered his phone call. There was no time now to ring him, she would do it later. Doubtless his purpose for ringing was to try and give her arm another twisting and persuade her to go to his wedding. He had phoned her last week, saying he wasn't prepared to take no for an answer. 'You're not scared to come, are you?' he'd asked her. As blunderingly close to the truth as the question was, it had been his jokey way to make her rise to the challenge and claim defiantly that she wasn't scared of anything.

'Of course I'm scared,' she'd joked back at him. 'I'm terrified of seeing you done up in a top hat looking like a top prat.'

'You've seen me in a far worse state,' he'd said.

How true that was.

It would be easy to say that it had all gone wrong for Seb during their last year as undergraduates, in particular those weeks in the run-up to finals, though really his problems had been going on for years. But the pressure of finals was what brought matters to a head.

True to her procrastinating nature, Floriana could put work off to the last minute with the best of them, but she was a rank amateur compared to Seb whose casual attitude towards attending lectures and handing in essays took brinkmanship to a whole new level. 'No sweat,' he'd say, 'I can knock that essay out in my sleep.' It became a sport for him to see just how far he could push the tutors. Although perhaps it was more of a sport to see how far he could push himself. But then Floriana realised it was no longer a game for him and what he was putting himself through had pushed him perilously close to the edge.

These days there was a lot of talk of so-called 'smart drugs', such as Modafinil and Ritalin used by students to get them through an essay crisis. There was also mkat which, apparently, was absurdly easy to get hold of online and was considered perfectly safe by many students who claimed it was nowhere near as strong as cocaine and ecstasy. Back then, Seb was using speed to keep him awake for as long as it took to complete an eleventh-hour essay. There was nothing wrong in what he was doing, he asserted when Floriana accidentally knocked over a cup of coffee in his room and, in the process of cleaning the mess up, found a small packet of pills. 'What are these?' she'd asked.

'Antihistamine,' he'd said, casually taking the packet from her and slipping it into his pocket.

A long silence jam-packed with tension followed. It was broken by Floriana: 'What are you allergic to, Seb, the truth?'

'Don't look at me like that. I'm just a little off my game, that's all. If I needed something to help me sleep you'd be cool with that, all I'm doing is the reverse.'

Furious, she'd called him an idiot. 'I honestly thought you were smarter than that.'

'Hey, we can't all be like you, effortlessly brilliant! Some of us have to slog our guts out. And come to think of it, you must be the only student here in Oxford not taking something to take the edge off things.'

'Oh yeah, that's right, that old safety in numbers thing – everyone's doing it so that makes it OK. What else are you taking?'

'None of your business!'

'You're my best friend, Seb, so that makes you, and what you get up to, very much my business.'

'Get off my case, will you?' he'd shouted – something he'd never done to her before. 'You're sounding like a poor imitation of my waste of a space useless mother!'

Out of all the insults he could have thrown at her, and knowing how much he despised his mother, to be likened to her was too much and Floriana had walked out of his room, quietly closing the door after her; no way was he going to fling that one at her: that just like his mother she had stormed out in a pique of door-slamming when she was losing the argument. Not that she was losing the argument, there was no argument: she was right, he was wrong. End of. Certain things in life had no fuzzy grey edges for her. As far as drugs were concerned, it was very much a black and white landscape.

She didn't see him again until a week later when he lay in wait for her at the porter's lodge of her college. The sun had not yet risen and she was on her way for the annual May Day celebrations on Magdalen Bridge.

'You surely weren't thinking of going without me, were you?' he said, pushing himself away from the wall when he saw her. Before they'd argued, they'd planned to go together, just as they had the previous two years. This time she had nominally agreed to go with a group from St Anne's.

Not another word exchanged, Seb linked arms with her and they turned out of the gate onto the Woodstock Road. Following the way he'd just come, they cut through St Giles' Church, crossed over the Banbury Road and were passing the back of Keble College Chapel when he spoke. 'I'm sorry,' he said. 'Please don't be cross with me any more. You're all I have.'

'I'm sorry too. I shouldn't have lectured you. It's just that drugs scare me. It's my default setting. You know how boringly provincial I am.'

'I know. That's why I didn't tell you. But it's no biggie, I just need something to keep me going. I only do it when I'm up against it. I'm not like you; I don't have your conscientiousness. Or your brains. If I was blessed with a near photographic memory like yours, I wouldn't need the extra help.'

'I've told you before,' she'd said, 'having a good memory just means I regurgitate what I've read. There's nothing clever in that.'

'Yeah, well, don't knock it because right now I'd be more than happy to settle for that ability.'

They walked on in silence. Up ahead of them, a lively group of May Day revellers were giving a boisterous rendition of 'Bohemian Rhapsody', which owed more to *Wayne's World* than Queen. After a bit, Floriana said, 'Seb, will you promise me something?'

'If it's within my power, sure.'

'You won't let things get out of hand, will you? Whatever it is you're taking, promise me it's only for now, that it's a short-term measure.'

'Course it is. Come on, let's not talk about it any more. I'm sick of the thought of exams and essays. I'd give anything to wake up tomorrow morning and find it's all over.'

Once more they walked on in silence and when they made it to Magdalen Bridge, the purplish sky lightened and a sense of anticipation went around the gathered crowd, most of whom had probably been up all night partying at the numerous May balls taking place. Last year Floriana and Seb had boycotted the May balls at their respective colleges and opted to do their own thing, which had been to spend the night watching camp horror movies from the sixties and seventies.

The sun had risen now, casting a rosy blush of dawn light over the Great Tower and as the bells rang out and the choristers began singing the Hymnus Eucharisticus, Floriana felt a wave of intense emotion engulf her. She knew it wasn't the done thing to admit it, but she loved every bit of Oxford's pomp and ridiculous circumstance. The city was steeped in ceremonial tradition and secretly she loved being a part of it – she particularly loved the idea that in her own small way she was adding her own insignificant footprint into the sands of time.

With nearly everyone now drifting away and following the morris dancers down to Radcliffe Square, Seb migrated towards a quiet spot on the bridge. Resting his elbows on the stone parapet, he leant over as if his eye had been caught by something in the water below. He was leaning so far over Floriana moved in closer and instinctively put a hand out to him.

'I wonder what would happen to me if I jumped,' he said morosely.

Unnerved by his tone, she kept a hand on his arm. 'You'd either die or break your neck,' she said. 'You're not Superman,' she added more lightly.

'I'm being serious,' he said.

'So am I.' Over the years there had been too many students either drunk or imagining themselves invincible who had come to grief by hurling themselves into the shallow waters of the Cherwell. The roll-call made for chilling reading.

As if she hadn't spoken, he said, 'If I jumped and broke my neck, what would happen to me? Who would care?'

'I'd care,' she said fiercely, dispensing with any attempt to lighten the mood, at the same time tugging at his arm to pull him back. 'I'd care more than words can say.'

'You'd be the only one,' he said.

She knew what he was saying, that he had no family to speak

of – these days neither his mother nor his father paid him more than a cursory interest. Guilt money, as Seb referred to the monthly payments which arrived in his bank account, was the only point of contact he had with his father. For years there hadn't even been that, but whether his financial situation had improved or his conscience had got the better of him, the man had a last done one decent thing for his son.

As for Seb's mother, she only got in touch to whinge tearfully that she was all alone and nobody cared, or to announce that she had just met the love of her life – the see-saw of self-absorption happening with increasing regularity.

'My parents would care if anything happened to you,' Floriana said, 'even my horrible sister Ann would care. God, can you just imagine her visiting you in hospital and you not being able to escape from her? Now that's what I call a fate worse than death!'

'Sometimes,' he said, again as though he was in his own world and hadn't heard her, 'I wish the whole thing was over.'

'What? Oxford?'

'No. Everything. I wish it was all over.'

He then turned and looked at her. Really looked at her and what she saw made her blood run cold. There was a terrible bleak emptiness to his eyes; the golden flecks of amber were hardly visible his pupils were so large. A stone of dread plunged deep inside her. This was not someone play-acting to get attention, this was real. Very likely Seb was depressed. Oxford did that to some people. It was the pressure. For some it even made them suicidal. Sorrow and fear surged through her. How had he hidden this from her? Why hadn't she guessed he felt this way? Was it the effect of the pills he'd been taking? Was he taking more than just something to help him meet an essay deadline?

She was about to say something, when he kicked at the stone-work of the bridge. 'Let's go,' he said, as though suddenly bored. 'I could murder some breakfast and a very large Bloody Mary.'

It was while they were tucking into their traditional May Day breakfast specials – eggs, bacon, sausages, fried bread, beans and tomatoes and two large Bloody Marys – that Seb looked around the café at the other students and shook his head in a display of withering disgust. 'I don't fit in here,' he said, 'I'm not like these people. I'm an outsider.'

'That's how most of us feel,' she countered, knowing he was

referring to the students who came from a very different background to theirs, the ones who had been kitted out at birth at Nobs & Toffs by royal appointment.

'No it's not. It's not how *you* feel, is it? Not really. *You* fit in.'

Feeling as if he was accusing her of something dreadful, she said, 'So do you. You have lots of friends here. More than me. You're always out doing stuff. And don't get me started on your high-speed love life!'

He puffed out his cheeks and exhaled deeply. 'It's all one big fake,' he said. 'I do what I have to just to keep pace, to look like I fit in. What I hate most is knowing how hard I try to conform; that's because I have nothing of any originality to offer. Whereas you, Florrie, you're a one-off, you go your own way because you have the confidence not to care what anyone thinks. You believe in yourself. I'm the same as your sister, Ann-without-an-E, I need to blend in.'

'Seb,' she said in stunned disbelief, 'how can you say that? You've never once indicated you felt this way. Where's this come from?'

He stabbed viciously at the yolk of his egg with a piece of fried bread. 'Maybe I used to be better at kidding myself. Now I'm facing up to the reality of just how pathetic I am.'

'There's nothing remotely pathetic about you,' she said, anguished. 'There never has been. And to me you're more of an original than I am. I've always looked up to you and been so proud to be your friend.'

He grimaced. 'Then you shouldn't. Trust me, you really shouldn't.'

She chewed on a piece of bacon, but found herself having to force it down with a large gulp of her Bloody Mary. Discovering how desperately unhappy her best friend was had taken away her appetite. 'I always thought the reason we get on so well is because we're two of a kind,' she said.

He shook his head. 'In some ways, yes, but one big defining difference between us right now is that you'll be sad to leave this place and I won't. I can't wait to leave.'

He was right; she was going to hate the day when she left. Already she had been thinking of ways to stay on in Oxford, but so far nothing had stuck. Typical her, she was putting the future on hold. She wasn't one of life's great planners; she just let things fall into her lap. Did that mean she also let things slide? Had she let her friendship slide with Seb and in so doing had she missed how depressed he was?

Looking across the table, she said, 'When did it change, Seb? When did your world become so black? When did I miss that happening? We used to tell each other everything. Now I feel like I don't know you.'

Except she didn't say any of that. She didn't get the chance. Downing his Bloody Mary and ordering another, Seb insisted that she cheer him up by agreeing to go backpacking round the Greek Islands with him, something they had talked about before but had never got around to doing.

Relieved to see his mood instantly lift, she played along with him, deciding she wouldn't push him now; it would keep for another time. Why drag him down yet further?

It was later that she realised she had been a coward for not pushing him to open up to her. It was yet another example of her putting something off.

Looking back on it now, it was nothing short of a miracle that Seb not only made it through his finals, but that he didn't end up dead.

Their faces lit up in the softly glowing lamplight, the party of schoolchildren were spellbound as they sat in the choir stalls in Christ Church Cathedral. They had started out the tour in Radcliffe Square full of high-spirited bravado, some of them giving off a-couldn't-care-less attitude of OK *then, show us what you've got!* She had seen it before and was always confident she could win them round. The highlight of the tour was always Christ Church College. In full Professor McGonagall mode, Floriana had shown them the cloisters and quads that had featured in the Harry Potter films, along with the spot where the Professor had first greeted Harry when he'd entered Hogwarts with the other first-year students. Next she had taken them to see the Great Dining Room that had been replicated in the film studio.

Watching the awed expressions on the faces of the children as they listened to the choir, Floriana thought of Esme and the utter relief she had experienced when the old lady had stirred. Her relief had been so great she had very nearly scooped her up in a big hug, but then that would have necessitated explaining why, and to admit she'd been terrified Esme was dead was perhaps not the most sensitive of things to say.

After the children had climbed aboard their coach with their teachers and she'd waved them goodbye, Floriana went back to the office to deal with some paperwork for Tony and then set off for home.

Once again, as she pedalled her way through the traffic, she remembered she had yet to ring Seb. Knowing she wouldn't get home for some time yet – she was going to call in on Esme and have an early supper with her – she stopped off on Parks Road, locked her bicycle to the railings and went into the park.

No more procrastinating, she told herself as she followed the path towards the area where she and Seb had often eaten their lunch while throwing chunks of bread to the ducks.

The sadness of remembering Seb's awful last term here had made her come to an important decision. Twice now she had very nearly lost him, now she had been given another chance to have him back in her life. It might not be how she wanted it to be between them, but having him as a friend again would be better than not at all.

She had promised once that she would never let him down, that she would always be there for him, now she was going to live up to that promise. She would somehow find the money and go to Lake Como and she would watch Seb marry the woman he loved and she would be happy for him. Because what was the alternative?

Settled on the bench where they had sat so many times before, Floriana took out her mobile. Do it now, she told herself. No more putting it off. Say you'll be there for him.

Chapter Thirty-Three

'What you need, and I believe this is the correct turn of phrase, is a plus-one. That would make it less of an ordeal for you, wouldn't it?'

In the week that had passed since Floriana had told Esme and Adam that she had decided to go to Seb's wedding, it hadn't crossed her mind to take anyone with her. Who would she take anyway?

In answer to her non-committal response, Esme raised her voice above the high-pitched scream of the hairdryer. 'You know who would be perfect to go with you, don't you?' she said.

Floriana switched off the hairdryer and regarded Esme in the dressing table mirror. 'Who?'

'Adam, of course. He'd be the ideal escort for you. Not only would he be a reassuring shoulder on which to lean, should things prove difficult, but he'd be marvellous company. Why don't you ask him?'

Floriana gave a short laugh. 'Have those antibiotics gone to your head?'

Esme tutted. 'Now why would you ask that? I think it's a perfectly reasonable suggestion.'

'Perfectly reasonable if Adam's mad enough to go all that way to spend a weekend in Italy with a bunch of people he's never met before, not to say pretend to be my partner.'

'Who said anything about him pretending to be your partner? Can't he be what he is, your friend?'

Glad that Adam was downstairs in the kitchen and there was no danger of him overhearing, Floriana said, 'But people will assume he's my partner. He'd hate that. It would be hideously embarrassing.'

'What tommyrot! He'd be proud to be there with you. What's more, you could treat it as a little holiday, a mini break. Heaven only knows the two of you could benefit from some fun in your lives. It's work, work, work with the two of you, you never stop. You need to live a little.' The old lady paused while she clipped on a pair of pearl earrings. 'Why don't you ask him, dear? I'm sure you'd enjoy yourself much more having him at your side. He would be great moral support for you.'

Outside on the landing, the door ajar, Adam waited to hear what Floriana said next. But all he heard was the sound of the hairdryer starting up again.

Thinking they might worry how much he had overheard, he decided not to tell them dinner would soon be ready; he'd come back in a few minutes. With Euridice padding alongside him, he went quietly back downstairs to the kitchen.

Taking the chicken out of the oven to rest, he covered it with foil then put a pan of water on the hob. When it was boiling he added frozen peas, lowered the heat to a gentle simmer, then went to announce that dinner would be served in ten minutes.

In the weeks that Esme had been ill, he had enjoyed the routine he and Floriana had slipped into. Originally the idea had been to share the load and divide the visits between them, but invariably, depending on their work commitments, they had spent many an evening together here at Trinity House. After they'd eaten, and if Esme was up to it, they would play cards or get the Scrabble board out. It went without saying that Scrabble was not his game, he was constantly misspelling words, but having a face made for poker – as Floriana teased him – he was on safer ground there. It was one evening while he was shuffling and dealing the cards for a game of rummy that he remembered that this was the very week when he and Jesse should have been on holiday in St Lucia. The trip had long since been cancelled and as surprising as it was to him, he could honestly say Jesse rarely figured in his thoughts these days. What would she make of his bizarre new social life? he wondered wryly.

It was an annoying expression, but he had actually achieved the inconceivable: he'd moved on. Moving in next door had helped, just as he'd hoped it would. He was happy here in Latimer Street, even if the house was a wreck, and would be so for some months yet. With so much time spent here with Esme and Floriana, he had yet to get stuck into the renovation work he had planned, but no matter, he was in no hurry.

Upstairs, Esme's bedroom door was still ajar, but there was no sound of the hairdryer now. He knocked loudly. 'Ladies,' he said in a commanding voice, 'your presence is requested in the dining room.'

There was a low laugh from Esme, followed by, 'What a wonderful butler you make, Adam, but don't whatever you do come in, we're in a state of undress!'

'I wouldn't dream of it.' Smiling, he added, 'Will your ladyship require assistance down the stairs?'

'I think we can manage,' came Floriana's voice and the sound of something being rustled.

He hurried back down the stairs and checked it was warm enough in the dining room. If the sight of Euridice lying stretched out on the hearthrug in front of the gas fire was anything to go by, then yes it was. This morning Dr Pardoe – or Dr Death as Esme referred to him – had declared his patient to be well and truly on the mend and to mark the occasion, Floriana had offered to help Esme get specially 'dressed up' for dinner this evening and do her hair for her.

In the kitchen, Adam served the meal into warmed serving dishes and by the time he'd ferried it through to the dining room, Floriana and Esme had appeared at the top of the stairs. He waited for them at the bottom, observing their steady progress. Esme might have made a good recovery, but watching her hold onto the banister with one hand and her other tucked into Floriana's, she was unquestionably looking less robust – as robust as any octogenarian could look. But despite that, there was no mistaking the effort that had gone into the pair of them dressing for dinner, which put his jeans and old sweater to shame.

Yet as smart as Esme looked in a charcoal-coloured woollen dress with a sort of lilac shawl draped around her shoulders, it was Floriana who caught his attention. No longer wearing the black leggings, the baggy top and the short stripy black and purple skirt she'd had on earlier, she was now almost unrecognisable. She looked ... He floundered. There was a word that instantly sprang to mind but he was reluctant to use it. Yet there was no getting away from it, Floriana looked *hot*.

When they reached the bottom step, Adam tipped his head

towards Esme. 'Dinner is served, and may I say how splendid your ladyship is looking this evening.'

'You may indeed, Adam, and as grateful as I am for the compliment, I think we both know that I'm utterly eclipsed by Floriana. Don't you think she looks ravishing?'

Ravishing worked for him, he thought, trying not to stare at the plunging neckline of the silvery-grey silk dress that hugged Floriana's every contour and stopped just below the knee. So used to seeing her submerged in multi-layered outfits with leggings or thick tights, he was stunned to see that she had the most amazing body. And great legs too. Who knew!

Before he could think how to respond, Floriana said, 'Her ladyship here insisted that seeing as this was a special occasion, I had to change out of my usual gear and choose something nice from her wardrobe.' She laughed in that refreshingly unconscious way she had. 'I was convinced nothing would fit. But hey, I squeezed into this slinky little number.'

'And as I kept telling you, I was bigger back then,' Esme said. 'I've shrunk with old age.'

Still laughing, Floriana raised an elegantly arched foot in a strappy sandal with a four-inch heel. 'What do you think to these little babies, Adam? They're genuine 1960s evening shoes. Gorgeous, aren't they?'

He swallowed. Never mind the shoes, *you* look gorgeous, he wanted to say, but something stopped him. It was that question he'd overheard upstairs, and not knowing what Floriana's answer had been. Just how did she perceive him? She had said that him being mistaken for her partner would be hideously embarrassing. Did she mean hideously embarrassing for him, or for her?

'I think I'm one very lucky guy to be having dinner with two such beautifully dressed women,' he said diplomatically. 'However,' he went on, reverting to the role he'd adopted for himself, 'as a lowly chef and waiter combined this evening, I would urge you to come through to the dining room before your dinner gets cold.'

Both Floriana and Esme laughed happily and led the way. Following behind, Adam now saw that the dress that was skimming Floriana's body in all the right places had a plunging back to it and with her hair tied up on the top of her head, her long neck and pale shoulders were fully exposed. He knew that it was supremely shallow of him, but the sight of her in that dress was making him view Floriana in a whole new light. He'd challenge any man not to.

Esme had enjoyed herself tremendously, but now she was running out of energy. As much as she wanted to continue the evening with her delightful young friends who had gone to so much trouble for her these last few weeks, she knew that she needed to retreat to her bed.

But before she did, there was something important she wanted to do. She wanted to make an announcement, something that would surprise them both. She just hoped they would agree to it, not just for her own sake, but theirs. Because if ever there were two people who were perfectly suited, it was these two. Oh, how she wished they could see that. And how she longed to nip things in the bud before they became too firmly entrenched in the belief that they could only be friends. Hadn't Floriana learnt that already with Seb?

While they'd been upstairs getting changed, and while Esme was trying to persuade her that Adam would make an ideal plus-one – and a lot more besides if she had her way – Floriana had said that ages ago Adam had shown her a photograph of Jesse which, she claimed, categorically proved that any girlfriend of Adam's had to have supermodel attributes. 'That's why we get on as well as we do,' Floriana had then said, 'there's no ambiguity, he can relax around me. So stop trying to fix us up,' she'd added with a kindly laugh. 'We're fine as we are, as *friends.*'

But Esme had seen the way Adam had looked at Floriana when they'd appeared on the stairs for dinner. His reaction had told her all she needed to know and had confirmed that she'd been right to meddle in the way she had by manipulating Floriana into wearing something sensationally different so that the scales would be lifted from Adam's eyes. It amused Esme that for all his customary playing his cards close to his chest, Adam had failed in this instance to hide his feelings; he'd patently been bowled over by the sight of Floriana. Question was, had Floriana noticed his reaction? Perhaps not, she was extraordinarily unaware of her own attractiveness.

For a long time now Esme had wanted to see Floriana dressed in something that would flatter her more; inviting the girl to ferret about in her wardrobes that were packed full of old clothes she hadn't been able to part with – they were like old friends to her – had been the perfect temptation to get Floriana to play at dressing up. The dear girl had been like a child in a sweet shop pulling dresses out and exclaiming ecstatically that she'd never seen such beautiful clothes. 'Wow, this is vintage heaven!' she kept exclaiming.

Pleased that Floriana liked what she saw, and tapping into the girl's natural inclination for theatricality, Esme had guided her towards a dress she knew would effect a spectacular transformation. She had been right. Ugly duckling to beautiful swan was too simplistic an analogy, because Floriana wasn't ugly, not even plain, she was a very pretty girl indeed, it was more a matter of changing her mindset, of making her see herself differently.

Now with Euridice purring on her lap, Esme watched her two young friends clear the table – they had insisted she did nothing but sit and eat. How good they were to her, how very generous they were with their time and friendship. They could almost be the children she had never had, she thought with a pang of sad regret. Or, perhaps more accurately, the grandchildren she'd never had.

When they returned from the kitchen Esme readied herself to make her announcement. It was while they had earlier been toasting her return to good health that the idea had come to her fully conceived – before then it had been nothing but a vague murmur of an unfeasible suggestion in her head. But suddenly there it was, a definite plan, and all it would take would be a straightforward request. She had no idea how Floriana and Adam would react; it was a lot to ask of them, and she knew she had to let it go if they said no. But she badly wanted them to say yes, for without their help she simply wouldn't be able to do it.

Marco's portrait was to blame for putting the idea into her head in the first place. Staring at his face for so many hours every day, and with Floriana's curiosity prompting more and more memories from the past, it was as if the very waves lapping at the shores of Lake Como were whispering to her, beckoning her to return. *Ritorn ... Ritorn ... Come back ... Come back ...*

Could she do it? Would her dear friends help her make it happen?

Chapter Thirty-Four

With his knee furiously jiggling up and down, Floriana could see that Seb was wired. The tension coming off him was wholly at odds with the quiet loveliness of their surroundings.

It was a glorious summer's day in June and they were sitting on their old bench in the park, the same bench where two months ago she had phoned him to say she had decided to blow all her worldly savings on attending his wedding, and he'd better be grateful! In response to her jokey bolshiness, he had returned the gesture in kind. 'Yeah, well, Florrie, just so long as I'm not putting you out.' The exchange meant that it was business as usual; they could both relax now. In short, his wedding invitation had been his way of apologising for what had happened between them and her agreeing to go had been her way of saying sorry. Later he'd texted to say that she'd made his day. To which she'd messaged back, *Must have been an awful day in that case.*

Not even close! he'd replied.

As tempting as it had been to invite him to unburden himself, a little warning voice inside her head had told her to back off. If he'd had a bad day, it was Imogen's job to listen and sympathise.

Today Floriana had had an art group from Chipping Norton booked on a Pre-Raphaelite tour – it was one of her favourite tours to conduct and included the collection of paintings at the Ashmolean, the stained glass in Harris Manchester College, the murals in the Oxford Union and the tapestries in Rhodes House and Exeter College and, of course, Keble College Chapel to see Holman Hunt's *The Light of the World*. It was at Keble, while she was waiting for a few stragglers in the group to finish photographing the front quad and catch up to go into the chapel, that she'd felt her mobile vibrating in her pocket.

To her surprise, it was Seb. She had just been thinking of him. But then she couldn't set foot in Keble without doing so. 'You'll never guess where I am,' she'd said, keeping her voice low and stepping away from her group who were mostly talking amongst themselves.

'Hmm ... let me have a stab at that. I'm going to guess that you're about five yards from entering my old college chapel.'

'How the hell—' She broke off, looked about her. There, over by the main entrance, just stepping out from behind a group of giant-sized rowers, was a familiar figure raising a hand in her direction.

'Surprise!' his voice said in her ear. 'Behold,' he went on, adopting a theatrically deep tone, 'I stand at the door and knock. If any man hear my voice and open the door I will come to him and will sup with him and he with me. How am I doing?'

'Word perfect. I'm surprised though, you hated that painting, dismissed it, and the whole of the Pre-Raphaelite movement, as nothing more than sloppy tosh.'

'Whereas you always had a fondness for that sort of thing.'

'You mean I had an open mind. What on the earth are you doing here?'

'If you're free later, I'll tell you.'

Seeing that the stragglers of the group had now caught up, she said, 'I'll be finished at about five-thirty.'

'Let's meet in the park. Usual place. I'll bring some bread for the ducks.'

Now, as Floriana tossed a handful of breadcrumbs at the greedy well-fed ducks around them, she thought of Seb's explanation for coming here – Imogen was in Paris on her hen weekend, leaving Seb at a loose end. He claimed he'd driven to Oxford on impulse, in the hope of seeing Floriana. On another impulse, he'd decided to call in at his old college and lay a few ghosts to rest, and that was when he'd spotted her. Serendipity, he called it.

The pragmatist in her maintained that a simple phone call was all that it would have taken to confirm that she was around and free to see him. Typical Seb, he could never do things the easy way. It was always last minute and leaving things to chance with him.

After a trio of panting joggers had gone by, he said, 'Come on then, tell me about this guy you're bringing with you to my wedding, who is he? I suppose he's a boffin type, isn't he, all brains and a dubious dress sense which he thinks gives him a personality.'

Floriana tossed another handful of crumbs at the ducks, one of which was pecking at her shoe. 'You know what, I'm just going to sit here and let you fine-tune that offensive tone of yours.'

He laughed. 'I'm right, aren't I? I've hit the nail slap-bang on the head. Well, I guess it stands to reason you'd end up with someone of that ilk, after all –' he spread his arms wide – 'this is your world.'

Dodging the arm that nearly caught her on the jaw, she said, 'He isn't a boyfriend, he's a friend.'

'Aha! Distancing yourself from him already. Shame on you, Florrie. Stand up for your man. Or as the song goes, stand by your man.'

'Seb.'

'Yes?'

'Shut up or I'll set these killer ducks on you.'

'Pecked to death, sounds eminently more fun than being nagged to death.'

'I haven't nagged you!' she said indignantly.

'I didn't mean you.'

'Who did you—' Floriana bit the question back, sensing she'd inadvertently entered a danger zone.

His knee, which had come to a rest momentarily, began jiggling again, its movement vibrating through the bench. 'Go on,' he prompted, 'finish what you were going to say.'

No, she wasn't going to play that game. Throwing the last of her bread to the ducks, she stood up. 'Let's go,' she said.

'Where to?' he asked, also on his feet. 'Your place?'

'If you promise to behave.'

'I'll even remove my shoes at the door,' he said. 'I'm very well trained. If nothing else, Imogen's done an extremely thorough job on domesticating me. I even put the loo seat down these days.'

He kept eye contact with her for a beat too long and sensing another trap, Floriana said, 'Where did you say you'd left your car?'

'Nice,' he said, standing in the sitting room and staring round. 'It's very you.'

'Is that code for cheap and arty?'

'It wouldn't be you otherwise. But honestly, it's nice; I like it. It feels comfortable, like a proper home.'

'Thank you. Drink?'

'What are you offering?'

'Not very much, I'm afraid.' She stepped through the archway into the kitchen. 'I wasn't expecting company.'

'Not even your *friend*?'

Ignoring him, and the emphasis he put on the word 'friend', she looked in the fridge. 'I have two bottles of beer and some white wine.' The wine had been a gift from Adam to thank her for helping to tackle the wilderness that had swallowed up his garden. Esme had helped as well, issuing commands as to what had to be dug up and what was worth keeping.

Having followed her into the kitchen, Seb peered into the fridge next to her. 'A bottle of Cloudy Bay, no less; I'll have some of that. Your taste in wine has obviously improved. Is it your *friend* who is responsible for introducing you to the world of decent wine? Is he an elitist North Oxford wine connoisseur?'

Smarting with annoyance, she gave Seb a cool look. 'Adam is no such thing.'

'Hallelujah! Finally we have a name for the mystery man!'

'You are aware, aren't you, that you're turning into a tedious bore with your sarcasm and constant snidey comments? What's the matter with you?'

He had the grace to pull a placatory face. 'Sorry. How about you pour the wine while I use your bathroom and then I'll let you decide what's wrong with me?'

Listening to Seb moving about upstairs, Floriana wondered how he would react to the news that her going to Lake Como to his wedding was no longer just about him and his marriage. It had become something far bigger and, very likely, a whole lot more interesting.

When Esme had first asked Floriana and Adam to accompany her to Lake Como, stressing that the most sensible thing to do would be to coincide the trip with Seb's wedding, and that she would meet all costs involved – that was non-negotiable – Floriana had been lost for words, not something that happened to her too frequently. Adam had been stunned into silence as well. An even more profound silence than usual from him.

'It's good to know that even at my age I can still surprise people,' Esme had said with a smile. 'I know it sounds like a madcap scheme, but please believe me, I haven't lost my marbles while being ill, I really couldn't be more serious about this.'

There had followed several days of intense discussion, mostly between Floriana and Adam as they came up with a list of reasons why the idea was barmy and shouldn't be considered, not for a single minute. It was the responsibility that frightened them. What if Esme was ill? What if it was all too much for her? Floriana even discussed it with her parents, who said it sounded like a wonderful thing to do and she should view it as an opportunity. An adventure. By then Floriana couldn't stop thinking about the irresistibly romantic prospect of retracing Esme's stay at the lake all those years ago. 'It's her swansong,' she said to Adam, after she'd checked with Tony in the office that she could take the time off, 'how could we have the heart to refuse her? And just think, what if we tracked down Marco?'

'What indeed?' had been Adam's less than enthusiastic response.

'Oh, don't be like that, it could be fun. And selfishly, it would certainly take my mind off Seb's wedding.'

Despite the doubts he kept airing, Adam finally gave in. 'I'm doing this against my better judgement,' he said, 'and on the basis that not only do you need a driver, since neither of you can drive, but more importantly you need a responsible adult on hand!'

'And nobody's more suited to that task than you,' Floriana had teased him.

Esme had been delighted when Floriana had called in to give her the news. She had clapped her hands like an excited child. 'Oh, how wonderful! And now, my dear, you won't have the worry of going to Seb's wedding unaccompanied, you'll be able to take Adam.'

'This might surprise you, but I wasn't that worried about going alone.'

'Well, I was worried for you; I hated the idea of you being all on your own. So much better this way, now you'll have a lovely handsome man to show off.'

With a laugh, Floriana had warned Esme not to let Adam catch her talking about him as if he were a piece of arm candy. 'Do that and he'll back out of the trip altogether!'

It was a few days after this conversation had taken place that Floriana admitted to herself that Esme was right – it would be much better to have Adam with her when she was forced to witness Seb and Imogen marry. So plucking up her courage, and making it very clear that she would quite understand if he'd rather not, she had asked Adam if he'd like to be her plus-one. To her surprise, he'd agreed. 'OK, why not?' he'd said. 'So long as I won't be an embarrassment to you.'

It had been such an odd comment for him to make, and it puzzled her still. Why would he think he would be an embarrassment to her? The other way round, she could understand.

After Seb had come down from the bathroom and apologised again for acting like an idiot, and after Floriana had listened to what he had to say, she shook her head at him. 'For heaven's sake, Seb, you've got a classic case of pre-wedding jitters, it's perfectly normal. All couples go through it.'

'I hope you're right because I'm beginning to think I've made a terrible mistake. She's ... she's changed.'

'Of course Imogen's changed! She has a wedding to organise and by definition that's turned her into Bridezilla.'

'I get that, but what about me? Why aren't I included in any of the arrangements? I'm not kidding, Florrie, it's like I don't exist. She and her parents talk about nothing but the wedding. If it's not worrying about the photographer or the flowers, it's the place settings, or declaring war on the Italians if they fail to deliver good weather on the day. Then there's the cost of it; it's obscene the amount they're lashing out.' He rubbed at his unshaved chin. 'And it's not just the wedding they've hijacked, it's everything, it's ... it's our relationship. They keep making plans for us. Holidays, Christmases, even what car we should consider buying. And naturally everything they say is disgustingly extravagant. When I point out to Imogen we can't afford whatever it is her father's just recommended, she tells me to relax and let her parents buy it for us.'

Surprised to hear Seb talking about money this way, she said, 'But I thought you earned staggeringly good money?' Three years ago Seb had landed a plum job with a prestigious advertising agency and within weeks had become their blue-eyed boy after he'd come up with an ad campaign for a mobile phone company that had gone viral on YouTube; its success had sent his earnings and creative reputation into the stratosphere.

He swatted her comment away with an impatient hand. 'I

do, but I like to live within my means. No one's immune from financial meltdown. And that's where we're heading if Imogen has her way, because I absolutely refuse to let her parents own me with their money.'

Sympathising with him on that score, Floriana said, 'All right, and putting the matter of money aside, you wouldn't be the first groom to feel like a spare part before getting married; it goes with the territory. You'd be doing yourself a huge favour if you just left Imogen and her parents to get on with it. What's more, her parents will want to do this for their only daughter, they'll want to give her a perfect day.'

Frowning, Seb let out his breath. 'What makes you such an expert?'

'Don't you remember Ann's wedding? The run-up to that very nearly brought about Armageddon.'

He suddenly smiled – the first time he had since they'd met in the park. 'God yes, your sister's wedding, what a day. I was your plus-one, wasn't I?'

'And you got spectacularly drunk. Much to my sister's disgust you tried to perform an excuse-me during her and Paul's first dance.'

'I couldn't have been that drunk as I clearly remember the look on her face. I thought she was going to deck me.'

'She would have if she hadn't been worried it would spoil her make-up. Which just goes to prove every bride turns into a monster. Just accept that Imogen's going to be suffering from the emotional bends and be outrageously cranky until the big day. You have exactly four weeks to get through and then life will return to the blissful state it was before.'

The smile dropped from his face. 'Trouble is, I can't remember a time when it was blissful. We used to laugh, I'm sure of it, but for the life of me I can't think when or why.'

The warning voice from earlier, accompanied by a loud klaxon, advised extreme caution. 'Seb,' Floriana said carefully, 'haven't you got any friends in London you can talk to about this?'

He shook his head. 'They're all mutual friends. I'd only have to utter a single negative word to any one of them and it would get back to Imogen in a flash.'

'What about your best man? Surely he's somebody you're close to and in whom you can confide?'

Draining his glass, he settled it on the arm of the sofa and contemplated it, as if hinting for Floriana to give him a refill. Mindful of his drive back to London, she didn't. 'Well?' she pressed.

'This is going to sound seriously weird, but I didn't get to choose my best man. Imogen insisted on her brother doing the job. About eighteen months ago he was in an accident and lost both legs, but he's since learnt to walk with prosthetic limbs and Imogen thought it would be great if he was given the honour of being my best man, so –' he shrugged – 'it was a done deal.'

Seb was right, it did sound weird that he hadn't been able to choose his own best man, but Floriana kept that thought to herself. 'I can see how Imogen would like that, but you could have suggested he was an usher and chosen who you really wanted. Didn't you try that?'

'I did. But she put her foot down. I mean, to a degree I can see her point, that it goes against convention, the person I wanted, but so what?'

'Who did you want that would be so unconventional?'

His knee started to jiggle again. 'You.'

Floriana spluttered on a mouthful of wine. 'You're joking?' she said when she'd recovered.

'Given that you've been my best friend since for ever, why not you? You know me better than anyone.'

'Because anyone can see that it would freak Imogen out. No wonder she's got an attack of the emotional bends!'

'I don't see why.'

Haven't you forgotten that excruciating day when I told you I loved you? Floriana wanted to say, but she couldn't bring herself to utter the words aloud. Instead she said, 'Don't be obtuse, Seb.'

'I know what you're thinking,' he said.

'If you really do, then you wouldn't need me to tell you what an idiot you are.'

'But that's all in the past,' he said with an annoyingly trivialising wave of his hand. He suddenly lurched forward in his seat, not noticing his elbow had knocked his empty glass to the floor. 'It was just a mad heat of the moment thing, wasn't it? Besides, you don't feel that way about me still, do you?'

'You've knocked your glass over,' she murmured, not knowing how to answer him. Could Seb really believe that the two years of silence between them had been the result of nothing more than a crazy heat of the moment thing, a meaningless tiff? Or was it his way of convincing himself they could pick up where they'd left off, no harm done?

He bent down to his glass and helped himself to the bottle on the table. 'This is my big day as well, not just Imogen's; I don't understand why she can't respect my wishes. Or at least respect just one important wish.'

'You're whinging like a spoilt child,' Floriana said gently. 'Isn't it enough for you to know that I'll be there to stick my tongue out at you as you walk down the aisle a happily married man?'

When he didn't say anything, just lifted his wineglass to his mouth and drank from it, she said, thinking once more of his drive back to London, 'How about something to eat?'

'What have you got in mind?'

'I could rustle something up or we can get a takeaway. There's a great Bangladeshi restaurant on North Parade.'

He smiled. 'Having seen the lacklustre contents of your fridge, let's have a takeaway.'

They set off to walk the short distance. It was a beautiful summer's evening, the air lightly perfumed with the sweet smell of freshly cut grass. The sound of birdsong rang out along with the persistent whirr of a low-powered lawnmower.

They turned into Latimer Street and when they were level with Trinity House, and as she always did, Floriana looked to see if there was any sign of Esme at the drawing room window. There wasn't; she was probably in the kitchen getting her supper ready.

Outside Adam's house there was a skip – they came and went with regularity – but the space where he parked his silver Mercedes was empty; he'd gone to spend the day with his family to celebrate his stepmother's seventieth birthday.

'So come on, then,' Seb said, linking his arm through hers, just like old times, 'put me out of my misery and tell me all about this guy you're bringing to my wedding. You've been annoyingly evasive so far. Which makes me think you either have something to hide or you're deliberately teasing me. Which is it?'

'I'm doing neither. His name's Adam and that's where he lives, just back there.'

Seb twisted his head to see. 'Ah, so he's a neighbour, how very cosy.'

'And how very jealous you keep sounding,' she said. 'It's as though you don't really want me to bring someone.'

'I suppose it's true, I don't like sharing you, I never have.'

'Really?'

'Don't sound so surprised, it's human nature to want to keep a best friend all to oneself.'

'You were never jealous here in Oxford.'

'Says who?'

'But you can't have been, you never once gave any indication that was how you felt.'

'I—' A ringing sound coming from Seb stopped him from continuing.

'It's Imogen,' he said, slipping his arm out from hers as he looked at the screen on his mobile. 'I'd better speak to her. Do you mind?'

'Of course not,' Floriana said, walking on ahead to give him space to talk in relative privacy.

'Hi, Imo,' he said brightly – too brightly to Floriana's thinking – 'how's it going? Having a good time?'

Not wanting to hear any more, Floriana quickened her step as Seb slowed his, presumably to give his wife-to-be his full attention.

When he came off the phone, he caught Floriana up outside the restaurant. A thought occurred to her. 'Does Imogen know you're here in Oxford?' she asked.

His face said it all. 'No, she doesn't.'

'And your thinking behind that is, what, exactly?'

'I don't want to give her anything else to worry about.'

'So you've lied to her?'

'Only by omission.'

Floriana shook her head and pushed open the door. 'That doesn't seem like a good way to run a relationship, Seb.'

'Don't spoil it,' he said, resting a hand on her arm. 'I'm enjoying being here with you. It's giving me perspective.'

Perspective of what precisely? wondered Floriana, her stomach queasy with the fear of what Imogen would say or do if she ever knew of his visit to see her.

Chapter Thirty-Five

So far so good. Another thirty minutes and they should be at Villa Sofia.

Surprised and relieved at how easily the journey had gone, Adam concentrated on the narrow winding road that lay parallel with the lake. In the back of their hire car, her hands folded on her lap, Esme was looking thoughtfully out of the open window at the view, and next to him in the front Floriana also had her gazed fixed intently on the smooth flat water to the right of them. Their earlier exuberance during the flight to Milan now gone, they had both fallen quiet at the same time, each, he imagined, mulling over their feelings about coming here.

When Esme asked for his and Floriana's help to bring her here, his initial reaction had been to reject the idea out of hand. Politely, of course. He had thought the idea would be no more than a passing whim and would soon be dismissed as merely a pleasant dalliance with a daydream. He'd been sure also, knowing how unapologetically proud and independent Floriana could be about money, that lack of her own funds would be a contributing factor to putting a stop to the plan. But instead of vociferously refusing Esme's offer to finance the enterprise, and after checking she could take a week off during the peak tourist season, Floriana had executed a complete U-turn and leapt to support Esme in her desire to go on a trip down memory lane. Moreover, she had then badgered him into dispensing with his common sense. 'Oh, Adam,' she'd said, 'you're Mr Fixer, you have to agree to help, no one makes things happen like you! Do say you'll do it. Pretty please.'

He should have known this would be Floriana's reaction, having seen her frequently veer from a state of acute procrastination to wholehearted impetuosity. She might be guilty of putting things off but, boy, when she put her mind to something, she

235

was one of the most determined people he knew. What was more dangerous was that her impulsive behaviour was infectious and before he knew it, he was caught up in her enthusiasm and looking forward to a week away in the sun.

A lot of Floriana's enthusiasm was based on the hopelessly idealistic notion that they would somehow stumble across Esme's first great love and the two of them would be reunited sixty years later.

'But what if we could make that happen?' Floriana had argued when he'd voiced his doubts of that coming to pass. 'Come on, Adam,' she'd pressed, 'I know how analytical you are, but even to a romantically challenged man like you, you can surely see how wonderful it would be for Esme and Marco to meet up again after all this time.'

Romantically challenged? It had stung, and still did, that Floriana viewed him so poorly.

He flicked his eyes to the rear-view mirror again to check on Esme. She looked exactly the same as before, her hands motionless and folded in her lap like a well-behaved child waiting for the party to begin.

He had severely misjudged Esme's character when they'd first met and he was forced to acknowledge he'd got it wrong again in underestimating the old lady's resolve to see something through. With an uncrushable will of iron, she was adamant that every last cost of the trip would be met by her. 'I won't hear a word from either of you two about money,' she'd said. 'In exchange for your help, you'll both be my guests throughout the duration of the trip. No, Adam, that's my final word!'

The first important decision they'd had to make was where to stay. A quick hunt on the internet established that Hotel Margherita was no longer in existence, which further endorsed Adam's pessimistic view on them somehow stumbling across the Bassani family. They were just considering other hotels, when, as luck would have it, Adam's brother came up trumps with friends who owned a villa at the lake and who would give them mates-rates for a week-long stay.

'Mr Fixer strikes again!' Floriana had laughed. 'Is there anything you can't arrange through people you know?'

'Hush, child,' Esme had said, giving Floriana a stern look of reprimand. 'Adam, we're very grateful to you that you know so many helpful people.'

Flights were then booked and in a flurry of paperwork, a new passport had to be organised for Esme – her last one having run out more than a decade ago. Travel insurance, which Adam insisted upon for Esme, proved somewhat problematic given her age, and the fact she'd been ill recently, but they got there in the end.

Next they had to find somebody to take care of Euridice. Buddy and Joe immediately stepped in and promised to call in twice a day to Trinity House to see that the cat was fed and watered.

The nuts and bolts of the trip arranged, Adam had left Esme and Floriana to fret over the mystical work of what to wear for the trip. Privately he was hoping for the reappearance of the silvery-grey silk dress Floriana had worn the evening of Esme's Lake Como announcement.

He'd been in a quandary ever since that evening, torn between feeling increasingly differently towards Floriana, alarmingly so at times, and trying to resist the attraction he felt. He cautioned himself that it was too soon after splitting with Jesse to consider a new relationship; his emotions couldn't be trusted.

There was also the small and worrying matter that he genuinely had no idea how Floriana would react if he so much as hinted at them being more than friends. From what he could tell, she didn't exactly view him as potential boyfriend material. Romantically challenged, she'd described him. Analytical as well. These were attributes that supported his belief that while she liked him as a friend – a good friend – she considered him too dull to be anything more.

He'd never considered the possibility before that he might be thought of as boring and it worried him. What worried him more, however, was doing anything that might jeopardise his friendship with Floriana. He would hate to lose that, especially as it had played such a vital part in helping to establish his new-found happiness following his split with Jesse.

Since the Night of the Silk Dress, as he now thought of it, he had begun to notice all sorts of things about Floriana he'd never seen before, like the telltale way the corners of her mouth would twitch when she was about to tease him over something.

And then there was the way her eyes widened ever so slightly before she laughed. She had a great laugh, natural and unforced, it seemed to wrap itself around him. He also liked the way she treated Esme, respectful yet never patronising. Would Jesse have been so quick to befriend an old lady and give up her limited holiday time to accompany her to Italy?

Wrong! He mustn't ever compare Floriana to Jesse. There was no comparison; they couldn't be more different. Maybe that was part of the attraction, that Floriana was quirkily individual and followed no one's trend but her own.

But putting all that to one side, there was the colossal elephant in the room to consider – how did Floriana feel about Seb? No way was he going to play second fiddle to someone with whom she might still be in love. He could be wrong, of course, and her feelings for Seb could now be a thing of the past, but because she seldom spoke about him in any detail, Adam couldn't be sure what the true picture was.

He was well aware that the fact he was reasoning everything out this way only went to confirm Floriana's opinion of him: that he was overly analytical and about as impulsive as an exhausted sloth.

True to his exacting nature, he'd studied the map during the flight and now, recognising the names of the villages they had so far driven through – Cernobbio, Moltrasio, Laglio, Brienno, Argegno – he spotted a sign for Colonno, which meant that according to the satnav they were now only fifteen minutes from Villa Sofia. Forced to slow his speed for a car in front towing a caravan with a Dutch number plate, he glanced in the rear-view mirror. 'Anything familiar to you, Esme?' he asked.

She smiled back at him. 'In some ways, yes. But it's much more built up than I remember.'

'That's inevitable, I suppose, but the property development that's gone on doesn't look too badly done.'

Breaking her silence, Floriana laughed. 'You wait, Esme, Adam will have sniffed out a property deal by the end of the week!'

'Hadn't crossed my mind,' he said innocently. Although, of course, it had; he'd spent a fair bit of time looking at Lake Como property online in the last few weeks. No harm in looking, was his motto.

'Oh, this I recognise!' Esme suddenly exclaimed, pointing

out of the window, her hair fluttering in the wind. 'It's Isola Comacina. My father and I took a boat there for lunch one day. It was a wonderful restaurant; it hadn't been open for very long. The owner was an extraordinarily mercurial gentleman.'

That was something else Adam had read about online. 'It's much the same today,' he said. 'What's more, the menu hasn't changed since it first opened, it's one of the things they pride themselves on.'

'Perhaps we could go there?' Floriana said eagerly. 'If it's not too expensive,' she added.

This last comment was met with a formidable tut from the back of the car.

Still following behind the Dutch caravan, Adam slowed his speed again at the sight of a German tour bus coming towards them on the other side of the particularly narrow road. There didn't seem to be enough space and despite pulling over as far as he could, the bus came so close to the car Adam instinctively breathed in as though making space for it. Driving on, the road widened and after another bend, Esme let out a cry.

'That's it! That's Hotel Margherita! Down there on the promontory.'

But a fleeting glimpse was all they got as the road steered them sharply away from an impressive gated entrance and a discreet sign with the words *Villa Margherita*. It confirmed what they had discovered online, that sometime in the 1970s the hotel had closed and the villa had been restored to use as a private residence, just as it had been before the Bassani family had run into money problems.

For the last leg of the journey, Floriana was in charge of reading the directions they'd been given – they'd been advised to ignore any satnav instructions at this stage as they petered out somewhat unhelpfully. Having turned off from the main road at the junction where there was a small supermarket and a bar, they were now climbing steadily up the hill on the lookout for an easy-to-miss turning to the right.

'There!' Floriana exclaimed excitedly, pointing towards a narrow opening in a bushy hedge that was marked with a small concrete post.

The cobbled road led them to an open gateway and a dusty potholed track that ran along the edge of an area of olive trees.

And finally, there in the brilliant sunshine, nestled amongst a cluster of other stone-built buildings, Villa Sofia stood before them. Three storeys high, its dusky-rose façade was topped with a low-pitched terracotta roof and two sturdy chimneys. On the upper floors each window had its own balcony with decorative wrought-iron railings. The ground floor was partially hidden beneath an extensive pergola that was covered with a vigorous vine. In front of the villa was a rectangular swimming pool with sun loungers grouped enticingly at one end of it.

Staring up at the sleep-shrouded villa with its closed peacock blue shutters, Floriana felt a happy thrill of anticipation as she pushed open the car door and stepped into the heat of the afternoon. Greeted by the sound of cicadas chirping noisily, she thought everything about the villa looked perfect, even better than it had in the photographs the owners had sent Adam.

Opening the rear passenger door, she helped Esme out. 'What do you think?' she asked. 'Will it do?'

'I think it will do splendidly,' Esme replied, looking up at their home for the next week. 'Adam, you have quite excelled yourself. Bravo!'

'Let's hope the interior matches the exterior,' he said. 'Do you need a hand up the steps?'

'No, no, I can manage, thank you.'

Eager to explore, they left the luggage till later and went to look for the key they'd been told would be placed under a pot of scarlet geraniums on the terrace. They found it easily enough but were distracted from rushing to unlock the door by realising that from their elevated position, they had a spectacular panoramic view of the lake. As far as the eye could see, it lay there as peaceful as a sleeping cat in the dazzling sunshine, and beyond it mountains, lush and green, rose majestically out of the water.

'It couldn't be more perfect,' Esme murmured with a wistful gaze. 'It's as enchanting as I remember it. Thank you both so much for making this possible for me.'

Hearing the catch of emotion in Esme's voice Floriana put an arm around her. She was about to say something herself when a stocky, elderly woman appeared from round the side of the villa. Wearing a flowery dress and with a head of luxuriantly black hair – for the woman's age it couldn't be anything but dyed – she greeted them with a warm and very welcoming smile.

'*Buongiorno! Buongiorno!*' her cheery voice rang out, while proffering a large plastic bowl of eggs and tomatoes. '*Sì, sì,*' she urged when Floriana dithered over whether to take the bowl.

This had to be Renata, the neighbour who they'd been told would be on hand to help with any problems they might have. It soon became evident that Renata was a woman of many words and not shy to share them round. The trouble was, the profusion of words coming from her were all Italian with one or two English words sporadically thrown in. The addition of hand gestures helped though, and having given some time to swotting up with *Teach Yourself Italian in Thirty Days*, Floriana hazarded a guess that Renata's brother – Domenico – would come tomorrow to check on the pool and water the garden. But Esme stunned them by smoothly replying in Italian and gaining for herself an extra wide beaming smile from Renata and the words, '*Piacere, signora. Piacere.*'

'You've been holding out on us,' Floriana said when Renata had left them. 'You never said you could speak Italian so well.'

'Oh, just a few words,' Esme said airily. 'Funny how it comes back to one.'

'It sounded more than a few words to me,' Adam said.

'What else haven't you told us?' Floriana asked.

Esme's answer was to suggest they fetch the luggage.

Chapter Thirty-Six

Esme woke early, but plainly not as early as Adam.

Looking out of her open bedroom window, she watched him pace barefoot up and down the length of the pool as he talked on his mobile phone. Wearing shorts and a T-shirt and a pair of sunglasses, he was dressed like a man on holiday, but the call said otherwise. Esme knew that his business concerns effectively meant he was never off duty, but she wished he would allow himself some time to relax. During dinner last night at a nearby restaurant, and under the intense spotlight of Floriana's interrogation, he'd admitted that he had never taken a holiday when he hadn't stayed in regular contact with his office. Esme wondered how he would cope without his mobile phone or laptop. Not that she would ever dream of saying anything to him. She was only too grateful that he was here, that along with Floriana he had made this trip possible for her.

In all the years since she and her father had stayed at Hotel Margherita, Esme had never wanted to return to the lake. Perhaps another person might have done so, if only to put the past to rest, but she had taken the stance that the past was the past and nothing would be gained from revisiting it in order to reopen old wounds that were better left untouched and healed.

Yet here she was. And at her own doing. Whatever the outcome, she had only herself to blame.

Despite sleeping with Marco's portrait on the wall opposite her bed all her adult life, there were days when its abiding familiarity meant she hardly noticed it; it was just there, a part of her life. Casting aside the many emotions the picture had provoked over the years, it had never before compelled her to return to Italy. But then along had come Floriana with her Lake Como wedding invitation and little by little the past had been reawakened and nudged at her. Gently at first, then more forcibly, until there was no ignoring it. *Go back before it's too late*, the softly spoken voice of her father murmured in her head.

Her father had lived and died with too many regrets, and in the last couple of days prior to their departure, when Esme had been assailed with eleventh-hour misgivings at the wisdom of making this trip, she had reminded herself that she didn't want to die as her father had, with an apology of regret on her lips. She had to do this. It was now or never.

Floriana, the dear girl, was full of hopelessly giddy expectations for their visit, whereas Esme was content merely to retrace her steps and linger a while in a place that had given her such pleasure, as well as such heartache. The chances of meeting Marco again were highly unlikely, and even if by some remote chance he still had a connection with the lake and it was possible to track him down, would he want to meet Esme? Would he even remember her?

More likely he was dead. Everyone else was.

But he wasn't dead, she was sure of it. She would have felt him parting from this world. Yet if he was alive, she couldn't imagine him as an old man, his handsome face withered by age, his dazzling blue eyes faded, his skin loose and pouchy, his joints creaking and aching with rheumatism.

Turning away from the window where Adam was still by the pool talking into his mobile phone, she faced the bedroom Floriana had insisted should be hers when they had brought in their luggage from the car yesterday afternoon. It was the largest of the bedrooms with its own bathroom. Simply furnished, it contained a large double bed, a dressing table, a wardrobe and an armchair to one side of the window and balcony. She could picture herself being very happy to sit here letting the memories wash over her.

Emerging washed and refreshed from the bathroom, she looked out of bedroom window again and saw Floriana coming up the steep path towards the villa. She was weighed down with two large bulging carrier bags – she must have been to the small supermarket at the bottom of the hill.

'Morning!' Floriana greeted her cheerily when Esme entered the kitchen – she was busy chopping fruit and Adam was spooning coffee into one of those fiddly coffee pots that went on the hob.

'Breakfast is on its way. We have croissants, bread, peaches, pears and apricots. How did you sleep?'

'Exceptionally well, thank you. The two of you are very industrious for so early in the morning. What time did you get up? It must have been the crack of dawn.'

'A little after six,' Adam said. 'What would you like to drink? Tea or coffee or mango juice?'

'Mango, how very exotic!'

'Sorry, I made a mistake,' Floriana said, pulling a face. 'I misread the label, thought it was orange.'

'Well, for now, I'll have some tea please. But I can make it.'

'Absolutely not! Adam, take Esme outside and make her comfortable on the terrace.'

'You heard the lady,' Adam said, raising his eyebrows. 'Best do as she says; she's in a very assertive mood. More to the point, she's holding a dangerously sharp knife.'

Esme happily allowed Adam to usher her outside where a table on the terrace in the shade of the vine-covered pergola had been set for breakfast. 'I don't wish to appear ungrateful but I do hope you're not going to boss me around the whole time we're here,' she said when Adam and Floriana had finished bringing out breakfast and were seated. 'I won't have you waiting on me hand and foot.'

'This is our way of thanking you for the opportunity to be here with you,' Floriana said. 'Oh, and by the way, I've had a text from Joe to say that you're not to worry about Euridice; she's fine. He went last night to check on her and will be going again this morning.'

'I still feel badly about leaving her,' Esme said with a frown. Leaving her beloved cat had been a terrible wrench, but there really had been no alternative. Forcing the anxiety from her mind, she helped herself to some slices of peach from the attractive fruit platter Floriana had prepared. 'Now what are our plans for today?' she asked, thinking more positively. 'What have you decided?'

'We thought we'd take it easy this morning,' Adam said, 'give us all a chance to catch our breath.'

'And by *us* I presume you mean me?' remarked Esme.

'Not at all,' Floriana said, 'a relaxing morning by the pool would suit me perfectly. We thought we could then find somewhere for lunch and afterwards pitch up on the doorstep of Villa Margherita. What do you think, are you ready to give that a go?'

It seemed the longest of shots that they could appear out of nowhere and persuade the current owner to let them have a look around the house for old times' sake, but as Adam and Floriana had both said when they'd discussed this before, what did they have to lose? Could they really come all this way and not try?

Later that morning, and lulled by the warmth of the day and the inexhaustible buzz of the cicadas in the nearby trees, Esme leant back in her chair in the shade of the pergola and with her eyes closed, listened to Adam and Floriana – Floriana's voice light and gaily animated, Adam's low and soothingly measured.

They were in the pool, floating on a pair of lilos Floriana had found in a large wooden chest at the far end of the terrace, along with a beach ball and an enormous inflatable hammer. She had also found some bats and a Swingball, which she'd immediately set up on the lawn and then challenged Adam to a game. Esme had watched him hesitate – he'd been reading something on his laptop. Don't you dare refuse, Esme had thought, leave that wretched computer alone for two minutes and have some fun! To her relief, he'd pulled off his T-shirt and taken hold of one of the bats. 'My game of choice as a child,' he'd said. 'I was county champion.'

'Hah! I was national champion,' Floriana had responded with a laugh.

They'd played with a raucous competitiveness that produced from each of them a great deal of noise, and with each claiming they were the victor at the end. It gladdened Esme's heart to see them enjoying themselves.

Now as they cooled off in the pool and their voices gradually receded into the background noise of the cicadas, and drowsy with rose scent, thick and seductive, Esme's thoughts began drifting away from her like balloons sailing off into the sky. Then she too was sailing away. But she wasn't floating off into the sky; she was on a boat, a small dinghy with a sail flapping in the soft breeze. And there was Marco. He was standing on the shore of the lake; he was waving to her. She tried to sail towards him but the breeze strengthened and whipped at the sail and steered the boat away from the shore. Marco was calling to her, but try as she might, she couldn't steer the boat towards him, the wind was taking her further and further away until she was in the middle of the lake and he was out of sight. Frightened, she stood up and at once the boat wobbled and rocked beneath her, then tipped over and she felt herself falling, down and down into the cold, dark water. And then she saw it, at the bottom of the lake, tangled in a mass of slippery pondweed, a small milky-white baby, its pale arms reaching out to her.

She woke with a violent start, her heart pounding painfully in her chest. Blinking in the sunlight, she turned to see the outline of a man looming over her. To her horror, he held what looked like a swaddled baby in his hands. Alarmed, she let out an involuntary cry, her heart beating even faster.

'*Mi perdoni*,' the man said, 'I am Domenico. I here to check on pool and water flowers.'

Her heart still thumping, her mouth dry, Esme rose awkwardly from her chair, realising now that this was Renata's brother and what he was carrying was, in fact, some sort of newspaper-wrapped bundle. 'Oh, please, do forgive me,' she said, her brain too fuggy to speak in Italian, 'I was fast asleep.'

Over by the pool, Adam was launching himself out of the water. 'It's Domenico,' she said, 'he's come to check on the pool.'

'Ah yes,' Adam said, grabbing a towel and coming over. Floriana was also now climbing out of the pool.

'If no good now, I come back later,' the man said with a congenial smile. He looked about seventy years old, was nut-brown and wiry with a head of thick grey hair; his Roman nose was prominent and his eyes as black as coal.

'No, no, stay and do whatever you need to do,' Esme said, still shaken from her dream but her composure beginning to return. 'Would you like a drink?' she asked, remembering her manners.

He shook his head. 'No thank you, *signora*. But I bring you this. From my garden. I grow all myself.' He handed her the bundle.

Surprised by the weight of it, Esme set it down on the table and opened it up. '*Che bello!*' she exclaimed. 'And how very kind of you.'

'What is it?' asked Floriana coming over.

'All sorts of delicious goodies,' Esme said. 'Courgettes, radishes, beetroot, lettuce and more tomatoes.' She turned to Domenico. '*Grazie mille*,' she said. '*Lei è molto gentile.*'

The man beamed back at her, revealing a row of surprisingly white and even teeth. '*Fa niente, signora*,' he replied, '*è un piacere.*'

'Well, I'd say you've just acquired yourself an admirer,' Floriana whispered when Domenico had disappeared round the side of the house to where the hose and outside tap was. 'A toy boy at that.'

Esme tutted. 'Behave yourself, young lady, or I shall be forced to take you in hand.'

Laughing, Floriana went and flopped down on a sun lounger next to Adam, who was once again doing something on his laptop.

'And put some sun cream on your back and shoulders,' Esme called after her, 'you're turning pink.' And if Adam doesn't offer to do it, I shall be very cross with him, she thought, taking Domenico's generous delivery of vegetables inside the villa.

Out of the corner of his eye as he answered an email from Denise in the office, Adam watched Floriana struggling to apply sun cream to her back. Go on, he told himself, offer to help, it's the most natural thing in the world to do. What's the problem? Touching her is suddenly a big deal?

Stupidly, everything about his feelings for Floriana were fast becoming a farcically big deal. Swimming with her just now, watching her dive into the water and then surfacing at the other end of the pool, her hair streaming down her back as shiny as an otter, had been as enjoyable to watch as it was torturous. How easy it would be to forget himself and do something regrettable!

More and more he was having to warn himself not to make the comparison, but it was impossible not to. Not only did Floriana look just as good in a bikini as Jesse always had – actually, she looked better because she had more curves – she was a lot more fun. Jesse had loved a beach holiday, but really it was the sun lounger she loved; swimming had held no attraction for her; she hated to get her face and hair wet. In contrast, Floriana was as natural in the water as she was at thrashing him at Swingball.

Uncomfortably aware that she was still straining to reach the middle of her back with sun cream, he forced himself to say: 'You're going to dislocate your shoulder if you carry on like that, how about I do it for you.'

'That's OK,' she said, 'you don't want to get your hands all greasy when you're trying to work.'

He hesitated. Was that her polite way of saying *touch me and you're dead?*

No, that was paranoia kicking in. 'It's no trouble,' he said. 'But Esme's right, you are looking a bit pink already.'

'Really?' She twisted round to try and get a better look over her shoulder.

Dispensing with his laptop, he put his hand out for the tube of sun cream.

He'd barely touched her when alarmingly she let out a long sigh. 'It's such a beautiful place, isn't it?' she said. 'I may never want to leave. I can quite understand how Esme fell in love here. How romantic it must have been for her, especially when you think how young she was.'

'Not that romantic,' he said, his hands moving slowly over her sun-warmed skin – pale skin not often exposed to the sun, he reflected. 'They parted before they really got to know each other, after all.'

'That doesn't mean it wasn't romantic the short time they were together.'

'Define romantic,' he said.

She laughed. 'That's like asking me to define intelligence, strictly speaking it can't be done as there's no empirical cast-iron test.'

'OK then, which is more romantic in your opinion: a happy or a tragic ending?'

'Hmm … good question. But if you think I'm going to cite Romeo and Juliet as the ultimate romantic couple, think again. I've always thought they were ridiculously ill-matched.'

'Hold your hair up a bit more,' he said, not wanting to dwell on that last comment. She did as he asked and it took all of his will power not to kiss the nape of her neck. Just one small kiss. Then maybe one of her right shoulder, and then her left and …

'Oh, look,' she said, stopping dead his thoughts and making him realise his hands had stopped moving and he'd leant in perilously close. 'Esme's chatting to Domenico. What a dark horse she's been, knowing how to speak Italian so well and not letting on. There's such a lot she hasn't told us. For instance, we don't even know for sure that she and Marco slept together.'

'I think we can take it as a given that they did,' Adam said. 'What we have no real idea about is what happened afterwards. We're assuming Marco went off to become a priest while Esme and her father returned to England and moved to Oxford.'

'What else could have happened?'

'That,' said Adam, 'is the million-dollar question. There, that's you done.'

He passed Floriana the tube of sun cream and went to cool off in the pool. And not because he was too hot.

Chapter Thirty-Seven

Floriana was worried that the heat was proving too much for Esme. It wasn't like her to be so quiet and withdrawn. Although it would be quite understandable if it was nervous anticipation that was causing her to be so pensive.

They were driving along the lake road to Hotel Margherita, or Villa Margherita as it was now. From the back of the car, Floriana observed Esme carefully, taking in how still and tense she was as she stared intently out of the window. During lunch, which they'd decided to have at the villa seeing as they had a fridge full of food care of Domenico and his sister Renata, Esme's sole contribution to the conversation had been to say that she had spoken to Domenico about the Bassani family. Apparently the name meant nothing to him, but then he had only moved to the lake twenty years ago when his wife had died. He'd promised to ask around. More than anything, Floriana hoped he came up with a lead for them. It would be so wonderful to know what had happened to Esme's first love.

So preoccupied with her elderly friend's happiness, Floriana had barely given her own a second thought since arriving here yesterday afternoon. By rights, the thought of Seb and Imogen's impending wedding on Saturday should fill her with dread, but it didn't. Mostly that was due to knowing she would have Adam at her side. Having him there would ensure she would get through the day with her dignity fully intact. There would be no yelling *It should have been me!* No drinking too much and disgracing herself. And no blubbing. Absolutely no blubbing. She would be a model of sobriety and self-control. She would be a noble and shining example of magnanimous goodwill. Well, that was the plan.

Admiring the passing scenery of lakeside villages, she had to admit that she was looking forward to showing Adam off as her plus-one – Imogen certainly wouldn't expect her to show up with anyone so attractive and so obviously out of her league. She'd expect a hairy-toed hobbit to be more Floriana's level! A small laugh escaped from her at the thought.

'Something amusing you?' Adam asked, raising his glance to her in the rear-view mirror.

'Don't ask, it involves hobbits and hairy feet.'

'Of course it does,' he said with a smile, 'doesn't it always?'

A short while later, he turned off the main road and drew to a stop in front of the closed wrought-iron gates of their destination. His window down, he leant out to press a button on the intercom when a car appeared on the other side of the gates. Reversing out of the way, the gates slowly swung open. The other car drew alongside and, lowering his window, the driver gave them an enquiring look.

They had decided earlier that Floriana would be the one to try and talk their way into Villa Margherita, that – in Adam's words – with her bubbling enthusiasm and colourful imagination she would be able to plead their case like no other. So stepping out of the car and dispensing with any attempt to stumble over the limited Italian words and phrases she'd learnt, she asked if the man spoke English.

'Of course,' he replied in a manner that implied she was mad to think he didn't. 'How can I help you?' He spoke with an impressively flawless English accent.

Working on the basis he could be the owner, she launched into the explanation for their visit, indicating Esme at the appropriate moment, who right on cue bestowed one of her most charming and regal smiles on the stranger, and then finishing up with an entreaty into which she hoped she poured sufficient heart and soul that would guarantee that only the most hard-hearted of souls would refuse to show them round their home.

'I see,' he said, when she'd brought her petition to a close, 'but I'm very sorry to tell you, the owner is not here.'

Floriana's heart sank. All that effort and he wasn't even the owner!

'But,' he went on, a smile beginning to work its way over his face, 'there is a way you could see the villa. It's for sale and I'm the estate agent selling it. Now if you were to say you were interested in buying it, then I could personally show you round.'

Floriana could have kissed him! She turned delightedly to Esme and Adam. 'Oh yes, we're very interested in buying the villa, aren't we?' To the man, she said, 'Would it be possible to see it now?'

He checked his watch. 'I was on my way back to the office in Menaggio, I only came to collect the mail, but ...'

'We could come back another time if it would be more convenient to you,' Esme called from the car. 'Would tomorrow be better?'

Still looking at his watch, as if struggling to make out what time it was, he came to a decision with a nod. 'No, now is better, I can make the call I need to later. Follow me down.'

With both cars parked, the agent – a tall angular man with curly black hair and an immaculately trimmed beard – introduced himself as Giovanni Zazzaroni and took them round to the main entrance that overlooked the lake. Standing on the gravel pathway and looking down the incline of lawn, Esme felt as if she had taken a step back in time. Little had changed. Or so it seemed.

Behind her, Adam was talking to the agent about property prices and how stable the market was in this part of Italy. Next to her, Floriana was silently taking in the view. 'Is it how you remembered it?' she asked eventually.

'It's entirely the same. I feel as though any minute I'll spot my father with his easel in a shady corner, and there –' she pointed beyond the stone fountain that wasn't working – 'will be the Kelly-Webbs holding hands, and then Elizabeth will come rushing across the terrace to tell me some snippet of gossip, and if I listen carefully I'll hear Elena scolding Alberto in the vegetable garden for some terrible crime he's committed.'

'And what about Angelo and Marco, are they here?'

Esme swallowed and her gaze travelled the length of the lawn to the stone steps flanked by two magnificent cypress trees. 'Yes,' she said simply, but not elaborating further.

Adam approached. 'He's unlocking the house for us now.'

She turned to see the agent taking a large bunch of keys out of the leather bag slung over his shoulder.

'Keep him talking at all times so I can take some photos,' Floriana whispered to Adam.

'Oh, I don't think we should do that,' Esme said anxiously, 'it seems too rude, let's not forget this is somebody's home.'

'I promise I'll be discreet,' Floriana said, 'and it's not like the photos will be for public consumption, only yours.'

The house was markedly cooler inside and as the hallway with its polished floor and heavy gilt-framed paintings stretched out before Esme, her bare arms prickled with gooseflesh. The doors leading off from the hall were all closed, adding further to the gloom. In front of her was the wide staircase and she remembered how she had stood at the top and witnessed Marco's arrival from Venice with his aunt Giulia.

She turned to their guide. 'Who is the present owner? Are you allowed to tell us that?'

'It's two sisters from Milan. Your friend –' he indicated Floriana – 'said earlier that the time you stayed here back in 1950 when the house was run as a hotel, it was owned by a Signora Bassani. I have heard of this name, but I know nothing about the family, other than the last remaining member of the family sold it in the late 1950s and then it was sold again in the 70s to a Signor Farella in Milan. On his death, his two sisters inherited the villa and now they themselves are too old to benefit from it so want to sell it. They've already sold some of the more valuable pieces of furniture and paintings.'

'How much do they want for the house?' asked Floriana. She gave a little laugh. 'Just out of curiosity.'

The agent smiled back at her and Esme couldn't fail to notice how with an Italian instinct born of old, he eyed Floriana from top to toe in a single sweep of his roguish eyes. 'It's on the market for ten million,' he said. 'That's euros. But,' he added with a teasing lilt to his voice, 'an offer would be considered.'

Floriana whistled. 'I'll bear that in mind.'

'And now, allow me to open the doors so you can have a proper look round.' He led the way into what Esme remembered as the drawing room. Opening the shutters, his voice echoing in the large semi-furnished room, he said, 'Forgive me if I don't open the shutters in all of the rooms, it would take too long; I have another appointment in an hour.'

'That's quite all right,' Esme said, 'I'm just so very grateful you've allowed me this opportunity to have a look.'

The ringing of his mobile had him apologising and excusing himself to take the call out in the hall. In his absence, Adam finished the job of opening windows and pushing back the shutters. With dust motes dancing in the sunlight now streaming into the room, Esme again had the profoundest sensation of stepping back in time. So much so, the hairs stood up on the back of her neck.

'It's quite extraordinary,' she said with a shiver, going over to the black marble fireplace, 'the furniture and furnishings are not that different from what I remember, though it has to have changed.'

Looking about him at the ornately decorated ceiling and intricate cornice picked out in gold, Adam said, 'Maybe the previous owner ... what was his name?'

'Signor Farella,' Floriana supplied, standing behind the open door and taking a photograph with her mobile phone.

'Maybe Signor Farella wanted to preserve the original look,' Adam continued. 'How old do you think the place is?'

'I believe it was built in the 1830s.'

'The *signora* is correct,' Giovanni Zazzaroni said, coming back into the room, the soft rubber soles of his shoes squeaking on the marble floor.

Behind him, and out of view, Floriana hastily pocketed her mobile.

'May we see the dining room, please?' Esme asked, flashing a warning look at Floriana.

'Certainly.'

'If it will help, Floriana and I will close the shutters here and catch the two of you up,' Adam said. The agent nodded his thanks and Esme walked on ahead with him, guessing that left alone with Adam, Floriana would use the opportunity to take more photographs.

The dining room was as grand as Esme remembered. The glorious *trompe l'oeil* effect of a vaulted ceiling was perfectly preserved – she had been worried it would have been painted over by some ghastly modernist philistine. To the contrary, it appeared to have been very carefully restored; the paintwork looked to be in pristine order.

'It's very fine, is it not?' the agent commented, after he'd opened the last of the windows and shutters and the room was flooded with sunlight.

'Indeed it is,' she murmured. 'I'm glad it has been so well looked after.'

'Tell me,' he said, 'did you know the Bassani family well?'

'I ...' She paused, wondering how much to tell this stranger. 'It was Giulia Bassani's nephew I knew best, Marco Bassani. But we lost touch when ... when he went on to become a priest. I must admit to being curious to know what happened to him.'

'Would you like me to try and find somebody who might know something? If you gave me some other names of the people who worked here at the time, there's a strong chance they'll be local and can help give you some answers.'

'I wouldn't like to put you to any trouble.'

'It would be a pleasure,' he said. 'I like to have a problem to solve.'

She gazed about her at the Wedgwood-blue walls and the marble floor. 'Do you think it will be a problem selling this house? It's very expensive.'

He smiled. 'I already have several interested parties. The location is exceptional.'

'I hope you sell it to the right person, somebody who will love and treasure it.'

'That, I'm afraid, I cannot guarantee.'

'Wow!' Floriana exclaimed as she and Adam entered the room. 'This is amazing! Signor Zazzaroni, I think I might just make an offer after all.'

'Please,' he said, his eyes once more raking her from top to toe, 'call me Giovanni.' He then stole a quick glance at his watch.

Taking his hint, Esme said, 'There's just one more room I'd like to see and then if I could have a last look around the garden, we'll be on our way.'

Upstairs, and while the others returned to the landing to admire a chandelier – it was a particularly fine copy, so Giovanni explained, of a traditional eighteenth-century Rezzonico chandelier with hand-cut Murano flowers and ornaments in white and clear glass – Esme remained alone in the bedroom where she had slept.

The cream and sunny-yellow decor and antique furniture was of no interest to her, she gave it and the canopied four-poster bed with its lace and frills no more than a cursory glance through eyes grown watery. It was the past, saturated with heartbreaking poignancy, that was more tangible to her than the furnishings, and all at once the memory of something buried deep inside her broke free and she was overcome with the painful ache and longing for what she had lost.

Her child.

The child she had never held.

The child she had never had the chance to cherish.

The child she and Marco had created in this very room and whose life, cut short so abruptly, had never been given the chance to blossom.

She squeezed her eyes shut against the memory. Not for a long, long time had she experienced the pain so acutely of what she had so nearly had within her grasp. That dreadful dream she'd had this morning had left her feeling unbearably shaken and upset. She used to dream all the time of her poor dead baby, but as time went by she was haunted less frequently by the dreams, until almost never at all.

She had learnt to live with her loss – a double loss, first Marco, then the baby – and had sworn she would never let regret and the emptiness of her heart consume her. For the most part she had succeeded in not letting the bottomless pit of grief claim her and had come to terms in accepting their romance had no real foundations in reality, that it had existed for so short a time, it really was no more than a dream. Again and again she had convinced herself that if reality had been allowed to creep in, love might not have flourished into something everlasting.

But the child had been real. The child should have been everlasting and with her still.

A light touch on her elbow made her jump.

It was Floriana. 'I'm sorry,' the girl said softly, 'I didn't mean to startle you. Are you all right?'

Esme swallowed and blinked hard, tears threatening to spill over. 'Forgive a foolish old woman for—' The words were so tightly bunched up in her throat it was a struggle to get them out. She tried again. 'For letting her emotions get the better of her.'

Floriana pressed her arm gently. 'Oh, Esme, there's nothing foolish about you.'

Tears welled in her eyes and she took several attempts to swallow. She mustn't cry. Not now. Not after all this time. Opening her handbag, she took out a handkerchief. 'We should leave now,' she said briskly, after she'd blown her nose and pulled herself together, 'we've taken up far too much of Signor Zazzaroni's time.'

Her expression tight with concern, Floriana said, 'Don't you want to look round the garden?'

Esme shook her head. 'I don't think we should give Signor Zazzaroni the opportunity to ogle you any more, my dear, the saucy fellow's done quite enough of that already. Another chance to undress you with his hungry eyes and I'd be surprised if Adam doesn't punch him on the nose.'

Floriana laughed. 'Really? I hadn't noticed him looking at me.'

Tutting at the absurd innocence of her, Esme said, 'That's your problem, young lady, you have no idea how others regard you.' Then linking her arm through Floriana's, she took her over to the window for one last look at the garden. In the distance, a *traghetto* was negotiating its way across the lake. When it was out of sight on the other side of the promontory, Esme turned to face Floriana.

'Now whether you want it or not,' she said, 'I'm going to give you some important advice. Don't let your life be full of regret, whatever chances come your way, grab them with both hands. And if you learn nothing else from this week, it must be that you don't make the same mistake with Adam as you made with your friend Seb.'

A look of startled shock on her face, Floriana opened her mouth to speak, but Esme hurried on, determined, once and for all, to open the girl's eyes. 'I want you to think very carefully why Adam is here with us. You surely can't be naive enough to believe he's here purely for my benefit.'

Chapter Thirty-Eight

That night Esme went to bed early saying she was tired. She *was* tired, she was *very* tired, but she couldn't sleep, she was too restless, just as their villa seemed to be – the wooden bones of its old construction relaxing and creaking in the cooling darkness after the torpid heat of the day.

Try as she might, she couldn't settle; her mind was racing, full of what she'd shared with Adam and Floriana over dinner. Adam had booked the restaurant, a beautiful place in Brienno directly overlooking the lake, but really it would have been better if they had gone on their own and enjoyed the romantic atmosphere just the two of them. She had suggested she stay behind, but they wouldn't hear of it.

So now they knew the full story, that when she had last seen Hotel Margherita she had left the lake pregnant, although she hadn't known it at the time. Later, back in Nottingham when a doctor confirmed her suspicions, the only other person to know her secret had been her father. Secrecy had been a matter of survival, a way to get through the shock and sadness.

It never failed to annoy her when she heard the voice of middle England rise up onto its haughty we-know-better haunches and condemn the many unfortunate young girls who found themselves pregnant. Always the poor girls were portrayed as ignorant and wilfully careless. Well, she too had been wilfully careless. So had Marco. They would have been classed as precisely the kind of people to know better. Nonetheless, they had been stupidly reckless, and not just once, but several times, tossing aside all reasoned thought in the pursuit of expressing their love for each other. Once could be justified as merely losing themselves in the moment, but after that first time Marco had returned to her room late that night when everyone was asleep. The following night also. And then he had left the lake to return to Venice and she never saw him again.

At the end of August, Esme and her father returned to England, and as time passed she began to suspect she was pregnant. In the brooding claustrophobic gloom of Hillside and planning their move to Oxford where she was due to take up her place to read English at St Hilda's, Esme confided in her father that she believed she was carrying Marco's child. He was bitterly upset, blamed not just Marco but himself for not doing a better job at keeping her safe – he regretted allowing her so much freedom, he thought he should have spent less time selfishly painting and more time with her. 'It's no one's fault but my own,' she told him. His anger and guilt persisted and he was all for writing to Giulia Bassani and informing her of the situation, making it clear that her nephew had a responsibility to do the right thing.

Esme begged her father not to write the letter, arguing that Marco's life was set on a particular course and she had no intention of forcing him to give up something he felt destined to pursue. 'But what about your life?' her father pleaded with her. 'Your future has been destroyed because of him.'

'Altered,' she maintained, reiterating her decision to keep the baby and forego her place at St Hilda's, 'not destroyed.'

Her father gave in and the planned move, now deferred until the following year, took on a greater importance. They would time the move to Oxford immediately after the baby was born and start afresh. Meanwhile, and with his help, Esme would have to hold her head up high and brave whatever malicious gossip circulated in the village where they lived.

In December of that year they received a Christmas card from Elizabeth in London saying that she was planning a return visit to Hotel Margherita in the spring, but before then she would love to visit them, would February be convenient? As fond as they were of Elizabeth, they couldn't agree to her visit; she would take one look at Esme and put two and two together, and being the incurable gossip she was, who knew who she would tell when she was back at the lake in the spring? They put her off with the excuse that they were in a state of chaos preparing to move house. For whatever reason, and perhaps fortuitously, they never heard from her again.

Four weeks before the baby was due Esme was rushed to

hospital and underwent an emergency Caesarean. When she came round from the anaesthetic she was given the news that she would never truly get over, that due to a prolapsed umbilical cord her baby – a girl – had been stillborn. Cruelly, she never saw her daughter, not so much as a glimpse. She didn't even know what happened to the body. Twenty-four hours later and following a massive haemorrhage, she had to have yet more emergency surgery and when she woke up she was given more devastating news – she would never be able to have a child of her own.

Still grieving for her baby daughter, who she secretly named Grace, Esme and her father left Hillside and moved into Norham Gardens in North Oxford on a warm summer's day. They settled into their new life with determination and knowing that the best way to recover from her loss was to be busy, Esme threw herself into making their new house a proper home in the way that Hillside never was.

Her father could have led a life of gentlemanly leisure, living off the money his wife had left him, but an opportunity arose for him to join a firm of solicitors in St Aldate's and he took it. He continued with his painting, turning part of the top floor of the house into an art studio. He even started to exhibit his paintings, but it wasn't in his nature to show off his artwork and he didn't pursue selling his work as he could have done.

The following year when the secretarial college opened in St Giles, Esme embarked on a course and twelve months later she started work at Wadham College in the bursar's office.

In time their lives became enriched with new friends and new opportunities. There were young men too; men with whom Esme was happy to go to the theatre or have dinner, but she couldn't bring herself to get close to them; she now had a fear of intimacy.

In her late twenties, she met Charles Penstow, an American professor of Economics who was at the university on a sabbatical year. Twelve years her senior and deemed a catch by her small circle of friends, he surprised her one evening over dinner by asking her to be his wife and return with him to his home in Boston. 'But we hardly know each other,' she'd said, astounded.

'I know all I need to know,' he'd replied, tapping the table with his forefinger. 'You're an eminently sensible and down-to-earth woman, there's never any fuss with you. What's more, you can do *The Times* crossword faster than anyone I know and you have impeccable manners and a stylish dress sense.'

He insisted that she didn't give her answer straight away; she was to give his proposal her full consideration while he was on a speaking tour in Australia promoting a weighty tome he'd recently had published. Somewhat bemused, she was pondering his extraordinary proposal when disaster struck: her father suffered a debilitating stroke. By the time Charles was back in Oxford, and based on the medical advice she'd been given, Esme had reached the only conclusion she could: her father would need constant care for the rest of his life and it was down to her to be the one to provide it. Charles took her rejection with the kind of equanimity that implied he was far from heartbroken. Which she wasn't either, not when she felt she had been damned with faint praise – being described as 'sensible' and 'down-to-earth' were hardly the romantic endearments a girl likes to hear from a prospective husband. They certainly didn't compare to the things Marco had said to her.

Her father spent the rest of his life in a wheelchair, and to add insult to injury, his eyesight began to fail. Many a day he wished he was dead, that he wasn't the burden he had become. 'I've imprisoned us both,' he would mumble through his brutally distorted mouth. She lovingly cared for him right up until he died, by which time she was in her early forties and the idea of marriage was no longer of interest to her; she was too set in her ways. Instead, she embraced life as a spinster and studied for the degree she had intended to do more than twenty years previously, and when she graduated, she joined the librarian staff in the magnificent library at Queen's College. Five years later the chance to work at the Bodleian came up and she took it. It was when she was approaching retirement that she decided to sell the house in Norham Gardens and buy something smaller and more manageable; that was when she moved to Trinity House.

On the whole she would say she'd had a life of comparative ease and privilege. Financially she had never had to worry, her work life had been absorbing and fulfilling, and she had been loved by a good father and had known, albeit briefly, love at its most poignant. She had no right to wallow in this pathetic self-pity to which she had surrendered. Plenty of women lost a child. Plenty also were never able to be a mother.

Tomorrow, for the sake of her two dear friends, she had to pull herself together and make the most of her time here. There would be no more tears from her. But even as she silently articulated the words, her heart ached for the baby girl she had so very nearly known. And for the man who had helped create her.

It was nearly midnight and Floriana and Adam were in the garden, sitting on the wooden swing seat, gently rocking to and fro. It was a beautiful night, still surprisingly warm and unnaturally still. Beneath them in the distance, the lake shimmered along the path of silvery light cast from the moon, and on the other side of the stretch of water clusters of lights twinkled like stars in the darkness.

They had opened a bottle of wine and were in a reflective mood. Their voices low, they were discussing Esme.

'I can't stop thinking how broken-hearted she must have been to have experienced all that pain and suffering at so young an age,' Floriana said sadly. 'How different her life could have been.'

'Life's like that,' Adam said, closely observing Floriana's upturned face as she regarded the inky sky. 'It's nothing but a series of what ifs. What if Esme had never met Marco? Or what if he hadn't been a priest in the making? Or what if the baby had lived?'

Lowering her gaze, Floriana sipped from her glass of wine, her expression thoughtful. 'What's your greatest *what if* moment?' she asked.

He considered the question, but chose to avoid answering it by turning the tables. 'I'm not really sure. How about you? What's yours?'

She drew her legs up, tucked her bare feet under her. 'I don't know about the greatest or most significant *what if*, but certainly I can't help but think what if I'd never received Seb's wedding invitation? If I hadn't, then I wouldn't have got hit by that car and you and Esme wouldn't have come to my rescue, which means I wouldn't be here now with you both.'

'There are definitely better ways to meet people,' he said with a smile, 'but I'm also glad that sequence of events happened. My life's been a lot more fun since I got to know the two of you.' *You in particular*, he wanted to say, but he couldn't bring himself to form the words.

'For me too,' she said softly, half turning to look at him.

He stared back at her nervously – at the face he was fast coming to know as well as his own. Right now her hazel eyes were like liquid pools of darkness and stirred within him the same desire he'd felt when he'd been rubbing sun cream onto her shoulders earlier that morning. His mouth suddenly dry, he wondered what the sequence of events would be if he was brave enough to put a hand to her cheek and kiss her lightly on the mouth. Would there ever be a better moment – a more romantic moment – than this to make his feelings clear, to tell her that he wanted to be so much more than friends?

But he couldn't do it. It was too big a risk. If she turned him down, their friendship would be as good as over no matter how hard they pretended otherwise. So instead, he cowardly raised his glass of wine. 'Here's to *what if* moments,' he said.

Chapter Thirty-Nine

Awake before anyone else, Floriana crept downstairs as quietly as she could. She made herself a mug of tea and went outside.

The soft morning air was tantalisingly fragrant. The scent was coming from the luscious velvety-red roses in front of the terrace; long arching sprays were heavily laden with blousy blooms that were intensely perfumed. Stepping barefoot down from the terrace onto the parched coarse grass, she stooped to a lavender bush and ran her hand through the flowers. She breathed in the delicious fragrance thinking that when she was back at home, she really must make more of an effort with her own small garden. It would be heavenly to fill it with wonderfully scented flowers.

But home wasn't what she wanted to think of right now. She just wanted to go on losing herself in this enchanting paradise where everything felt different. Not to say distinctly perplexing.

And that was thanks to Esme and her accusation that basically Floriana didn't have a clue what was going on right under her nose and that Adam wasn't here solely for Esme's benefit. Just what was Floriana supposed to make of that? Other than to be completely confused.

It was a matter of pure conjecture on Esme's part as to whether Adam had wanted to punch a cheeky Italian on the nose for looking at Floriana inappropriately, but it did beg the question why she hadn't noticed Giovanni Zazzaroni checking her out. And if she'd missed that, what else had she missed? Particularly when it came to Adam?

Since that extraordinary conversation with Esme in her old bedroom at Villa Margherita, and with every chance she had when she could do so unobserved, Floriana had found herself studying Adam, searching for a sign from him that would corroborate what Esme had said. Yet try as she might, she could detect nothing in his manner that proved he viewed her any more than as a friend.

But then late last night, there was that moment on the swing seat when, out of the blue, she had truly believed he was about to kiss her. But he hadn't. She had gone to bed not long afterwards wondering if that had been a *what if* moment between them. Would Esme class that as a lost opportunity?

Or was it no more than this magical place casting a bewitching spell on its visitors and putting thoughts into their heads that had no right to be there?

Oh, Esme, Floriana thought with a heartfelt sigh, how muddled you've made me feel.

Twenty-four hours ago and the idea of Adam kissing her hadn't crossed her mind, now she couldn't shake the thought of him out of her head!

But why would he be interested in her? They were chalk and cheese. Besides, she'd seen that photograph of Jesse with her stunning catwalk figure and her glossy long hair; there wasn't a chance in hell of Floriana following an act like that. It was a great pity Esme hadn't seen the photo as then she wouldn't be so keen to fan the flames of romance, she'd give it up as a lost cause. Because one thing was a definite in this life, attractive men like Adam sought out equally attractive women, they didn't settle for less.

She went over to the pool, sat down and dangled her feet into the cool water. Sipping her tea, she couldn't resist replaying the cosy little scene in her mind of sitting on the swing seat with Adam last night. Whichever way she viewed it, she couldn't rule out the gut feeling she'd had, that Adam really had been on the verge of kissing her. So why hadn't he?

More importantly, would she have kissed him back? Yes, she would have, and for two reasons. Firstly out of curiosity, because let's face it, who wouldn't mind being kissed by such an attractive man? And secondly, nobody knew better than her that to be rebuffed was hideously humiliating. If afterwards Adam had shown any regret or embarrassment, she would have laughed it off as though being kissed by accident happened to her all the time.

It was a shame Seb couldn't have done the same, she thought with sadness. If he had reacted with less horror when she'd made the mistake of kissing him, their friendship might not have suffered the way it had.

A short distance away, further up the hillside, a church bell chimed the hour – it was seven o'clock. The bells were different here, not at all like the ones in Oxford; these bells had a softer less intrusive clang to them.

With her head tilted back and her eyes closed against the bright sun, she thought of Oxford and a young heartbroken Esme moving there to start a new life. Imagining the strength it must have taken for her to put her grief behind her, Floriana realised that the heartbreak she had gone through with Seb was nothing compared to what Esme had endured.

She opened her eyes and sat up, suddenly understanding very clearly that the time had come for her to let go of Seb. He was the past. She had to look to the future now.

After breakfast, and after he'd touched base with Denise in the office, Adam announced his intention to find Villa Belmonte where Mussolini and his mistress had been shot. As far as he could work out, the scene of the execution in Giulino di Mezzegra was practically on their doorstep.

Esme pulled a face when he asked her if she'd like to join him. 'I'll pass on that grisly outing, if you don't mind,' she said.

He looked at Floriana over in the pool. 'It's probably not your kind of thing either, so don't feel you have to come,' he said. 'I had the misfortune to go there once before.'

Putting the book down that she was reading, Esme regarded him over the top of her reading glasses. 'Really, Adam,' she said, 'could you make the poor girl feel any less welcome?'

Thinking that Esme was more her usual self this morning, he frowned. 'I didn't mean it that way, I just meant that I'd understand if no one fancied coming with me. As you said, it's a bit grisly wanting to see where two people were executed. It's not everyone's cup of tea.'

'I wouldn't mind going,' Floriana said, swimming towards the edge of the pool, 'but if you'd rather I stayed here with you, Esme, I'm—'

'I'm not in need of babysitting if that's what you're suggesting,' Esme interrupted her. 'I'll be quite happy here on my own saving my energy for this afternoon when we go to Villa Balbianello. So off you go, the pair of you. Go on, *shoo!'*

The hot sun was already high in the sky and blazing down on them when they set off on foot with a roughly drawn map – a map which Adam had found in the file of local information provided by the owner of the villa.

Having caught the sun yesterday on her shoulders, Floriana was wearing a white long-sleeved top with shorts and a pair of flip-flops. Her head was covered with a large floppy-brimmed hat that Esme had insisted she borrow from her. 'I'm not having you come down with heatstroke,' she'd fussed. The downside of the hat was that Adam couldn't see Floriana's face, or more to the point, her expression, which he was anxious at all times to read. More than ever now.

'Does it feel weird being a tourist and not being in charge as a guide?' he asked her.

He winced at how dumb the question sounded, like they'd only just met and he was making polite small talk. But that's what he had been reduced to. He was so busy watching himself around her, he'd become awkward and self-conscious and didn't seem able to say anything right. Especially after last night. In some ways he wished he'd just seized the moment and kissed her. At least then he'd know where he stood. As it was, he was behaving like an idiot with the situation fast spinning out of his control. And likely to get a lot worse if he didn't do something about it. He couldn't go on like this. It was ridiculous. It wasn't as if he was a novice in these matters, there had been plenty of girlfriends before Jesse. But none like Floriana, he reminded himself, she was in a class of her own. He could honestly say he'd never known anyone like her, or admired anyone as much. There were times when he wanted to say, 'Go on, just once make me feel half as clever as you!'

'You didn't hear a word of what I just said, did you?'

Oh hell! What was happening to him? He couldn't even keep up with a simple conversation now. 'Sorry,' he said, 'what did you say?'

'I was saying I have no problem switching off from work. Unlike you. I bet that's what you were just thinking about, wasn't it?'

He made a half-hearted murmur of apologetic assent.

'So exactly how many work phone calls have you made this morning?' she asked.

'A few.'

'And how many emails have you sent?'

Her questions were an echo of what Denise had said earlier, when he'd called to check she'd spoken with the electrician about the faulty wiring in the house on Walton Street. 'This may come as a shock to you, Adam,' she'd said, 'but I can manage perfectly well without you. Now get on with enjoying your holiday and leave me alone!'

Indicating the turning to the right which they needed to take according to the map, he said, 'I'm not a workaholic or a control freak, if that's what you're getting at. It's just in my nature to get things done.'

'I know,' she said. Then lifting up the floppy brim of her hat, she peered out at him, the corners of her mouth twitching with a smile. 'But you know what happens to control freaks and dictators round here, don't you?' She mimed a gun raised to her temple. '*Pop!*'

He laughed, and at last felt himself relax. 'Actually, I think my assistant, Denise, is more of a dictator than me. But thanks for the warning, I'll be on my guard.'

When she heard the sound of their voices approaching, Esme felt like jumping from her seat and rushing to greet Adam and Floriana.

For the last thirty minutes she had sat here patiently waiting for their return, bursting to tell them her news. Domenico had visited shortly after they'd left, bringing with him the name and address of someone who might be able to throw some light on the whereabouts of the Bassani family.

Chapter Forty

With their afternoon trip to the Villa Balbianello cancelled they were on their way to Bellagio.

At Tremezzo they boarded the crowded *traghetto* and with a protective hand placed at Esme's elbow, Adam – part Moses, part Superman – cleared a path for them to squeeze through the tightly packed tourists to get to the prow of the boat. There were no empty seats, but luckily an Australian man kindly offered his to Esme and immediately struck up conversation with Adam, while the woman he was with started chatting to Esme.

Standing a few feet away from Adam, Floriana caught the odd word of his conversation with the other man – cricket seemed to the topic of interest. Adam liked cricket? That was news to her. But then as she was rapidly discovering, there was a lot about him she was learning this week.

Partially hidden behind a couple of girls with huge rucksacks on their backs, she continued to watch Adam. Since Esme had put the cat amongst the pigeons yesterday afternoon, Floriana kept looking at him through new eyes and unnervingly always came back to the same thing: she could no longer regard him in the way she once had. His attractiveness, which familiarity had ensured she had taken for granted, now had a habit of catching her unawares, forcing her to sit up and take extra notice. Right now he stood out from just about every other man on the boat because he wasn't dressed as a tourist in unattractive sandals, ill-fitting baggy shorts and a T-shirt boasting a previous holiday destination. In contrast, he was wearing slim-fit jeans and a pair of deck shoes, and a smart blue and white check shirt, the sleeves rolled up to his elbows with the creases from where it had been folded in his case just discernible. Clean-shaven, his light-brown hair ruffled by the wind and with Ray-Ban Aviator sunglasses in place, he looked effortlessly cool.

Not for the first time Floriana wondered if his ex-girlfriend ever regretted ending their relationship. From what Adam had said, Jesse had simply stopped fancying him. It happened. It had happened to Floriana with a number of her old boyfriends. With hindsight it had been because she was always trying to kid herself that they were as fun to be with as Seb; eventually she would accept they weren't and the attraction she had originally felt would die in an instant.

Still hidden behind the girls and their rucksacks – she had decided they were German – Floriana continued furtively to observe Adam. She thought back to when she had met him that cold December night and the solicitous way he'd taken care of her while they'd waited for the ambulance to arrive. She had never forgotten how reassured and safe he'd made her feel. She had since come to know that was how she always felt when she was with him.

It was the opposite to how Seb had made her feel. With Seb she had always felt she was precariously on the edge of the unknown. It had, she now admitted to herself, been a strain at times, as though she was carrying him, bearing the heavy burden of whatever was troubling him. She supposed she had got so used to doing it, it had become second nature for her. Even recently she had been the one to whom he had turned for help when he'd been worrying about his approaching wedding.

But that was what you did when you cared for someone; you willingly shared the load. But had Seb ever done the same for her? She had never asked herself this before and the answer made Floriana think just how one-sided their friendship had been. Perhaps some relationships were meant to be that way. But wouldn't a balanced relationship feel more secure and satisfying? And would it be like that with Adam?

No! No thinking along those lines.

Squeezing past the two German girls, she managed to find a free space against the rail of the boat. Leaning on it and staring out at the lake, she thought of their walk this morning when they'd gone in search of the site where Mussolini and his mistress had been executed. It was hardly an outing to foster any romantic declarations, but even so, Adam had been exactly the same as he always was with her, which threw further doubt on Esme's claims.

No. That wasn't entirely true. He'd been quieter. More thoughtful. Even a bit distracted at one point. Was that a sign? Or was she clutching at straws to try and make sense of an old lady's attempt at matchmaking?

With the wind whipping at her hair, Floriana pushed her sunglasses back, tipped her head up to the sun and closed her eyes. There was really only one question that counted for anything in all this, and it was the most fundamental and obvious question of the lot – how did she really feel about Adam? Did she feel sexually attracted to him? No sooner had she articulated the thought, than a picture of the two of them popped into her head – to her surprise, it was of *her* taking the initiative and kissing Adam. But then, just as suddenly, she saw it wasn't Adam she was kissing, but Seb. She snapped her eyes open with alarm. Was that an omen, her subconscious telling her not to risk ruining things with Adam?

'It's not a bad view, is it?'

'Not bad at all,' she said awkwardly as the man himself materialised next to her. She hastily lowered her sunglasses and hid behind them, worried that her face would betray what she'd just been thinking. He rested his elbows on the rail beside her, his already tanned arm touching her much paler one.

'Where's your new Australian buddy?' she asked.

'With his wife now and being thoroughly charmed by Esme. I'll be disappointed if by the time we reach Bellagio they haven't invited her to visit them in Perth.'

Floriana smiled. 'Esme's not the only one who can turn on the charm.'

'Meaning?'

'Meaning you don't do so badly yourself. You have a way with people.'

'That sounds horribly like you're accusing me of being Mr Smooth.'

Her equilibrium fully restored now, she nudged his arm playfully. 'More like Mr Overly Sensitive!'

'I can't win with you, can I?'

'Damn straight! Just accept that I'm Miss Perfect.'

He laughed. 'Trust me, I did that a long time ago.'

The boat was drawing nearer to their destination and looking at the outline of the pretty town of Bellagio in the distance,

Floriana said, 'I hope meeting this woman this afternoon doesn't upset Esme as much as going to Villa Margherita did yesterday. I'm beginning to wonder if it wasn't a mistake her coming here. I feel so responsible.'

'What for?'

'For her happiness. If I'd never received Seb's wedding invitation, the memories might not have got so stirred up for her and she wouldn't have left Oxford; she'd be at home perfectly happy with Euridice.'

'We're back to those *what if* moments, aren't we?' he said. 'But I honestly don't think she'll regret this trip, and maybe it's down to us to make sure that doesn't happen.'

Touched by his comment, Floriana smiled and watched him take a photo with his mobile of where they were heading. 'Has anyone ever told you, you are one of the really good guys?'

'Hell yes! I get that a lot. All the time, in fact.'

She laughed. 'I retract that statement, you're nothing but a honking great *blagueur*!'

'Wow, a *blagueur*. Honk, honk! Can I claim that as our word of the day?' Then turning his mobile around so the screen was facing towards them at arm's length, he said, 'How does Miss Perfect feel about posing with Monsieur *Blagueur* for a photo?'

She smiled. 'No problem, so long as you get my best side.'

Their heads close together, they struck up a series of poses, with Floriana then getting her own mobile out and doing the same.

From her seat next to the woman from Perth whose husband had given up his place for her, Esme watched Adam and Floriana fondly. Better and better, she thought with happy satisfaction as she watched their grinning antics and heard Floriana's uninhibited laughter, while Adam had his arm casually placed around her as they posed for the camera.

The sight of them made Esme's brain make a rapid connection to that day when she'd been on the boat with Angelo and he'd put his arm around her. The memory filled her with a rush of reminiscences so strong she felt an ache in her chest, and her head spun with details she should have long since forgotten.

How devious Angelo had been with her and what a silly innocent she'd been for trying to appear so worldly-wise with him.

How easily he must have seen through her veneer of sophistication and her desperate need to be taken seriously as a woman.

Her gaze moving away from Adam and Floriana, and over to the lakeshore, she stared at a large building that was partly covered in scaffolding. It took her a few moments to realise what it was: it was the Hotel Grand Bretagne. Adam had shown her photographs of the hotel on the internet, how it had fallen into disrepair and that numerous attempts had been made to revive it, but without success. How sad that such a fine and beautiful building had been stripped of its dignity and glory days.

Amidst the jostle of people disembarking the boat, Esme was grateful for Adam's steadying hand. When they were clear of the terminus, she looked up and down the length of the main street. There at the far end was Hotel Metropole and Hotel Suisse, and in front of her was the covered promenade and Hotel du Lac with its balconies gaily adorned with scarlet geraniums; to her left was Hotel Florence. It all seemed more colourful than she remembered, more vibrantly alive, but then that was probably because there were so many more tourists here now.

Thanks to Domenico, everything had been arranged and they were to be met at the terminus; they were to look out for a *ragazza* – a young girl – in a silver Fiat. Sure enough, there was a car that fitted the description and standing behind it was an attractive young girl in sunglasses. Catching sight of them, she came over. She was of a similar age to Floriana with long dark hair tied back into a ponytail. 'Signora Silcox?' she said to Esme.

'*Sì*,' Esme replied, '*sono io.*'

With a smile of happy relief, the girl shook hands with all three of them and introduced herself as Maddalena. 'Please to come,' she said, ushering them towards the car, 'my grandmother is most curious to meet you.'

She drove at breakneck speed out of the centre of Bellagio, away from the lake and the bustling streets of tourists. Climbing up and up the hillside and taking hairpin bends so fast the wheels of her little car squealed, she suddenly turned sharply to the right, then slowed to turn again before coming to a stop in front of a two-storey house with a circular bed of red roses in the garden.

Leading the way, Maddalena took them to the front door and stepping inside, she called out to her grandmother. '*Nonna!*' In return, Esme heard an indistinct response, and following behind the girl they passed through a short hallway. The house was dark and quiet, and very cool compared to the baking heat outside.

They came to a stop in a room that was filled with too much cumbersome furniture and a large stone fireplace with blackened stonework. The room, by no means small, was dark and oppressive, the sunlight kept out by heavy net curtains at the windows. A pair of open glass doors led out to the garden, but the opaque net curtain remained perfectly still. Framed photographs on the walls charted the progress of a growing family. Above the fireplace there was a crucified Christ and rosary beads hanging from the crucifix.

At the other end of the room was a dining room table with six chairs and an ornate display cabinet. To the left of this was an archway and coming through it, her movements slow and stiff, was a stocky woman with short iron-grey hair.

Esme stared at her, and with equal curiosity the other woman stared back at her from behind a pair of spectacles.

Was it really Maria? Could this woman really be the young, spirited waitress from Hotel Margherita? The girl with the flashing eyes, the smooth olive skin, who had been jealous of Esme dancing with Angelo?

'You don't recognise me, do you?' the other woman said, raising her sagging chin. 'But yes, I am Maria.'

'I expect you don't recognise me either,' Esme replied. She was surprised how tremulous her voice sounded in the oppressive atmosphere.

'This is true,' Maria replied, 'but I remember your name and how you looked all those years ago.' She motioned for them to sit down, while also dispatching Maddalena to the kitchen for drinks.

Then, as if only now noticing Adam and Floriana, she gave them a long hard look. 'These are your grandchildren?' she asked.

Esme explained that they were friends and would be attending a wedding on Saturday – putting the emphasis on their coming to the lake for a wedding sounded better than a foolish old woman wanting a sentimental trip down memory lane.

'You speak excellent English,' Esme complimented her, after Maria had said the lake was a very popular place for weddings these days, that it was good for the local economy.

Maria shook her head. 'No, no, it is only what I have picked up over the years.'

Reappearing with their drinks – glasses of iced tea – Maddalena said, 'As usual, my grandmother is being modest. She speaks very well the English and helped me with my homework when I was at school. My cousins also. She helped us all. We all say she should have been a teacher.'

Glancing round at the photographs on the walls, Esme said, 'You have a big family, I see.'

With obvious pride, Maria said, 'I have two sons and a daughter and seven grandchildren and one great-grandson. And you?'

'I never married.'

'Then you have been spared the sadness of losing a husband,' she replied matter-of-factly. 'My husband Vittorio died five years ago. We had a good life together. He was a ...' she hesitated, seeming to search for the right word, 'an electrician,' she said finally. 'He had his own business.' She said this with yet more pride. 'I remember your father; he was always very polite. He loved to paint, didn't he?'

Pleased that Maria could remember her father so clearly, and after Maddalena had excused herself saying she would return later to drive them back to the boat terminus, Esme said, 'I don't know how much Domenico told you, but I'm interested to know what happened to the Bassani family. I know Hotel Margherita was sold many years ago, but do you know what happened to Giulia and Angelo and Marco?'

Maria's expression hardened and behind her spectacles, her watery eyes sparked. 'The Bassani family attracted nothing but bad luck,' she said, her heavily knuckled hands clenched in her lap, 'and their misfortune spread to everyone who came in contact with them.'

Chapter Forty-One

In the leaden stillness of the room Maria took a long and deliberate sip of her drink. And then another. The ponderous silence seemed to go on for ever and was so intense Esme could literally feel her pulse ticking as she waited for the woman to speak.

'Bad luck was in their blood,' Maria said finally. 'The family was cursed. First Marco's parents died in a car crash, then Giulia's husband killed himself.'

'I thought he died from a heart attack,' Esme said. 'That it was the strain of coping with the pressure of trying to keep the family business going during the war that proved too much for him.'

'That was what the family wanted people to think. But we all secretly knew he started that fire which destroyed the Bassani factory, he did it for the insurance money and when he feared he would be found out, he hung himself. He was a coward. Just like his son, Angelo.' The bitterness in Maria's voice was palpable and out of the corner of her eye, Esme noticed Adam and Floriana exchanging a glance.

'Angelo was not only a coward,' Maria continued, 'he was ...' She hesitated, while leaning forward to put her glass down on the table. 'In Italian we say, he was *furbo*. I believe in English the word is "cunning". He could make people do whatever he wanted them to do. I think maybe you know what I mean by that.'

She looked at Esme meaningfully and a moment of shared understanding passed between them.

'Yes,' Esme said, 'I didn't know Angelo for long but in that short space of time I came to realise that he knew precisely how to use his charm to get what he wanted. I was very naive with him.'

'I was too,' Maria responded, with a slight lifting of her shoulders. 'All women were. I remember I was jealous of you. You

276

were so beautiful with your blond hair and blue eyes and your shy and modest English ways. You were like a perfect little china doll. I hope you did not give Angelo what he wanted.' She shot Esme another meaningful look.

To which Esme shook her head. 'No, I didn't.'

'Good, because you would have given yourself to a man who had the cold heart of a murderer.'

'A murderer? Surely not?'

'It is true, I tell you!' Maria exclaimed vehemently, bringing her hand down on the arm of her chair with a fierce slap. 'Believe me, Angelo was no angel, he was a devil! It was he who caused the death of my oldest brother. Federico's death broke my parents' hearts. And mine. My family never recovered from the sadness.'

'I'm sorry,' Esme said gently, sensing that whenever this brother had died, Maria still felt that loss keenly. 'What did Angelo do?'

A faint welcome breeze blew in at the open glass doors, causing the heavy net curtains to sway and stir the stagnant air. 'You knew about the *spalloni* at the lake, didn't you?' Maria said. 'The *contrabbando*?'

'The smugglers? Yes, I was told that it was a way of life for many, a way to survive. I know also that Angelo was involved.'

Maria gave a short sour laugh. 'He played at being involved. He was nothing but *un mammone* – a spoilt mamma's boy – looking for excitement. His own life bored him. He wanted the life of a *spallone*. He saw it as heroic. Which it was for those whose lives depended upon it. It was not enough for him to be part of the organisation in Lecco and Milano that helped fund things. For that was his role, you see, that was what he was suited to do – with his smart appearance and family name, it meant he was above suspicion. But he wanted more; he wanted the excitement of hiding from the border police in the mountains, of beating them. To him it was nothing but a game, an adventure. For my brothers who knew the dangers, who risked their lives again and again, they did not want him with them, but he persuaded them. To them he was a fool, full of talk and hot air.'

She paused to take another sip of her drink, giving Esme the opportunity to glance across to the sofa where Adam and Floriana were sitting. They each gave her a small acknowledging nod.

'He boasted that he was as strong as my brothers,' Maria

went on, 'but he wasn't. How could he be when every day he sat behind his desk in his safe office in Milano? Not for him the hard physical labour my brothers were used to as builders.'

'So what happened?'

'What happened is carved on my heart,' Maria said. 'The story has been told in our family many, many times. For us, Matteo and Federico were true heroes. And for me personally, Federico was the brother I loved most when I was a child. I adored him.' With a shaking hand, she leant forward to place her now empty glass on the table. She cleared her throat and sat back stiffly, her eyes fixed on Esme.

'Reluctantly my brothers agreed for Angelo to go with them one night after he promised to do exactly what they told him. The easy part was crossing the border into Switzerland, but the return journey, with the heavy *bricolla* on his back, is what truly tests a man. After all his big talk, Angelo could not carry his sack of *bionde* – that was what cigarettes were known as. He was too slow and many times Federico and Matteo had to wait for him. He was a vain man and his pride hurt, he became angry and accused them of deliberately making his *bricolla* heavier than the ones they carried. He was nothing but a child. An angry child used to getting his own way. They had warned him before that it would be hard, that the sacks would weigh as much as thirty kilos and so they told him to stop behaving like a child and to be a man, it was time he grew up!'

Esme could just imagine how furious that would have made Angelo.

'There were other men there too,' Maria pressed on. 'It wasn't just Federico and Matteo; they were part of a team that had to work together. But Angelo was not a man to play in a team or to share. He wanted only the glory for himself. Before long, he had forced Federico and Matteo to slow down so much they had lost sight of the rest of the men; they were on their own in the dark. Again Angelo began to complain that his *bricolla* must be heavier than theirs, so Federico swapped with him to prove it was not the case. Of course, the truth of this only made him look more stupid. By now Matteo was angry, he understood the danger, and he insisted they hurry to catch up with the others, but that was when they heard noises and suddenly the path behind them was bright with flashing lights: it was the Swiss border police.

Federico shouted for them to run, but the police started firing their guns and that was when Matteo saw Angelo push Federico out of the way so he could escape. He cared only about himself.'

Pausing to take a deep breath, Maria's gaze shifted from Esme to a group of framed black and white photographs on the wall to her left – they were too far away for Esme to make out the people in them, but she assumed they included Maria's brothers.

'Thanks to Angelo,' Maria said, turning to face Esme once more, 'Federico was shot in the head and died instantly, and Matteo was captured and spent a year in prison, and all for agreeing to let Angelo go with them. It was a decision Matteo has regretted all his life. If you asked him today about it, he would tell you word for word what I have said and then he would spit on the name of Angelo Bassani.' With a weary shake of her head, she took off her spectacles and rubbed her eyes. 'Poor Matteo, he wasn't allowed to go to his own brother's funeral. It was terrible. A disgrace.'

Out of respect for Maria, not wanting to seem uncaring, Esme counted to twenty before saying, 'What happened to Angelo? Was he caught?'

Her spectacles back in place, Maria said, 'He escaped. But he did not escape judgement entirely. His body was found in the lake a year later.'

'An accident?'

'Possibly. Possibly an act of justice from God. Who knows? He had many enemies. He owed money to people in Milano. He gambled. There was talk of debts.'

'When did all this happen?'

'It was August 1955 when his half-rotted body was found. I know exactly because that was when I married. I was twenty-one.'

Five years on from when she and her father had left Hotel Margherita, Esme thought. 'How did his mother take the news of his death?' she asked.

'It was the end for her. Signora Bassani became an old woman almost overnight and died of ...' Maria waved her hand around in the air, as though conjuring the right words. 'It was something growing on her brain. A lump. She was not an easy woman to feel sorry for, she was too proud and she loved her son too much. It was a love that made her blind; she could not see the bad in him.'

'I'm not so sure that was true,' Esme said carefully. 'Angelo was jealous of his cousin, he seemed to think his mother thought more of Marco than him.'

'That was typical Angelo, he was jealous of anyone he thought might be more popular than him.'

Thinking of the way Angelo had reacted when he'd suspected she and Marco were growing close, Esme said, 'You've been very kind to share all this with me, especially as it must bring back a lot of painful memories, but do you know anything about Marco? Do you know what happened to him? Did he become a priest?'

Maria's expression immediately changed and she gave Esme another uncomfortably meaningful look. 'I thought you might ask about him. For that is what you really came to ask me, isn't it?'

The directness of Maria's question, and knowing that little had got past her all those years ago, Esme felt her neck and face flush.

'Yes,' she said simply.

Chapter Forty-Two

In the silence that followed, the ring of her mobile made Floriana start.

'Sorry,' she apologised, fumbling in her bag for the phone as it kept on ringing. Unable to find it, and not wanting to spoil the crucial moment any more than she already had, she went outside to the garden to deal with whoever was calling her. It had better not be one of those wretched PPI people.

It wasn't. It was worse than that. Far worse.

'Floriana, it's me, Imogen.'

'Oh, hi, Imogen,' she said, trying to pitch her response on the right side of pleasantly surprised rather than all-out panic accompanied with flashing lights and sirens blaring. Why was Imogen calling her? She had never phoned her before. That was 'never' in the sense of *NEVER* in very large italicised capitals and in bold for good measure. What could she possibly want?

'I hope you don't mind me ringing,' Imogen said, 'I got your number from Seb.'

'Absolutely no problem at all,' she said, nearly choking on her forced cheerfulness. 'So how's the bride-to-be?'

'Oh, you know, frantic with organising a million and one things. We're at the lake now, we got here yesterday.'

The thought of Imogen being so close made Floriana's stomach lurch with a swirl of queasy apprehension. Which was ridiculous. She had known all along Seb and Imogen would be arriving a few days before the big day on Saturday, but since she and Esme and Adam had settled in at Villa Sofia, the wedding – the actual reality of it – had conveniently receded to the far reaches of her cluttered mind, hidden at the back with all the other things she preferred not to deal with. But now it was right back up there at the top of her list of *Things She Would Rather Not Do*, a list that included *Avoid Speaking to Imogen on the Phone*.

'The hotel's super,' Imogen blithely carried on. 'Mummy and I are booked into the spa for the rest of the afternoon, leaving Seb to enjoy some boy-time with Daddy and Jules.'

'Jules?'

'My brother.'

Ah yes, the foisted best man. 'That's nice,' Floriana said. So much for being frantic, she thought unkindly while grimacing at the words *Mummy* and *Daddy*. And who described something as *super* without being ironic? 'Sounds like you have everything under control.'

'That's what Seb keeps saying. He says I'm worrying too much, that it'll all come together with or without me beating it into submission with a big stick. Such a typical Seb thing to say, don't you think? He has no real grasp of what's involved.'

Piggy in the middle, Floriana warned herself. 'That's a man for you,' she said, matching Imogen's blithe tone.

'Anyway,' Imogen said, her voice suddenly stepping up a gear. 'According to what Seb's told me, you're already here on holiday with friends, but if you could tear yourself away from them for an hour or so, how about you and I having some girl time this evening?'

'Err ...'

'Come to the hotel and I'll meet you in the bar at six-thirty. No need to dress up. Yes, Mummy, I'm coming. Don't fuss, the spa can wait until we're there! Sorry, Floriana, like I say, a million things to do. See you then!'

'Hold on, where are you staying? Which hotel?'

'Grand Hotel Tremezzo. You can't miss it; it's the impressive one with a large swimming pool across the road from it. Catch you later!'

Imagining a perfectly manicured fluttery hand waving goodbye to her, Floriana ended the call and stood very still. She was in shock, and in spite of the hot sun pressing down on her, she shivered. That was no invitation she had just received, it was a royal command. Princess Imogen had summoned her to the royal court. But why? Girl time? What was that all about? When had Imogen ever wanted that with her?

The net curtains at the glass door behind her swished to one side and Adam stepped out into the garden. 'Everything OK?' he asked.

'I'll tell you later,' she said. 'How's it going in there? Does Maria know anything helpful about Marco?'

'Yes and no. She knows plenty from years ago, but nothing about him in the last decade or so.'

'Did he become a priest?'

'He did.'

'Don't tell me, he's now a high-ranking player in the Vatican and rubbing shoulders with the Pope.' Rattled by Imogen's call, she had no problem in directing her anger towards this Marco character. There he was, piously going about his business while all these years poor Esme had suffered in secret about the loss of her baby. *His* baby. Hah, what would his precious Church have to say about that!

Adam squinted at her in the sun. 'The last Maria heard he was working as a parish priest somewhere near Turin.'

'Hmm ... well,' she muttered, trying to pull herself together, 'perhaps reaching a dead end might be best, given the circumstances. Especially when you consider that wherever the Bassani family goes bad luck is but a breath away.'

Pushing his hands into his trouser pockets, Adam nudged at a weed growing through the gap in the paving slabs with his foot. 'Seems a shame when we've come so far in the story.' He looked up. 'You're not telling me you believe an old woman who claims the family was cursed?'

She shrugged. 'Esme lost her baby and the chance to have any more through her connection with them, I wouldn't want anything else bad to happen to her.'

'But that could have happened with any pregnancy she had and with any man as the father. There was nothing mysterious about it. It was a genuine medical emergency she suffered. Medical facts, Miss Day,' he added with a small smile. 'No superstitious hokum.'

Realising he had picked up on her less than cheery mood and was trying to lighten it, she affected a Scarlett O'Hara voice. 'Why, Mr Strong, I do declare you're putting me in my place.'

He laughed, raised his hands in mock surrender. 'Do I look mad enough to attempt that?'

Grateful to him for making her smile, and for taking her mind off Imogen, she linked her arm through his. 'Now if you were Rhett Butler you would take delicious delight in rubbing my nose in my so-called hokum. Come on, let's go back inside and see if Maria's remembered anything remotely useful about Don Marco.'

Yes, she thought, I need all the distraction I can get to stop me from dwelling on why Imogen wants to meet.

From what Floriana could see of Grand Hotel Tremezzo, it certainly lived up to its name; it was very grand indeed.

Everywhere she looked, her eyes fell upon five-star grandeur and opulence, from the vine-covered exterior that commanded a spectacular view of the lake with Bellagio in the distance, to the shiny gold- and mirror-lined lift that rose smoothly from the ground floor entrance up to the vast reception area furnished with red and gold rugs and enough sofas and armchairs to kit out DFS for a bank holiday sale. On the website Adam had shown her, the hotel was described as an authentic art nouveau palace historically frequented by the elite. Which made it the perfect hotel for Imogen and her family.

OK, Little Miss Snidey, that's enough, get back into your box!

Warning herself to behave, Floriana felt horribly under-dressed in her cheap Zara gypsy skirt and vest top. They'd got back from Bellagio only a short while before she had to be here, so there had been no time to shower or wash her hair. So here she was, hot and sweaty and feeling like a grubby social misfit.

Not having a clue where the bar was, she caught the attention of a member of staff hurrying by in a cream jacket. She knew that places like this were notorious for snooty staff and after explaining that she was meeting a guest for a drink and half expecting to be led towards the back entrance where the bins were kept, she was relieved when the waiter gave her a friendly smile and offered to escort her to the bar himself.

But there was no sign of Imogen; the bar was empty. 'Perhaps you would like to go outside on the terrace?' the friendly waiter suggested in faultless English.

'Thank you,' she said, following him once again.

Clearly this was where the smart set hung out with their pre-dinner drinks and nibbles waiting for that perfect sunset moment, and after Floriana had established there was no sign of Imogen here either, she was shown to a table. She ordered a glass of Prosecco. Heaven only knew how much it would cost, but she would worry about that later. Right now she needed a drink.

Waiting for it to arrive, and surrounded by so many elegantly dressed guests – all of them couples – she couldn't have felt more conspicuous. Moving her seat so she could look out across the lake, she wished Adam and Esme were with her.

They had both agreed with her that it did seem a little odd that Imogen wanted to meet her alone – why not with Seb? 'Perhaps she now recognises how important your friendship with Seb is to him and feels she wants to clear the air between the two of you with a private one-to-one chat,' Esme had suggested when they were on the boat coming back from Bellagio.

'It's feasible, I suppose,' Floriana had said doubtfully. But Esme didn't know the full story. No one did, apart from Floriana and Seb, and Imogen.

However, the real basis of her doubt was the growing suspicion that Imogen now knew that Seb had come to Oxford when she'd been in Paris on her hen weekend and wanted to know exactly what had gone on. Most brides-to-be probably would. She had felt extremely uneasy at the time that Seb hadn't been honest with Imogen; his keeping quiet about his visit only made things look worse.

The trouble was, things did end up having the potential to appear a lot worse because Seb had stayed the night with her. She hadn't mentioned this to anyone, not even Adam or Esme; she hadn't wanted them to point out the obvious, that she'd been playing with fire by letting Seb stay.

And now she was terrified Imogen had got wind of it and had spent the afternoon in the hotel spa having her nails sharpened in readiness for a pre-wedding showdown. Moreover, she genuinely had no idea how to respond. For the simple reason she didn't know how much Imogen knew. If she knew anything at all. But if she did, what would Seb have told her? With that worry uppermost in her mind, she had tried ringing Seb when they'd been waiting to catch the boat back from Bellagio, but had got no reply. She had left a message on his voicemail – a carefully worded message in case Imogen listened to it – but he hadn't replied. With hindsight the sensible thing to have done would have been to call Imogen and cancel their get-together.

Her drink arrived and she practically pounced on it before the waiter had scarcely arranged the segmented dish of olives and nuts and paper napkins on the table.

With two gulps of nerve-settling fizz down the hatch, she glanced at her watch.

Imogen was now twenty minutes late.

How tempting it was to down her drink in one and make a dash for it and later claim that Imogen had been a no-show.

But no such luck, for there, at last, was Imogen coming towards her.

If it were possible she looked even more beautiful than the last time Floriana had set eyes on her. She was utterly perfect, from the top of her naturally blond hair to the tips of her varnished toenails. She was simply dressed in vertiginous high-heeled sandals, white jeans and a peach-coloured off-the-shoulder top – one of those asymmetrical tops that whenever Floriana saw one, she felt the urge to straighten it like she would a crooked painting on the wall. Judging from the glances of the other guests, Imogen's wattage was burning so brightly all that was missing from her ensemble was a diamond crown upon her head so that people could freely bow down and worship her. Dear God, if she looked this stunning for a girly drink, how amazing was she going to look on her wedding day?

'Floriana!' she called out, weaving her way through the tables and dropped jaws. 'How lovely to see you. No, don't get up. Stay there.' Bending down, and making Floriana feel even more awkward, Imogen air-kissed her cheeks. 'You look so well,' she gushed, her perfume washing over Floriana. 'You're positively glowing. You've caught the sun, haven't you?'

No, thought Floriana, that's just fear and guilt scorching my skin. 'You look pretty well yourself,' she managed to say when Imogen had finally brought the floorshow to an end and had parked her size zero bum on the chair opposite. 'You don't look at all stressed by the approaching big day. What's your secret?' An unfortunate choice of words, she thought with a further reddening of her face, at the same time noting the big sparkly ring on Imogen's finger.

'Three hours in the most divine spa,' Imogen cooed, 'that's my secret weapon for de-stressing. I'm determined not to let it get to me. I'm also determined to stay out of the sun until the honeymoon. No strap marks on my shoulders for the wedding photographs! Seriously, though, you do look a little pink. What sun cream are you using? You might want to consider a higher factor.'

Before she could reply Floriana's friendly waiter appeared. '*Signora?*' he said to Imogen. 'What can I get for you to drink?' From now on Floriana guessed she would be as good as invisible to him.

'If that's Prosecco my friend is drinking,' Imogen said – with the kind of wide-eyed enchanting smile that would have the man tearing out his heart and serving it on a platter for her – 'I'll have the same.'

He nodded and disappeared, leaving Floriana wishing she could go with him. Oh, how she wished she was enjoying a relaxing drink with Adam and Esme.

At an open-air bar overlooking the lake, Esme tapped her glass of Prosecco lightly against Adam's glass of water – as their driver for the night he was saving himself for wine later when they would return to Grand Hotel Tremezzo to collect Floriana and then go for dinner.

'*Salute,*' she said, 'and apologies for being stuck with me. As I said before in the car after we'd dropped Floriana off, it's a shame you have to make do with the company of an old woman instead of a lively attractive girl.'

He leant back in his chair, stretched his legs out in front of him. 'If it makes you feel any better, I promise to do my best to make do with you. How's that?' He gave her one of his delight-fully sardonic looks and nudged the dish of crisps that had come with their drinks towards her.

Smiling, she helped herself to a couple of crisps. Glad that the intense heat of the day had given way to a more bearable warmth, she watched a *traghetto* passing across the lake en route for Bellagio; in the low evening sun, the picturesque town glowed with a roseate radiance.

She thought of Maria, who had gone to live on that side of the lake ever since her marriage. It had been a strange encounter today between them. Maria had been neither hostile nor particu-larly friendly, but she had been of help and for that Esme was enormously grateful.

The nature of Angelo's death didn't surprise her. All in all, he had been the epitome of a man who needed to sail dangerously

287

close to the wind just to feel alive, the sort of man who would either survive on guile and cunning, or come to a less than honourable end. It seemed that his moral connection with humanity had been an extremely fine thread. The opposite to his cousin, Marco.

As if picking up on her thoughts, Adam said, 'Have you decided what we do next regarding Marco?'

During their journey back from Bellagio, Esme's initial reaction had been to accept they'd come as far as they could. Wasn't it enough to know that Marco had fulfilled his wish to be a priest? Coming here hadn't been about meeting him, that would have been a wholly implausible expectation; it had been about revisiting the past, to walk where she had once walked, to see things she had once seen and maybe experience a new perspective on that past.

'I honestly think we've done as much as we can,' she said in answer to Adam's question, 'and I'm quite content with what we've learnt. Though I doubt Floriana will be happy to hear that. Bless the dear girl, I know she had a hopelessly romantic picture in her mind of Marco and I having a marvellously poignant reunion. I never once thought that would happen.'

'Actually,' Adam said, leaning over to help himself to some crisps, 'she's no longer of that opinion. After what we heard today, in particular about the Bassani family bringing bad luck on anyone who comes in contact with them, she's anxious that you're not hurt all over again.'

Touched by Floriana's concern, even if it was somewhat misguided, Esme shook her head. 'As if that could happen at my age.'

'Does age really make one invincible to emotional hurt?' Adam asked.

'Less sensitive, perhaps. One toughens up with experience.'

While he seemed to consider this and turned to stare out at the lake, Esme decided to be brave. Who knew when she might have the chance to be alone with him again? 'Adam,' she said, 'can I ask you something of a personal nature?'

He turned to face her. He was still looking his affable self, but she knew him well enough to see there was now wariness in his expression; his guard was up. 'That would rather depend just how personal,' he replied, reaching for a paper napkin and wiping his hands, slowly and with care.

She took a fortifying sip of her Prosecco, then leapt in with both feet. 'How exactly do you view Floriana?'

His eyes narrowed fractionally. 'She's one of the nicest people I know.'

'Oh, come on, you can do better than that.'

'I didn't realise there was a right or a wrong answer. What's the answer you're hoping for?'

She fixed him with a hard stare. 'I believe you know exactly what I'm asking.'

He laughed abruptly. 'What a marvellously uncompromising woman you are, Esme.'

'That's as may be, but are you going to answer my question?'

He stared back at her unblinkingly. 'All right,' he said with a deep sigh, 'I can see that the path of least resistance would be simply to give in, so I'll tell you what you want to know and then that will be an end to the matter. Yes? No more interrogating questions. Deal?'

'Certainly not!'

He tipped his head back and let out another laugh. A couple at a nearby table glanced their way. Shifting his chair, he moved in closer to her. 'OK,' he said, 'I'll tell you what you want to know and then you can give me the benefit of your immense wisdom.'

Chapter Forty-Three

Time was getting on and still Floriana didn't know why she was here.

For nearly an hour she had been forced to listen to Imogen bemoaning the tiresome business of organising a long-distance wedding via a wedding planner, and then prattling on about the guests flying in from all over the world, many of whom were school and university friends who had not met Seb before. Apparently they were just dying to check him out – how Seb must be looking forward to that, Floriana thought. And all the while, she kept waiting for Imogen to lower the wattage of her dazzling charm and get to the point. To lean across the table and hiss a litany of venomous accusations at Floriana.

Or was Seb's bride-to-be being genuinely right-from-the-bottom-of-her-heart nice? Had she changed? And had Floriana's view of Imogen been coloured by toxic jealousy to the point of blindness? After all, what was there to dislike about her?

Hmm ... how about too beautiful?

Or too frivolous?

And let's not forget too controlling and a blatant liar.

Oh, it was no good, Floriana couldn't pretend that this girl was anything but just too wrong for Seb. He needed someone with more depth and sincerity. He needed someone who really cared about him. Someone who understood him to his very troubled core and would anchor him. Imogen simply wasn't that person; she was too self-absorbed. The truth was, they were two highly strung, high-maintenance people and their coming together could only ever be an explosive disaster.

Wanting this meaningless charade of a let's-get-together-for-a-girly-chat to be over, Floriana looked pointedly at her watch.

Fair play to Imogen, she picked up on it. 'Yes, of course,' she said, 'I mustn't keep you. But there's just one thing I wanted to ask you.'

Relieved that the end was in sight and she could give Adam and Esme a call so they could come and get her, Floriana said, 'Sure, ask away.'

'I want to know why Seb stayed the night with you the weekend I was away in Paris.'

There it was! The words *How do you know he did?* leapt to Floriana's lips, but she clamped her mouth shut.

'You can see how it looks from my perspective, can't you?' Imogen went on. 'First time I go away for a weekend without him and he's off to Oxford to see you. Why was that?'

'We're friends,' Floriana said, doing her damnedest to sound calm and with nothing to hide. 'We go way back. You know that.'

Up until this point, Imogen had looked and sounded perfectly good-natured and unruffled, but now the act was showing signs of cracking. 'You just can't let go of him, can you?' she said heatedly.

'It's not like that. I didn't know he was coming; he turned up out of the blue. You know what he's like, he's always doing things like that, he hates to be predictable.'

'That may have been how he used to be, but he's changed.'

'Has he?'

'Yes he has!' Imogen snapped. There was steel in her voice now. In her eyes too. 'But I think you're deliberately missing the point.'

'No, it's you who's missing the point,' Floriana said with a flare of anger. 'If you can't trust Seb, then you need to ask yourself why that is.'

'I've asked myself that again and again and always I come back to the same thing – how can I trust him with you constantly trying to get your claws into him?'

'I'm afraid that says more about your insecurity than anything I've ever done. And for the record, Seb stayed the night with me because he'd drunk too much and driving back to London wasn't an option. He crashed out on the sofa and that was where he spent the night. Absolutely nothing happened. Would you rather he'd risked killing himself by driving in that state than staying safe in Oxford?'

'I'd rather he'd stayed in London in the first place, that he hadn't gone to see you.'

Wondering what Imogen would say if she told her all the things Seb had poured out that day he'd come to see her and how she had tried to reassure him that it was nothing more than jittery pre-wedding nerves, Floriana held her tongue. Imogen wouldn't believe any of it; she would merely accuse her of lying and of trying to drive a wedge between them.

'What's your plan, Imogen?' she said instead. 'To cut Seb off from anyone he used to know before you appeared in his life? You couldn't even let him choose his own best man; you had to force your brother on to him.'

'How dare you! He was more than happy to have Jules. Jules is a good friend to him. They're extremely close.'

'I'm glad to hear it. Does Seb know you and I are here having this chat?'

'No.'

'I thought not. Did he actually give you my number, or did you help yourself to it on his mobile? Yes, just as I thought. So what have you done with him while we're having this cosy tête-à-tête, locked him in your room until you give him permission to come out?'

'Please don't be childish, he's with Daddy and Jules in Menaggio hiring a boat for tomorrow.'

'Still begs the question why you didn't tell him about meeting me. Afraid to let him know you don't trust him, is that it? And to satisfy my curiosity, how did you know he'd been to Oxford to see me? Did he tell you or, and my money's on this, did his mobile just happen to fall into your hand when you returned from Paris and you thought, oh, why not, I'll check his texts to see if he got up to anything interesting in my absence?'

Imogen glared back at her. 'With you still trying to steal him, no one in my shoes would do differently. And the fact he didn't mention his visit makes you look guiltier still.'

She had a point, of course, and that was precisely what Floriana had feared. 'He probably didn't mention it because he knew you'd be upset and overreact,' she said reasonably. 'Which is exactly what you're doing.'

'And with good grounds!'

Oh Seb, thought Floriana sadly, what do you see in this girl?

She's too insecure and possessive for you. And why didn't you delete those messages on your mobile? Because he'd probably seen them as perfectly innocent. Because he'd probably never imagined his girlfriend would be devious enough to read them behind his back.

'So inviting me here this evening, was all about what, exactly?' Floriana said. 'To ban me from the wedding because you're scared I might try a last-ditch attempt to steal Seb at the altar?'

Imogen rose slowly and elegantly to her feet. Looking down at Floriana, she said, 'I wouldn't put anything past you.'

'I'm glad you think that highly of me.'

'Please don't try and be funny. I'd give anything in the world to be able to make you stay away on Saturday, but since that would upset Seb, this is what I want you to do.' She leant down so her face was just a few inches away from Floriana's. 'You can come to the wedding but you have to promise never to see him again.'

'Why would I do that?'

'If you care about Seb's happiness, you'll do as I ask. I want to make him happy and I can't do that with you undermining our marriage. I want you out of his life permanently. I tried once before to make him realise there was no place for you in our relationship, that it was you or me, and he made his choice: me.'

'You gave him an ultimatum?'

'It was the only way he could be free of you.'

Floriana was stunned But it explained so much. Now she knew why Seb had ignored her attempts to apologise and put things right between them. 'But I don't understand why you then allowed him to invite me to your wedding,' she said.

'Stupidly I thought it would be all right after all this time. I was wrong.'

More wrong than you could ever imagine, Floriana thought as she watched Imogen walk away.

Chapter Forty-Four

'It strikes me that it's been an eventful day and one I'm more than happy to bring to an end by going to bed,' Esme said.

From where he was opening a bottle of wine on the terrace, Adam watched Esme hug Floriana and kiss her goodnight. 'Sleep well, sweet thing, and no dwelling on that ghastly encounter with Imogen.'

'Don't worry,' Floriana said, hugging Esme back, 'it'll take more than a crazy bride to cheat me out of a good night's sleep.'

Esme came over to Adam next and patted him on the shoulder. 'Goodnight and thank you for booking such an excellent restaurant for us this evening, it couldn't have been more perfect.' Glancing over to where Floriana had wandered off to inspect a rose bush, and lowering her voice, she added, 'Please do bear in mind my advice, won't you?'

He tugged the cork out of the bottle. 'Sleep well, Esme,' he said non-committally. 'It's going to be another warm night, are you sure you wouldn't like me to switch on the air con in your room?'

'No, no, I'll be fine thank you with the window open.'

Watching the old lady go inside the villa and hoping Floriana hadn't overheard what Esme had said, Adam called out to her. 'What are you up to over there, Floriana?'

'What does it look like? I'm gathering rose petals.'

Kneeling on the grass, she was indeed gathering rose petals. Cupping them in her hands, she raised them to her face and breathed in deeply.

'Glass of wine?' he asked.

'Yes, please,' she replied, joining him on the terrace. She held her hands out for him to smell the petals.

'Very nice,' he said.

'"Very nice",' she repeated. 'Is that all you have to say? Adam,

294

this is the most exquisite perfume on earth. It doesn't get any better.'

He went back to pouring out the wine. 'I'm sorry, I'm just a simple man with a limited vocabulary at his disposal.'

'What a shame,' she said with a teasing smile.

No, he thought, the real shame is I can't express myself the way I really want to, that I'm rapidly losing the power of speech when I'm alone with you. Esme was right. He needed to sort this situation. And soon. He was still shocked that she'd guessed at his feelings towards Floriana; he'd been convinced he'd given nothing away, that outwardly his behaviour hadn't changed. But according to Esme he'd shown his hand by trying too hard to conceal the attraction; she'd spotted the signs weeks ago. His concern was that if Esme had guessed, then surely Floriana had, so why hadn't she done anything about it? Unless she wasn't interested?

In answer to this worry, Esme had been adamant. 'It's not her place to make the first move, Adam. A girl shouldn't be the one to do that.'

When he'd suggested politely that that was an outmoded form of etiquette as far as modern-day dating went, she'd dismissed his comment with an exasperated sigh and told him to stop making excuses and get on with it. 'Unless, of course,' she'd said, 'you're not truly over Jesse yet?'

Now it was his turn to be adamant. 'There's no danger of that,' he'd replied truthfully. 'But what if Floriana's still in love with Seb?'

'Take it from me, she isn't.'

'You have actual irrefutable proof of that?' he'd asked. 'Has she told you she isn't?'

'No. But I feel it in my bones. Moreover, you're the one to prove to her that she isn't. You know, a very long time ago someone once told me that most of our hurts in life come through relationships, equally, so does our healing.'

'But I don't want to jeopardise our friendship.'

'Adam, presumably you take risks all the time during your working day and they all come off to your satisfaction. Am I right?'

'On the whole, yes. But they're calculated risks weighted heavily in my favour. I don't like taking risks in my private life, especially one with an outcome that could end so badly.'

'But think of the reverse! What if it ended well? Gloriously well! Come on, Adam, faint heart never won fair lady.'

With those words echoing in his head, and too tense now to sit down with Floriana, he said, 'How about a swim to cool off?'

'Brilliant idea!' she said, unexpectedly flinging her hands into the air and twirling on her toes as the rose petals fluttered to the ground, covering her in a shower of pale pink confetti.

He laughed. 'Miss Day, are you just a little bit drunk? Because if you are, maybe a swim isn't such a good idea.'

'I'm as sober as a judge,' she said, coming to a stop, her lovely hazel eyes resting on his. 'Besides, you'll be there to save me, won't you?'

'What if *I* need saving?'

'Then I'm your girl. Hand on heart, and despite those glasses of limoncello I had after dinner, I won't let anything happen to you.'

Too late, he thought as they went to change, *you've* happened to me.

In the quiet dark of the night, the underwater lighting that illuminated the pool was so luminously white it made Floriana look like she was carved from alabaster. Oh yes, Adam thought ruefully, he could think such poetic things; he just couldn't say them aloud.

He watched her swimming with slow smooth strokes, her chin skimming the surface of the water, her body gliding noiselessly through the water. 'You look so serious,' she said, 'what are you thinking?'

'Oh, this and that.'

'If you don't mind me saying, you've been very serious for most of the evening.'

'You should know by now, that's how I roll.'

She came to a stop in front of him at the deepest end of the pool. Treading water, her arms stretched out either side of her, she raised her eyes to the dark night sky. 'If you tell someone there's a hundred thousand million stars in the Milky Way, they'll believe you, but tell someone a plate is too hot to touch and they'll touch it to be sure.'

'And your point?'

She grinned and flipped over onto her back and floated away from him. He swam after her. 'Your point, Miss Day?'

Her face turned upwards, her hair fanning out in the water, she said, 'My point is that people will always question what they feel able to challenge, and I'm no different. I'm convinced something is bothering you.'

'Nothing's bothering me,' he lied.

'So what's the advice Esme's given you and which you have to bear in mind?'

He felt his face redden. 'You did hear then!'

'What? I'm suddenly supposed to be hard of hearing?'

Taking a breath, he dived beneath the water and swam back to the deepest end of the pool. When he surfaced and was shaking the water from his ears and pushing back his hair, he looked for Floriana, but there was no sign of her. Not until she surfaced right behind him. Holding onto the side of the pool and mimicking a horror movie voiceover, she said, 'You can run but you can't hide. What's Esme been advising you to do?'

He wiped a hand over his face, playing for time. 'OK,' he forced himself to say, 'I'll tell you. But honesty deserves honesty in kind. Right? And I warn you, this could turn awkward, which is what I was anxious to avoid.'

She nodded and he pushed on. It was now or never. 'Are you still in love with Seb?' he asked. 'I need to know that. Otherwise there's ... there's no point in me saying what else I want to say.'

He could see that his question had surprised her. More worrying, he could also see a flicker of something in her face that didn't encourage him. He fought his disappointment. 'OK, I'll take that as a yes,' he said. 'Thanks for being straight with me. I appreciate that.'

She frowned. 'But I didn't say anything.'

'It's fine. You didn't need to.'

'No, Adam, you don't understand. I—'

'You really don't have to say anything more,' he said quickly, not wanting to prolong his embarrassment any further. 'You don't need to explain yourself. It's OK.'

He was about to launch himself away from the side of the pool, when she put a hand out to him. 'Adam, you've got it wrong. I don't love Seb. At least not in the sense you mean.'

'What sense do I mean?' he asked.

'You want to know if I'm *in* love with Seb,' she said softly. 'I'm not. I care about him deeply, but the feelings I used to have for him have gone. I think now I mostly feel sorry for him. He doesn't seem at all happy.'

'When did you realise you felt differently?'

'Probably it started when he came to see me in Oxford in June, when Imogen was away on her hen weekend in Paris. I told you and Esme earlier that I knew it had been a risk to let Seb stay the night, but think about it, if I'd loved him, I mean, if I'd been *in* love with him and not cared about the consequences, I wouldn't have left him to sleep on the sofa that night; I would have seized my opportunity.'

He stared at her, but didn't know what to say next.

'I didn't sleep with him,' she said firmly. 'It didn't cross my mind. And now that I've been so honest with you, I think it's only right you have to be honest with me. Why did you need to know this?'

He hesitated.

She continued to stare at him, not a flicker of movement in her eyes or face.

'You're a smart girl,' he murmured, 'I think you can work it out for yourself, can't you?'

'You've got me all wrong,' she said with a small smile, her body inclined towards his, the strength of her gaze boring into him. 'I'm really not that smart. Some things I need spelling out for me.'

He moved in closer to her. Really close. 'Now is not the time to play the cute-but-dumb card. Or make fun of me.'

'Not even a little bit?'

'I can think of better uses to which you could put your considerable talent.'

'Why, Mr Strong, are you flirting with me?'

'Bloody hell, I certainly hope so. It may not seem much to you, but I'm working my arse off here!'

She laughed. 'And to great effect, I might add.'

He was so close now he could practically count the lashes around her shining eyes. 'Please,' he said, 'I'm asking nicely, put me out of my misery and give a sign that it would be all right to kiss you.'

'What kind of sign would be clear enough for you?'

'I'd settle for one that indicates you won't bite me.'

She laughed again and lifted her chin so that her mouth was just a few tantalising inches from his. He could feel the warmth of her breath against his skin.

'How's this?' she whispered. She brushed her lips against his, first his top lip, then his lower lip. As erotic moments went, it was right up there. 'Is that obvious enough for you?' she asked, tipping her head back and looking into his eyes.

'I can't be sure, but what the heck, I'm happy to take my chances.' With one hand holding onto the side of the pool, he placed the other to her neck and kissed her.

Restless and unable to sleep, Esme got out of bed and went and stood at the open window. Looking down to the pool that was still brightly lit, she saw Adam and Floriana. She hastily backed away from the window.

Her work was done, she thought happily. All they'd needed was a jolly good shove in the right direction.

Chapter Forty-Five

Everyone slept in the following morning.

Up first, and with no sound of activity coming from the others, Floriana was in the kitchen pouring herself a glass of water and contemplating whether she had the energy to fetch some croissants for breakfast.

It was not all she was contemplating. Drinking the water thirstily – she'd drunk more red wine and limoncello than perhaps was good for her last night – she went outside and looked over to the pool, its flawless surface gleaming in the bright sunshine. *Here kissed Adam Strong and Floriana Day*, she thought with a happy smile, picturing a blue plaque proclaiming the historic moment to future guests who stayed here.

Walking barefoot across the parched grass, she went over to the swing seat where, after their late night swim, she and Adam had sat wrapped in the warm, still, night air. In the glow of light from the pool, her head resting against his shoulder and his arm around her, she had begun the process of recalibrating the balance of their relationship. Funny how one kiss could change things. It was going to take some getting used to.

It had been nearly two o'clock when finally, and with her hand slipped inside his, they'd walked back up to the villa to go to bed. Kissing her one last time outside her bedroom door, he'd turned away and taken the stairs quietly up to his own room on the top floor.

Playing her feet over the dry grass beneath her, Floriana hoped Adam believed her about Seb; that she no longer loved him in the way she once had. Her feelings for him really had undergone a change. It was difficult to explain, even to herself, but for the first time in a long while, she felt free – free from the self-inflicted pain caused by loving someone who didn't love her in return.

Nonetheless, Seb was still immensely important to her and if Adam couldn't accept that Seb would always figure in her life, it would be better to stop things right now. Was it asking too much of him – or any man, for that matter – to accept that situation?

She sighed deeply, wondering for the millionth time what on earth had possessed Seb to propose to Imogen. Why couldn't he see how wrong she was for him? And what would he think of his wife-to-be and her conversation with Floriana last night?

She thought how miserable he had been when he'd stayed with her in Oxford, his mood worsening exponentially with each glass of wine he drank. Whenever the memory of how melancholy he'd been came to mind, she couldn't help but recall an earlier time in his life when depression had plunged him terrifyingly close to rock bottom.

It had happened in their final term as undergraduates and some weeks after May Day when Seb had spoken so disconsolately on Magdalen Bridge and then again over breakfast. The concern she had felt for him that day had been lessened by his absolute conviction shortly afterwards that he was fine, that he'd just been having a bad day. Maybe it was relief that had allowed her to believe him for she instantly threw herself into revising for finals, as well as taking up with a new boyfriend. With hindsight, Angus – a second-year PPE student at St Peter's – had been nothing more than an amusing distraction from the pressure of revising.

The day of her last exam, Angus had arrived outside the Examination Schools to help celebrate in the time-honoured fashion by trashing her with eggs and flour. No sooner had he kissed her and hurled the first egg than she caught sight of Seb standing awkwardly back from the raucous group gathered in the High. He was holding a bottle of champagne and sporting a half-hearted beard that couldn't have suited him less – it was a stark reminder that it was some weeks since she had seen him. The last she'd heard from him was that he was revising hard and didn't want to be disturbed. 'No distractions!' he'd insisted when she'd suggested they meet to relax over a pizza and a beer. But seeing the state of him now, how drawn and dishevelled he was, she was concerned that he'd been hiding from her.

She pushed her way through the noisy crowd to reach him. Close up she was alarmed just how ill he looked – his cheeks were sunken and deep violet shadows dragged at his dull eyes;

he'd lost weight too and his hair needed a good wash. She said the first thing that came into her head. 'You OK?'

'Never better. You?'

'Relieved I have no more exams to do.'

'Lucky you, mine don't start for another ten days.' His eyes darted to glance over her shoulder. 'Yonder lover-boy's not looking too happy. If you don't mind me saying, he doesn't seem your type, he's got tosser stamped all over him. Correction, *posh* tosser. What his name?'

'Angus.'

'So what's the deal with him, you trying a social experiment to see how the other half behave close up?'

'And what's your social experiment?' she said, annoyed at the criticism. 'To see how many chemicals your body can withstand until it finally wastes away?'

'Don't be like that. I'm here to say sorry.'

'What for?'

'For being as big a jackass as your boyfriend.'

'That's an apology?'

Hands thrust deep into his pockets, he'd smiled. 'You know the old adage, can't gild a turd.'

She'd laughed at that and, linking arms with him, not caring about Angus, she'd said, 'Let's get out of here.'

They'd gone down to the river where Seb prised open the champagne and apologised for his absence for the last few weeks. 'I couldn't face anyone,' he said, passing her the bottle.

'Not even me?'

'Especially not you. You're too censorious these days.'

Handing the bottle back to him, she watched him take a long swig. Then another. 'Tell me what's wrong, Seb. Tell me why you look so awful. It's more than finals, isn't it? What's happened?'

'Censorious *and* perceptive.' He took another long swill. 'It's my father.'

Surprised, she waited for him to elaborate. Apart from funding him through college, Seb's father had all but detached himself from his son. It was a situation that Seb had long since accepted. Or so she thought. 'What about him?' Floriana asked when Seb appeared to have retreated behind a wall of silence.

'I did what I always swore I wouldn't, I got in touch with him, to see if, you know, we could actually meet up, get to know each other, make some sort of relationship actually happen between us.'

Never before had Seb spoken about wanting to meet the man who had left him and his mother for another woman and with whom he'd created a new family. 'What made you do that?' she asked, watching Seb snatching at the grass to his right. 'Why the change of heart?'

He shrugged his thin shoulders. 'It's Mum's doing. You remember that bloke I told you about, the one she met online who lived in Spain?'

'Yes, I remember, we joked he'd turn out to be a gangster hiding out on the Costa del Crime.'

'Who knows, he may yet prove us right. Anyway, Mum went to stay with him and low and behold, they got married. She wrote to tell me the glad tidings of her nuptials a couple of weeks ago. She's selling up here, lock, stock and near-empty barrel. She said if I was stuck for somewhere to stay when term's over I could either go to her in Spain, or try my luck with my father.'

Floriana was incredulous. Although in truth she shouldn't have been, Seb's mother was one of the most selfish people she knew and had never taken her parental role seriously, telling Seb repeatedly that he was better off without any input from her.

'Do you think it will last,' Floriana asked, 'this latest whirlwind romance?'

'Who knows? But we're getting off-track, this isn't about my mother, it's about my father.'

'Sorry. Go on then, what did he say when you asked to meet?'

'He said something like, "I suppose we could work something out", like it was some kind of debatable point.'

'It was probably surprise,' Floriana said, trying to be generous. 'Perhaps it was something he'd been waiting to hear for years and suddenly there it was and you took the wind out of his sails.'

'Nice try, Florrie, but all I subsequently got from him were excuses to any date or time I suggested. He was either busy with work or travelling, or was occupied with some family occasion with his kids.'

Floriana's heart went out to Seb. How it must have pained him to take that first step only to be rebuffed so cruelly. She couldn't imagine how it must feel to be so summarily rejected by a parent. By both, to all intents and purposes.

In comparison her own parents had been much more caring towards Seb. They always gave him birthday and Christmas presents and Dad had even given him driving lessons, despite having been terrified half to death when he'd tried to teach Floriana – she'd failed her test and never attempted it again, whereas Seb had passed first go.

'Did you manage to pin him down in the end?' she asked.

'Yeah, he said he'd come here to Oxford and take me out for dinner.' He fell silent again, snatched at a long blade of grass and tapped it against his chin. 'But he never showed. Not even a phone call or a text to say he was running late or couldn't make it. I emailed him the next day to ask what the hell he thought he was playing at and all he said was something had come up.'

'Oh, Seb, I'm sorry.'

He tossed the blade of grass away from him. 'No! No sympathy. Anything but that. Give me anger. Give me anything but pity!'

'Seb, don't you dare ever confuse my sympathy for pity. Not when it hurts me so much to see you like this.'

'Like what?' He sounded angrily defensive.

'Looking like hell,' she said bluntly. 'Like you've given up on yourself.' She hated to admit it, but right now with his crumpled clothes smelling as if they hadn't been washed in a long time, his shaggy hair dull with grease and his patchy beard, he could easily pass muster as one of Oxford's many down-and-outs.

'Why shouldn't I give up on myself? Everybody else has.'

'I haven't,' she replied vehemently. 'And you bloody well know that!'

'Could have fooled me. I've seen precious little of you since you took up with Angus the rugger-bugger.'

She gave him a playful nudge with her foot; it was a gesture that belied the hurtful sting of his accusation. An accusation that wasn't without an element of truth. 'He doesn't play rugby, he's a rower,' she said, 'and besides, it was you who said you didn't want to be disturbed. If you'd wanted me you only had to call or come and knock on my door.'

'And catch you in flagrante? I think not.'

'So torturing yourself in isolation was preferable?'

'You know me, the tortured soul sits well on my shoulders, better than that of a happy camper. You know how I hate false notes.'

The following day Floriana realised that Seb had been fooling her with a whole symphony of catastrophic false notes. The extent of what he'd been hiding from her was made clear when she received a call from the John Radcliffe Hospital and was told that Seb had been admitted early that morning and was asking for her.

'Don't believe a word they tell you,' he said gruffly when she sat by the side of his bed. 'It wasn't intentional; it was just a binge that got out of hand. If I'd wanted to kill myself, I'd have succeeded. And for God's sake, don't look at me like that, or I'll wish I had!'

'I'm looking at you like this because you're frightening me, Seb. Why do you always have to do everything in the extreme?'

'You want half measures from me? Never!'

'I want you to be happy. Is that so very terrible?'

'Happiness is beyond my reach.' Yawning deeply, he'd closed his eyes and fallen asleep.

The hospital staff didn't believe Seb's story either and after checking his medical records with the GP he'd signed up with in Oxford, it was revealed he'd been taking anti-depressants for the last eight months.

He was discharged the following day with an appointment made to see a psychiatrist. Floriana took him back to the house he shared with two Chinese physicists – it was they who had found him collapsed on the floor in the bathroom. Moving in with him, Floriana watched over Seb day and night and then very gently reminded him that his finals were only two days away. He'd laughed at her, declaring her madder than he was if she thought he gave a damn about his degree. She begged him to reconsider, if for no other reason than to please her. 'I swear this is the only thing I'll ever ask you to do,' she said. 'What have you got to lose by giving it a go? I'll help you prepare all I can.' Amazingly he gave in and when the exams were over, she took him home to Mum and Dad where for two and a half weeks he did nothing but sleep and eat. When he surfaced and resembled something more like his old self, he thanked her for not giving up on him. She promised she never would, that she would always be there for him.

*

Having found the energy to go down to the supermarket, Floriana was now climbing back up the hill with a bag of croissants and a carton of milk. She was just wondering if Seb had ever shared with Imogen just how close he'd come to ending his life when her mobile buzzed. Fishing it out from her shorts' pocket, she saw that it was Seb. 'That's weird,' she said, more than a little spooked, 'I was just thinking of you.'

'You were? Good or bad? No, don't answer that. Are you free this afternoon?'

'It's the day before your wedding, Seb, I hardly think it's appropriate for you to—'

'It's really important,' he cut in.

'Does Imogen know you're ringing me?'

'No.'

'Then I don't think we should meet.'

'Florrie, please! Just give me an hour. That's all I need.'

God help her, but she agreed.

Chapter Forty-Six

Esme wasn't happy. Not happy at all. Just as things were coming together so nicely, up pops this infuriating Seb fellow to put a spanner in the works. As usual, Adam was keeping his own counsel, but Esme knew from the gravity of his tense expression that his mind was quietly ticking over.

After lunch, and watching from the terrace as Floriana set off on foot to meet Seb, Esme regretted not encouraging her to invite him to the villa where she could keep an eye on him. Based on what Floriana had said, Esme's fear was that he had a bad case of cold feet and was on the verge of backing out of his wedding, and who better to turn to than the one person in the world who would support him in the way she always had? And where would that lead? Oh, it was all so damnably annoying! Why couldn't the path of love run smoothly? Why did it always have to be so difficult?

As a ploy to keep Adam occupied, Esme had asked him to take her to see Villa Carlotta, and as they drove the short distance along the lake road, he could not have been more subdued. Esme longed to reassure him that he had nothing to worry about, but she couldn't bring herself to offer him false hope. Less than twenty-four hours ago she had been steadfastly of the opinion that Floriana had successfully worked Seb out of her system, now, after one click of his fingers, the girl was running back to him, leaving Esme – and Adam – on much less surer ground.

Having dropped her off as close to the main entrance as he could, Adam drove further on to park the car. While Esme waited for him to return, two large parties of tourists arrived, one from a German coach and the other a group of Brits who streamed across the road from the nearby boat stop. What a contrast it was to when she had come here with her father. There had been no crowds then, and with no more than a handful of tourists exploring the house and garden, her father had been allowed to set up his easel and paint in the peace and quiet for as long as he wanted.

Surrounded on all sides by the noisy jostling crowd, the fiercely hot sun beating down on her, her cotton blouse clinging to her back and shoulders, Esme suddenly felt trapped. Her heart began to race and panic seized her. Struggling to find her breath, she looked frantically about her. She wanted to escape, to push through the surging mass of bodies pressing against her. What was she doing here in this sticky heat? Why wasn't she sitting comfortably in the cool shade of her garden watching Euridice trying to creep up on that bossy blackbird? Oh, how she missed the quiet company of her beloved little cat! This was all a terrible mistake; she should never have come. And she should never have put Adam and Floriana through this. Especially Adam. What had she thought she was doing meddling in their lives? Why couldn't she have left them alone?

But then she spotted Adam and at the sight of his calm de-meanour and the effortlessly forceful way he created a pathway through the crowd to reach her, she pulled herself together. On top of everything else, the last thing Adam needed was a foolish old woman falling apart.

On edge and fidgeting in his chair, alternating between fiddling with the strap of his watch and the drinks menu on the table, Seb looked as if it was killing him to be here with her. Every few seconds he glanced anxiously round the al fresco bar in the small square overlooking the lake; he was terrified they might be seen. Away from the main road, Floriana very much doubted any of the wedding guests would stumble across them. She had read about the bar – La Magnolia – in the visitors' book back at the villa and because it was within easy walking distance, it had been the obvious choice for her. No way had she wanted to ask Adam to drive her to meet Seb, nor had she wanted Seb to meet her at the villa.

With the arrival of two ice-cold Peroni beers, Floriana hoped Seb would relax and explain why he had been so desperate to see her. But if anything, as he gulped at his drink, he seemed even twitchier.

'Seb,' she said when she could take it no longer, 'for heaven's sake, stop looking so ludicrously shifty!'

He dragged a hand across his forehead that was beading with sweat. 'Sorry, I can't help it.'

'Then perhaps you shouldn't have called me.'

'But I had to. Now was the only time I knew I'd be able to see you – Imogen and her bridesmaids have gone shopping in Menaggio.'

'But you're scared stiff we'll be seen together. Which isn't exactly making me feel at ease being with you.'

He took another gulp of his beer.

'So come on, what is it you had to see me about?' Her question came out more impatiently than she'd intended, but he didn't seem to notice.

'There's something I can't stop thinking about,' he said, 'it's—' He stopped himself short. He swallowed and again wiped his forehead with the back of his hand.

Floriana studied him closely, her concern growing that he was here to confide in her that he couldn't go through with tomorrow. If so, what did he want from her? Assurance he was doing the right thing in backing out? Or was she supposed to provide the steadying voice of common sense as she'd done before and remind him that it would be fine, that nearly all grooms suffered with nerves. If the former, all it would take from her was one word about last night's chat with Imogen and he would have the perfect excuse to call it off. But Floriana wasn't going to do that. Seb had to figure this one out for himself. Just as he should have figured out that agreeing to Imogen's ultimatum to ditch his oldest friend was a mistake. Knowing that he had been capable of such a decision hurt Floriana deeply. Had she counted for so little? Or had he simply loved Imogen so much he'd been blind to reason? And how would he react if she were to tell him she knew of the choice he'd made?

'I need to know something,' he said quietly. 'Something important.' He met her gaze. 'I know you've never approved of Imogen, it's OK, you don't have to pretend that you do, but what I need to know is, is that simply because ... because you loved me and were jealous of her?'

Floriana turned away, pretended to be fascinated by an elegantly stylish boat coming into view on the lake. It was made of highly polished wood and gleamed like glass in the sunlight. When the boat had passed, and choosing her words with care, she said, 'It really doesn't matter how I feel about Imogen, or for that matter, how I once felt about you. What's important is that you know exactly what you feel for the woman you're marrying tomorrow.'

'What if I said I didn't know how I felt because there was something unfinished between us?'

A pulse of alarm ran through her and she tensed. 'I'd tell you the truth, that there isn't anything unfinished between us.'

Very slowly he shook his head. 'You're wrong. To my shame, it's taken until now to realise that.'

Her response swelled in her throat and she had to force the words to come out. 'Seb, don't. You mustn't. It's too late.'

'Too late for what?'

'You mustn't ruin everything.'

He reached across the table and covered her hand with his. 'Do you still love me? Yes or no?'

'It's not as simple as that.' She tried to slip her hand away from under his, but he wouldn't let her.

'It should be,' he said. 'All you have to do is say you still love me and I'll put an end to tomorrow's fiasco. I love you, Florrie. I probably always have, I just didn't recognise my feelings for what they were until I saw you again in Oxford.'

From nowhere anger sparked within her and she snatched her hand from beneath his. '*No!* I will not allow you to use me as an excuse to get out of marrying Imogen!'

He looked horror-struck. 'I'm not using you.'

'Then why aren't you having this conversation with Imogen? Why aren't you telling her that you're not in love with her?'

'Because I'm a coward,' he said flatly. 'I always have been. You're the one with all the courage. You were the one who had the guts to be honest and say you loved me. If I'd been a better man, I'd have behaved differently back then. But I didn't. And I'm sorry for that. More sorry than I can say.'

'I don't want to hear any more.'

'But I need to know. I'm begging you, Florrie.'

'No, Seb, you need to know what's in your own head before you ask anything of me. Why on earth have you left it until now? And while we're about it, were you ever really in love with Imogen?'

'For a time, yes,' he said with a grimace. 'She made me feel different about myself. I liked the idea of making her happy. And I wanted to fit in ... to be a part of her family. I thought I'd found somewhere I could call home, and for that I was prepared to change, to raise my game and live up to Imogen's expectations. I can do this, I kept telling myself.'

'So what changed?'

'*You* changed things. It felt so uncomplicated being in your company again. I didn't have to try with you; I could be myself. With Imogen, I ... I was playing at being someone she wanted me to be. I suppose I liked the challenge of that to begin with, I was reinventing myself, acting a role. It felt good, like I'd got rid of all the crap from before. But then when I had lunch with you that day in January, everything began to feel shallow and false.' He leant in close. 'Florrie, it's only when I'm with you that I feel real, that the world feels real. Without you, it's just a hollow sham.'

It was too much for Floriana to take in. What on earth could she say? Why did he have to say this now? Why not two and a half years ago? Why hadn't he believed her back then when she'd told him what she'd seen? But no, he'd called her a liar, had accused her of jealousy, of wanting to destroy his one and only chance to be happy.

She had been jealous, that much was true, but destroying his happiness had not been what she'd set out to do. But how could you tell someone that their partner was cheating on them without inflicting pain?

And Imogen had cheated on Seb; Floriana had caught her red-handed. Whether it had been a one-off event, Floriana never knew. She still didn't. But she hoped it had only happened the once, she had hated the thought of Seb being made a fool of. To this day it amazed her that Imogen could face her without squirming, knowing as she did that Floriana knew the truth. It explained why she was so keen to get rid of Floriana though. How tempting it had been last night to lean across the table and whisper in Imogen's ear exactly what she had seen. But for Seb's sake, for the sake of his happiness, she had promised herself she would never succumb to doing that, or speak again of what she'd seen with her own eyes.

It had been in late November – almost two and a half years

ago – when she had gone to London for an exhibition at the Royal Academy and afterwards, when she'd emerged onto the street and was buttoning her coat and pulling on her gloves, that she did a double take.

It was one of those weird moments when you recognise a person but immediately think, *Hang on, that can't be right.* In this instance, Floriana's brain was telling her it couldn't be Imogen on the pavement a few yards from her because the man in the smart overcoat and tartan scarf with whom she was so cosily arm in arm was not the man it should be. At the same time, her brain was reminding Floriana that Seb was away with work this week, so who the hell was this?

Following them was the right thing to do, she told herself; it was a need to be sure she wasn't imagining things. But really, and to her shame, it was nothing but a need to gloat, for here was the proof she needed to convince Seb that he should end it with Imogen.

And in that same moment, picturing Imogen out of the way, Floriana had promised herself she would find the courage to tell Seb how she felt about him. Then, please God, he would realise that deep down he felt the same way about her and they would laugh over the absurdity of the situation, that it had taken so long for them to appreciate they were each what the other had been looking for all these years.

Armed with that rock-solid certainty, she had scurried cloak-and-dagger-style across the road and into the Ritz Hotel, where she watched the man with the tartan scarf ask for his room key at the desk. With this in hand, he then nuzzled Imogen's neck, producing from her a giggle and a lingering kiss as they made their way towards the lifts.

Hiding behind a pillar, Floriana watched with grim satisfaction as they stepped into the lift together. *Gotcha!* she thought, when the doors closed on them and they disappeared. *Imogen Morgan, consider yourself history!*

How wrong she'd been.

'Florrie, say something. Tell me I'm not wrong to think you still love me?'

Wrenching herself away from the excruciating memory of what had then happened when she'd told Seb what she'd seen – how angry he'd been, how he'd pushed her away when she'd been crying and had tried to kiss him, to prove her feelings for him – Floriana said, 'Why didn't you believe me when I told you that Imogen cheated on you? Why did you believe her story of meeting an ex-work colleague for a drink?'

He frowned. 'Because ... because you were jealous and wanted to split us up.'

'That's what Imogen wanted you to think. But surely, Seb, it must have dawned on you at some point that she was pathologically jealous of our friendship and was hell-bent on turning you against me? And the worst of it is, you let her. You have no idea how much that hurt. I laid myself bare to you, told you that I loved you, and what did you do? You accused me of everything Imogen had so cleverly filled your head with. You broke my heart when you did that.'

'I'm sorry. I think deep down I knew that Imogen had cheated on me, but I didn't want to believe it. I didn't want to lose what I had, I'd invested so much in it.'

'So it was easier to live a lie?'

'Yes.' He turned his glass of beer round on the table in front of him. Round and round. 'You haven't answered my question,' he said, looking up at her. 'Do you still love me?'

Floriana stared back at him sadly. 'You've left it too late, Seb.'

A haunted look came over his face. 'Don't say that.'

'But it's true.'

'Are you saying a choice can't be unmade?'

When she didn't say anything, he said, 'Give me your hand.'

She did as he asked. 'Look,' he said, tracing a finger across her palm and making her shiver despite the sultry heat of the day, 'it says here that we're meant to be together. Can't you see it?'

Chapter Forty-Seven

The last wedding Adam attended had been a catalyst for change for him; it was when he'd met Jesse. He didn't like to think what the outcome of today's wedding might be.

When he and Esme had returned from Villa Carlotta yesterday afternoon there had been no sign of Floriana. She didn't appear until early evening and despite her attempts to avoid looking at them, it was obvious she'd been crying. It was equally obvious that she didn't want to talk about what had gone on between her and Seb.

They had planned to go to Menaggio for dinner, but Floriana had said she had a headache and they should go without her as all she was fit for was a shower and bed. With Floriana upstairs in her room, Esme had then said she was too tired for an evening out and so he had offered to fetch takeaway pizzas from a nearby restaurant. No sooner had he arrived back than a flash of lightning lit up the sky followed by a clap of thunder so sudden and loud it had made Esme start and drop the cutlery she was putting on the table on the terrace. Heavy rain had driven them inside and, gathering momentum, the storm had raged for the rest of the evening and well into the night. The power had gone off at one point and after he'd found the fuse box and flicked the switch and the lamps in the sitting room came back on, Esme urged him to go up and talk to Floriana.

'No,' he'd said. 'If she wanted to talk, she would. I'm not going to pester her.'

'Don't be stubborn, Adam. I know what you're thinking, that you dared to trust your feelings and now you don't know where you stand with her.'

'Please, Esme,' he'd snapped, unsure just how much she knew, he'd said nothing to her about kissing Floriana, 'I don't want to talk about it!'

Now, as the morning sun shone down from a faultless blue sky and the lake and mountains looked scrubbed fresh and clean, Adam regretted the sharpness of his words to Esme. She meant well, he knew, but really this was something she had to stay out of.

Using the net provided, he skimmed the surface of the swimming pool to clear it of storm debris. As he worked methodically at the task, he repeatedly warned himself not to leap to any conclusions. In particular, where Floriana was right now.

On his way downstairs, he'd noticed her bedroom door was ajar, and hoping she was awake and might be ready to talk, he'd knocked and pushed it further open, only to find that her bed was empty. The thought flashed through his mind that she'd slipped off in the night to be with Seb. He'd known it was a crazily irrational thought, but he couldn't stop himself from casting his gaze round the room to check her things were still there. She's gone down to the supermarket, he'd told himself angrily. Just as she's done every morning.

The pool now clear of leaves and twigs, he put the net away. It was almost nine o'clock. And still no sign of Floriana. Or Esme. Odd that she should be sleeping in so late, but then perhaps, as it had with him, the thunder had kept her awake last night. Already wearing his swimming shorts, he pulled off his T-shirt and went to the deep end of the pool. He dived in. He swam two lengths under water, surfaced for breath, then did the same again. Next he tried swimming three lengths under water. Then four. It was as good a way as any to rid himself of his frustration. All he wanted was to know where he stood. Was that so much to ask?

When he'd pushed his lungs to the limit, he floated on his back, his eyes closed against the dazzling sunshine. Sensing he wasn't alone, he looked up to see Floriana sitting on the edge of the pool at the shallow end, her feet dangling in the water. He'd never seen her look more serious. Or more sad.

'Hello,' he said cautiously. On the sun lounger behind her was a carrier bag from the supermarket. *See*, he told himself.

'Sorry about last night,' she said quietly. 'I just needed to be alone. Are you very upset with me?'

He flipped over onto his front and swam towards her. 'Should I be?'

315

'I don't know. I don't know anything at the moment.'

He stood up. 'Is there anything I can do or say that would help?'

She held her arms out. 'A hug would be nice.'

'A wet hug?'

She nodded.

Putting his arms around her, he held her sun-warmed body to him and, fully clothed, she slipped into the water with him. Her mouth came to rest against his and he kissed her. It should have reassured him, but it didn't. Her sadness was palpable and it added to his own.

'Where's Esme?' she asked when she drew away from him.

'I don't know, I haven't seen her yet.'

She frowned. 'It's not like her to sleep in so late.'

'I thought the same about twenty minutes ago.'

They were both looking up towards Esme's bedroom where the shutters were still closed after the storm last night, when Esme appeared through the open kitchen door.

'Your mobile, Adam,' she called to him. 'It was ringing, but I'm afraid it's stopped now, I was too slow in bringing it to you.'

Out of the pool, Adam grabbed a towel. 'That's OK,' he said, roughly drying his hair then wrapping the towel around his waist. 'Whoever it was I'll call them back.'

Handing the phone to him, Esme looked at Floriana, who was now climbing out of the pool. 'And how are you this morning, young lady? Did you sleep well? Headache all gone?'

Floriana pulled at her clinging vest top and dripping shorts. 'I'm fine,' she said. 'I'll go and change and then I'll get us some breakfast.'

'That's all right,' Esme said crisply, 'I'll see to that. When you're ready, I want to have a chat with you.'

Adam didn't doubt for a minute what Esme wanted to discuss with Floriana, but he lacked the will to intervene. Frankly, he didn't think she could say anything that would make the situation any worse than it already was. He sensed also that she had woken in a combative mood and would take no prisoners. So he went upstairs to change and to deal with the missed call; it was probably Denise.

But the message left on his voicemail proved him wrong; it was from the estate agent, Giovanni Zazzaroni, and he wanted

Adam to call him back. He did, but getting no reply, he left a message.

Her mind in as many knots as her stomach, Floriana felt awful. She hadn't eaten since lunchtime yesterday and didn't think she'd be able to tackle the breakfast Esme was downstairs making – or the lecture she was to be subjected to. She had the strongest feeling Esme disapproved of her meeting Seb yesterday.

All last night she had dreaded her mobile going off with a call or a text from Seb. Or worse, receiving a communication from a member of Imogen's family. The fact that no one had been in touch implied the wedding was going ahead. Floriana couldn't believe that it would. How could Seb go through with marrying someone he claimed he didn't love?

Although there was still time yet for it to be cancelled, she thought, as she stripped off her wet clothes and stepped into the shower. Two and three-quarter hours, to be precise.

There had been so many times in the past when Floriana had worried about Seb, but never more so than now. He'd effectively begged her yesterday afternoon to save him from what he was about to do because he lacked the courage to save himself. Just a few words from her and he would be free from the doomed-to-failure situation he'd got himself into, he'd bargained with her.

She had parted from him in tears, knowing that unable to do the one thing he'd begged her to do, she had failed him.

'Stop manipulating me,' she had cried, 'I can't do it. I won't have this on my conscience.' Then she had really hurt him. 'I don't love you, Seb. I don't love this man you've become. If you had any respect for yourself, or me, you wouldn't be trying to make me your scapegoat. I'll never forgive you for this.'

'Don't say that. I need you, Florrie.'

'But I don't need you. I have Adam in my life now.'

She'd hit home with that and his stricken face showed the extent of his hurt. When he'd recovered, he'd said, 'Will you promise me something, will you come tomorrow? If I know you're there, I'll have the courage to go through with it. Because at least then you'll think better of me.'

His logic was skewed beyond belief. How could she think better of him when he was deceiving not just himself, but Imogen?

And why? To save Imogen's feelings? To save her from the shame of being jilted at the altar?

'If that's what you want,' she'd replied, 'then I'll be there.'

'You promise?'

'Yes, Seb, I promise. And now I'm going.'

She had left him sitting in the bar; he hadn't come after her and she hadn't looked back.

Unable to face returning to the villa straight away, where she knew Esme and Adam would be waiting for her, she had gone for a walk. She had walked and walked, fast and furiously, following a path that wound its way along the lake. At times it was nothing more than a shaded narrow cobbled track between ivy-covered stone walls that were so close she could almost touch them either side of her. In other places the path took her away from the lake, up into the hillside before dropping down onto the busy main road.

Eventually, when the sky had begun to darken with storm clouds and she'd reached the town of Menaggio, she came across a taxi rank and got a lift back to Mezzegra. One look at Adam's concerned expression was enough to have her retreating to the sanctuary of her room. She hadn't wanted him to see her so upset, knowing it would give him the wrong idea. Yet with hindsight, she had done exactly that, had given him all the cause in the world to believe she was still in love with Seb.

Out of the shower now, she heard a sharp knock at the door. 'May I come in, please?'

At the sound of Esme's voice, Floriana's stomach tied itself into yet more of a knot.

Chapter Forty-Eight

The instructions that accompanied the wedding invitation explained that guests were to be shuttled to the Villa Balbianello by motorboat and it looked like Floriana and Adam were amongst the last of the guests to set off from the waterfront in Lenno.

Rounding the promontory where the magnificent villa stood, the spectacular view had everyone in the boat, including Adam, reaching for their cameras. Floriana was the exception; she couldn't bring herself to record the view, she just wanted to get the day over and done with and then remove all trace of it from her memory.

His photo taken, Adam put his mobile away in his jacket pocket and leant in closer to her. He slipped his hand inside hers. 'How're you doing?' he asked quietly.

'Fine. I think.'

'You know, I was wrong earlier when I said you looked lovely; you look beautiful.'

She smiled gratefully. 'It's the dress that's beautiful.'

'I disagree, it's the combination of *you* and the dress, and that's my final word on the subject.'

The dress was Esme's doing. As so much was, Floriana was beginning to realise.

When the old lady had knocked on her door earlier, it hadn't been to interrogate her about Seb, but to present her with the grey silk dress she had worn once before – a dress that far outshone the one she had brought with her.

'You don't have to wear it,' Esme had explained, 'but knowing how well it suits you, I thought you might want to consider it for today. I've ironed it for you, and I brought this little bead bag to go with it, the shoes as well. Do you think you can manage to walk in them for the day?'

Floriana hadn't been at all sure about wearing the dress; she hadn't wanted to make anything of her appearance – she'd wished to be as inconspicuous as possible – but not wanting to hurt her elderly friend's feelings, she had agreed to wear it. So after Esme had insisted Floriana ate some breakfast, she then helped her to get dressed and do her hair, sweeping it up into a sophisticated French pleat, a style Floriana would never have accomplished on her own. Lastly, Esme had put a double string of very fine pearls around her neck. 'There now,' she'd said, 'you look perfect.'

Having expected Esme to cross-examine her as to why she'd been so upset last night, she had been surprised when the old lady had made no mention of it. When curiosity had got the better of her and Floriana had queried the absence of any questioning, Esme had responded by asking if there was anything in particular she wanted to get off her chest. 'If there's anything troubling you,' she'd said, 'you know you can always talk to me. Is there something troubling you?'

'You know there is,' Floriana had replied. 'Seb shouldn't be going through with this travesty of a marriage.'

'That's for him to decide.'

'He told me yesterday that he doesn't love Imogen.'

'That's as maybe, but it's still his decision to do the right thing, whatever that is. You must stay out of it.'

'I know, but the thing is—'

There had been no chance to talk more as Adam had knocked on the door to say it was time to go.

The boat had slowed its speed now; they were approaching a landing stage that was decorated with pink and white ribbons and balloons.

'You thinking what I'm thinking?' Adam muttered.

'What?'

'Ken and Barbie.'

Floriana smiled.

'Sorry, cheap shot on my behalf to make jokes about your friend's big day.'

'That's all right, I doubt he played any part in the arrangements.'

Standing aside to let the others off the boat before them, they followed behind, making their way up the stone steps from the small dock and its wrought-iron gates.

'Somebody must have been busy this morning clearing this lot up after last night's storm,' Floriana remarked when they found themselves on a gently sloping path flanked either side by manicured lawns with not a stray leaf or twig in sight. Majestic cedar, cypress, magnolia and pollarded plane trees provided some welcome shade from the hot sun blazing down from a crystal-clear blue sky.

In bed last night she had listened to the thunder crashing overhead and hoped that the storm would rage on so violently for the next twenty-four hours, the wedding would have to be cancelled. But the weather gods had come through for Imogen and given her the gift of a perfect day.

When the ground levelled out to reveal the palazzo in all its splendour, music drifted across the expanse of lawn, accompanied by the buzz of chatter and happy laughter of guests mingling. A string quartet was playing Vivaldi's *Four Seasons* and in the shade of the central loggia that was covered by creeping vine ornately clipped into an interlocking design, chairs had been set out; each chair decorated with pink and white ribbons. Through the central arcade of the loggia, there was a marquee where, presumably, lunch would be served. The way her stomach was churning, Floriana didn't think she'd make it as far as lunch. Sick with worry, she was terrified Seb was going to do something appallingly dramatic. Or more accurately, something ruinously destructive.

Taking in the smartly dressed gathering and unsurprisingly not recognising a single face, Floriana wondered how many of the guests Seb actually knew. His parents wouldn't be here – he'd told her back in January that he hadn't even informed them he was getting married; he'd as good as cut himself off from them. Just as he'd done with her in his attempt to start a new life.

Aware that Adam was no longer at her side, Floriana turned to look for him. Over by the balustrade, he was leaning against it with his back to the view of the lake, one leg crossed over the other, his hands behind his back. His head tipped to one side, he gave the impression of being very relaxed, as though he were quite at home here. Impeccably dressed in a light grey suit and white shirt that showed off his tan, he looked eye-catchingly handsome.

Filled with a warm glow of deep affection for this one-in-a-million man, she recalled the pair of them sitting on the swing seat together two nights ago. She remembered especially the way her body had fitted against his and how good it had felt. She wished she could turn back the clock and be there with him again, to when she had felt so refreshingly carefree.

'What were you thinking just then?' he asked, when she joined him by the balustrade.

'That you're one in a million. What were you thinking?'

'That you look bloody fantastic and I'm lucky to be here with you. To which no response is required. Instead, take a gander at this view, it's quite something.'

Facing the lake, she linked arms with him. 'Thank you,' she said.

'What for?'

'For everything. But mostly for fixing things so it was possible for Esme to return here. It wouldn't have happened without you.'

'I had an ulterior motive; I wanted to spend time with you.'

She smiled at him. 'I'm glad you did.'

He raised his sunglasses and gave her a penetrating stare. 'Really?'

Before she could reply, Vivaldi's *Four Seasons* came to an end and the abrupt silence gave way to a murmur of anticipation: it was time for everyone to sit down; the service was about to start.

An usher showed them to mid-row seats and while Adam struck up polite conversation with the couple on his left, Floriana, who had an aisle seat, scanned the front row of chairs for Seb. There was no sign of him. There was, however, a blond-haired woman elegantly dressed in a lilac-coloured two-piece suit and a feathery fascinator perched on her head – the bride's mother, Floriana assumed. Straining to get a better look, she watched her talking to a woman with an iPad in her hands. The wedding planner, perhaps? What must this shindig be costing? Floriana pondered. A venue like this one wouldn't come cheap.

From somewhere close by she heard the trill of a mobile. *Uh-oh*, she thought, glad it wasn't hers – first social breach of wedding etiquette committed.

She felt a nudge at her elbow. 'Is that *your* mobile?' asked Adam.

Convinced it was somebody else's, she opened Esme's beaded

bag on her lap to prove she wasn't the guilty offender. She was wrong. Seb had texted her: *Are you here?*

Oh God, what was he thinking, texting her just minutes before his wedding? Was he mad? And what should she do? Ignore or reply?

For his peace of mind, she decided to reply with just one word: *Yes.*

Then for her own peace of mind she switched off the phone.

'Everything all right?' asked Adam, when she slipped the phone back inside her bag.

She nodded. Time will tell, she thought grimly.

The string quartet had started up again and the only chairs that remained empty were the ones right at the front. The service should have started fifteen minutes ago and with every minute that passed, Floriana's anxiety increased. Her experience of weddings was minimal and of the few she'd attended she couldn't remember if they'd started late. The wedding that stuck out most in her memory was her sister's. Ann had been adamant that as with everything else in her life, it would run like clockwork and start on time. Sure enough, Ann had arrived at the church, with Floriana in tow as a bridesmaid, bang on the appointed hour. The fact that Ann had very nearly suffered a nervous breakdown to make it happen was neither here nor there.

'Perhaps they've given the formalities a miss and eloped,' Adam whispered in her ear when another five minutes had passed and the bride's mother was exchanging don't-worry-every-bride-is-late looks with those immediately around her.

Over by one of the ivy-clad pillars, the wedding planner was talking to a short, barrel-chested man in a well-worn suit. He didn't look like a guest, rather he had an official air about him; perhaps he would be the one to make Seb and Imogen man and wife.

Another five minutes passed. Floriana's head throbbed with a low and steady beat as countless plausible and wholly innocent reasons for the delay spooled through her mind. But then a stir of activity rippled around the gathering and everyone glanced towards the front.

Floriana's heart did a little leap: there was Seb! Behind him was a tall fair-haired man, presumably his best man and Imogen's brother, Jules. They both approached the bride's mother – Imogen's brother walking slowly with a pronounced limp – then took their seats. But not before Seb turned and surveyed the expectant faces all looking his way. Floriana knew what he was doing; he was seeking her out. In the time it took for him to locate her, Floriana's apprehension was compounded by the bleakness of his expression. Why was he doing this? Why go through with something that was obviously making him so miserable?

When his gaze settled on her, and flickered towards Adam, he didn't smile or give her a friendly wave, instead the grimness of his expression intensified to such an extent that when he turned his back on her and sat down she could almost believe he held her accountable for his being here against his will.

I can't watch him do this, she thought when behind her someone joked about never having seen such a nervy groom. 'He looks like he's about to throw up,' a man said. Adam reached for her hand. She tried to muster a smile for him, but failed hopelessly.

There was a pause in the music and then Bach's 'Jesu, Joy of Man's Desiring' began. A few chords in and, at the front, Seb and his best man rose to their feet. The latter looked over his shoulder to watch for his sister's arrival; Seb stayed facing the front.

The first to appear was a pair of flower girls in pretty marshmallow-pink dresses and carrying baskets, from which they clumsily distributed pink rose petals as they made their way forward. They looked about four years old and drew predictable *oohs* and *aahs* of delight from the guests. Behind the two little girls came the main event – the bride with her father and a posse of older bridesmaids in the same soft pink.

There was no disputing that with her slender body and ice-blond hair, Imogen made a stunning bride; she looked exquisite. The dress – white and elegantly simple – had a sweetheart neckline with a ruched bodice that fell to a fish-tailed skirt that trailed behind her and was embellished with pearls and sparkling crystals; the back plunged in a deep V to her waist. She looked utterly radiant, a vision of breathtaking loveliness.

Only when Imogen had reached her destination by Seb's side, and after she had passed her bouquet of pink and white roses to one of the bridesmaids and they'd taken their seats behind her mother, did Seb truly look at his bride.

The official conducting the service now took over, delivering his lines in Italian and pausing, as he explained, at the required moments for an interpreter to fulfil the legal requirement of translation. This, so he said, was so that the parties concerned could not claim at a later date the marriage wasn't legal because they had misunderstood what they were taking on.

'Love is the force that allows us to face fear and uncertainty with courage,' the translator addressed the bride and groom, 'and the challenge of marriage is to preserve your integrity and your individuality when you become as one with your partner. This takes commitment and great honesty.'

Oh, Seb, Floriana thought miserably, where's your honesty and integrity in all this? She lowered her head, closed her eyes and tuned out of the service. She didn't want to hear any more. But what did she want of him now? To back out at this late stage for the sake of his integrity? Better, surely, to do the deed and extricate himself later when Imogen's feelings wouldn't be hurt so much.

And how ironic was it that Floriana should care about Imogen's feelings?

A sudden squeezing of her hand made her jerk her head up. She looked at Adam. His brows drawn, he directed her attention to the front where Seb was now speaking.

'I'm sorry,' he was saying, his eyes darting over the rows of guests, 'and I know you've all travelled a hell of a long way to participate in this day, but—'

Her face as white as her dress, Imogen looked aghast. Floriana felt the colour drain from her own face and her heart raced wildly. She gripped Adam's hand as if she might fall.

'But the thing is,' Seb continued, 'I'd be a liar if I stood here and professed to love Imogen in the way I should.'

Imogen gasped.

Other people gasped too.

'I'm sorry, Imogen, but I just can't do it.'

'*No!*' she cried. 'Don't do this.'

'You'll thank me in the end,' he said. 'Why would you want to be married to me when I'm in love with somebody else?'

With *Schadenfreude* pulsing in the air, the translator and official exchanged frantic glances of panic. Imogen's parents were on their feet. So was her brother. The wedding planner looked like she wanted make a run for it; this had to be her worst nightmare.

Floriana was tempted to make a run for it as well. Then to her horror, above the rumble of prurient excitement breaking out amongst the guests, she heard Imogen say, 'It's that bloody Floriana, isn't it?' Her voice had risen to a loud screech. 'This is her doing! Where is she? Where is that bitch?'

Seb's guilt-riddled body language immediately alerted Imogen to where she was sitting and, mortified, Floriana felt herself become the focus of everyone present. *I've done nothing wrong!* she wanted to scream.

But she had. She should never have agreed to come here.

Chapter Forty-Nine

Next to him Floriana may have become rooted to her chair with shock, but Adam quickly rose from his with a potent surge of adrenalin. If there was going to be any kind of a confrontation, he was going to deal with it on his feet, and with Imogen bearing down on Floriana, he stepped neatly into the aisle to position himself squarely between the avenging bride and her prey.

Objectively, the poor girl had every right to be furious and in need of a retributive face-off, but no way was he going to let Floriana be used for that purpose. If Imogen needed to blame anyone, she had to look to the idiot of a man who'd led her to this disastrous point. A man who was now chasing after her. Along with her stunned parents and brother.

'Out of my way,' the jilted bride hissed at Adam. 'Let me see her.'

'Imogen, please don't. Not here.'

She rounded on the man she had been about to marry. 'Not *here*?' she screeched, her whole body quivering. 'Where then? On our cancelled honeymoon? Or perhaps back in London in our house where you're *never* setting foot again?' Drawing breath, but for no more than a split second, she started to scream at him. 'How dare you do this to me! How dare you do this in front of all my friends and family! Why did you have to humiliate me this way? Why?'

'Darling,' her mother pleaded, 'I hate to agree with him –' she shot Seb an accusatory glare – 'but please, not in front of everybody.'

'I want answers,' Imogen shrieked, 'and I want them now! I want to know how you –' she jabbed a finger in the air at Seb – 'could go through with all the arrangements when you never really loved me.'

'I did love you. You must believe that.'

'*Liar!*' Her voice wobbled and she began to sob. 'It's Floriana you've always loved!' She suddenly tried to push past Adam, to get at the person she clearly blamed, but he stood securely and resolutely blocking her way.

Thwarted, she thrust a hand out at Floriana. 'That's who you love! Right there!' She then turned to the other guests. 'And the worst of it is, she just wouldn't leave him alone. This is her doing!'

On her feet now, visibly trembling, her eyes large and dark, her face flushed, Floriana shook her head. 'You've got it all wrong. We've only ever been friends. Nothing more. He's like a brother to me.'

Imogen's father pressed in close. 'Imogen, enough. No more. Don't put yourself through this.' To Seb, and above the noise of Imogen gulping for air as she collapsed into her mother's arms, he said, 'I don't know what the hell's going on here, but you've got some explaining to do. We'll speak later, when Imogen's calmed down. For now, I think it would be better if you left us alone, this is family time.'

Perhaps sensing it was safe to do so, and clutching her iPad like it was a protective shield, the wedding planner approached. 'What do you want me to do?' she asked, looking apprehensively around the group.

'Get everyone into the marquee,' Imogen's father instructed in the manner of a man who was used to taking charge and giving out orders. 'Give them something to drink.'

Seemingly oblivious to everything going on around her – people scraping back chairs and reluctantly leaving the scene of so much high drama – Imogen launched herself away from her mother and tried again to get at Floriana. Once more Adam ensured her way was blocked.

'I bet you're really pleased with yourself, aren't you?' she threw at Floriana. 'You've got what you've always wanted. Well, you're welcome to him! Everyone told me I was too good for him, now I know they were right. But you two deserve each other. I hope you'll be perfectly miserable together!'

Out of the corner of his eye, Adam noticed one of the guests holding up a mobile phone to film them. Enough really was enough, he decided. 'Floriana,' he said firmly, 'I think we should go now.'

'Yes, why don't you?' Imogen said bitterly. 'And whoever you are –' this was to Adam – 'I hope you're not a serious boyfriend, because take it from me; you won't stand a chance of breaking these two up; they're inseparable, joined at the bloody hip.'

With that last piece of invective issued, she allowed herself to be led away by her parents and brother, leaving the three of them alone and isolated in what Adam felt was the wreckage of their very own ground zero.

Shock still crashing through her, her stomach clenching and her cheeks flaming, her breath trapped in the tension of her chest, Floriana stared at her oldest and closest friend and experienced an emotion she never dreamt she would ever feel: she was ashamed of Seb.

'I'm sorry, Florrie,' he said, loosening his tie.

'So you should be,' she snapped back at him, taut with anger. 'You've made me out to be something I'm not.'

'I'm sorry,' he repeated. 'Really sorry. I'm sorry for everything.'

'Stop it!' she cried. 'Saying the same thing over and over doesn't make everything suddenly right.'

'Please don't be cross with me.'

Exasperated, she flung her hands in the air. 'I don't know what else you expect me to be.'

'It wasn't my finest hour, I agree.'

'My God, Seb, even by your standards that has to be an understatement of monumental proportions! I'd say that what you've just done is a personal best in cruel wickedness. What are you going to do now?'

He shrugged. It was the shrug of a thoroughly defeated man and caught Floriana off guard; it gave compassion a chance to suffuse her fury with him. 'I have no idea,' he said. 'Other than go home. Except I don't have a home now. Not really.' He yanked off his tie, shoved it into his jacket pocket, and undid the top button of his shirt. 'You must be Adam,' he said, as though only now aware of his presence. 'You're not what I expected.'

'Funnily enough, you're exactly what I expected,' Adam replied coolly.

He raised an eyebrow. 'A total bastard?'

'Something like that, yes.'

'Fair play to your honesty. I can respect that.'

Just when Floriana thought the situation had reached its

zenith, the sound of soothing music flowed out incongruously from the marquee – like the musicians on the *Titanic*, the string quartet must have been given orders to play.

'I guess they're going to go ahead with the reception,' Seb said morosely. 'Why not? It's all paid for; the guests might just as well enjoy something of the day. Along with my disgrace. They'll be able to dine out on that for years to come.'

'Oh, for heaven's sake!' Floriana rebuked him sharply. 'Don't start feeling sorry for yourself. Anything but that. Adam, let's go. And, Seb, you'd better come with us.'

They both looked at her, surprised.

'You can hardly stick around here, Seb, can you? Unless you're hungry and fancy lunch?'

For an awful moment she didn't know whether he was going to laugh or cry. Thankfully he did neither, just nodded and silently fell in step.

What on earth am I going to do with him? she thought. And why do I always end up feeling responsible for him?

Because, she answered herself as they followed the winding path down to where the boat had dropped them off earlier, he's a part of your life and always will be.

Chapter Fifty

A light sleeper all her life, Esme was no stranger to waking in the middle of the night. And that night Villa Sofia seemed determined to disrupt her sleep with its aged structure shifting and creaking in the silence of the hot, airless night. She had been wakened by an extra loud creak, followed by another and, seconds later, she'd heard the sound of a door opening.

The luminous hands on her travel clock told her it was ten minutes past two. She turned over onto her back, stretching out her legs and arms either side of her in search of a cooler spot in the bed. She closed her eyes and tried to get back to sleep, but her mind was instantly too active, picking over the day's events, to allow her to drift off.

She had been helping Domenico deadhead the roses in the garden when Adam and Floriana had returned long before she had expected them. But they hadn't been alone. Introductions and apologies had followed, along with a request that Seb stay the night with them as he didn't have anywhere else to go. Anywhere else where the rascal dared show his face, more like it!

While Floriana had shown him upstairs, taking with him his luggage which they'd collected from the Grand Hotel Tremezzo, Adam, as impassive as ever, had filled Esme in on what had taken place. It was exactly what she had feared since yesterday when Floriana had agreed to meet Seb.

Esme tossed and turned some more, then gave in to the need to go to the lavatory. Back in her bedroom, she paused at the open window and thought she saw someone on the swing seat down in the garden. Straining her eyes in the darkness, she saw that it was Floriana and Seb, their heads bent close together. She turned away, not wanting to see any more.

But was it such a surprise that they were there together? Wasn't it to be expected they would want to be alone so that Seb could unburden himself fully while Floriana listened? Until now he hadn't emerged from his room; apparently he hadn't been able to cope with facing people. Floriana had taken a meal up to him, but she had later returned with the tray untouched. More than ever Esme was convinced that the dynamics of their relationship was based on the simplest of laws: Floriana was the giver and Seb was the taker. It was not a healthy arrangement, to her mind.

Yet Esme wasn't without sympathy for Seb. Here was a young man who, at the eleventh hour, had realised that he'd got it hopelessly wrong. Though heaven only knew why he'd had to bail out quite so dramatically. Unless it had been his way to prove to Floriana what he was capable of doing for her sake, a profoundly public gesture that declared the extent of his love for her; the ultimate showy display of romantic muscle. What woman wouldn't be flattered and succumb to such a gesture?

But where did it leave poor Adam? How could he possibly compete with not just the immeasurable depth of what Floriana and Seb shared, but with the inevitable seismic shift in their relationship now that Seb had revealed his feelings for Floriana? This, after all, was what she had wanted so badly two and a half years ago.

Back in bed now, Esme closed her eyes and tried to shut out her misgivings for coming here. She should have left well alone. If she hadn't encouraged Floriana to attend Seb's wedding in an attempt to draw a line under matters, none of this would be happening. But selfishly she had allowed her needs to manipulate the situation, transferring her own desire for closure – of her nineteen-year-old self – onto Floriana.

And what of that closure? All she had achieved in coming here was confirmation of what she had known all along: that Angelo had been a bad lot. As for Marco, she knew nothing more about him, nothing that would put to rest the emotions that had been so thoroughly stirred up these last few months.

She sighed deeply and yet again tried to find a cooler spot on which to lie. Just a few days more and this would be all over, she thought, and then she would be back at home. She couldn't wait to be gone. To lie peacefully in her own cool bed and to have Euridice at her side.

*

The following morning, before anyone was up, and before it became too hot, Adam went for a run. Running was good for clearing the mind, so he told himself as he pounded down the hillside. At the bottom of the hill he paused for the traffic to pass, then turned left onto the main road that ran parallel with the lake. There was no pavement to speak of, and despite the early hour, a surprising number of cars, trucks and scooters were hurtling by. Keeping his wits about him, he pressed on, checking over his shoulder every so often to keep an eye on the traffic from behind. Strictly speaking he should be on the other side of the narrow stretch of road, facing the oncoming traffic, but there was a complete absence of pavement there.

Eventually the road widened, giving him the safety of a wide tree-lined promenade of pavement and an impressive view of the lake where, across the smooth water, Bellagio could be seen rising through the early morning dusky-rose haze. He was tempted to stop and admire the view, but his legs were programmed now to keep moving, just as his mind was programmed not to dwell on Floriana and Seb. Whatever will be, he'd told himself last night while trying to sleep. If Floriana was meant to be with Seb, then so be it. Besides, there was no commitment between himself and Floriana, no more than a friendship that had tipped over into something more. He could easily detach himself from that, couldn't he? All it would take would be a slight readjustment of thinking. It wasn't the same as when Jesse left him. Nothing like it. It was disappointing, but not the end of the world. Very little was, when push came to shove.

Maybe it would never have worked out between them anyway. After all, what did he and Floriana really have in common? No, she was better off with Seb. He would bow out with good grace. His pride required that at the very least.

He upped his speed, gritted his teeth and pushed on.

He was passing the Grand Hotel Tremezzo where Seb had been staying, when the music he was listening to on his iPhone was interrupted by a call. He slammed to a stop, bent over to catch his breath, then answered it.

It was Giovanni Zazzaroni. 'Signor Strong, I'm sorry to ring you so early, but I'm due out of town today and didn't want to miss you again. Is this a good time to speak?'

Still fighting for his breath, Adam said, 'Yes, it's fine, but

333

you'll have to excuse me, I'm out for a run and I'm not as fit as I should be.'

The other man laughed. 'I admire your discipline, exercising on holiday and this early in the day. *Bravo!*'

'So what can I do for you?'

'No, it is what I can do for you. I have news for you regarding the Bassani family, in particular Marco Bassani.'

His breath still ragged, Adam said, 'Go on.'

Floriana had seen Adam going out and was anxiously waiting for him to return; she badly wanted to talk to him. He'd been gone nearly an hour now. How long a run was he doing? To Switzerland and back?

It upset her to think how he might be feeling, and how could she blame him after she'd brought Seb back with them yesterday? But she couldn't have abandoned Seb. She'd made a promise in Oxford when he'd tried to end his life that she would never give up on him, she wasn't about to break that promise now, not when he needed her more than he ever had.

Could she explain that to Adam? Would he understand that Seb literally had no one else to whom he could turn? He was alone in the world. As he'd admitted last night in the garden, he had become isolated from the few friends he had in London because Imogen hadn't liked them; she had wanted her circle of friends to be his friends. Which was totally in keeping with a possessive and jealous nature – isolate the object of your desire and keep that person all to yourself. It was one of the reasons Imogen had been so determined to be rid of Floriana.

For the first time they had discussed in real and objective detail what Floriana had witnessed that day in London when she'd followed Imogen to the Ritz. 'I don't understand how she could have done that if she loved you,' Floriana had said.

'It is possible to love more than one person at the same time, I guess,' Seb had said. 'And from your description, it sounds like it was a previous boyfriend you saw her with. She was probably still figuring out what she felt for him.'

'That seems remarkably fair-minded of you,' Floriana had commented.

'I'm not always as blinkered as you think I am. Just as I'm

not blind to noticing that your friends – Adam and Esme – don't approve of me being here with you.'

'They don't know you, that's all,' she'd said. 'And nor will they if you keep hiding in your room from them.'

'I'm not hiding there now, am I?' he'd replied, bending down to the bottle of wine they'd brought out with them and topping up their glasses.

'Only because they're not around,' she'd countered. 'Don't be a coward, Seb, avoiding people isn't the answer.'

'What is the answer?'

'Try asking for help. That would do for starters.'

'I'm not good at that.'

'I know, it's why you get yourself into such a mess. But you're going to have to learn to do it, because otherwise I won't ever be able to stop worrying about you.'

'But I like you worrying about me,' he'd said, his tone light. 'It makes me feel loved.'

'You are loved, Seb. You always have been. Even when you shut me out.' She had told him then about meeting Imogen and learning about the ultimatum he had been given.

'I'm sorry I made the choice I did. It was wrong. Like so many things I've done. But I didn't want to lose Imogen. I really did love her.' In the warm, still darkness he'd put his arm around Floriana. 'What I know now, and without a shred of doubt, is that it should have been you I was marrying today.'

'Well, it wasn't.'

'I've messed up spectacularly, haven't I?'

'No question.'

'You could at least sugar-coat it for me.'

'Would that really make you feel any better?'

'No, but sitting here with you does. Wouldn't it be great if we could just stay here for ever and grow happily old together?'

'I'm not ready to grow old yet.'

'Don't be so pedantic. You know what I mean.'

Yes, she thought now, pulling on a pair of shorts and a vest top to go down to the shop for that morning's fresh bread, she knew exactly what Seb had meant. He wanted to avoid returning home to face the fallout of his actions.

She was creeping down the stairs as quietly as she could, trying not to disturb Esme or Seb, when she realised Esme was already in the kitchen.

'You're up early,' Floriana said.

'I couldn't sleep.'

'Me neither.'

'What about our guest?'

Esme's gaze was as pointed as her question and Floriana felt the colour rush to her face. Shocked that Esme thought she had slept with Seb, she opened her mouth to respond, but closed it abruptly at the sight of Adam appearing through the open kitchen door.

Breathing hard, sweat pouring from him, his T-shirt damp and clinging to his chest and shoulders, he said, 'Esme, I think you might want to sit down.'

Chapter Fifty-One

From her table at the open-air restaurant of the Hotel Danieli and while listening to the early morning bells ring out, Esme sipped her coffee and watched boats of all shapes and sizes busily traversing the lagoon. In the distance was the island of San Giorgio and to her right was the Basilica of Santa Maria della Salute and the Punta della Dogana marking the entrance to the Grand Canal. Venice; there was no other place like it in the world.

A lifetime ago she had stared with the same fascinated wonder at this uniquely magnificent view; now here she was again. Then she had been with her father, this time she was here with Adam and Floriana.

Though less than a four-hour drive from Lake Como, she had been concerned that the trip would be too tiring for her to do in one day and so she had made the suggestion that if they could find rooms at such short notice, she would pay for the three of them to stay at the Danieli. It seemed a fitting way to go about things, completing the circle.

They had arrived last night, leaving Seb on his own back at Villa Sofia. Esme had dreaded Floriana wanting to bring him along for the ride, but to her very great relief there had been no mention of him joining them. His predicament had taken rather a back seat in the face of Adam's news that Giovanni Zazzaroni had asked around the elderly members of his family and discovered that one of his great-uncles had been an *avvocato* in Como and had overseen Giulia Bassani's will following her death. From there, and following a series of addresses given to him, Giovanni had tracked down Marco's present whereabouts and actually spoken to him. She had to admire the man's tenacity in pursuing the task he'd taken on so readily.

The first decision that had to be made and which only Esme

could make, was whether or not to meet Marco face to face. After Giovanni had explained the purpose of contacting him, Marco had apparently expressed a keen desire for Esme to ring him with a view to meeting. As absurd as it was, she hadn't been able to bring herself to ring the number and speak directly to him after all these years. Fearing she would become tongue-tied and embarrassingly inarticulate, she had asked Adam to speak to him on her behalf.

'How did he sound?' she'd asked the second he'd ended the call – a call that had been conducted with Floriana jammed close to him in order to hear what was said.

'Curious would be a fair description,' Adam had replied.

'He's invited you to have lunch with him in Venice!' Floriana had chipped in excitedly. 'You will go, won't you?'

'My, how you've changed your tune,' Esme had remarked. 'I was under the impression you weren't in favour of taking things any further?'

'That was then. This is *now*. And who knows, this might be the only chance you ever get to meet Marco.'

'Writing me off, are you?'

'You know what I mean. We've come this far, let's go. Let's go to Venice!'

It was so good to see Floriana's spirits returned to their normally highly animated state, Esme could do nothing but be swept along by her enthusiasm.

But now, now that in a few short hours she would be face to face with Marco, Esme's enthusiasm was tempered by a growing sense of doubt about the enterprise. Was lunch such a good idea? What if they had nothing to say to each other? Perhaps a brief exchange over a drink would have been better, at least then there would be a built-in easy way out should the conversation falter and dry up completely. But whatever they discussed, she knew with absolute certainty she would never tell him about the baby. What would be the point? What was done, was done.

A large passenger ferry came into view across the lagoon. So many people on the move, she reflected, and each and every one of them on board the ship had a story to tell. Some perfectly ordinary, some perfectly extraordinary. And no two exactly alike.

What would be Marco's story? Had he been a good priest? Had the priesthood been as fulfilling as he'd imagined it would be? Had there been any moments of regret for him, having given his life to the Church to the exclusion of all else?

Oh, what arrogance of her to think that he might, she chided herself. Any regrets she had were hers and hers alone, it was not something to inflict on others.

Her coffee and breakfast finished, she decided she would go for a walk, leaving Adam and Floriana to have breakfast on their own. Heaven only knew they needed some time alone to sort themselves out.

Adam knocked on Floriana's door to see if she was ready to go for breakfast. When there was no response from her, he tried Esme's door, but again drew a blank. Maybe they were already upstairs on the roof terrace.

He found Floriana there alone and talking intently on her mobile. Seb, again, he thought irritably.

Seeing him, Floriana beckoned him over, at the same time mouthing an apology. He sat down and tried to ignore her conversation by concentrating on the view. He'd never been to Venice before and couldn't think for the life of him why he hadn't. A shame they were here for such a short time. A shame also that he and Floriana hadn't had a chance yet to talk properly. He kept waiting for the right opportunity, but either Esme had been around, or Seb had monopolised Floriana.

It was impossible not to overhear what Floriana was saying and he soon realised it wasn't Seb she was talking to. Whoever it was, there was a problem going on somewhere back at home. Finally she said goodbye to the caller. 'Stay in touch, Robert, and if I hear anything, I'll let you know.'

'I don't believe it,' she said, putting her phone down on the table. 'That was my brother-in-law – he says my sister's left her husband.'

'Why?'

'Ann discovered he was having an affair.' She shook her head. 'It just doesn't seem possible. If you'd asked me, and I know this will sound unkind, but I'd have said Paul was too dull to have an affair.'

'Where's your sister now?'

'Nobody knows. She left a message for Paul last night telling him he was welcome to see as many women as he wanted, and while he was about it, he could take care of the children as well.'

Without warning, Floriana suddenly stood up, bumping the table, nearly knocking over an empty water glass. 'I'm sorry,' she said with a frown, 'do you mind having breakfast on your own? I really ought to speak to my parents to see if they know what's going on.'

Adam watched her go. There goes another lost opportunity, he thought.

Leaning out of her bedroom window to get the best signal for her mobile, Floriana listened in stunned silence to her mother.

It was true. Paul really had been having an affair, and Ann really had walked out on him. How had it happened? Yes, they bickered and sniped and got on each other's nerves, but that was their thing, it was what stoked their relationship.

'So where is she, Mum?' Floriana asked.

'She won't say. She says she's staying where she is until she's decided what she's going to do.'

'Is Paul serious about this other woman?'

'He says it was a terrible mistake, just one of those office situations that got out of hand.'

Floriana scoffed. 'Oh yes, we've all done that, haven't we?'

'Sarcasm won't help, darling.'

'Well, you can hardly blame Ann for reacting the way she has.'

'I agree, but what about the children? They're caught in the middle. Your father and I have offered to look after them but Ann is adamant we mustn't. Your father says this is her way of punishing Paul, to make him appreciate all that she does. And I know the two of you haven't always seen eye to eye, but Ann's trouble is that she's not like you, she takes life too seriously and works too hard.'

'Are you saying I'm a slacker blithely sailing through life without a care in the world?'

'You know exactly what I mean. You're more relaxed, you let yourself enjoy life.'

Thinking how she'd been anything but relaxed in the last couple of days, Floriana said, 'So when did this happen?'

'Three days ago.'

'Mum, why didn't you tell me?'

'The same reason you didn't tell us about your accident last

December; we didn't want to spoil your holiday. I'm very cross with Robert for disturbing you; he should never have done that. How's it going, by the way?'

'We're in Venice now.'

'Venice! Lucky you. What about the wedding? How did that go?'

Floriana took a breath. 'It didn't. Seb literally jilted Imogen at the altar. Although strictly speaking there wasn't an altar.'

'Good God! But why?'

Not wanting to explain, she said, 'Look, Mum, this is costing me a fortune; I'd better go. But ring me if there's anything I can do. I'll be home tomorrow. Meanwhile, give my love to Dad and tell Ann she can call me if she wants to.'

The call ended, Floriana continued leaning out of the window, resting her elbows on the sill. Down on the waterfront tourists were streaming off a *vaporetto* and adding to the crowds that were already gathering. She wondered what Seb was doing right now. He would like it here. So many people he could be anonymous amongst, so many narrow winding streets in which to lose himself.

Annoyed with herself that she should think of Seb at a time like this, she switched her thoughts back to Ann. It wasn't often she felt sorry for her sister, but right now she genuinely did. What must Ann be going through? And where was she?

It had been one of Ann's proud boasts that she had never been apart from the children for more than a night, and Floriana supposed it was a mark of just how hurt and angry she was that she was using Clare and Thomas to punish Paul, who really, when it came down to it, had not been the poster boy for hands-on fathers.

But had Ann given him a chance to be a more interactive father? Or had she, with her superwoman efficiency, frozen Paul out? Even if she had, it didn't give Paul carte blanche to shag some work colleague over the photocopier! How about telling Ann how he felt? How about thrashing things out and being honest?

But then who was Floriana to talk when she still hadn't found the ideal moment to talk to Adam about Seb?

During the drive here yesterday, and sitting in the back of the car, her gaze snagging on Adam's in the rear-view mirror as he drove, she had longed to say something to him, but the conversation they needed to have had to be done in private. And privacy seemed to be in short supply just now.

Last night, after they'd arrived and had eaten dinner, she had patiently waited for Esme to go to bed so she could be alone with Adam. But then Seb had ruined things by ringing her, complaining that he was bored. The moment Adam had realised who it was, he'd said goodnight and disappeared. She had knocked on his door when she'd finished talking with Seb, but he'd either gone for a late night walk or had gone to bed. Disappointed, and too wired to sleep, she had decided to go for a walk herself, despite it being gone midnight.

Wandering around the eerily quiet piazza, the basilica beautifully illuminated beneath the velvety night sky, the campanile looming unfeasibly tall in the darkness, she had hoped she might bump into Adam. But, of course, she hadn't.

She was losing him, she knew. As with a number of her boyfriends, he couldn't handle the Seb situation.

She was beginning to think she couldn't either.

Chapter Fifty-Two

At Floriana's suggestion they were secretly keeping watch over Esme. As surveillance work went, it wasn't easy given that St Mark's was chock-a-block with tourists and pigeons.

'I feel like something out of *Spooks*,' Floriana said from the other side of the pillar they were hiding behind in the colonnaded walkway. 'I have this overwhelming urge to start muttering into my sleeve while glancing furtively over my shoulder.'

'Esme would be furious if she knew we're doing what she expressly told us not to do,' Adam said.

'If she finds out, I'll say it was in a good cause, that I wanted to make sure she was all right.'

'And she'll ask you precisely what harm you imagined an octogenarian could inflict on her.'

'Fair point. But you must think the same or you wouldn't be here with me.'

Where else would I be? Adam thought dismally. When else was he going to get the chance to be alone with Floriana and actually talk?

He continued to stare across the piazza to where Esme was standing in front of the campanile and facing the clock tower. She looked so small and vulnerable, lost amongst the sea of people. 'Have you heard anything more from Seb today?' he casually asked.

There was a noticeable pause from the other side of the pillar. 'No. He's gone quiet.'

'Is that a good or a bad sign?'

'I don't know. That's the thing about Seb, you never really know what he's thinking.'

'Are you very worried about him?'

'I've always been worried about Seb; it goes with the territory.

343

But if I'm completely honest, I'm more worried about you at the moment.'

'Me?' Adam said guardedly, resisting the urge to lean forward to look at her. 'Why's that?

'You've become distant with me. It's because of Seb, isn't it?'

He swallowed. He should have known that once he referred to the elephant in the room, even under the guise of an innocent query, Floriana would seize on it and answer with unnerving directness. 'I was thinking the same about you,' he said. 'That you've been distant with me.'

'And why would you think that?'

'Because, without putting too fine a point on it, you're the reason your friend abandoned his wedding.'

'Are you saying I'm to blame?'

'No. But it's the consequences. I . . . I saw the two of you in the garden the other night and . . .' He stopped himself from going any further; to do so would reveal just how pitifully jealous he was. He'd tried not to give in to it, he really had, but it had got hold of him and wouldn't let go. Especially after he'd seen the two of them in the very same spot where he and Floriana had sat. The extent of his jealousy had brought him up short and made him realise the depths of his feelings for Floriana, that he had fallen in love with her. But what use was that when he knew he couldn't compete with Seb?

'And what exactly did you see, Adam?' asked Floriana. Her voice was tight with recrimination.

'I'm sorry,' he said. 'Forget I said anything.'

He waited for her to say something and when she didn't, he leant forward and peered round to her side of the pillar. She wasn't there.

'I knew this would happen.'

He turned on his heel and found her standing behind him. 'You knew what would happen?' he asked.

'That Seb would ruin things between us.'

'And has he?'

She gave him a long unsettling stare. 'Only if you let it, Adam.'

'You don't think you need me to step back, to give you space to decide what you want to do?'

'You think I don't know what I want?'

'I think you need to be sure,' he said carefully. 'I don't want there to be any confusion. Nor do I want to get in the way of you making a reasoned decision.'

She frowned. 'Sometimes reason doesn't come in to it. You just know when a thing is right.'

'Or sometimes emotions get in the way and—' He broke off abruptly; his mobile was ringing in his pocket. *Damn!* Of all the times.

'Go on,' she said with a small sigh. 'I can wait.'

Esme spotted him straight away. One look at the smartly dressed man walking purposely across the piazza in the blindingly bright sunshine, weaving his way through the crowds, and she knew at once that it was Marco.

Not because he was instantly recognisable to her, but because he walked with such deliberate intention, and directly towards her. Though, of course, what he was really doing was merely aiming for the bell tower.

She had half expected him to be dressed as a priest – not in full robes, but in a black suit with a clerical collar. He was actually wearing taupe trousers, chestnut-brown loafers, a cream polo shirt and a navy-blue sweater draped over his shoulders, the sleeves loosely tied at his chest. Tucked under one arm, he carried a slim wallet-style briefcase. His hair was salt-and-pepper grey but was still thick and abundant. He looked effortlessly suave, effortlessly Italian. In old age, as in his youth, his appearance was startlingly arresting, the passing of years and the acquisition of lines and wrinkles had done nothing to diminish it. He looked so very at ease.

In contrast, Esme felt flustered and full of nerves – just as she had as a young girl. She wished she could freshen her make-up with a dab of powder from her compact; she was perspiring like mad in the baking heat. 'How do I look?' she had asked Floriana earlier when she had been patting her hair into place for the hundredth time.

'As elegantly composed as you always do,' the dear girl had responded with a hug. 'You'll knock him for six!'

'That's hardly my intention, but thank you for your vote of confidence.'

He was a few yards from her when his step faltered, then resumed pace. Convinced he was thinking what a ghastly old crone she had grown into, she took a deep breath and swallowed down her nerves.

'Hello, Marco,' she greeted him when he was standing directly in front of her. 'It's been a long time.'

'My God,' he murmured, as though not quite believing his own eyes. 'It really is you, Esme. It *is* unmistakably you.' He stooped to kiss her on the cheek, first her right, then her left. Standing back, he shook his head. 'It doesn't seem possible. All these years and here we are again. It's incredible!'

'And how very clever of you to suggest to Adam that we meet where we first saw each other.'

'Forgive an old man a moment of theatrical sentimentality, but I could not resist it.'

'I'm astonished that you remembered.'

His eyes twinkled. '*Cara*, how could I have forgotten? I can see you now, spinning around in your red skirt. Such a sight it was!' He offered his arm to her. 'Come, let us go for lunch, I have a table booked.'

And just like that, she found herself being propelled back in time to when she and Marco were young and had their whole lives before them.

Yet how could it be as simple as this, Esme thought when they had walked the short distance from the piazza to the welcome cool shade of the Calle Vallaresso and were settled at a table in Harry's Bar.

After all these years, it defied belief that they could be sitting down for lunch as though it were the most natural thing in the world, as though the years had melted away and they'd been doing this all their lives. Indeed, a stranger observing them might even mistake them for an elderly married couple as they sat side by side on a comfortable banquette at a corner table – a table that was positioned so they faced out towards the other diners. At least they would have something to look at should they run out of conversation, she thought. Although she doubted that would be the case, now that she was with Marco.

While he chatted to a waiter – they clearly knew each other – Esme recalled the times she and her father had eaten here during their brief stay in Venice. On one occasion there had been a tremendous stir of excitement amongst the diners when word went round that Sophia Loren would be making an appearance. Much to her father's disappointment, the great actress hadn't material-ised. Looking about her, Esme thought how extraordinary it was that the place seemed just the same, as though nothing had changed. The tables and chairs were the same, as was the decor. Or was she imagining that?

Breaking off from his conversation with the waiter, Marco turned to Esme. 'What would you like to drink? A Bellini?'

She shook her head. 'I'll have a vodka martini, please. With a twist of lemon.'

With a slight lifting of an eyebrow that was much darker than his hair and gave his expression extra definition, he said, 'An excellent idea, I will have the same. *Due*,' he instructed the waiter.

'*Allora*,' he said, when they were alone. 'Where do we start in trying to catch up?'

'Perhaps,' she said cautiously, a thousand questions on her tongue hovering to take flight, 'I should say I know about your cousin Angelo and how he died.'

He looked surprised. 'How do you know this?'

'It's a long story, but my friends and I met Maria a few days ago. Do you remember her? She was the young waitress at your aunt's hotel. She lives in Bellagio.'

Marco nodded, his expression suddenly grave. 'Yes, of course I remember her. Did she tell you about her brother?'

'Yes.'

'Poor Maria, she was so very angry with my cousin for what he did.'

Reluctant to waste any more time discussing Angelo, Esme changed the subject. 'But what about you, tell me about your life as a priest. Are you still a priest? You don't look like one. I don't mean that as a criticism.'

His face softened with a smile. 'I was a parish priest for over twenty-five years, then something changed in me and no matter how hard I tried to resist the doubts, I could not do so. I lived this way for nearly two years.'

'Did you experience a loss of faith?'

'No, a loss of belief that I was doing what God really wanted of me. I felt I was being called to serve in a different way. Eventually I—'

He broke off, interrupted by their waiter appearing and setting their drinks on the table with an unhurried pedantic preciseness that made Esme want to slap his hand and hasten him away. When at last he'd left them alone, she urged Marco to continue. 'Eventually you did what?' she prompted.

'After much searching of my soul, I left the Church and re-trained to be a teacher. I taught English and History to high school children in Turin for nearly ten years until I was offered the chance to teach English here in Venice at the university. Naturally I retired a long time ago and now I live simply and quietly, filling my days reading and occasionally tutoring students in English.'

'It's ironic that you should end up here, a place Elena was convinced was so harmful for someone with a weak chest.'

'Ah, yes, dear Elena, she was such a worrier. But as you can see, I have survived perfectly well.'

He picked up his glass. 'A toast,' he said, his blue eyes poignantly faded with age and fixed on hers, 'to survival, and to you, Esme, for giving me this opportunity today to do something I should have done a long time ago, but which, to my shame, I never had the courage to do.'

Chapter Fifty-Three

'But first, I want to hear all about you.'

'Goodness,' she said lightly after taking a sip of her drink, its distinctive glowing warmth spreading through her, 'there's so little to tell. I've had a very dull life really.'

'I'm sure that's not true, I cannot imagine the young girl I knew living a life that was not rich with love and happiness.'

She tutted. 'Shame on you for trying to flatter an old lady.'

'Not so,' he said with a tender smile that was wholly reminiscent of the smile that had once melted her heart. 'You married, surely?'

She shook her head.

'*No?*' His voice was as incredulous as the look on his face. 'Does that mean there's a string of broken-hearted men in England?'

'It means we should order lunch now,' she said crisply. She reached for her menu. 'What do you recommend?'

He took his cue. 'The *carpaccio* is always excellent, as is the *scampi all'Armoricaine*, and the *Cipriani risotto*. And please, do me the courtesy not to look at the prices, they are for my attention only.'

Registering that the cost for anything was eye-wateringly expensive, Esme remarked, 'Presumably a retired teacher of English here in Venice exists on a good deal more than his counterpart in Britain.'

'I doubt that, but as the last of the Bassani family, I inherited Hotel Margherita from my aunt Giulia on her death. It was impossible for me to continue running the hotel, and with no need of such a large house to live in, I sold it. I kept a portion of the proceeds and divided the rest between two children's homes in Milan where I was then a priest. In general I live modestly, but an occasion as important as this warrants a little extravagance, does it not? Although it is reward enough for me to be here with you again, something I never dreamt would happen.'

She tutted once more. 'There you go again with your flattery, you really must stop it.'

He merely smiled and acknowledged the approach of their waiter.

Their lunch order taken, Marco leant in a little closer to Esme. 'You have cleverly distracted me enough, *cara*, now I want to learn more about you.' He laid a warm smooth hand on top of hers. 'I want to know what sort of life *you* have experienced.'

It was such a seemingly simple question, yet freighted with immense complexity if she were to be wholly honest with him. She didn't doubt for a second that he had matured into a man of considerable intellect and to be anything other than candid with him would be an insult. 'It would be fair to say that at my own choosing, I have lived a life of compromise,' she said at length.

His lips pursed together, he nodded solemnly, waited for her to expand. When she had given him an edited potted history of her life in Oxford, he said, 'I once had the opportunity to visit Oxford with a group of students, but sadly I was ill and could not accompany them. Just think, our paths might have crossed!'

'But would we have recognised each other if we had passed in the street? I doubt it.'

His soft beguiling gaze fell on hers. 'I would have known you anywhere.'

From nowhere, she was filled with a burning sensation deep within her and to her alarm, she felt herself blush. Ridiculous, she told herself. Perfectly ridiculous that she could still react this way! 'You're not going to say you recognised me instantly in the piazza, are you?' she asked, willing her voice to remain steady.

'Certainly I did. Did you not recognise me?'

'I'll concede to a degree of familiarity, but let's not fool ourselves, we were each waiting to spot someone our own age who vaguely matched the image we had in mind.'

He laughed. 'I give in; my foolish vanity is no match for your pragmatism! Unwisely I was hoping for a *piccolissima* admission from you that I was still the same Marco that loved you.'

Hearing him use the word love, she felt another absurd rush of heat spread through her. She tried to quench it with a sip of her vodka martini. 'You know as well as I do,' she said, 'we are not the same people we once were. Thank God, I am far less naive than I was when I was a silly young girl who thought she knew it all.'

His pale blue eyes narrowed as he studied her face. 'We were both naive, *cara*, but we knew one very important thing, and that was how we felt about each other.'

Their waiter materialising with their starters conveniently saved her from responding. Identical plates of the *carpaccio* were set before them with an extravagant flourish, which now – now that Esme had relaxed – she felt no inclination to hurry, appreciating instead that their dining experience came with a generous side order of theatrical show.

'*Buon appetito*,' Marco said when once more they were alone.

Minutes passed while they ate in companionable silence until Marco put down his knife and fork. 'I hope you never doubted my love for you, Esme,' he said unexpectedly. 'I truly did love you. Perhaps you think that it was such a long time ago and how could I possibly remember how I felt, but I never forgot that summer we shared. It has stayed with me all these many years.'

When she didn't say anything, he went on: 'I have always wanted to apologise to you for what I allowed to happen between us, knowing, as I did, that it could go no further. But now, finally, I have the chance to say sorry. Can you forgive me after all this time?'

'Is it that important to you? Did you not confess your sin to God and receive his forgiveness?'

He flinched at her comment. 'Do you ask that with cynicism?'

'Not at all. I couldn't be less cynical. I'm assuming that it was very much a minor sin in the eyes of a red-blooded Italian, so I merely assume you would have found yourself forgiven in an instant.'

'You believe I made a habit of such behaviour, do you?'

'If you did or did not it's really none of my business.'

Again he flinched, his brows drawn. He looked far from happy. 'Then let me assure you, once I entered the priesthood I took my vows of celibacy most seriously.'

The severity of his words jolted her and shocked that she was being so transparently rude, she murmured a chastened apology. 'I'm sorry, it wasn't my intention to accuse you of anything.'

Wasn't it? she thought. Hadn't she, in the darkest moments

of her grief, often imagined such a scene between them when she could hold him accountable for the pain she had endured? Hadn't there been many a time when she thought the sorrow of losing their child would never leave her, instilling in her a violent need to lash out at the man who was the cause of that anguish? The man who had simply carried on with his life blissfully ignorant of the wreckage he'd helped to create.

'No,' he said more gently, his voice low and halting her rapidly spiralling thoughts, 'it is I who should apologise. You are perfectly entitled to question my sincerity; after all, I gave you every reason to think badly of me.'

She could think of nothing to say in response, and as if by tacit agreement, they each concentrated on eating.

When they'd finished, Esme said, 'You asked me if I'd ever married, but did you? Did you marry when you left the priesthood?' She had a sudden mental picture of a wife waiting for him at home.

He shook his head with a smile. 'I became that terrible cliché an academic bachelor who spent all his time with his books and his students. There was no woman who would put up with me.'

'I find that hard to believe.'

'Now it is you who resorts to flattery. But it is true. No relationship ever lasted very long with me. I am too set in my ways. But tell me, *cara*, what brought you to Italy? And who is the young man I spoke with on the telephone?'

While their waiter reappeared and removed their empty plates and carefully repositioned things just so, Esme explained about the wedding to which Floriana had been invited and how it had led to Esme reminiscing about the summer she had spent at the lake with her father.

'So this Floriana and Adam, they are like children to you? You have taken them under your loving wing?'

She laughed. 'More like they have taken *me* under their wing. They're extraordinarily protective of me. Floriana particularly so. She was concerned I shouldn't be upset in any way by meeting you.'

'Upset?' he repeated, his expression one of puzzlement. 'Is there a danger that you will be upset by having lunch with me?'

Having unwittingly opened up a line of conversation she hadn't intended to touch on, she said airily, 'Oh, you know how it is, trips down memory lane are not always the positive experience one hopes they'll be.'

'I agree. But for us, surely it can only be a good thing that we have met again after more than sixty years? For me, this is certainly the case.'

His easy tone rankled. Yet at the same time she knew it wasn't his fault. He was ignorant of one key fact.

The sight of their attentive waiter coming towards them with their main course filled her with relief; further explanation could now be avoided. The waiter's performance complete, and after their drinks had been replenished, she took charge of the conversation.

'Maybe later, before my friends and I leave, you would like to meet them? I know they're curious to meet you.'

He nodded. 'Yes, I would. For if it were not for them, we would not be here together. I should like to thank them for that.' Then more seriously, he said, 'How much do they know about me?'

More than you'd like them to know, she thought. 'That you were my first love,' she said, meeting his gaze with bold directness.

He hesitated. Then: 'When do you leave?'

'This evening Adam will drive us back to the lake. Tomorrow we fly home to England.'

He looked crestfallen. 'That is such a great shame. I wish you could stay longer.'

'You're sure you'll be all right?'

'Of course we'll be OK. You're not to worry about us; I'll sort out everything here. Esme and I will take the train back to the lake, just as I told you.'

'But the hire car?'

Floriana shook her head at him. 'Adam, stop it. I can deal with the car hire firm. What's important is that you get home as fast as you can.' She hugged him. 'Let me know how you get on. And please try to stay positive; there's every chance your father will pull through and he'll be just fine.'

Adam hugged Floriana tightly. He could have stayed there indefinitely, letting her certainty wash over him. But knowing he had to, he reluctantly tore himself away and stepped down into the private water taxi. The concierge at the hotel had said it was the fastest way to get to the airport; the *vaporetto* was cheaper but it would take twice as long. And time was against him. If he didn't get to the airport in the next fifty minutes he'd miss the flight Floriana had managed to book for him.

He looked back one last time to Floriana as she waved goodbye, then called his brother to say he was on his way. He tried not to think of the day twelve years ago when Dad had phoned him to say he'd better get to the hospital fast, that Mum wouldn't make it through the night. She hadn't. And he'd arrived ten minutes too late.

Floriana stayed watching the water taxi until it steered away from the lagoon and disappeared from view. Even then she remained rooted to the spot.

Her heart went out to Adam. She hoped to God that she never received a phone call like the one he'd had earlier from his brother with the news their father was in intensive care having suffered a massive heart attack.

She had never seen Adam anything other than coolly in control of any situation; he was the most capable and decisive person she knew; the kind of person to whom people would naturally turn in a crisis. But the news of his father had knocked him sideways and she'd found herself having to take control and make decisions for him; namely getting him on the first available flight home. She knew that he feared the worst, that he wouldn't make it in time.

Eventually she dragged herself away from the pontoon to make her way back to the hotel. Her first task was to ask the concierge to help her arrange the necessary train tickets for Como and then she needed to ring the car hire firm. Then she had to wait for Esme to return after her lunch with Marco.

And heaven only knew what was going on with her sister! How many more shocks lay in wait for them?

Chapter Fifty-Four

It had been a long and tiring day and Esme was more than ready for bed when they finally made it back to Villa Sofia. She was too old for running around Italy like this.

The train journey from Venice – reminiscent of the same trip Esme had made with her father more than sixty years ago – had involved a tiresome one-hour wait at Milan for the train to Como which had stopped at almost every small town and village along the way, and from there they had taken a taxi for the last forty-five minutes.

Their taxi driver very kindly helped carry their luggage up to the villa, which was in darkness. Inside it was airless and stiflingly hot – the windows were all shut, but the shutters had been left open. Floriana called out to Seb.

'It's quite late,' Esme said, noting Floriana's concerned expression when there was no reply from him, 'he's probably in bed asleep.' During the journey back to the lake, Floriana had mentioned several times how odd it was that there'd been no word from Seb since yesterday and odder still that he hadn't responded to the text messages she had sent him today.

In contrast to Seb's lack of communication, Adam had been in touch to say he was at the hospital where his father was still in intensive care.

Switching on lights, Floriana called out again to Seb. Still not getting a response, she ran lightly up the stairs. Seconds later, she was down in the kitchen again, her expression doubly concerned now. 'He's not here,' she said. 'All his stuff's gone as well. I knew something was wrong. I just knew it!'

It was then they spotted what looked like a letter on the kitchen table: it was addressed to Floriana.

'I'll make us a cup of tea,' Esme said, giving herself something useful to do while Floriana read the letter, which she could see ran to several pages.

The kettle hadn't yet boiled when Floriana gasped. 'I don't believe it, why does he always have to—'

To Esme's dismay, Floriana's face crumpled and she began to cry. Dreading what Seb had done now, Esme stopped what she was doing and put her arms around Floriana. 'Oh, my dear girl, what on earth has he said to upset you so much?'

'You can read it for yourself,' Floriana said when she had calmed down. 'I'll make the tea.'

Finding her spectacles, Esme sat at the table.

Dear Florrie,

I've given this a lot of thought and there's only one thing I can do to make things right.

I owe many people an apology but I owe you the biggest apology of all. You've been the best friend anyone could have and there's no way in the world I could ever kid myself that I deserved your friendship. I was horrible to you when I met Imogen – maybe it was because deep down I knew you were right, that she was wrong for me. But you know how stubborn I am, how could I possibly admit I was making a mistake?

I'll always regret that we lost two years of our friendship, but it meant everything to me that, in the end, you agreed to be there at my farce of a wedding. It says a lot about the strength of your character that you were there. Even if it was ultimately only to witness me hit the self-destruct button.

So what can I say? Other than the obvious. I'm a mess, Florrie, I've screwed up big time, and now there's only one thing I can do that feels right – I must leave you before I mess anything else up, especially for you.

But before that, I'm going to give you some advice – forget I ever said it should have been you I was marrying. Wipe that from your memory, I was wrong; I'd only bring you trouble. You'd be better off with someone like Adam, somebody decent and steady who will put you first. You know as well as I do, I'm selfish, I always put myself first.

What I'm trying to say is, don't let Adam go, he'll make you far happier than I ever could. And if it doesn't work out, so what? You'll have tried and that's what counts. But one thing you have to accept, the whole you-and-Adam thing won't work with me hanging about. That wouldn't be fair to him.

As for me, #cantfacethemusic would be an appropriate hashtag to this letter, so I'm going to do everyone a massive favour and perform a vanishing act. Cowardly, I know, but it's the best I can do in the circumstances.

Remember how we always used to dream of travelling together? That's what I have in mind to do, and then, who knows, I might become a hairy old hermit living in a cave somewhere. How does that sound?

But for now, I want you to know that despite the uphill struggle, you always managed to bring out the best in me. Such as it was. Being the smart-arse that you are, you'll know who said this, something about 'We think caged birds sing, when indeed they cry'. That just about sums me up. And you, Florrie, you always got that about me.

Take care,
  Seb.

P.S. I'm trusting Adam to be the decent bloke I believe him to be, but if he messes you about, pass the message on that I'll be sure to come and find him. He's been warned!

P.P.S. Hold out your hand. Yes, see that line there, it's just as I thought, it says you must stop procrastinating about Adam and put him out of his misery. He's clearly got it bad for you.

Esme took off her spectacles and cleared her throat. 'A very insightful and eloquently written letter,' she said, looking up at Floriana. 'He's right, of course. You know that, don't you?'

Passing her one of the mugs of tea, her eyes still glistening with tears, Floriana nodded and sat opposite Esme. She took a deep breath. 'I thought it was a suicide note. I thought he was leaving me for ever. I ... I couldn't bear that.' Fresh tears spilled over and ran down her cheeks. 'I nearly lost him once before, I never want to go through that again.'

'You won't have to,' Esme said soothingly. 'He knows what he means to you, that's why he's doing what he is, he doesn't want to do anything that will upset or hurt you. I admire him enormously for that, for recognising the sacrifice he needs to make for the sake of your happiness. That takes a special kind of love.'

'But he could have told me this face to face. Or failing that, why not leave me some clue as to where he's going? I hate not knowing where he is.'

'I would imagine he's returned to London to organise his finances and resign from his job, if he really is going to go travelling.'

'It's so typically and unnecessarily overly dramatic of him!' Floriana said with exasperation. She pressed the palms of her hands against her eyes and sighed deeply. When she looked up, she said, 'You didn't like him very much, did you?'

It was a characteristically direct question from her young friend. 'In fairness I didn't know the young man,' Esme replied. 'Now I wish I had been able to spend more time with him. But any antipathy I displayed was down to my worry that he'd upset the apple cart with you and Adam. Which he did, didn't he? He unsettled Adam terribly.'

'You're right, he did.'

'But the important question is, has he unsettled you?'

Floriana blew on her tea and took a sip. 'Just how much do you know about Adam and me? Has he spoken to you about us?'

'You know as well as I do how little Adam willingly gives away, but after – and I make no apology for this – but after I applied a degree of pressure, he reluctantly confided in me. But to answer you properly, I'd say I know enough to be aware that for a brief time, despite how discreet you both were, the two of you had realised how you felt about each other, that there was an attraction; something more than mere friendship. Has that changed as a result of Seb's actions?'

'In some ways yes,' Floriana said, 'I'd be a liar to say anything different, but it was for no more than a blink of an eye. Yet as sudden and short-lived as the shift was, it was sufficient to make me appreciate what Adam means to me and how he makes me feel.'

'And what does he make you feel?'

'One word covers it: happy. I feel happy when I'm with him. Which is the opposite of what Seb makes me feel. I never understood until now just what a great weight of sadness I carry around when I'm with Seb.'

'Did you tell Adam this? Did you reassure him?'

'I wanted to but I never got the chance, we were never alone long enough to talk properly. Then when we were, when you were waiting to meet Marco, I was about to, but his brother phoned and then nothing else mattered apart from getting Adam back to England as fast as possible.'

Esme thought about Adam travelling home worrying about his father and not knowing where he stood with Floriana. It must have been a tortuous journey for him. 'You were watching me in San Marco, weren't you?' she said.

'Did you see us?'

Taking the opportunity to cheer Floriana up with a small distraction, she said, 'Of course I did. I knew you wouldn't be able to resist catching a glimpse of Marco.'

'I wish I'd taken a photograph of the two of you now; it would have been a lovely keepsake for you to have at home.'

'A nice idea, but keepsakes at my age are somewhat superfluous. Besides, it's all in here.' She tapped the side of her head. But at the same time, her mind's eye conjured up the keepsake Marco had kept all these years – her much-loved copy of *Room With a View*, which she had read to him when he was ill in bed and subsequently given to him as a parting gift to remember her by when he'd left the lake. Today, when they'd finished their meal, he had stunned her by pulling the book out of his leather briefcase and shown her a faded black and white photograph contained within the yellowed pages – it was a picture her father had taken of the two of them in Venice when they'd first met.

'Well, anyway, I'm glad lunch went well for you both,' Floriana said, breaking into Esme's thoughts, 'and that I was able to meet Marco. He was charming. And still quite the looker.'

Esme smiled. 'Yes, I rather thought so too.'

Following their lunch Marco had escorted Esme back to the Danieli and it was there that they found Floriana waiting for her in the foyer of the hotel with the news that Adam had left and they would now be travelling back to the lake by train. Marco had insisted they let him arrange a private water taxi to the station as well as accompany them there.

Saying goodbye to Marco on the crowded platform had been poignantly evocative of the time he'd done it before, when he'd waved Esme and her father *arrivederci* and said he hoped very much to see them again one day. 'I remember saying that,' he'd said earlier this evening on the platform when Esme had reminded him of their first parting. 'And I'm going to say it again because, *cara mia*, this cannot be the end. Not yet. Promise me that.'

'I promise,' she'd said, having no idea how such a promise could be kept.

Holding her against him as a group of noisy teenage girls jostled around them, he'd kissed her lightly on the mouth. 'Write to me. You have my address, yes?'

'It's in my handbag,' she said.

'And maybe your friends will make a modern woman of you and teach you how to use a computer so you can email me?'

'They will!' Floriana had butted in. 'I'll personally see to that. Come on, Esme,' she'd added, 'the train's about to go, we need to get a move on, unless you're planning to stay.'

'*Arrivederci, cara,*' Marco had said as Esme had passed her case to Floriana and climbed up the steps onto the train.

With the train moving slowing out of the station, she had waved back at Marco until he was lost in the distance and she could no longer see him. Even then she continued waving; her vision blurred with tears. '*Arrivederci, caro,*' she'd murmured. '*Arrivederci …*'

'It was John Webster,' Floriana said.

'Who's John Webster?' Esme asked, reluctantly letting go of the lingering memory of waving goodbye to Marco.

'Seb's quote about caged birds not singing, but crying. It's from a seventeenth-century play called *The White Devil* by John Webster, the English playwright. It's a revenge tragedy. Did you tell Marco about the baby?'

'No,' Esme said, thinking she was far too tired to keep up with the flow of Floriana's thought process. 'Why lay something as immense as that on his conscience?'

'You've had to carry it alone for a lifetime, shouldn't he be allowed to share some of the responsibility? Doesn't he have a right to know? And wouldn't sharing it with him bring you two closer together?'

Three questions for which Esme had no answer.

Chapter Fifty-Five

Back in Oxford and with Esme safely installed at Trinity House and reunited with her beloved Euridice, Floriana wheeled her suitcase the short distance down Latimer Street in the warm evening sunshine. After the intense heat of Italy, the gentle warmth of an Oxford summer accompanied by the familiar and wholly English sound of a chirruping blackbird was a pleasant welcome home. She had been away for less than a week yet it felt so much longer.

No sooner had she unlocked her front door and pushed it open, than a sixth sense kicked in and she knew something was wrong: there was an intruder in her house.

Adrenalin pumping through her, she stood very still on the doorstep, her every sense on full alert. Somebody was speaking. No, strike that, *several* people were speaking. There was laughter too. What was going on? At the sound of clapping she realised it was the television she could hear. No way had she left that on. The next noise she heard was the unmistakable sound of the toilet flushing upstairs. Who the hell was here and making themselves so at home? A burglar who'd taken a liking to her house? Squatters?

Furious indignant anger outweighed her fear now and she stepped over the threshold ready to confront whoever it was who had the brass neck to break in. But then in open-mouthed disbelief, she saw her sister coming nonchalantly down the stairs and looking as comfortably at home as Goldilocks.

'Of course I don't mind that you came here,' Floriana said, trying to sound like she meant it.

Actually, she did mind. She minded very much that Ann had taken it upon herself to use her just-in-case key without Floriana's permission. It was an obsession of Mum's that they all had a just-in-case key to one another's houses in case of an emergency,

362

but did Ann leaving Paul constitute an emergency? Perhaps it did.

'You can't stay here indefinitely,' she said as kindly as she could, 'you'll have to go home at some point.'

In a passable imitation of seven-year-old Thomas when he was in one of his sullen moods, Ann said, 'Who says I'll ever go home?'

'But the children, they must be missing you terribly. And it's not really fair to leave them in the dark like this, is it?'

'They're not in the dark; I speak to both Thomas and Clare every day. It's not as if I've abandoned them on the street in their slippers and pyjamas. They're with their father, for heaven's sake! And doubtless Paul's mother has stepped in and is in her element, cooking and washing and bitching about me, claiming I drove her precious son into the arms of another woman.'

'Forget about Gillian,' Floriana said firmly, 'she bad-mouths everyone. What do the children think you're doing?'

'I've told them I'm having a holiday, that I needed a rest. And you know what, I did! I'm so tired. Tired of everything! It's all right for you; you have your commitment-free life just skipping along any old how. You do exactly what you want, when and how you want. Look how you've just been swanning off on an all-expenses paid holiday to Italy. What wouldn't I give to be able to do that! But every second of my day is accounted for. I have no free time. Not a single minute. I do nothing that isn't for Paul or the children. Or those lazy ingrates at work. What do I ever do that's entirely for me? I'll tell you what, a big fat nothing!'

'But I thought you loved being busy and on the go all the time,' Floriana said, although what she really wanted to say was – *I thought you loved being in charge and bossing everyone about.*

'I do, mostly, but it would be nice, just once, if someone showed they appreciated the hard work I put in!'

Until now, Ann had been prowling about like a seriously agitated tiger looking for something to eat. Now she came and stood in the archway between the kitchen and sitting room. With her arms crossed in front of her chest, she looked on grimly as Floriana resorted to filling the kettle to make some tea to combat the shock of finding her sister here. Well, she would make some tea if she could find the teabags. 'Where've the teabags gone?'

she asked, hunting through the cupboard above the kettle.

'They're over here,' Ann said, 'above the fridge, which is a much more sensible place to keep them. I tidied your cupboards, by the way; they were in a dreadful mess, no order to them whatsoever. I also cleaned out the fridge. Or should I say, I mucked it out. You had stuff in there that was hopelessly past its sell-by date. It's a wonder you haven't died of food poisoning before now. Don't forget to make me a decaf.'

Much more of this and dying from botulism would be a mercy, Floriana thought. 'Let's sit in the garden,' she said brightly, when she'd made the tea, 'and then we can talk about how we're going to get you and Paul sorted.'

Ignoring her sister's snort of derision, she gritted her teeth and resolved that her number-one priority was to get her sister and brother-in-law back together again, and as soon as possible. There wasn't a chance in hell of Floriana living in peace and harmony with Ann for more than twenty-four hours. If that long! Just as soon as Ann's back was turned, she would ring Mum and Dad and get them onside.

'And don't even think about speaking to Mum and Dad about me being here,' Ann said in a spooky bit of mind-reading. 'Do that and I'll never speak to you again.'

'So what's your plan?' Floriana asked, when they were settled in the postage-stamp-sized garden – how different it was to the garden at Villa Sofia with its panoramic view of the lake. 'If you're not going to speak to Mum and Dad, or Paul, then who are you going to talk to? What about someone objective who could mediate between the two of you? Have you thought of marriage counselling?'

'No!' Ann said vehemently. 'What I need is for everyone to leave me alone. And how can you even suggest marriage counselling when I have no marriage – Paul saw to that!'

'He made a mistake,' Floriana said, aware that she was risking her sister's wrath. 'A considerable mistake, I'll grant you, but you should at least give him the chance to explain why he did what he—'

Ann held up a hand. 'Don't even think about saying it takes two for a marriage to go wrong.'

'Doesn't it?'

'Oh, so suddenly you're an expert!' Ann exploded, her eyes

flashing contemptuously. 'Not a husband or family in sight, but you think you can advise me? That takes some doing!'

Very slowly, Floriana mentally counted to ten. This is not going to work, she thought with growing consternation. Her sister just simply wasn't going to listen to anyone but her own hurt and outrage. But then how would she feel if the man she loved betrayed her? What possible justification on his part would enable her to forgive him?

'Ann,' she said with great patience, 'I'm absolutely no expert when it comes to relationships, my track record speaks for itself, but tell me what it is you want to happen. Do you want to find a way to forgive Paul? Do you think that would be at all possible? Do you still love him?'

To Floriana's alarm, her words made the inconceivable happen: the implacable and wholly indignant expression on her sister's face disintegrated. Gone was the assertive defiance Floriana knew of old and in place – just as when her niece was about to cry – was a wobbly lip as Ann battled to stay in control. But then her body went slack and the battle was lost to choking sobs. Floriana couldn't remember the last time she saw her sister cry, it just never happened. Ann never showed weakness. She never showed she was anything other than ruthlessly capable. Poor Ann, so resolute in her belief that she and she alone was in charge of controlling the universe, and now here she was heartbroken and vulnerably exposed to the very worst kind of betrayal.

Holding her sister tightly, Floriana did her best to soothe the pain away. She was rubbing Ann's back when she recalled something Esme had said last year, that maybe Ann was jealous of her, for her seemingly carefree lifestyle. But who really lived a carefree existence? She didn't, for sure. The truth was, everyone had their burden of commitment and anxiety, and despite what we all thought at some time or other, the grass was never greener than one's own patch. It was just a different type of grass with its own inherent problems.

When her tears had finally subsided, Ann shook herself free from Floriana's embrace. 'Sorry,' she mumbled, embarrassment coming off her in a wave of awkwardness as she searched her skirt pockets for a tissue, finding only a folded shopping list. Her face blotched and her eyes red and swollen, she said, 'It's tiredness, that's all, I haven't been sleeping well.'

'That's hardly a surprise,' Floriana said gently, 'but there's really no need to apologise.' Up on her feet, she went to fetch the tissue box in the kitchen. She eventually located it hidden out of sight inside a cupboard and not on the shelf above the toaster where she normally kept it. There was a pile of post there too. Oh, Ann, she thought with sadness, what was the point in hiding everything?

After a monumental amount of urging on Floriana's part, she managed to persuade Ann to have a long relaxing soak in the bath with a glass of wine, and with her sister out of the way – more crucially out of earshot – she phoned Mum and Dad. No way was she going to harbour Ann without letting them know where she was. Which, she knew, in turn, would mean they would probably tell Paul. And because she hadn't made an actual promise to Ann not to speak to them, she didn't feel too guilty over what she was doing.

That's what she told herself as she listened to the ringing tone in her ear while she waited for Mum or Dad to pick up at their end. But the longer the call went unanswered, the less sure she felt about speaking to them. How would she feel if the boot was on the other foot and she'd asked Ann to keep something quiet?

She ended the call and immediately rang another number.

But there was no answer from Adam either. There'd been nothing from him since yesterday. Hoping his father was OK, Floriana wished she could be with him at this difficult time, but in all likelihood she would be the last thing on his mind right now.

Maybe she would never be truly on his mind ever again. Almost certainly he had convinced himself she was too tangled up with Seb for him to want to risk a relationship with her. And who could blame him for reaching that conclusion?

Chapter Fifty-Six

Carissima Esme,

I cannot tell you how much I enjoyed reading your letter and how it made me wish I could be there with you so that I could meet Euridice and acquaint myself better with your friend Floriana and get to know Adam. You are truly fortunate to have two such wonderful young people in your life.

I have so little to share with you in comparison. But this one thing I will share this with you – in the belief that it will make you smile. Crina, the Moldavian woman who keeps my apartment from falling into a state of chaos, has declared that I have a secret lover! She says that this is as obvious to her as the sun shining through the clouds, as she has never seen me looking so happy. I have told her that I am far too old to have a lover, but she just wags her finger and says her grandfather back at home in Chisinau married for the third time last year and he is ninety-one and that it is not too late for me to contemplate marriage. I fear her head is full of romantic thinking right now for she is very much in love with a young man from Mestre on the mainland.

One thing Crina has right, you have brought the sunshine into my life. As I sit here at my desk looking down onto the small square where a neighbour's little girl is chasing the pigeons, I want to thank you for bringing back so many happy memories for me. How clearly I can picture you when I first met you and then again later at the lake when you nursed me with such tender care.

Our time together was brief, but I never forgot you. Occasionally, a fragment of memory would pop into my mind and I would wonder where you were and how your life had turned out. Now when I look back I feel as if we were connected by an invisible thread and that we were destined to meet again, and that there is more of our story to come.

But for now I must finish and go to the bank before it closes for lunch, as well as post this letter. Write to me again and soon! I want to know what happens next between your young friends, Adam and Floriana.

Un abbraccio,
Marco.

PS When time is so short, email would be so much easier and quicker for us ...

Esme took off her spectacles. 'And what do you make of that?' she asked Euridice who was on the floor at her feet and washing herself with concentrated effort, paying particular attention to her ears.

'What?' Esme asked, when the cat ignored her. 'You're not interested in Marco's letter? Or are you still sulking because I left you in Joe and Buddy's care? Is that it? Well, I suppose it's true, cats do have long memories.'

Just as Marco and I do, she thought with a wry smile. She really hadn't bargained on him remembering things as well as she had. In that respect she had wildly underestimated him. It made her consider the possibility that she might be wrong to withhold the one thing that could very well be the invisible thread between them: the child they had created and lost.

There is more of our story to come ... Yes, Marco, there is.

But for now there was Adam and Floriana's story that was far more pressing.

It was self-centred of her, but Esme was saddened not to have seen more of her young friends in the two weeks since arriving home from Italy. But what else could she expect when Adam was dividing his time between work and the John Radcliffe where, as far as Esme knew, and following surgery, his father was making steady progress. Meanwhile, not only was Oxford teeming with visitors and keeping Floriana busy from morning till night, but she'd had her own family problems to deal with, namely her sister who had only recently been persuaded to return home to her husband and children. With so much going on in their lives, it was only natural they hadn't had the time to visit her as they did before. What upset her more was the fear that they hadn't had time for each other either, which probably meant matters had not been resolved between them.

It was later in the day, as she was putting away the shopping she'd just fetched from Buddy Joe's, that she had a surprise and very welcome visitor: Adam.

'If you've got a moment, I wondered if I could have a word with you before going to see my father,' he said.

'It's about Floriana,' he explained, when she'd ushered him through to the garden and he was settled in a chair with Euridice on his lap. 'Have you spoken to her recently?'

'No more than a few words. Like you, she's had her hands rather full of late. Is there something specific you want to know?' Esme asked. As if she couldn't guess.

'Floriana and Seb,' he said bluntly. 'What's the situation there now?'

Esme waved a wasp away that was making a nuisance of itself around her. 'Shouldn't you be asking Floriana that?'

'I ... we haven't spoken since ... well, not since Venice.'

'Not even on the phone?'

'Just a couple of texts when the two of you arrived back.'

It was exactly as Esme had feared. 'I know you've been pre-occupied with your father, Adam, but are you sure you haven't been avoiding Floriana?'

He shifted his position, stirring Euridice to rise up and paddle his lap with her paws to get comfortable again. 'Actually, I was under the impression that she was avoiding me. Has she spoken to you about Seb?'

The wasp was back again. This time Esme ignored it. 'What is it you're really asking me? Is it – do I think she's still in love with him?'

'In a nutshell, yes. Before Seb's aborted wedding she told me she wasn't in love with him, but perhaps that's changed since, well, since circumstances have changed. It would be understand-able if it had.'

'And would you suddenly decide you loved Jesse again if she

reappeared and claimed she'd made a mistake?' Esme asked.

He drew his brows together. 'No, not now. It's too late.'

'Then give Floriana the credit for being in exactly the same position: Seb left it too late to say he loved her. But one thing you have to accept, she cares deeply about him and probably always will. Do you know about the letter he wrote to her when we returned to the lake from Venice?'

Adam shook his head. 'What letter?'

Exasperated that two such intelligent people could let things slide so easily, Esme decided to fill Adam in.

'But why didn't she tell me this?' Adam said when she'd finished.

'Perhaps your behaviour gave her the impression you were no longer interested. Or worse, she suspected that jealousy had got the better of you. I'm sure you don't need me to tell you that jealousy is one of the most destructive of emotions and can wreck the best of relationships, which means you'll have to come to terms with the fact that Floriana won't want to cut Seb out of her life entirely.'

'I wouldn't expect her to.'

'Easy to say, but only you will know if you really mean it. But if I may offer you some advice, Adam, Floriana needs to be as sure about your feelings for her as you need to feel about hers for you.'

Adam knew Esme was right, jealousy and pride had kept him from speaking to Floriana, and the longer the silence had gone on between them, the more he convinced himself that he had lost out to Seb, and the more resigned he became.

But then last night, after spending the evening with Joyce at his father's bedside, and witnessing the depth of affection and closeness between them, he had been struck by how lucky they both were to have found happiness second time around. It had made him really think about Floriana and how much he missed her. He missed the brightness she'd brought into his life, the way she could always do or say something to surprise or challenge him. It had prompted him to take the radical step of telling his father and Joyce about her.

'Stop buggering around and do something about it,' his father had said, not mincing his words, 'that's my best advice. If you care about the girl and think there's a chance you can make a go of things, then seize the day. After all, what else would I say lying here having just escaped death by the skin of my teeth? Cliché or not, Adam, we only get one life, so make the most of it.'

His father's words had nudged at him throughout today and eventually made him seek Esme's advice before approaching Floriana directly.

Now, after visiting his father, he was on his way home, his mind made up to speak to Floriana. He would see her tonight; it was time to get this sorted. He would lay out his cards, tell her he loved her, and if she rejected him, so be it. At least he would know. At least he would know he had tried. The challenge would be to convince her – and maybe himself – that Seb was no longer an issue for him. As Esme had rightly said, a relationship between them would be doomed if Floriana was constantly worrying that he was jealous of her oldest friend.

He parked outside his house on Latimer Street and walked the short distance to Church Close. There were no lights on at Floriana's, but then it wasn't fully dark yet.

After he'd rung the doorbell three times and looked discreetly through the front window, he had to accept he'd had a wasted journey. Disappointed, he turned around to go home. The sensible thing would have been to text or even ring Floriana to check she would be in, but he'd been led by the desire to act on impulse – something she would doubtless have smiled at. 'Ooh, spontaneity, Mr Strong,' he imagined her saying, 'whatever next?' He had a sudden mental image of the snowball fight she had instigated on this very spot last December. Then a more recent image came to him, of her in the garden at Villa Sofia gathering rose petals and flinging them in the air above her head. Both recollections made him smile.

He was halfway home when he saw Floriana coming towards him on her bicycle. She was wearing a long white cotton skirt that was sliding up and down her bare legs with each rotation of the pedals, and with one hand casually resting on the handlebar, she held a strawberry ice lolly in the other.

Seeing him, she came to a stop alongside and hopped off the bike. 'Hi,' he said, resisting the urge to remind her that she ought to wear a cycling helmet, as he and Esme had repeatedly nagged her, 'I've just been to see you.'

'That's funny,' she said without missing a beat, 'because I've just been to see you. I left a note for you.'

Her lips were faintly stained from the lolly and had the unexpected effect of making him want to kiss her, to run his tongue lightly over her lips to taste the— He stopped himself short and swallowed. 'What does it say?' he asked.

'Oh, this and that. How's your father?'

'Beginning to grumble about being bored and wanting to get home, which we're taking as an encouraging sign. So this note, should I rush back to read it?'

She licked the side of her hand where the lolly had dribbled and left a strawberry coloured trail. 'No hurry.'

A white van drove by, its windows down, loud indistinguishable music blaring. When it had driven past, he said, 'Esme tells me your sister's gone home to her husband.'

'Yes, she went two days ago. I think I've just about recovered from the trauma.'

'Was it really as bad as that?'

She gave an exaggerated shudder. 'Off-the-scale bad.'

OK, he thought, that's the niceties covered, time now to give it his best shot. 'It seems ages since we last spoke,' he said. 'I've missed you.'

Her eyes settled softly on his. 'I've missed you too, but I didn't like to bother you, what with your dad and all.'

Do *not*, Adam warned himself, on pain of death, ask if that was the only reason she hadn't been in touch. 'Was that the only reason you didn't get in touch?' he asked. *Oh, perfect, mouth clearly disengaged from brain!*

Her gaze strengthened on his. 'I wasn't sure you'd want to speak to me.'

'Why would you think that?'

'You know why.'

She was right. Of course she was. Only an idiot would ask such a dumb question. 'Can we talk now?' he said. 'I mean, can we talk properly? And somewhere else,' he added as a car drove slowly by, its driver staring at them as though they had no right to be there. 'Somewhere more private. Like my place, for instance. Although it's a bit of a tip still. We could go to yours, if you'd prefer.'

She sucked hard on the last remains of the fast melting lolly, then looked over his shoulder, up the road towards her house, then back towards his, before glancing down at the pavement. 'This is our very own personal equator, isn't it?' she said, drawing a line across the pavement with her foot. 'We're standing exactly equidistant from my house to yours. You choose what we do.'

Knowing what she was really asking of him and knowing also that he had never been more sure of anything in his life, he said, 'Come home with me.'

'You're sure about that?'

'Yes. One hundred per cent sure.'

She smiled. It was like an explosion of sunshine bursting between them. He put a hand to her cheek and kissed her, and kept on kissing her, all the doubts and uncertainty of the last two weeks swept away in an instant. And yes, her lips tasted of strawberries, sweet and luscious.

When they drew apart, she matter-of-factly tossed the lolly stick into the basket on the handlebars of her bike. 'Hop on,' she said, indicating the saddle, 'and I'll give you a lift.'

'Better still,' he said, 'you go on the back and I'll pedal.'

'Only if you agree to sing "Raindrops Keep Fallin' on my Head",' she countered.

He laughed. 'A tribute to *Butch Cassidy and the Sundance Kid*, I wouldn't have it any other way!'

Chapter Fifty-Seven

A beautiful Sunday morning in mid-September and to the sound of bells calling out across the rooftops, Floriana was cycling to work. It was one of those flawless sun-drenched days when, in a show of golden mellowed splendour, Oxford reminded her, as if she ever needed reminding, that she couldn't live anywhere else. This was her home and always would be.

With the university term yet to start, the city was in that slumberous state of taking a deep breath to recharge itself before the onset of a new academic year. A soft early morning mist had hung over the University Parks when Floriana and Adam had gone for a run before breakfast. It was years since she had donned a pair of trainers to go running, but inspired by Adam's efforts to keep fit, she'd joined him and surprised herself by how much she enjoyed it.

But then, as cheesy as it sounded, she enjoyed most things she did with Adam. It still made her smile that they were now officially an item and that things were going so well between them. Better than well, they were going brilliantly well! He frequently stayed over with her in Church Close, and though nothing had been said, she had the sneaky feeling he was building up to ask her to move in with him when he had the bulk of the renovation work completed on his house. Certainly that's what Esme believed his intentions to be. And had the wise oracle that was Esme Silcox been wrong thus far? No she hadn't!

Occasionally Floriana imagined herself living with Adam in his Latimer Street house; oddly it was always a Christmassy scene she pictured, a sort of soft-focus, Disneyfied version with snow steadily falling, and in the bay window of the front room, a ceiling-high tree tastefully decorated with just the right amount of sparkly baubles and twinkly lights and she, stealthily padding down the stairs in her pyjamas on Christmas Eve to hide Adam's presents under the tree. As rosy-tinged imaginings went, it didn't get any rosier. But really, that's how life felt right now for her.

Just as she'd expected, Floriana's parents had taken to Adam straight away and even her sister had given him her approval. 'He seems like a fully formed adult,' Ann had remarked, 'not a bit like your usual haphazard choice.' Praise indeed!

Amazingly, Ann had taken Floriana's advice and she and Paul were now seeing a marriage guidance counsellor. It was early days, but there were signs that things were moving in the right direction for them as a couple – Ann was learning to relinquish her iron fist of control, and Paul was learning to be more involved with the children and to do more around the house. Floriana guessed it would be a long time before Paul got over the embarrassment of the rest of the family knowing he'd had an affair, as brief as it was, but they were all doing their best to move on and behave normally around him. What else could they do?

The same week Ann and Paul attended their first counselling session, Adam's father was discharged from hospital. A couple of days later Adam took Floriana to meet him and his stepmother, and his brother Giles. It was when they'd been driving back to Oxford that Floriana had confessed to Adam that she'd actually been a bundle of nerves beforehand. Meeting a boyfriend's family had been a first for her – it was a relationship milestone she'd always managed to avoid in the past, for the simple reason no relationship had lasted long enough, or was committed enough, to warrant such a step.

Meanwhile in Buenos Aires, Sara was demanding to be kept up to date with regular news bulletins and photographs. She had also invited Floriana and Adam to stay with her when she'd found herself an apartment. Floriana couldn't see that happening any time soon, but Adam was all for it.

Her group that morning had signed up for the City Highlights tour. Amongst them was a Swedish couple and every now and then the husband would translate for his wife when she nudged him with her elbow.

Leaving behind them the cobbled quaintness of Merton Street and the gargoyle delights of Merton College, Floriana led the group back towards the High, cutting through Magpie Lane and omitting to tell them the narrow street's original name in case its earthiness caused offence. A more polite variation on the name was Grope Lane – so given because back in the thirteenth century it was an area where prostitutes plied their trade.

When they were once again outside the office for Dreaming Spires Tours, Floriana said goodbye to the group and after checking in with Tony, she headed for home. She was pedalling across the junction between Catte Street and Parks Road when her mobile rang. Thinking it might be Adam asking if she could stop off for something he'd forgotten for their lunch with Esme, she reached into her bag in the handlebar basket. 'Yes, Chef, what do you need?' she asked.

'That's a strange way to answer your phone,' said the last voice on earth she expected to hear.

'*Seb!*'

'The one and only. How's it hanging?'

How wonderful it was after all this time to hear from him! 'It's hanging just fine,' she said, pedalling nearer to the kerb as a car swept by. 'Couldn't be better. How are you? And where are you?'

'It's neither here nor there where I am; all that's important is that you're OK. Are you OK? Is Adam behaving himself? Does he make you happy?'

'Yes to all three questions. What about you? Are you happy?'

'Yeah, I'm doing fine.'

'Really?'

'Would I lie to you?'

'It's been known.'

Ahead of her was Keble College, and remembering how Seb had surprised her once with a phone call there, she said, 'Go on, give me a clue where you are.'

'Not a hope. It's better you don't know.'

'Why?'

'No special reason, I just prefer it that way.'

'You're not in prison, are you?'

He laughed. 'Nothing like expecting the worst of me! How's that old lady friend of yours?'

'She's on excellent form. Remember I told you about her first love who became a priest? Well, he came to stay with Esme a few weeks ago for her birthday. I keep teasing her that she's finally going to get her man and marry him. It would be the perfect romantic ending to their—'

But she didn't get to finish what she was going to say, as to her left, and pulling out of Keble Road, was a van. It was upon her before she could register that the driver hadn't seen her and she could do nothing to avoid it. The impact caught her side on and threw her into the air and as she lost all sense of what was up and what was down, she heard a terrible noise: it was the sound of her screaming.

Feeling weirdly suspended in time and motion, she thought how unfair it was that she would never see Adam again.

She was told that because she'd been wearing the cycling helmet Adam had bought her just a few weeks ago, and which he'd made her promise she would always wear, she had been spared a serious head injury. Or worse. Up until he'd given her the helmet, and despite all the statistical evidence to prove she was an idiot not to wear one, she hadn't bothered. It was another of the many things she had told herself she would eventually get around to doing.

But while her head had miraculously survived unscathed, the rest of her had not fared so well. She had two cracked ribs, a badly grazed knee and a bruised hip, and a shoulder that had been dislocated and then very painfully manipulated back into place.

'Sorry about spoiling lunch,' she said, when Adam was allowed to see her in the curtained-off cubicle. 'Sorry too for putting you through this, I know how you hate hospitals.' A distressed child in the cubicle to her left started to cry. Floriana suddenly felt like crying herself.

'Doesn't matter,' he said. 'None of that matters.' He bent down and kissed her lightly on the mouth. 'How're you feeling?'

'Funnily enough, like I've been hit by a truck. And a bit paranoid that maybe I'm wearing a target on my back – knocked over twice in less than a year, do you think that's a record?'

'Record or not, let's hope that's your lifetime quota of accidents, because I never want to go through another scare like that again.'

At the gravity of his expression, she said, 'It really wasn't my fault, you know, the driver, he just came straight at—' She flinched as she recalled the exact moment when the van hit her and threw her off her bike.

'Don't think about it,' he urged, taking her hand in his. He perched carefully on the edge of the bed. 'You might not want to hear this, but the van driver's here. I've spoken to him.'

'Is he hurt as well?'

'No, but he's very shaken at what he's done and wants to know that you're all right. He knows it's his fault and that he's probably going to be charged for dangerous driving, but he wants to say sorry to you. You don't have to see him, not if you don't want to. There's a policeman here as well.'

'Queuing up to see me, eh? We should charge an entry fee.'

Two hours later Adam took Floriana home to Church Close. After he'd helped her change into her pyjamas, he settled her on the sofa with a blanket, made her a cup of tea and then telephoned her parents. Next he spoke to Esme to put her mind at rest. Esme had been with him when the police had telephoned; she'd just arrived at Floriana's where he was cooking them lunch.

It was thanks to Seb that Adam had received the call. Speaking to Floriana from New York where he was currently working, Seb had heard the accident actually happen and had immediately alerted the emergency services in Oxford and told them to get in touch with Adam Strong who lived in Latimer Street.

'Do you want anything to eat?' Adam asked Floriana when he'd said goodbye to Esme and passed on her love and best wishes.

'No, thank you. Come and sit next to me. I feel like I never want to be more than a few feet away from you.'

He knelt on the floor beside the sofa and, taking in how vulnerably pale and drawn she looked, he was suddenly overcome with the intensity of his love for her. The thought that she could have gone off to work this morning and not return filled him with an anguish he couldn't put into words. Perhaps it was delayed shock, but he found he couldn't speak. All he could do was gently squeeze her hand.

'Do you want to know what went through my head when the van hit me?' she said.

He nodded.

'That it would be so unfair if I never saw you again. It made me realise something very important.'

'What was that?'

She smiled. 'That I love you, Adam.'

He cleared his throat, managed somehow to find his voice. 'I love you too.'

'Really? You're not just saying that because I said it?'

He shook his head and smiled. 'I've known since we were in Italy that I loved you.'

'And you kept it to yourself?'

'You know what I'm like.'

'I do indeed. You take inscrutableness and reticence to a whole new level.'

'Guilty as charged.'

'But admit it, I'm wearing you down and gradually easing open that clamshell demeanour of yours.'

He stroked her cheek. 'You've been doing that since the first day we met.'

'Nice to know my efforts haven't been in vain.' She put a hand to her mouth and yawned.

'How about you get some sleep now?' he said.

She gripped his hand. 'You won't leave me, will you?'

'I'll stay right here with you.'

'You promise?'

'I promise.'

Her eyes fluttered and then closed. 'That's good,' she murmured sleepily.

He watched the steady rise and fall of her breathing, and was just considering changing his position to stretch his legs, when her lips began to move. 'Adam?'

'Yes.'

'What would you like for Christmas?'

The question took him by surprise. 'But it's only September,' he said.

'I know, but I'm planning ahead.'

'In that case, I'd like *you*, please.'

'But you've got me already.'

'I want you for ever.'

She opened her eyes.

'No more talking,' he said, placing a finger lightly against her mouth. 'Go to sleep. You need to rest.'

Chapter Fifty-Eight

Almost a fortnight after Floriana's accident, Esme received a letter from Marco. It was a letter she had been dreading.

Carissima Esme,

I have read your letter again and again and with a heart that grows heavier with each repeated reading. I find there are no adequate words to express how I feel. Why did you not tell me this when I stayed with you in Oxford?

Never will I be able to repair the damage I have inflicted on you. To my dying day, I will live with the guilt of my actions. Yes, cara, I know you have said there is no guilt to be suffered on my part, but I am afraid that is not so. If it were within my power to turn back time, then I would surely do things differently. If I had known you were pregnant with our child – our daughter, Grace – I would have married you. How I wish you had not hidden it from me, but I do understand that you behaved selflessly, believing you were doing the right thing for my sake.

You say in your letter that you did not want to change the course of history that lay ahead for me, but perhaps you did, perhaps the true course of history was for us to be together, to be husband and wife, mother and father. You also say in your letter that you wish for me to forgive you for withholding the truth, but it is I who must beg forgiveness of you.

After much reflection, and prayer, I have no answer for why our lives followed the path they did, it would be too easy and convenient for me to say it was God's will. Not for the first time in my life I am left trying to understand the unfathomable.

What I do believe is that we have been brought together

*at last for a reason and we should make the most of it. I
so enjoyed my stay with you in Oxford and would like
to invite you to spend some time here in Venice with me.
Please let me know if that would be possible.*

*This letter would be a mockery of the depth of my
feelings for you and the extent of my mortification if I
did not beg you to pardon me for my behaviour all those
years ago when I should have shown more self-control. I
could argue that I was young and naive, but the result is
the same, my actions resulted in causing you unimaginable
sadness. I have no right to ask this of you, but I hope you
can find it in your heart to forgive me.*

*With love and great esteem for you,
Marco.*

Esme removed her spectacles and sat back in her chair. There
was not a trace of anger from Marco in his letter. That's what
she had dreaded: that he would be furious he had been kept in
ignorance all these years. Oh, what a relief it was finally to have
shared it with him and to know his reaction. Several times during
his stay with her, she had come close to telling him – especially
when he had seen his portrait in her bedroom and shed a tear
over it – but her courage had failed her. As cowardly as it was, a
letter had seemed the easier way.

As for Marco's invitation to visit him in Venice, she most
certainly would go. Why not?

For so long her world had been shrinking until it was hardly
more than a tiny bubble of existence, but that changed the day
Adam and Floriana came into her life. Through their friendship,
she had been given a new lease of life; they had opened her eyes
to the opportunities that still lay ahead for her.

To her dismay, she saw now that before they'd befriended her,
she had been effectively waiting for the end, believing the best
had gone. But it was not the case. While she still had her health,
there was plenty yet for her to enjoy. Gone were the days when
she would be satisfied to fill her time listening to the radio while
doing the crossword, she was now a woman who had things to
do and plans to make!

Her first task was to start using the laptop Adam had given

her. It was an unwanted cast-off from the office, he'd explained last night when he presented her with it, together with a small box with flashing lights that would magically hook her up to the internet. He had given her a lesson in what to do, as well as writing out clear and very precise step-by-step instructions, which he assured her would enable her to communicate by email. 'Just remember, you learnt to use a mobile phone,' he'd said, 'so there's no reason why you can't do this.' Under his expert and extremely patient tutelage, she had sent an email to Floriana, and within minutes had received a reply.

Sitting at the table in the window of her drawing room, Esme decided now was as good a time as any to try sending her first email unaided. Carefully following Adam's instructions, and putting in the email address she had been given, she began tapping very slowly at the keyboard. Really it wasn't so very different to using an old-fashioned typewriter – she had been a dab hand with those back in the dark ages of technology. Actually, this was a lot easier. With a little laugh, the expression old dogs and new tricks popped into her head. Aha! Not such a dinosaur after all, she thought cheerfully.

When she had finished her short message, she read what she had written, checking it for any errors. After she'd erased a few glaring typos, she nodded with satisfaction and read it through one last time.

Dear Marco,

Thank you for your invitation to visit you in Venice, I would love to come. When do you suggest?

As for forgiving you, I already have. So please, can we now accept that no one is to blame for what happened?

With love,
Esme.

P.S. I do hope you're impressed with my newly learnt computer skills. You have Adam to thank for that.

It was then, and with enormous trepidation, she carefully positioned the cursor over the little arrow icon and tapped it momentously.

'There now,' she said to Euridice who, from her lookout post on the window sill, pricked up her ears at the whooshing sound of the message launching itself into the ether, 'what do you think to that?'

Plainly unimpressed, the cat swished her tail and returned her attention to looking out of the window. She was instantly rewarded with the sight of Adam and Floriana walking by towards Adam's house next door. They waved to Esme and pointing to her watch, Floriana held up a hand to indicate the number five, meaning they'd be round in five minutes.

'Time to get the kettle on,' Esme said to the cat. 'And you know, if it wasn't so early in the morning, I'd suggest something stronger as I suddenly feel in the mood to celebrate. After all, there's so much to be thankful for, isn't there?'

Euridice jumped down from the window sill and followed Esme to the kitchen. A few minutes later, returning to the drawing room, Esme heard a pinging sound coming from the laptop. She looked at the screen and with a smile of delight, she saw she had received an email all the way from Venice.

Oh, what a strange and wonderful world it was she now inhabited, she thought happily, as she sat down to read Marco's reply.